ST. MARTIN'S

MINOTAUR

MYSTERIES

Praise for JANE HADDAM'S
GREGOR DEMARKIAN NOVELS

HARDSCRABBLE ROAD

"Outstanding."

—*Library Journal* (starred review)

"Gregor Demarkian is as compelling and intriguing as ever."

—*Booklist*

THE HEADMASTER'S WIFE

"Sharp, intelligent and inventive—the kind of mysteries a Dorothy L. Sayers or Josephine Tey might have been proud to come up with."

—*Chicago Tribune*

"Campus politics and intrigue intermingle with sex, suicide and possibly murder in . . . [this] compelling portrait of a closed society rife with sleaze under its veneer of respectability and prestige."

—*Publishers Weekly* (starred review)

CONSPIRACY THEORY

"Devotees of strongly written, intelligent mysteries will be pleased that Haddam remains hard at work."

—*Booklist*

"[A] fascinating study in conspiracies and those who adhere to them. . . . The book is as up-to-date as today's headlines."

—*Romantic Times BOOKreviews*

MORE . . .

HARDSCRABBLE ROAD

A GREGOR DEMARKIAN NOVEL

JANE HADDAM

St. Martin's Paperbacks

This is a work of fiction. All of the characters, organizations and events portrayed in this novel are either products of the author's imagination or are used fictitiously.

HARDSCRABBLE ROAD

Copyright © 2006 by Orania Papazoglou.
Excerpt from *Glass Houses* copyright © 2007 by Orania Papazoglou.

Cover photo of background image © David H. Wells/Corbis. Cover photo of woman © Helen Rogers/Alamy.

Library of Congress Catalog Card Number: 2005054793

ISBN: 0-312-98912-1
EAN: 9780312-98912-5

Printed in the United States of America

St. Martin's Press hardcover edition / April 2006
St. Martin's Paperbacks edition / February 2007

St. Martin's Paperbacks are published by St. Martin's Press, 175 Fifth Avenue, New York, NY 10010.

10 9 8 7 6 5 4 3 2

For Carol Stone and Richard Siddall,
who saved this book.
Literally.

ACKNOWLEDGMENTS

Most of the time I let books go by without acknowledgment pages, because I never seem to have the kind of things to say that everybody else does. This time, though, I have two things to mention.

First, the dedication is no joke. Through a series of absolutely impossible coincidences and screwups—my publisher was moving, I forgot to send a back-up copy to my agent, my computer hard drive disintegrated—this book was nearly lost. Completely lost. Gone into digital hell. Carol Stone and Richard Siddall retrieved it when it looked unretrievable, and I thought I would have to write it over from scratch. They keep my Web site running, too.

Second, Holli Zampano brought the cats—Creamsicle and Holli (named Holliday, since he turned out to be a boy)—who now make writing an adventure every morning. And they're so much help.

I also want to thank Joan of Green Bay from RAM, for sending the Cheesehead. Which I wear. While working.

And finally, thanks are due to Don Maass, my agent; Keith Kahla, my editor; and Steve and Gregory, editorial assistants, and all the people at St. Martin's who keep this series going by putting in far more work than I do.

—*Litchfield County, Connecticut*
11 November 2005

PROLOGUE

Monday, January 27
High 9F, Low –11F

And the work which we collective children of God do, our grand centre of life, our *city* which we have builded for us to dwell in, is London! London, with its unutterable external hideousness, and with its internal canker of publice egestas, privatim opulentia... unequaled in the world!

—MATTHEW ARNOLD

Oh, what a great act of charity and what a service to God a nun would perform if when she sees she cannot follow the customs of this house she would recognize the fact and leave! And she ought to do so if she doesn't want to go through a hell here on earth....

—ST. TERESA OF AVILA

Where it comes close to an ideal of disinterested, shared progress, scientific discovery is the most mature construct of human freedom.

—GEORGE STEINER

I

There was no thermometer outside the door of Our Lady of Mount Carmel Monastery, but Sister Maria Beata of the Incarnation didn't need one to tell her that the temperature was well below zero and getting worse. She reached through the heavy wool folds of her habit for the leather sack purse she had pinned to the pocket of her skirt. The pocket was pinned, too, rather than sewn on, and for a moment she found herself thinking the kind of thought—*Why in the name of God can't we at least force ourselves into the eighteenth century?*—that had kept her doing penance in Chapter for most of her formation. Behind her, Sister Mary Immaculata of the Child Jesus was unwinding herself from the bowels of the cab. There was a wind coming down the dark street, whipping stray pieces of litter into the air and then sucking them out of sight, heavenward. The old men who materialized out of nowhere to sleep in the monastery's barn on cold winter nights were already lined up at the door. One of them was wearing a bright red cap that was not only clean but looked new. Beata found the correct change and enough of a tip not to embarrass herself, and paid the cabbie.

"Sister," she said, as Immaculata came around to the curb, shaking out the folds of her cape against the wind.

Immaculata didn't say anything, but Beata didn't expect

her to. Immaculata was a very old nun, old chronologically and old in the order. She didn't approve of much of anything. Beata didn't think she ever spoke unless she was spoken to, and even then she seemed to hate it, as if the act of speech had been taught to her as the one necessary element of any mortal sin. And maybe it had, Beata thought. It was hard to know what people had been taught in Immaculata's day.

Beata went up the stone steps to the monastery's front door and rang the bell. Sister Marie Bernadette of the Holy Innocents opened up and stepped back to let them pass, holding out her hand for the briefcase Beata carried in the process. Beata shook her head, and Marie Bernadette retreated.

"You must be frozen," she said. "I've rung upstairs for Mother. She left word you were to meet her in the office as soon as you got back. Immaculata, you ought to go somewhere and have a cup of tea."

Immaculata inclined her head. Beata bit her lip to keep from laughing. "I'll go on through to the enclosure," she said. "The Cardinal asked us all to pray for him. I told him we already did, every day. I didn't tell him we prayed for him to retire. Somebody ought to open up for the men out there."

"Are they out there already? We're not supposed to open until six o'clock."

"It's cold," Beata said.

Marie Bernadette had her keys out and was fumbling with the door to the enclosure. It had an old-fashioned lock, the kind that took a heavy iron key with a little cutout square hanging at the end. The door swung back and Beata went through it.

"If we don't get someone out there soon, we're going to have at least one corpse before morning," she said. "Their bodies can't handle this cold."

The enclosure started with a hallway, long and narrow, with a crucifix in a wall niche at the very end. Beata unhooked her cape and pulled it off her shoulders. It was as hot in here as it was cold out there. She put the cape over her arm and went down the hall, genuflecting quickly when she got to the crucifix. Then she turned to the right and went down yet another hall to Mother Constanzia's office. At least the ceilings were high, she thought. It was odd that it had never occurred to her that enclosure could cause claustrophobia.

Mother Constanzia of the Assumption of Mary was already waiting, standing at the window that looked out onto the enclosure courtyard as if there was something she could see out there that she hadn't seen a thousand times before. Beata cleared her throat.

"I knew you were there," Constanzia said. "I was just thinking. I tried to talk you out of becoming an extern sister, didn't I?"

"You threatened not to admit me to Carmel if I insisted on becoming an extern sister."

"It's another example of how God knows better than we do what we need. I've got to admit that I never did think we'd need a lawyer."

"We have lawyers."

"I mean a lawyer we could trust." Constanzia turned around. "I'm not going to say that I don't trust the Cardinal or his lawyers, or that I don't trust the order and its lawyers, but—"

"You don't trust either."

"Something like that. You did well in law school, didn't you?"

"Tolerably well," Beata said. "I was only ninth in my class, but it was a fairly big class, and it was Yale."

"Sorry." Constanzia motioned to the chair in front of the desk. "I'm a little on edge. This hasn't been the best month of my life, let me tell you. Are we in as much trouble as you thought we were?"

"Pretty much." Beata let her cape fall over the back of the chair, put the briefcase on the desk, and sat down. "First, let me confirm what I thought this morning. The Justice Project *is* taking this very seriously. They're bringing in Kate Daniel herself to handle it—"

"Good grief. That woman."

"She's a very smart woman. She's a brilliant attorney."

"She's an anti-Catholic bigot."

"I don't know that she is. She does see this as an opportunity, and I don't blame her. But the game she's after isn't the Catholic Church."

"It's the game she's going to get."

"Then she'll count it as a loss. What she wants is Drew Harrigan, stuffed like a turkey and served up for Thanksgiving dinner, and if you ask me, she's going to get him. In the process, she may drive us into bankruptcy, or worse, but I don't think that's what she's after."

"She won't mind if she does."

"Maybe not," Beata said. "But Reverend Mother, the issue here is procedural, really. It's a matter of timing. Mr. Harrigan deeded the Holland Street lots to the monastery two weeks ago Wednesday. That was after he'd been indicted for illegal possession of prescription drugs, along with about two dozen other things, and after Sherman Markey filed suit against him for defamation and false accusation. After. It's the after that's the problem."

"Because it looks like Drew was trying to shield his property from the lawsuit."

"Exactly."

"Because it looks like an *arrangement*," Mother Constanzia said. "It looks like the whole thing is fake. That Drew deeded us the property so that Mr. Markey couldn't get it in a court settlement, and then we'd give it back to him when Mr. Markey was taken care of and had gone away."

"That's it, yes."

"Does it matter that none of that is true?" Constanzia said. "Oh, I'm not saying Drew didn't deed it to us out of spite against Mr. Markey. Drew is Drew. But there isn't any arrangement. The fact that we want to sell the properties ought to be proof that there isn't any arrangement."

"We might want to sell them, keep the cash, and turn the cash over to Drew after his legal troubles were over."

"Does the general public actually think that nuns are that Machiavellian?"

"It's not the general public we have to convince. It's one

sitting judge, and he's going to side with Markey. He has to, really. The fact of the timing looks bad. The fact that the buyer insists on remaining anonymous looks bad. The fact that Mr. Harrigan is your brother looks worse."

"I ought to go in there and tell that idiot that Drew may be my brother, but I've been a registered Democrat all my life."

"I think that would break enclosure."

"I'd wear a veil. And it can't break enclosure any worse to testify in a court than to vote, and we always vote."

"I'm trying to get a handle on what it would look like on the news. You sitting on the witness stand with your face covered by an exclaustration veil—"

"Be serious," Constanzia said. "Where are we now? What can we do?"

"Not much," Beata said. "We can't sell those properties as long as the court forbids us to, and the court is forbidding us to. We're going to have to find some other way to solve the problem."

"There is no other way to solve the problem. We have a bank note coming due in six weeks."

"I know."

"And if we don't pay it, there's going to be a first-rate dustup about this monastery's finances, and it's not going to be confined to the screaming fit the Cardinal is going to subject us to."

"The Cardinal doesn't usually scream, does he?" Beata said. "I've always thought of him as a go-stone-cold-silent type."

"The distinction is too fine to excite my interest."

"Possibly. But Mother, seriously. It's time to tell the Cardinal, and let him straighten this out. Maybe he could talk to the mystery buyer, or the buyer's lawyers. Maybe he could advance us enough to make the payment or countersign to roll over the loan. The Archdiocese does that kind of thing all the time."

"It used to."

"Mother, it's going to be a lot more willing to do that kind of thing than it will be to go on the legal defensive against Markey, who's going to be very easy to portray as a poor, downtrodden, unjustly harassed homeless person. It's going to be easy to do that even if it turns out Markey did sell Mr. Harrigan the drugs."

"Procured them," Constanzia said automatically. "Is he really homeless?"

"Not now. The Justice Project has him in a hotel. He was homeless when Mr. Harrigan says he was paying him to pick up the drugs for him."

"You've got to wonder how a person like that could keep himself together long enough to do all this nonsense he's supposed to have done to pick up the OxyContin and whatever else there was supposed to be. You read all these things in the papers. Going to a different pharmacy every time. Going to different doctors' offices. It's like a spy film with James Bond."

"The Justice Project doesn't think Markey did do any of that. They don't think he's capable. They think Mr. Harrigan is accusing him because he's handy."

"Because Drew doesn't want to admit that he did it all himself?"

"Because Mr. Harrigan is shielding somebody else, somebody he has more—respect for. Somebody whose life he doesn't think is a waste."

"I'd like to get my hands around Drew's throat and squeeze until he turns blue."

"Well, you can't for the next forty days. He's in rehab. The enclosure there makes the enclosure here look like wide-open access. Do you want me to try to get in touch with the Justice Project people?"

"Would it do any good?"

"Probably not but I wouldn't mind meeting Kate Daniel."

"Then go do whatever it is you do at this time of night."

"I go out to look at the barn."

"I remember when we had sheep in that barn," Constanzia said. "It's strange, really, the way things have changed since I've been in Carmel. I thought when I came here that if things changed in the outside world, I wouldn't know about it. But I do."

"I thought that if I came to Carmel, I'd find nuns who were all actively engaged in an ecstatic union with God. That was why I didn't want to make a solemn profession, did you know that? I'd read St. John of the Cross and St. Teresa, and I couldn't see myself in the throes of that kind of, that kind of—"

"Sexual hysteria?"

"We have to assume that that isn't what that was, don't we?"

"Get something to eat before you go out to the barn," Constanzia said. "I have to think. And thank you for everything you did today."

"There's nothing to thank me for. I'm a member of this community."

"I know. Go now. You look exhausted."

Beata hesitated for a moment, and then turned and left the office, back into the hallway, back down the hallway to the niche where the crucifix was. She genuflected again, absentmindedly. Around her, the monastery was silent. Even the clocks didn't tick.

"Everybody who comes to Carmel has a different story," Mother Constanzia had said, the day Beata had shown up at the monastery door, dressed in an Armani power suit and carrying a burgundy leather SoHo briefcase from Coach.

She didn't miss the power suit, but she missed the sound of music, all kinds of music, even the bad kind. She kept listening to hear the voice of God.

2

The name on the plastic nameplate screwed to the outside of the door was Richard Alden Tyler, but nobody in the world had ever called him anything but Jig. Even the king of Sweden, congratulating him on the first of two Nobel prizes, raising his voice a little to be sure the right people could hear, had called him "Jig"—or rather "Yig," because of the problems Scandinavian pronunciation had with the letter "J," and after that, for half a year, people had called out to him in bars and named him "Yig." Whatever. It was a sign of just how badly off he was that he was thinking about bars and 1974, instead of the 140 things he had on his mind these days, instead of the problem with Drew Harrigan. If there was one thing Jig Tyler knew, it was that the problem with Drew Harrigan was not about to go away. This was the calm before the storm. This was every cliché that had ever been written in every third-rate novel about the McCarthy era. This was idiocy, because Drew Harrigan himself was idiocy. This was—

Delmore Krantz had opened the office door and switched on the lights and stepped back a little to let Jig pass first. It was the kind of thing graduate students did when they were in awe of their professors and had no hope in hell of ever equaling them. Delmore was the kind of graduate student Jig attracted these days, in droves. There was a time when students came to him for the science. That time was gone. It was odd the way things worked out. Two Nobel prizes, one in mathematics, one in chemistry: that was science. Forty-two years of teaching in the Department of Mathematics at the University of Pennsylvania: that was science. Only the books that had landed him on the *New York Times* bestseller lists every couple of years for the last two decades or so were not science, and they were . . . they were . . .

With the light on in the office, it was obvious that he'd left his desk in a mess. He hadn't used to do that. He had this odd feeling, standing in the middle of the empty room, that he had turned into that character in *The Nightmare Before Christmas*. He was tall. He was thin. He was cadaverous. Delmore was Central Casting's idea of a sidekick. If he were any shorter or fatter, he'd be a mushroom.

"You left the tape machine playing," Delmore said, sounding worried. Delmore always sounded worried, except when he sounded put-upon, which was anytime anybody anywhere mentioned Israel. Delmore resented the fact that other Jewish students on campus expected him to defend Israel. He also resented the fact that non-Jewish students on campus expected him to criticize it. Jig thought he could see Delmore's future as clearly as he could see anything at all. There would be a job in a fifth-rate department somewhere in the Midwest, a wife with a career as a dentist, a child named Zara or Joe Hill, and forty-two million letters to the editor of the local paper, upholding Socialism and the High Art Tradition in the face of Midwestern anti-intellectual cant.

The voice on the tape machine was Drew Harrigan's. It would be, because that was what Jig had been listening to when he'd left to go to the department meeting. He hated department meetings. In the end they all came down to the same long whining complaint about parking.

"This man," Drew Harrigan was saying, "this fool, who thinks he's smarter than everybody else in the universe because they gave him a couple of Nobel prizes, who thinks he knows everything there is to know because he can move a few molecules around, who thinks you—I mean seriously, where do guys like this get off? What difference is there between what he's doing and flat-out treason? We're at war. We're in a big war. We—"

Jig reached up to the top shelf of the bookcase and turned the recorder off. How many hours of Drew Harrigan's voice had he taped?

"It doesn't matter," Delmore said loyally. "Nobody pays attention to Drew Harrigan. He's a fascist attack dog."

"He's the most popular radio talk show host in the country."

"Well, okay," Delmore said. "Those people pay attention to him. But nobody pays any attention to those people. Nobody here pays attention to them. This is a private university."

Jig couldn't help himself. Sometimes he couldn't. Stupidity fascinated him.

"I thought you didn't approve of the fact that this was a private university," he said. "I thought you said that Ivy League universities like this one were bastions of capitalist reaction and ought to be abolished."

"Yes, I did," Delmore said, looking confused, but only for

a moment. "But you have to work with reality. You have to play the game in real time. The fascists have control of the White House. They've got control of the state governments. You'd have a harder time right now in a public university."

"Does it ever bother you that so many people vote for the, um, fascists?"

"They don't," Delmore said. "Nearly half the people don't vote at all. They're discouraged. They think their voices don't count."

"And if you could get them to vote, they'd elect progressive politicians who would put an end to corporate hegemony, expand the welfare state, withdraw American troops from around the world, and institute social justice?"

"They'd *demand* that politicians do those things."

Jig dropped into the chair behind his desk. "You're delusional," he said. "The great American public is a mob of anti-intellectual celebrity worshipers. If they all started to vote at once, they'd install a monarchy in ten seconds flat. They'd probably give it to the Rockefellers. And do you know why?"

"No," Delmore said, looking stiff.

"Because the Rockefellers are just as stupid as they are. So are the Vanderbilts. So are the Cabots and the Lodges and the Goulds. That's one thing I learned in prep school. There are two kinds of people at places like Taft—poor kids with brains, and rich kids who can't think their way out of paper bags."

"Bill Gates," Delmore said tentatively.

"If Bill Gates had had any talent, he would have stayed at Harvard and gone into physics. I'm going to have to do something about this. I'm going to have to do it soon."

Delmore cleared his throat and sat down in the only other chair in the room besides the one Jig himself was sitting in. Jig liked students to stand when they came to see him. Lately, Jig preferred not to have students come to see him. Delmore's bulk didn't quite fit between the chair's arms. It oozed out the open spaces at the sides.

"The thing I think you have to worry about," he said carefully, "isn't the university, but the Department of Justice. The Patriot Act. They could be coming for you that way.

They could charge you with anything they wanted to, and you couldn't really fight back. They could arrest you and not tell anybody where you were, or let you see a lawyer."

"Do you really think they could do that?" Jig said. "I'm not exactly Joe Six-pack off the street. You don't think that would be *huge* news?"

"Well, um, yes, maybe, but the news organizations are in the hands of repressive capitalism. They support the administration and its efforts to criminalize dissent. In the context of reactionary hegemonic discourse—"

"I've told you, Delmore, no hegemonic discourse."

"It's the best available language to describe—"

"It's not the best available language for anything. It's window dressing meant to make banal ideas sound profound. The country is run by a horde of capitalist shits. Given the chance to get away with it, they behave as what they are. No hegemonic discourse required."

"But they own the language. They make it impossible for us even to think of dissenting, because they control—"

"Have they made it impossible for you to even think of dissenting?"

"I was thinking of ordinary people. People who haven't been trained to deconstruct . . . to deconstruct . . ."

"What?"

"Reactionary hegemonic discourse," Delmore said.

Jig sighed. "You'd depress me less if I thought you knew what it meant," he said, "but that's impossible, because nobody really knows what it means anymore. How any of you expect to have any effect at all on the general public is beyond me. You go into a bar in South Philly and start talking about reactionary hegemonic discourse, and you'll be lucky to get out to the street alive, assuming they pay any attention to you at all."

"But that's just it," Delmore said, sliding to the edge of his chair. "They've been brainwashed. They've been dumbed down by advertising and infotainment. They're addicted to media schlock. If we can pull them out of that, if we can break the spell and show them—"

"What? That NASCAR is for stupid people and they've really wanted to be listening to the London Philharmonic instead of Garth Brooks all along?"

"The High Art Tradition is a culture trap," Delmore said. "It exists to make ordinary people feel bad about themselves. The first step progressives have to take if they're going to advance the cause of social justice is to validate the cultural instincts of working people."

"Right. Give the Nobel in literature to J. K. Rowling."

"Magic is a culture trap, too," Delmore said. "It—"

But Jig had turned away. He had had to turn away. He was about to burst out laughing. He looked out the window onto the small, cramped quad that looked as uninviting as the brutal weather that enveloped it. He was sixty-two years old. His best days of scientific work were behind him. Science was a young man's medium. Mathematicians were washed up by the time they were forty. Physicists rarely lasted past fifty. He was at that part of his life when he was supposed to do something else, and he was being stymied by a man who ran to fat and stale ideas like a racehorse running to a finish line. The only difference was that the racehorse would at least be beautiful, and Drew Harrigan was not.

"The thing is," Jig said, not turning around, "we've got a window of opportunity. He's going to be in rehab how much longer? A month, forty days, something like that. So for another month or forty days, there are no more hour-long screeds on radio about how I'm selling out the American government and the American people, how I'm Benedict Arnold—except he never says Benedict Arnold, did you notice that? He either doesn't know the reference or he doesn't think his listeners will. How I'm a traitor and a Communist."

"You are a Communist," Delmore said. "All decent people are Communists at heart."

"He means a member of the Communist Party, which I most certainly am not. I don't join parties. I haven't even joined the Greens. The question is how to shut him up. It would be a very good thing for me if he'd go to jail."

"I don't believe he will go to jail," Delmore said. "He's

too useful to the special interests that run this country. That run this world. He keeps the masses content and focused in the wrong direction."

"At the moment, he's keeping the masses focused on me," Jig said. "Or maybe not at the moment. Up until the moment before this one. And when he comes out of rehab, you know what he's going to do. He's going to blame all this on a plot by Communists and liberals and left-wing nuts. Which he seems to think are all the same thing."

"He's going to push it all off onto that handyman of his, Sherman Markey."

"He's trying very hard."

"You know he will. They'll put Markey in jail for being a dealer and let Harrigan off with probation or something. He'll never go to jail."

"Didn't I hear that Markey was suing him?"

"Through the Justice Project, yeah. They do good work, but they're a little too middle-of-the-road. I think progressive organizations hurt themselves when they temper their message to appeal to what they think is the mainstream, because I don't think the mainstream is really the mainstream. People aren't going to take you seriously if you don't stick to your principles."

The quad looked dead and empty. Jig was tired of looking at it. He turned back and saw that Delmore was now more off his chair than on it. Sometimes he didn't understand why people like Delmore went on living. He understood Joe Six-pack. Joe Six-pack liked what he liked and was satisfied with it. Delmore was half one thing and half another, intelligent but not quite intelligent enough, erudite but not quite erudite enough, cultivated but not quite cultivated enough. No wonder he went in for "progressive" politics. It was the only place on campus where he wouldn't expose himself as a mistake on the part of the committee on admissions.

This was not someplace he wanted to go.

He picked up a few of the things on his desk: a graphing calculator; a snow globe with a miniature plastic replica of the Cathedral of Notre Dame inside it; a copy of his book,

Selling Suicide. It wasn't that Drew Harrigan was calling him a traitor that was the problem. It was the other things he was saying, the things about contacts with Al Qaeda, about aiding and abetting Islamicist cells on campus and in the city, about money laundered and money sent. It was a laundry list of things that could easily become criminal charges under the right circumstances. They were well on their way to the right circumstances. Jig Tyler wasn't Delmore Krantz. He could see the writing on the wall and the look in the eye of the dean, who remembered McCarthy but had his own skin to save first.

It was cold out there and it was going to get colder. If the news these days proved anything, it was that it was easy as hell for an innocent man to die in the electric chair.

"Lethal injection," Jig said, realizing only afterwards that he'd spoken out loud.

Delmore looked confused. "What?"

"Lethal injection. They use lethal injection these days to execute people, not the electric chair, not most places."

"You expect them to try to execute you?"

"No," Jig said, sighing. "I was just thinking about innocent people being punished for crimes they hadn't committed. That it happened all the time. That we know that because of the work done on the death penalty at this very university, in case you hadn't heard."

"The Death Penalty Project does very important work in the fight against global capitalism and domestic repression."

Jig sighed again. "Sherman Markey is being defended by the Justice Project, though, isn't he? They're bringing in Kate Daniel?"

"Kate Daniel is a heroine in the struggle against reactionary—"

"Don't say it."

Delmore looked away.

"Listen, tomorrow morning, let's get Ms. Daniel on the line and have a talk, why don't we? That might help, strategically. Don't you think?"

Delmore nodded. He was staring at the floor. He was staring at the bottom of the bookcases. He was staring anywhere in the room but at Jig himself, which was how all their conversations ended these days. Jig couldn't help himself. He really couldn't. There were people who hated blacks and people who hated Jews and people who hated broccoli, but Jig Tyler hated stupidity. He hated it with the same passion with which Martin Luther had hated the Catholic Church and Mary Tudor had hated all Protestants. He hated it with a fine white fire that was so pure and so intense, it made the problems between the Israelis and the Palestinians look like a high school football rivalry. He hated it to the point where he sometimes thought that that hatred was all that was really left of him, the Jig Tyler who had shown up on the campus of the Taft School in 1956, thin and raw and intense, able to read the math textbook in forty minutes and understand it all, able to read Kant's *Critique of Pure Reason* in two days and understand it all, a searchlight on a campus full of dimmer bulbs, a legend in a week. He was still a legend. He just no longer knew what he was legendary for.

"We'll call Kate Daniel in the morning," he said, suddenly wanting nothing more than to get Delmore Krantz out of that room and out of his sight. "We'll see what she can do."

Delmore still wasn't looking at him, but he knew a dismissal when he heard it. He mumbled something and made his way out, a thin flush of red creeping up his fat neck like vomit coming up a gullet at the end of a long night of drinking. Delmore was beginning to resent him, Jig knew that.

No matter how worshipful they were in the beginning, they all resented him in the end.

3

Kate Daniel was as cold as she'd ever been, cold enough so that she thought she could shatter her teeth by tapping them with a straw. The heater in the car wasn't working right, or something. She didn't want to think it was so cold that the heater in the car wasn't up to the occasion. She kept getting bulletins on the oldies' station she'd been listening to since she crossed the Pennsylvania border. She'd have listened to NPR if she could have, but she couldn't find it no matter how many times she punched the scan button, and she was afraid it would put her to sleep. She was not, really, the right sort of person to be a liberal. She was not, really, convinced that it was possible for the temperature to get down to minus eleven degrees. The old joke about global warming kept running through her head. She fervently wished she had never quit smoking.

Up at the far end of the street, a man in a long overcoat was waiting, leaning forward slightly to see if her car was the one he was looking for. That would be Mr. Whoever, from the Philadelphia Coalition for the Homeless, Kate thought. He'd look the car over and either approve of it (in which case she would hate him) or take it as a sign that she was one of those people who took every possible opportunity to burnish her credentials for revolutionary sainthood. The truth of it was that she truly hated buying cars. She wasn't good at it. She never walked off the lot without feeling she'd been cheated. She spent the next six weeks unable to think about anything but the car negotiations and how she had failed them. It wasn't worth it. The '84 Grand Prix was a good car. This one only had 250,000 miles on it.

The man in the overcoat was nodding vigorously. Kate was close enough now to notice that he was very young. He waved her to the left and she saw that there was a small driveway going to the back of the buildings. In the dark, she couldn't tell if it was as strewn with debris as the rest of the street. This was the kind of neighborhood where Coalitions for the Homeless hung out. It was supposed to be half-full of vacant lots and half-full of drug garbage. She hated the word "coalition." She hated it more than she hated the word "committee." She was already sick of this year's presidential race, and she didn't care who won.

She pulled through the driveway, wedged narrowly between two buildings that both looked as if they should have been demolished in 1966. She found a neat little parking lot in back, complete with overhead security lights and parking spaces marked by clean white painted stripes. She pulled in next to the only other car and opened her driver's side door. It really was minus eleven degrees out there. There was a wind, too, and it got up under her long wool skirt.

"Ms. Daniel?" the man in the overcoat said.

Kate's own overcoat was on the backseat. She never wore a coat when she drove. It got in the way of . . . something. Now she reached back and pulled her coat up to her, a good camel's hair one she'd splurged for at Brooks Brothers after the first time she'd seen herself on CNN, looking like she shopped at the Goodwill Dumpsters, never mind the Goodwill store. She got out onto the asphalt and pulled the coat around her shoulders. She leaned into the car and got her pocketbook and briefcase. She locked the car door and shut it.

"Hi," she said. "I've got a suitcase, in the trunk. Am I sleeping here?"

The man in the overcoat sucked in air. "Ah," he said. "Well. We've got you booked at the Hyatt. I mean, if it's not your kind of thing, we could always—"

"It's exactly my kind of thing. I love room service. I won't bother to get the suitcase out of the car until I get over there. There's nothing I need in it now. Are you the one who's going to be my aide?"

"What? Oh, yes. I'm, uh, I'm Edmund George, yes."

"Do they call you Ed?"

He looked uncomfortable. "Most people don't call me anything," he said. "My professors at Penn call me Mr. George."

"Do you want me to call you Mr. George?"

"No."

This was interesting, Kate thought. She got her pocketbook strap over her shoulder. She shouldn't call it a pocketbook. It was at least as big as her suitcase. She looked around the parking lot. It backed on a vacant lot. The buildings around them were squat and dirty and mostly dark.

"Well," she said, "maybe we should go inside and you can lay out the situation for me. I'm sorry I got here so late.

I kept trying to leave New York and getting held up by odd things happening in traffic. I should have taken Amtrak."

If Mr. George was thinking that any sane person would have taken Amtrak, he didn't say it. He just gestured in the direction of the back door to the building and started leading the way there. They'd gone to all this trouble about security lights and painted parking spaces, but what they should have done was hire a security guard. At least her car would be safe. It wasn't the kind of thing your ordinary cocaine addict was interested in breaking into.

Inside, the halls were clean but narrow, and the ceilings were blessedly high. The place seemed to be deserted. Mr. George led her down a small flight of stairs—they'd bought a new carpet fairly recently, Kate noticed; she wondered if that was because they'd had a sudden influx of money or because the old stuff had gotten so awful they'd had no choice—and then around a corner to a tiny office that looked as if it had been entirely papered in manila legal folders. There was a desk and a chair. There was a phone, a black one, in a "princess" style that was at least two decades out-of-date. There was a single poster on the wall, advertising Leontyne Price in *Aida* at the Metropolitan Opera in New York.

"We're not going to ask you to work in here," Mr. George said. "This is my office, actually. I've got all the files you need. We're cleaning out a space for you up at the front. We thought you could mess it up for yourself without any help from us."

"We didn't go there, why?"

"Because it isn't open." Mr. George flushed. "It was supposed to be, but Sheila must have forgotten and I don't know where she keeps the spare set of keys. I'm sorry. I'm, you know, a law student. I work here part-time. It's, I don't know. I'm not really up on all the detail stuff with the building and that kind of thing."

"Okay," Kate said. She didn't need the office right away anyway. She needed the files and he said he had them. She took a stack of papers off the seat of the one chair in the center of the room and sat down, stretching her legs out in front of her in the long line that had once made Wolf Blitzer say to her, at a party, that if they ever made a movie about her life, they'd have to get Sigourney Weaver to play her. She was still wearing her coat. She hated wearing coats indoors. She stood up again and took it off.

"Okay," she said, sitting down for the second time. "So tell me. Is our client in jail?"

"No," Mr. George said. "We managed to get him out on bail. He isn't really a flight risk, not in the normal sense of the term. The trouble with Sherman is that he wanders. He's not very all there, if that makes sense."

"Drug addict?"

"Alcoholic, mostly," Mr. George said. "Although, if you ask me, it's mostly a matter of opportunity. Sherman ingests whatever's around to ingest. Drugs are more expensive than wine, so wine is what he usually has. One of the things we want to do is get him to a doctor and have him checked out, but he's resisting. He says he doesn't see any point in getting bad news he can't do anything about."

"That's sensible."

"It is, really. Sherman can be very sensible, sometimes. Most times, though, he's not. He does seem to understand that he's got court dates he has to make."

"Where does he live?"

"We've got him put up at an SRO about five blocks from here, but he's practically never there. He forgets, or maybe he just doesn't want to. Usually, we find him at Holy Innocents over on Farraday Street."

"That's a church?"

"It's a Benedictine convent. Sorry, monastery. They call them monasteries, even though it's a place for nuns."

"Benedictine monasteries are usually enclosed," Kate said. "This one isn't."

"Do you mean cloistered?" Mr. George asked. "No, this one is cloistered. You can't see most of the nuns to talk to, not even the Mother Superior, or whatever she is."

"Abbess."

"Yes, okay. Abbess. You can't see her except behind bars, sort of. You go into this room and there's a wall with bars, but not just up and down, also across, like an open waffle—"

"It's called a grille."

"That's it. Margaret Mary told me what the word was, but I forgot."

"Who's Margaret Mary?"

"A friend of mine. She's a nun in training. A novice, I think."

"At Holy Innocents on Farraday Street?"

"No," Mr. George said. "At the Sisters of Divine Grace in upstate New York. It's not a cloistered order. Anyway, that's the only way you can talk to the nuns, except for two or three of them, who come out. Extern sisters, they're called. That's one I remember. They have a big barn on their property, heated, and they open it for homeless people when the weather gets cold. That's the Cardinal Archbishop of Philadelphia. His idea, I mean. There used to be a church in the city that did that, and he got the idea that all Catholic facilities should do that, so they do. And Sherman likes it there. It's on the edge of the city; it doesn't hardly look part of the city, really. And they don't get picky about the state he's in, or search him for drugs or alcohol."

"The place must be a zoo."

"Apparently not. I've been out there a couple of times. It's very calm. And clean, which I think may be part of the point. Anyway, Sherman likes it there better than he likes the SRO, so that's where we look for him when we want to bring him in to court dates. I know it's practically dogma around here never to become enmeshed in a belief in a client's innocence, but I do think Sherman is innocent. I don't think he got prescription drugs for Drew Harrigan or anybody else. I don't think he could have kept himself together long enough to do it, and if he did, I think he'd forget about why and take the stuff himself."

Kate thought about it for a minute. "He got stopped, didn't he? Drew Harrigan. He was exceeding the posted speed limit in a residential zone and he got stopped by a cop. He had a couple of fistfuls of pills in a bowl of some sort sitting next to him on the front passenger seat."

"It was a Tupperware container, a small one. With the lid off."

"So the cop pulled him over and there were the pills. So then what? They took him down to the police station while they checked out the pills? What about Harrigan's lawyer?"

"Harrigan's got lawyers," Mr. George said. "A couple of dozen of them. But they did charge him that night, if that's what you mean."

"That's what I mean. And they arraigned him, when?"

"About three days later."

"Is that when he started to accuse Sherman Markey of procuring the pills for him?"

"Sort of," Mr. George said. "It was odd, really. There was the arraignment. He entered a plea. He made the bail arrangements. He walked out of the courthouse door and held a press conference on the courthouse steps. I saw it on local TV. It looked like it had been planned."

"It should have been planned. If I was one of his lawyers, I'd have planned it to death. What did he do at the press conference?"

"He did a twelve-step number," Mr. George said. "He admitted to being addicted to prescription medication. And that's where he did it. It was in the middle of this statement that he said something like, 'For the last three years, I have used a man who works for me, Sherman Markey, to gain access to drugs I knew I would be unable . . .' Yada, yada, yada. He didn't actually accuse him. He just said—"

"That Markey was getting him the stuff, yes. So the police arrested Sherman Markey."

"Not right away. That took a couple of days. First Drew Harrigan disappeared into rehab. And I do mean disappeared. We don't even know the name of the facility, or its whereabouts, or anything."

"Does the court?"

"It must, don't you think?" Mr. George said. "I mean, they wouldn't let him go off like that and not know where he was, would they?"

"I don't know," Kate said. "He's a celebrity client. It's not as if he could disappear."

"He has disappeared."

"I meant in the long run. He's a very recognizable man. He's big. He's tall. He's loud. And even if they could manage to do something about all of that, he's got that anomaly. 'My heart's in the right place, on the *right* side of my chest.' "

"You can't see that he was born with situs inversus."

"No, you can't, but it's a rare condition. He couldn't go to a doctor without the doctor noticing it, or having to be told. It's something everybody knows about. He can't shut up about it. His heart is on the right side of his chest."

"So . . ."

"So he couldn't disappear for long," Kate said again. "He's the seven hundred pound elephant in the middle of the living room. How long is he supposed to be incommunicado in rehab?"

"Sixty days. There are about forty, forty-two left."

"And in the meantime the legal case against him has stopped?"

"I don't think they've stopped investigating, but, yeah, they're leaving him alone. Rehab is sacred. Instead, they're going after Sherman as a dealer," Mr. George said. "They're going after him on federal as well as state charges. It's insane. It's as if he were a Colombian drug lord."

"Are they going to charge Harrigan with anything?"

"They've charged him with possession of illegally obtained prescription medication. I don't think he's going to trial. I think they're going to bargain it out to probation or even less. I don't think he's going to spend a day in jail."

"What does Markey say about it all?"

"Not much. That he doesn't know anything. That the only work he did for Harrigan was around the apartment, scut work, cleaning up. Harrigan claims he got Sherman off the street holding one of those 'Will Work for Food' signs."

"Is that possible?"

"I don't think Sherman would take the time to make a sign," Mr. George said. "But Harrigan could have gotten him off the street. That's where Sherman usually is."

"It's odd, though, isn't it? That he took this guy off the street, somebody like Harrigan, who's always saying we should ship all the bums off to labor camps or let them die in their shoes. When was it? How long ago?"

"He didn't say. Harrigan didn't. I don't know if anybody asked Sherman. If they did, they probably didn't get a straight answer. Sherman isn't too good with time."

"Still," Kate said, looking down at the palms of her hands as if they could tell her something, maybe about stock prices. "It doesn't read right. Hiring him doesn't read right. Keeping him around when he was as messed up as you say doesn't read right. It's as if he knew he was going to need a diversion."

"You mean he knew he was going to be arrested?"

"Maybe. Or maybe he just knew he was going to be outed. If Markey wasn't getting him the drugs, I wonder who was."

"You think Sherman's innocent?"

"I can't tell yet," Kate said. "We'll straighten it out in the morning—can we find him in the morning?"

"Sure. We can go out to Holy Innocents first thing, if you want. Meaning about six. Or we could catch him when he gets to the Liberty Bell. That's where Sherman hangs out. At the Liberty Bell."

"That must be interesting for the tourists. Look, put the files I need together so I can look them over tonight, and let's go someplace where I can get a Scotch the size of Detroit. Then you can tell me about your name."

"My name?"

"Why you're having so much trouble telling me what to call you."

Mr. George looked away. He had, Kate thought, a remarkably *chiseled* face, the kind of face that belonged to a male model more than to a law student. He looked back and blinked.

"Chickie," he said. "People call me Chickie. Or they used to."

"Used to?"

"I'm gay. I used to, ah, before law school, I used to . . . camp it up. A lot. Not drag, you know, but swish, really. And then I gave that up. But I'm still gay. And I'm used to Chickie, so that's what people call me who've known me for a while, but people are odd about it."

"You thought I'd mind that you were gay?"

"I thought you might mind that I'm called Chickie. Except I'm trying not to be. The name is . . . I don't know. Something."

"I'll call you Ed, if you want. You ought to go for Edmund, though, to sound suitably Ivy League law school. But Ed?"

"What?"

"As long as you're first-rate at legal research, I don't give a flying damn if you fuck squid."

4

Neil Elliot Savage disliked the Catholic Church in the same way he disliked Philly steaks, and Chinatown, and that god-awful street where the silly detective lived. It was not hate. He wasn't about to put a sheet over his head and ride into the nearest Chinese movie theater screeching about the rights of white people and real Americans. He wasn't even about to write the kind of letter to the editor that always got quoted in fund-raising mailings for organizations like the NAACP and the ACLU. If he could have, he would simply have retreated to a place where he wouldn't be bothered by it all. But, of course, there was no such place anymore in America. The real Americans—and he did consider himself a *real* American, even if the words wouldn't come into his mind fully formed—had so thoroughly lost this battle that they had become irrelevant. The culture was Hispanic, or Italian, or Jewish, or decadent, or dead, but it was not the culture of Emerson and Thoreau, of Jefferson and Adams, of New England brains and Virginia elegance. If the men who had signed the Declaration of Independence were to show up today on the steps of Independence Hall, they would be branded a bunch of liberal intellectual elitists and rendered unelectable in any state but Massachusetts. If his own several times great-grandfather was to rematerialize in the middle of the small plot of land he had settled on when Philadelphia was still a colony, he would find himself in the middle of a restaurant catering to food from the Caucasus. It was all wrong, but there was nothing he could do about it. The best he could manage was to support people like Drew Harrigan, who at least stood against the tide of foreignness that had risen everywhere and would go on rising if something wasn't done to make it stop. That was odd, because in a way Neil Elliot Savage disliked Drew Harrigan more than he disliked the foreignness. With Drew, he came perilously close to hate.

The firm's offices were in a set of interlocking brick houses near Rittenhouse Square. They had been there for over a hundred years, and would be there for a hundred more, unless the neighborhood went to hell. The driver pulled up to the curb outside the main entrance. Neil got his briefcase and his coat and waited for the man to come around to open the door. He had spent all day arguing with a tall, thin, majestic young nun, and his head was throbbing because of it. Besides, she looked familiar. He was sure he'd seen her somewhere before, but he couldn't place where. He didn't know a lot of nuns. He didn't meet them in the ordinary course of his business. His partners knew better than to throw him into contact with the Catholic Church, and especially with anything to do with the Cardinal Archbishop of Philadelphia.

The driver opened the door. Neil got out, went across the sidewalk and up the steps, and rang the bell. Miss Hallworth opened up almost immediately, as if she'd been waiting at the window.

"Good evening, Miss Hallworth," he said, handing her the coat he hadn't bothered to put on. Miss Hallworth was black, but he didn't mind her. He really wasn't a candidate for a white sheet. "Is Marian in the office?"

"She's waiting for you in the conference room."

Miss Hallworth was taking his coat to the walk-in cedar closet where all the partners' coats were kept, and only the partners' coats. The nun this afternoon had had a long wool cloak, like something out of a medieval drama. He couldn't remember what she'd done with it when she'd sat down. He wondered what Drew Harrigan would have done about her if they'd had to meet face-to-face. It gave him a shameful feeling of triumphant glee just to imagine it. Drew Harrigan wasn't the most secure person on the face of the earth. He was especially insecure about his intelligence, which was meager. That nun would have ripped him up one side and down the other.

The problem was, Drew probably wouldn't have minded it. Neil let himself into the conference room. Marian Fuller was sitting in one of the chairs along the side of the table, tapping on a laptop.

"Come in and sit down," she said. "I'm not being serious. I'm on the Internet."

"I didn't know you could get on the Internet in the conference room."

"You can get on the Internet anywhere in these offices. Even the bathrooms. Don't ask me. It was Grayson Barden's idea. Bringing the firm into the twenty-first century."

"The twenty-first century seems to be starting with an ice age. I think it's below zero out there."

"It's minus eleven," Marian said. "So, what did you think? How was Sister Maria Beata of the Incarnation?"

Neil dropped his briefcase on the table and dropped into a chair. "She reminded me of somebody, I'm not sure who. She was bright as hell."

"She didn't remind you of someone, Neil, you know her. At least in passing. Her name used to be Susan Titus Alderman. She was within a week of a partnership at Coatley, Amis when she decided to enter the convent."

"Are you serious? A Catholic at Coatley?"

"She wasn't a Catholic when they hired her. She's Evan Alderman's daughter."

Neil sat up a little straighter. "That's who she reminded

me of, Evan. And not just in the way she looks. She has that same style of argumentation. She's very good."

"She's supposed to be. I meant to tell you about it before you left this morning, but I was late getting in and you went out early. It didn't matter much, though, did it? It wasn't an adversarial situation. You're both on the same side."

"We both want the monastery to be able to sell the property, if that's what you mean."

"That's what I meant, yes," Marian said. "Although you know, I'm getting a little nervous about the buyer. You don't suppose that Drew could be so stupid as to try to be buying the property himself? Behind our backs, I mean."

"Drew is stupid enough for anything and you know it."

"We're using the word differently," Marian said patiently. "He's stupid, yes, in that academic sense that matters so much to people like us, but he's shrewd, too. He's got a good eye for what's best for him. What worries me is that he's greedy, too, and greed gets in the way of judgment far too often. If it didn't, we wouldn't have jobs."

"Well," Neil said, "that's true enough. But the isolation in rehab is real. He has to stay incommunicado for sixty days. He's got forty more of them left. He can't be communicating with lawyers trying to buy the property we're trying to sell for him any more than he can be communicating with us. If he got caught at it, they'd kick him out the door. And then the legal problems would land on his head."

"They're going to land anyway."

"I know. He knows. But time matters."

"True," Marian said. "Of course, in a way, that almost makes it worse. It's not that hot a property. Who would want to buy it?"

"Maybe somebody who wants to help out the nuns without letting it go public that he's contributing to the Archdiocese," Neil said. "The scandals have made a lot of people unhappy to have a public connection."

"This is one and a half million dollars we're talking about. People don't lay out one and a half million dollars anonymously. And there's only so anonymous it can be.

Whoever it is is going to have to file tax forms, I don't know what else. Why the anonymity?"

"Presumably because there's something about the sale we might not like."

"Exactly."

Neil looked away. He liked Philadelphia in the winter. He liked the bleakness of it, the darkly clouded skies, the cold. He thought there was something stronger and finer about people who could live through that without having to run off to someplace southern and sunny, a happyface place without mind and without soul. Mostly without mind, he thought. That was why he hated Drew Harrigan. Drew Harrigan stood for all the crap he had to put up with these days, the alliances he had to make to be allowed to exist in his own country at all.

"Neil?" Marian said.

"Nothing," Neil said. "I was thinking about the Republican Party."

"Why?"

"Drew Harrigan," Neil said. "The new face of the Republican Party. Pork rinds and stock car races. Don't you just get sick of all those people sometimes, the local yokel, we're all small-town folks people? The religious people."

"I don't think Drew Harrigan is religious."

"I don't either. But he's part of it. Part of this whole movement to see intelligence and erudition and cultivation as—I don't know what."

"The hallmark of the liberal Democrat?"

"FDR has a lot to answer for," Neil said. Then he shook his head hard, as if to clear it. "I'm sorry. I'm behaving like an idiot. It's been a long day."

"Because of the nun?"

"The nun was all right. She really is very bright. It was a nice change from Drew."

"Drew's in rehab. You've got a respite. But I think we should take this seriously, Neil. I don't like the fact that the buyer is anonymous, and so anonymous that we can't even trace the lines of influence. I don't like it that he's got a law firm from Wilmington, and one we don't do business with."

"It could be a her," Neil said. "Maybe it's a woman. Maybe Drew put Ellen up to it."

"If he did, he's a dead man," Marian said, "which he may be no matter what, but that would tear it. Have you talked to Ellen?"

"A couple of times."

"And?"

"She didn't say anything in particular. The last time she really thought anything through was when she decided to go out for cheerleader instead of drum majorette in high school. She cries a lot. She's convinced there's a conspiracy to bring Drew down—"

"Drew's convinced of that," Marian said quickly. "And I don't think it's completely out of the question. You've got to wonder why there's this level of fuss—"

"No, you don't," Neil said. "The man was caught with a Tupperware container full of illegally acquired prescription drugs on the seat beside him in the car, while he was driving erratically—assuming we'd like a polite word for it—and then he damn near threatened to blow the cop's head off when he was asked to get out of the car. There's a point at which even the most accommodating district attorney has his hands tied. Or forced, as the case may be. We ought to be grateful that Drew didn't actually have the gun to carry out the threat, or we might be going to a funeral right now."

"There were no guns," Marian said.

Neil sighed. "I don't understand how these people live like that," he said. "The . . . confusion of it, I suppose. The constant upheavals. Drunk and stoned and fighting and I don't know what. He's no different than any of the rest of them."

"We need to do something about the buyer," Marian said. "We need to find out who that is. We need to cover our asses, not to put too fine a point on it."

"I know."

"And?"

"And I don't know," Neil said. "I'll go back to work on it in the morning. We've tried all the usual things. I'll see if there's something we haven't thought of before. Not that it really matters at the moment anyway, since the Justice Project has the injunction and the monastery can't sell the property anyway. Has it ever occurred to you that our lives would be a lot easier if Sherman Markey was just dead?"

"Going to get a gun and start trolling all the SROs and homeless shelters in Philadelphia?"

"No. But it's true. Without Markey making a fuss, nobody would care about the property. Nobody would care about the buyer. This whole thing would disappear in a few weeks. The DA doesn't want to prosecute Drew. It's going to be a pain and a half. He'd be more than happy to agree to a plea bargain on pretty good terms, if nobody was watching. Markey's making everybody watch."

"It was Drew's idea to stick Markey with the procurement charge."

"I know."

"And Markey wasn't procuring anything for anybody."

"I know that, too. So does the DA. Drew's an idiot and an ass. But we knew that already."

Marian turned off her computer and folded it up. "Maybe you ought to go home and get some rest. Go out and have a drink first, if you need to. Get some Johnny Walker Blue."

"If I start drinking Johnny Walker Blue, you're going to have to start paying my mortgage. Do you wonder who it is that Drew's shielding? Who got him the drugs?"

"No," Marian said. "It's not my business to wonder. It's not yours, either."

"No, it isn't. And I suppose it could be Ellen. Of course, she's got the same problem as Sherman Markey. She's a brain-dead ditz. And she's not exactly retiring. She'd walk into a drugstore wearing four-inch heels and thirty thousand dollars' worth of chinchilla and they'd be talking about it for months afterwards."

"Go home," Marian said. "It doesn't matter who got him

the drugs. It doesn't matter that he's an idiot. He's sitting in rehab and he can stay there for the moment."

"He'd better stay there."

"Exactly. Go home."

"If you were going to murder Sherman Markey, the thing to do would be to poison his booze. It wouldn't even be hard. You'd just doctor a bottle and hand it to him, and he'd take it and drink it. Nobody can think his way out of a paper bag these days. It's incredible."

"*I'm* going to go home," Marian said. "Imagine me sitting in front of my fireplace with the cat on my lap, reading P. D. James. Imagine yourself doing the same."

"Emerson," Neil said. "That's what I'm reading. Ralph Waldo Emerson. He couldn't think his way out of a paper bag, either."

Marian tucked the laptop under her arm and left. Neil looked back up out the window. It was not, he thought, about money. Drew was richer than he was by several magnitudes, and he doubted that Drew's family had had any less than his own when they were both growing up. It was not about money but about commitment, and most important, about commitment to those things that made civilization—what? That made civilization civilization. That made civilization *possible*. There was no civilization at all in a world full of people who were proud of their ignorance, who wore their willful stupidity as a mark of honor, who used the words "educated" and "intellectual" as epithets more worthy of scorn than pederasty or treason. It was not about money. It was not even about "Americanism." It was about the life of the mind.

He got up and looked around. The conference room was the same as he remembered it from his father's time. There was good mahogany paneling on the walls. There was good oak flooring underfoot. The Persian carpets had been cleaned a month or so ago, but they hadn't been replaced in fifty years.

Maybe he was wrong to think of the difference in the terms he did. Maybe he was so quick to recoil at the excesses of Drew Harrigan and his followers that he missed the good in them. Maybe the world had not been better and finer and more honorable when he was a boy—but it had been more uncompromisingly respectful of intelligence and achievement, and it had not been so enamored of the populist skew. He was sick of the jokes of people who could only laugh at what they did because they didn't understand it. He was sick of the kind of religion that pressed relentlessly to compress all life into the intellectual provincialism of the sort of small towns that had once made Sinclair Lewis despair. His America was not the America of creationism and WWJD bracelets any more than it was the America of bodegas and barrios. There were days when he wanted to torch the entire city of Philadelphia just to see what would rise from the ashes.

He wouldn't do it, because he was scared to death, deep down, that what would rise would be a rap band and a Bible-believing Christian.

He had to go home. Marian was right. It had been a long day, a long week, a long month, a long year, and he had gotten to that point in the day when killing somebody felt like a rational response to the conditions he was forced to live under.

It wouldn't do him any good to murder Sherman Markey—but he was right about the fact that everybody he knew would be better off if Sherman Markey showed up dead.

5

To Ellen O'Bannion Harrigan, life often seemed like a jigsaw puzzle with a couple of pieces missing—or like the English classes she had been required to take in high school, where the teacher and all the other students had been part of a joke she had not been let into, and kept claiming to see Meaning and Symbolism and Complexity in poems Ellen knew made no sense. There was a lot of that second thing going around in the world at large, as far as Ellen could see. Even the people who worked in Drew's office liked to talk about Iconography and Semiotics and the Politics of Meaning, which Ellen had finally figured out was the idea that people voted in order to make sure their lives Meant Something in the long run. She had no idea what it was people were supposed to want their lives to Mean.

Right now, what Ellen knew was that she wanted the city of Philadelphia to do something about the homeless people. This was the fourth little knot of them she had seen in the ride back from the dentist's office, huddled together over the steam grates that were set into the sidewalk every block in the middle of the city. There were two women and two men. They were all impossibly dirty.

The city of Philadelphia should move them, Ellen thought, sitting back. *The city should send them to shelters, or arrest them for vagrancy.* She didn't trust people who chose to live like that. Sherman Markey was a homeless person, after all, and he was responsible for Drew taking drugs and being in all the trouble he was in. Drew would never have taken drugs if he'd been left to himself. He wasn't a drug kind of person. It was the homeless people who took drugs.

The apartment was just up ahead, not a block and a half away. There were no homeless people here. The doormen chased them away. They sometimes got into trouble for doing it—apparently, you weren't supposed to be able to make citizens get off the public sidewalks, even if they were dirty and smelled and might be dangerous to the people who lived in the neighborhood—but they did it anyway, and most of the time nobody complained. She just wanted to get home and take a couple of Advil to keep her jaw from aching. This was the fourth root canal she'd had in as many weeks.

The driver pulled up to the curb and Ellen waited patiently for him to come around and open her door. This was important. Drew had drilled it into her over and over again. This wasn't a cab. This was his personal car and his personal driver. That made it her personal car and her personal driver. It wasn't her job to behave as if the driver were doing her any favors. She was also supposed to remember not to call him a *"chauffeur."*

The driver came and opened the door. She got out into the wind and flinched. It was really very, very cold. You would think that a night like this would make those people living on the street realize they had to change their lives and learn to be better. People called her stupid, but even she wasn't so stupid that she couldn't have picked up on a point like that one.

She said good evening to the doorman and went in through the big glass doors into the lobby, and then she stopped. There was a woman in the lobby, sitting in one of the big leather armchairs with her coat thrown off to the back of her, reading something Ellen thought at first might be a monthly magazine called *First Things*—and if that had been the case, the woman would have been Martha Iles, Drew's chief assistant. Ellen truly hated Martha Iles, in spite of the fact that she knew Drew would never be attracted to her, never in a million years. Actually, no man anywhere would ever be attracted to Martha. She was a frump, a pudgy little woman who wore skirts just long enough to make her legs look thicker. She was also a right royal bitch—which was a word, like *"chauffeur,"* that Ellen was supposed to remember never to say.

The woman in the chair wasn't reading *First Things*, but *Vanity Fair*, which was kept on the coffee table in the lobby to give visitors something to do while the people they were waiting for were taking too long to come down and get them. She was too tall and too thin to be Martha, too, and her hair had been colored recently, where Martha's had never been colored at all. Ellen relaxed a little. It was Danielle Underwood, Drew's media assistant, the one he had hired to prove that he wasn't some kind of anti-woman sexist Neanderthal.

Of course, as far as Ellen was concerned, women really should spend their time in kitchens, but that was just her opinion. It was just because she thought children were more important than money, even if she couldn't have any right now, because it would make things too complicated.

Danielle had seen her come in and put the magazine back on the coffee table. She stood up and got her coat by its collar.

"Ellen," she said. "It's good to see you."

Ellen did not think it was all that good to see Danielle, but she couldn't say that kind of thing. The ideal was to be always gracious and polite and absolutely vacuous, so that nobody could tell what you were thinking.

"Danielle," she said. "Has something happened? Isn't it late for you to be out?"

"I've been talking to the lawyers. To Neil Savage. I thought I'd come over and tell you what was going on."

"I don't really understand what's going on," Ellen said. "There's no use explaining it to me. Drew will be back in about a month. You should tell it all to him, then. He handles that kind of thing."

"Yes," Danielle said. "Well." She looked at the doorman.

There was going to be no way to avoid having this woman up to the apartment. It drove Ellen crazy.

"Why don't you come up to the apartment?" Ellen asked Danielle. Then she headed for the elevators, biting the insides of her cheeks so that she wouldn't scream. Her jaw hurt. She'd just had a root canal. She wanted to take painkillers and go to bed and watch *Titanic* on DVD.

The apartment took up half the top floor of this building. It could only be reached if you had a special key to put into the board next to the floor buttons. Ellen keyed them in and waited for the elevator doors to open up on the penthouse lobby.

She went across the lobby and opened the apartment with another key. Drew was always talking about getting full-time staff, including a maid to open up for them when they came home, but Ellen thought it would make things seem too cramped even in a large apartment. They could wait for the full-time staff for when they bought a place out on the Main Line.

Danielle walked through the foyer and threw her coat on the back of the couch. Ellen followed her, trying to look helpful and upbeat.

"Can I get you anything? Coffee? I can't offer you a drink, because we threw all that out just before Drew went into rehab. Not that Drew's an alcoholic, you understand, but it's supposed to be bad for somebody who's getting over a problem with pills. I don't understand why it's legal to sell pills like that if they're addictive. I mean, isn't that why drugs are illegal? Because they're addictive?"

"I don't know," Danielle said. "I've never thought about it. I don't need coffee, Ellen, thank you. I just wanted to tell you what the lawyers said."

"It's not going to do any good telling me what the lawyers said. I'm not going to understand it, because I don't know the background. Drew can take care of it when he gets home."

"Right," Danielle said. "Look, Ellen, you've got to try to understand that Drew may not be able to handle things when he gets home. Even assuming the course of treatment in re-hab is one hundred percent successful—"

"—Why shouldn't it be one hundred percent successful? Drew doesn't want to be addicted to anything. It's just a matter of strength of character. Drew has a lot of strength of character. The problem with most people who take drugs is that they don't care. They don't want to get up out of their little cocoons and get some work done."

"Right," Danielle said again. "The thing is, even assuming success, Drew's going to have a lot of legal problems to deal with. You've got to get used to the fact that he might have to spend some time in jail."

Ellen blinked. "Nonsense," she said. "Why should he spend any time in jail? He hasn't done anything wrong."

"He was caught in possession of dozens of pills that he had no right to have."

"But they were legal pills," Ellen said. "They were pills doctors gave him."

"The doctors only gave him the pills because he lied to them and said no other doctors were giving him the same pills. Which is against the law. And then there are the pills the doctors didn't give him, that he got on the black market—"

"From that man Sherman Markey. I know. I saw him on

the news the other night. I don't understand why he isn't in jail."

"He's out on bail."

"He shouldn't be out on bail, though, should he? He should be in jail."

"Ellen, at the moment, *Drew* is out on bail."

"They've got those people being Sherman Markey's lawyers. The Justice Project. They're Communists, did you know that? Drew told me. During the Cold War, they actively worked for the destruction of the United States and the victory of her enemies. That's just how Drew put it. Aren't people given the death penalty for treason?"

Danielle ran her tongue slowly over her upper lip, and all of a sudden Ellen didn't want to be in the same room with her anymore. For all she knew, Danielle could be a lesbian. So many people were, these days.

"I'm going to make coffee," she said. "And I'm going to take some Advil. I just had a root canal."

"I'm sorry, Ellen. I didn't mean to barge in on you at a bad moment."

"Advil is all right, isn't it? It's not illegal? I won't go to jail for having a whole bottle of Advil in the medicine cabinet, a big one, with two hundred fifty pills?"

"No, of course you won't. Ellen, listen, it's about the property on Hardscrabble Road that Drew deeded to the Our Lady of Mount Carmel Monastery. The nuns want to sell it."

"Well, it's their property now, isn't it? That's what Drew said. They can sell it if they want to."

"Ordinarily yes, of course, they could. But now, you see, there's a problem, because the lawyers at the Justice Project have gone to court and gotten an injunction to stop the sale until Mr. Markey's suit against Drew can be settled—"

"I can't believe that man is suing Drew. I can't believe it. It's the money, you know. He thinks Drew is rich. He ought to be in jail."

"Yes, well, the thing is, the reason why the judge agreed to stop the sale—hold it up, temporarily, really—anyway, the reason is that the judge thinks there's a chance that the entire transaction, giving the property to the convent, the sale, that the entire thing is a setup. That Drew has somebody pretending to be a buyer who isn't a real buyer. And that the sale will look all right on paper, but no money will actually change hands, so Drew will end up owning the property but at the same time the paperwork will look like he doesn't and therefore it won't be taken away from him if he's ordered to pay Sherman Markey any money."

"You're being ridiculous. You sound like a mystery story."

"It's not at all ridiculous, Ellen. People do it all the time. They shield money from taxes, from lawsuits, from spouses they're divorcing."

"Drew isn't divorcing me."

"No, of course he's not. I just mean that people do that kind of maneuver very often if they're afraid a court is going to attach their assets. And this is just the kind of case where a court could attach Drew's assets. Sherman Markey may win his lawsuit. There's no telling. And Drew could have—"

"He's in rehab," Ellen said triumphantly. "He couldn't have. He isn't allowed to talk to anybody. He isn't even allowed to talk to me."

"I know. I don't think anybody thinks he's trying to run this from rehab. Drew isn't that stupid. It's possible he set it up before he went in, with somebody he could trust."

"Who?"

Danielle coughed. "Well, not to put too fine a point on it, you."

"Me?"

"You're his wife, Ellen. You can't even be required to testify against him in court."

"And I'm supposed to be doing what, trying to buy this property Drew just gave away? Except I wouldn't be really buying it, because I wouldn't be using money?"

"Ellen, please. The Abbess of Our Lady of Mount Carmel is Drew's sister. She—"

"She could be in on it, too? A nun?"

"You've got to understand that the Catholic Church

doesn't have a great reputation for honesty in this country at the moment."

"I'm getting my Advil," Ellen said. "This is ridiculous. You're making it all up. Drew gave some property to a convent. He was giving to charity, for God's sake."

"He didn't give to charity until after Sherman Markey filed his suit."

"And it's no use thinking he and that awful woman have some kind of scheme going together. They can barely stand to be in the same room with each other. She's a liberal, you know, politically. She hates everything Drew stands for. She hates me."

"I didn't know nuns had politics," Danielle said. "Never mind, Ellen, I'm sorry I bothered you. I know it's ridiculous, under the circumstances, knowing the people involved. But I did think you needed to know what people are thinking, and what they're going to go on thinking. This isn't going to go away, not even when Drew gets out of rehab. You're both going to have to deal with it."

"I don't have to deal with anything. Drew deals with it."

"Yes," Danielle said. "Right. Okay, Ellen, I'm going to go and let you take your Advil and get some rest. I'm sorry I bothered you. It's just that we thought, and the lawyers thought, we thought it was important you understood what's going on."

"I understand what's going on," Ellen said. "It's that Sherman Markey. He got caught and now he's trying to put it all off on Drew. He should learn to take responsibility for himself and live like a decent person."

"Yes," Danielle said. "Well."

She was all packed up and ready to go. Ellen didn't move to follow her into the foyer and out the door. She didn't care how gracious and polite she was supposed to be. Her jaw hurt, and she wanted nothing more than to claw the skin off Danielle Underwood's face—or Sherman Markey's, if she could find him anywhere close.

There was something she hadn't gotten again, something she was being stupid about. She could see it in the way

Danielle was looking at her, but she'd be damned if she'd come out and ask about what it was.

That was the kind of mistake she used to make in high school, and she was never going to make it again.

6

Marla Hildebrande cared nothing about politics. She cared nothing about religion, either, beyond the sort of vague fuzzy-happy feeling that there probably had to be a God out there somewhere, watching out for her. It only made sense. If people asked her whether she prayed, she said yes, because she sent up heartfelt wishes for deliverance several times a day. It was the kind of thing anybody would do if they had to work with the kind of people she had to work with. If people asked her what she thought of the president of the United States or gun control or gay marriage or tax cuts, she tended to mumble a lot and look bright but mentally disabled. She only rarely knew what they were talking about anyway, and President George W. Bush had been in office for two years before she realized he was in office at all. When people said "President Bush" to her, she thought they were talking about the first one, whom she rather liked, because he reminded her of a boy she had dated her freshman year in college. She was shocked to find out that gay people were demanding the right to marry. Why would they want to, when marriage was mostly a hellhole for the heterosexual people who already had the right to do it? The one issue that sounded vaguely interesting to her was tax cuts, because cuts seemed to imply that she would pay fewer taxes and take home more money, although she wasn't sure of that. Political people got her confused, and they were angry all the time. Religious people weren't angry *all* the time, but they were angry a lot, and too many of them seemed to go to jail for tax fraud. She couldn't understand why any of it mattered anyway. It was only people talking, and the more they talked, the less sense they made. She was not registered to vote, which probably didn't matter either. She would never remember to go to the polling place and do it.

She would remember what night the election was on, because so many of the people she managed cared so much about elections, and so many of the programs she handled wound themselves around election results when the time came. She looked on them the way she looked on Oscar nights and the nights Miss America was crowned. It was the contest that mattered. Contests created conflict and conflict created narrative drive and narrative drive created radio programs people wanted to listen to, and if people wanted to listen to your programs, advertisers wanted to advertise on them. It didn't even matter if the conflict was controversial, or what kind of controversial it was. Rush Limbaugh and Howard Stern both made a lot of money.

Now she looked at the pile of papers on her desk and bit her lip. It was cold. There was a draft from the window at her back. Every time the pane rattled in the wind she could feel needles of ice running up and down her spine. Her story was simple, uncomplicated, and mostly (she thought) uninteresting. She had grown up in a suburb of Lehigh in a family that had been well-off enough that she'd never really thought about money, but not as well-off as the families of the two doctors and three lawyers in town, whose daughters sent away to New York for handbags and panty hose from Lord & Taylor. She had worked hard at school and gotten good grades, because that's what you did. It was your job, and it was important to be conscientious at your job. She had joined the school newspaper and later the school yearbook staff. It was a matter of getting up every morning and doing what you were supposed to do. She knew that she was neither a genius nor an idiot, in the same way she knew that she was neither a beauty nor a beast. She had friends without being popular, a place on the honor roll without being valedictorian, was good for a game of basketball in gym class without being athletic in a way likely to get her noticed by a scout from one of the bigger universities. When the time came, she had gone off to Gettysburg College, one of those good enough schools that were not quite up to being first tier, never mind Ivy League. On the day she graduated, she was like a thousand other girls at good-but-not-great colleges from one end of the country to the other. The only thing she had going for her was that steady conscientiousness that was the closest she had come to finding a moral center to her life. Other people debated the existence and definition of good and evil. Marla did not debate. She only insisted—for herself as well as everybody else—that work get done when it was supposed to and as it was supposed to, that records be kept with thoroughness and care, that letters and phone calls be answered within the day if at all possible, and that no problem be left unattended until there was time to attend to it. Marla Hildebrande hated procrastination.

At the moment, she also hated Drew Harrigan, and this Markey person, and every single lawyer in the city of Philadelphia. If she had been susceptible to migraines, she would have gotten one. As it was, her teeth hurt. Conscientiousness buys you things. She didn't know when she'd first understood that, but it had been a long time before she'd landed at LibertyHeart Communications, and what it had bought her at the moment was the fact that she was the youngest network programming executive in American radio. She was so young that there had even been speculation in the trades that she'd only gotten this last promotion because she was sleeping with Frank Sheehy, the president and CEO and chairman of the board and founder—which was a good damned trick, since Frank was as gay as she was straight and made no secret of it. When she surfaced long enough to consider conditions in the real world around her, Marla sometimes wondered how Frank got away with it. You would have thought Drew Harrigan's devoted fans would have had a hissy fit long ago about his show being carried on a network that belonged to a "pervert," but they never did. It made Marla think that she must have it a lot more right than the talking heads she saw on CNN on the odd night she decided to tune it in. Nobody really cared about any of the stuff they said they cared about. They only said they cared about it to give themselves something to do, and keep from being bored.

Personally, Marla preferred to stave off boredom with steak, wine, chocolate, and a good mystery novel, but it was probably a good thing other people didn't agree with her, because if they did there would be no LibertyHeart Communications for her to run the programming for.

Of course, if this kept up, there might not be any Liberty-Heart Communications to run the programming for anyway. That was why Frank was sitting on her couch—all right, lying half off it and half on it—and she was pawing through reports at six o'clock in the evening. She had been in the office since before six in the morning, and it was time to go home.

"I just can't believe that so much of our income depends on one man," Frank said. "I mean, he's only one man. Granted, he's the size of a house, and he probably takes up two seats on any airplane he flies on that he doesn't actually own, the principle remains the same. Was that smart of us, relying so much on one man?"

"We didn't do it on purpose, Frank. We were putting together a lineup, we were putting together a network, we were putting together a syndicate, and along came Drew."

"Do you ever wonder about that? I mean, he's got nothing to speak of. No credentials. The level of his commentary barely rises to the standard of a high school debating team— no, he'd get kicked off a high school debating team. He spends too much time shouting. Whatever made Drew Harrigan the biggest thing on radio since rock 'n' roll?"

"The same thing that made Father Coughlin the biggest thing on radio since radio, back in the day when Father Coughlin was a force to be reckoned with."

"Meaning racism and xenophobia?"

"Meaning that radio reaches a downscale audience," Marla said, blocking out the thought that she'd already had to explain this at least a dozen times over the years. "The kind of people you never met at Princeton. Or, what was it? Andover—"

"Exeter."

"Same difference."

"We don't think so."

"Everybody else does. Trust me, Frank. Anyway, it's a downscale audience. Mostly white men in blue-collar jobs or, worse, who've lost them. Guys who are worried about making the next car payment and worried about making the rent and worried about the state of their credit card bills. Guys who wake up in the morning and look in the mirror and find themselves staring straight into the face of a loser."

"And Drew is what? One of their own?"

"Sort of."

"You'd think they'd all be socialists."

"They aren't 'ists.' They don't go that far. They just know that they've got to put up with being embarrassed every single day, and it's always by the local doctor or lawyer or professor at the community college, the guys who went and got the education they didn't get and probably couldn't have gotten because they didn't have the academic talent, those guys. And they hate them. They truly hate them."

"So the whole phenomenon runs on hate."

"The whole phenomenon runs on resentment. Drew makes them feel real. He says what they think and says it's okay and makes millions of dollars doing it. They feel like they're getting their own back. I think of Drew as an addiction. When they can't have him, they get depressed. They go into withdrawal."

"And they haven't abandoned him because of the, ah, legal trouble?"

"You mean, because it turns out he's been broadcasting high for the last three years? No, of course not. Half of them think he's the victim of some left-wing plot. All of them have or have had alcohol and drug problems of their own. They sympathize."

"Then I don't understand. Why are we having a problem with the numbers?"

"Well," Marla said, "think of it this way. Their addiction is to Drew, not to right-wing politics. Oh, some of them have an addiction to right-wing politics, and those people will go on listening no matter who's putting out the message. But most of these guys want Drew, personally. And Drew isn't here. Drew is in rehab."

"And they don't like his replacement?"

"We've had three replacements in three weeks. None of them has gone over, and I don't think any of the others we're going to try will. Drew is a true phenomenon. He's practically sui generis. Even Limbaugh doesn't generate the kind of blind loyalty he does. Our numbers are off by fifty percent since the day Drew announced the drug thing, and that isn't the worst news. The worst news is that they're still falling, and they're falling fast."

Frank thought about it. "But it's temporary, isn't it? Drew will be out of rehab, in, what, forty days?"

"Forty-two. I've got the replacements doing a countdown. But Frank, you've got to face some facts. One is that even though Drew may get out of rehab, he may not be available to work right away. Or if he is, maybe not for long."

"Meaning what?"

"Meaning that the DA isn't going to let this go. He can't let this go. People would scream bloody murder. He's going to have to prosecute."

"But there won't be a trial," Frank said. "There never is in cases like this. There'll be a plea bargain. I know Drew is stupid, but he's not stupid enough to go to trial and risk getting sent to a penitentiary."

"No, he's not. But the DA still has that problem, and my guess is that he's going to insist on Drew doing at least some jail time. The Feds won't. No matter which side is in power when the time comes to do something about Drew's case, they'll back away. The Republicans will do it because they don't want to slam one of their own. The Democrats will do it because they don't want to be accused of playing politics. But the DA, Frank, the DA is stuck between a rock and a hard place. He's going to have to insist on something serious. Especially if he's going after Sherman Markey. I mean, how would it look—you stick the addled old homeless guy in jail for delivering the drugs but you let the rich celebrity go free because you think he's a victim?"

"Crap," Frank said.

"I've talked to the legal department. They say we should get ready for at least ten months' incarceration when this all shakes out."

"Worse crap."

"I know. You're right, by the way. We shouldn't be relying so much on just one man, and the fact that we do goes a long way to explaining the fact that we aren't bigger than we are, when we should be. And I think that it would definitely be a good idea if we started looked around to expand our roster, maybe even expand our scope."

"You mean actually hire liberals for once? Can't be done. Most of them can read."

"I meant looking into shock jocks. But in the meantime, we've got a big problem, and we need to think of something we can do about it."

"Have you thought of something?" Frank looked curious.

Marla sighed. "No. Aside from murdering Sherman Markey, I can't think of anything to do at the moment. We've got the replacements doing the countdown and pleading for the fans to support Drew, which they do; they just don't want to listen to somebody else. We'd be better off if Drew could make the pleas for support himself from rehab, but of course if he did that the DA would land on him and we'd be in the same mess, except there'd be pictures of Drew with a number plate under his chin running in all the daily papers. But we do need to think of something, Frank, and we need to think of it fast."

"Are we losing money?"

"Now? No. Most of our advertisers are on long-term contracts. But long-term contracts run out, and they're not happy. If Drew does have to go to jail for ten months, we'll be eviscerated. I mean it. They won't stand for it."

"The contracts are all coming due?"

"The contracts all have escape clauses in them. The advertisers aren't using them now because this is supposed to be a short-term thing and they don't want the fans to get mad at them, but they won't put up with ten months. They really won't."

"How would killing Sherman Markey help?"

"What? Oh. It's what I said. It's the contrast. The DA can't be seen to be hounding this poor old man into prison and letting the celebrity go free. If there was no poor old man to hound, it would be easier to let Drew off, run the process out for a year or two, and then quietly, when nobody was looking, give him probation. Do you see what I mean?"

"I suppose so."

"Of course, we could have something really interesting happen and find out who was really getting Drew the drugs, but I'm not expecting that anytime soon. Doesn't it bother you any? Who do you think was really procuring for him?"

"Ellen, probably."

"Ellen can barely procure coffee at Starbucks. Oh, never mind. I'm just fussing now. It will all work itself out in the wash. But we've got the next forty-two days, plus probably another six to eight months after that, to save our asses from this thing, and we'd better do it. We're not going to survive as a network or a syndicate with only one property."

"I know," Frank said. He stood up. "Do you know what I wanted to do when I started this network? I wanted to do rock 'n' roll. I wanted to be the place that wouldn't fire Alan Freed. I don't know if there's a disc jockey anywhere these days who's like Alan Freed."

"Rock 'n' roll is a wholly owned subsidiary of global capitalism. Or so says Jig Tyler. There's somebody you could put on the air. We'd probably get firebombed by the local militia."

"I'm going to go find someplace where there isn't a draft. It's freezing in here. You should get that window fixed."

"It's not broken."

"It's letting in cold air."

Actually, there was a thin film of ice along the bottom of it, right where the pane connected to the frame. Marla started pulling the papers on her desk into stacks.

"Lucy can do this tomorrow," she said. "But I don't want you to go to bed tonight without thinking about this. Thinking about what you want to do. Come in in the morning and be ready to give me my marching orders on our next step. If you don't, we're all going to be out of work in eighteen months."

"And killing what's his name isn't really an option, I take it?"

Marla would have said no, but it seemed superfluous, so she just went on stacking papers. She wished there was something she could do to change the world so that Frank could have the rock 'n' roll radio network he'd always wanted, and she could run it.

Instead, she was going to have to go home with the car radio tuned in to this station, and listen to one more good old boy with a down-home accent ranting about liberal elitists, pinko abortionists, and the homosexual agenda.

7

Ray Dean Ballard had spent most of the evening looking out his window and wishing for snow, but the best the weather had been able to do was a few ice crystals around five o'clock. Most of the time, Ray Dean hated snow. Snow meant the benches in the parks would be wet as soon as anybody lay down on them. Snow meant too much traffic in the streets and too many car accidents. Snow meant yet another story in the *Philadelphia Inquirer* about some homeless person somewhere pissing on the tires of a Volvo some doctor had parked at the curb while he ran into the store for the paper and hot coffee. From a public relations standpoint, extreme cold was much better than snow. In extreme cold, the story in the *Philadelphia Inquirer* was always about some homeless person who had frozen to death under a bridge because there wasn't enough room for him in the shelters.

There really wasn't enough room in the shelters for nights like this, but Ray Dean knew that the homeless person who died under the bridge tonight would not be there because he had been refused a bed. Ray Dean was twenty-six years old. He had been out of Vanderbilt for less than half a decade, and at work in this organization for even less time than that, and he already knew more than he wanted to about the homeless problem in America's cities. At least, he assumed it was the same homeless problem in all of America's cities. Part of the problem with being young and on your first job was that you lacked the breadth of experience you needed to judge whether your situation was atypical or not. He didn't think Philadelphia was atypical, but he knew he was. He couldn't imagine a bigger difference between this place and the place he grew up. He didn't know what it said about him that he was fourteen years old before he rode in a car without a uniformed driver.

Why exactly he'd majored in English literature, he didn't know. Maybe it was because he got more of an insight into the things he was dealing with by reading Dickens than by going to lectures in sociology and social work, which always seemed to assume that the homeless were not only a problem but a "problem," and something to be solved.

He looked up at the chart on his wall and the arrows he'd been drawing on it all day, from the parks to the shelters, from the soup kitchens to the shelters, from the alleys to the . . . where? The fact was, if they hid out in the alleys, they didn't want to go into the shelters. They weren't even happy going into the soup kitchens, for fear someone would force them into the shelters. There was, out there in America, a wave of paranoia the like of which he had never suspected—even though he'd been sitting in Nashville, the very heart of it. It wasn't just the homeless people who were defensive and afraid. It was everybody. If one half of Congress proposed the institution of a universal health care system, the other half was sure the first half were only doing it so that they could spy on the private lives of ordinary people and force them to eat wine and Brie instead of cheeseburgers and Cokes. If the part of Congress that was afraid of the universal health care system wanted to set up a universal database to track serial killers who went from state to state seeking victims, the part of Congress that had wanted the universal health care system would be convinced that the tracking project was a way to worm Big Brother into the lives of ordinary citizens and track their every move so that they could be picked up as soon as they showed any sign of opposing government initiatives. People owned guns not to protect themselves from crime in bad neighborhoods but in case the government came to the door wanting to lock them up for being Christians or socialists. At least the socialists had history on their side, if only vaguely. McCarthy had really existed. So had the Red Scares.

Even so, it was as if the entire world had gone completely insane. It was impossible to get anything done. It was impossible to talk calmly and sensibly about solving a problem or even alleviating it. The Republicans thought the Democrats wanted to make it a law, on penalty of imprisonment, that everybody had to exercise and eat like vegans. The Democrats thought the Republicans were going to tamper with the new digital voting machines so that votes for Democrats would be counted as votes for Republicans and nobody would be able to check. It had gone beyond craziness and into some Twilight Zone of schizophrenic delusion where there were enemies around every corner, secret agendas behind every closet door, and evil lurking in the hearts of anybody who didn't drive the kind of car you drove, listen to the kind of music you listened to, and eat the kind of food you ate.

In the meantime, Ray Dean was sitting here worrying about 318 people who were living on the streets in this city, a good 50 of whom would refuse to come in out of the cold even when cold meant minus eleven degrees, or worse. He had exactly four vans, each of which could carry seven people besides the driver. One of those vans was in the shop with brake problems, and one of the others was holding two large garbage bags of clothes it had to deliver to one of the shelters, reducing its passenger capacity to six. They were going to be out there all night, first collecting the easy ones at the soup kitchens, then going through the parks, then looking through the alleys and under the bridges and in the abandoned buildings where the drug addicts shot up to be out of sight of the police until they could get high enough not to care if they got arrested. They would look and look, but they would miss some nonetheless, and tomorrow the *Inquirer* would run its story about the people who had frozen to death and how the people trying to help them were understaffed and underfunded. It was true, Ray Dean thought, they were understaffed and underfunded. The newspaper people meant well.

There was a knock at the door and he called out to whoever it was to come in. His attention had suddenly been caught by the books on the floor-to-ceiling built-in shelves that made up one of his walls: Henry James. George Steiner. W. B. Yeats. Lionel Trilling. John Donne. His parents had expected him to give it all up and get a business degree as soon as he graduated and come to his senses. He thought he might do that, one of these days, out of exhaustion or desperation. At the moment, he only wondered how the two things could exist in the world at the same time: those old men dying of cold under the bridges; John Donne telling us all that no man is an island, entire of itself.

There seemed to be many men who wanted to be islands. Women, too.

The door popped open and Shelley Balducci stuck her head in, looking frazzled. "I've just been on the phone to Chickie George. He says they've lost Sherman."

"Lost him? How do you lose Sherman?"

"Well, he's wandered off, you know what he means. And the thing is, Chickie's afraid he might be hard to spot. They got him cleaned up. He's had a shower, and a shave, and a haircut—does Sherman need haircuts? Isn't he practically bald? Anyway, he's had all that and he's got entirely new clothes on. So he doesn't smell, and he might not necessarily look like a homeless person. And they don't know where he is."

"Did they go down to that place, the Benedictine place?"

"Yes, they did, and there was no sign of him. The nuns

haven't seen him. And you know Sherman. He's a creature of habit. So they're worried. He looks prosperous from the perspective of other homeless people and drug addicts. They're afraid he might have been rolled."

Ray Dean considered this. One of the things he hadn't expected when he first came to work here—it hadn't been true in the place he'd volunteered in Nashville in college—was that he would develop relationships with some of the people who needed his services. They weren't the kind of relationships he had with his parents, or his friends, or even Shelley, but they were relationships nonetheless, with histories, and futures, and private understandings. He could honestly say that Sherman was one of the people he had developed a relationship with. Sherman was not as addled as he liked to look. He could keep the contents of a conversation in his head, if he hadn't had too much to drink too recently, and he remembered things over time in a way that the mentally ill homeless never could. There weren't many clients who made Ray Dean wonder how they had ever ended up the way they had ended up, but Sherman was one of them.

"Sherman's pretty good about neighborhoods," he said now. "It wouldn't be like him to get rolled."

"He's pretty good about neighborhoods when he's on his own, yes, but the Justice Project people put him up in an SRO. Not that I said anything about that to Chickie, of course. I mean, they meant well. I just wish all the people who meant well would think before they ran around doing things to 'solve' the problems of the homeless. What I'm thinking is that he'd have had to have left the SRO room and made his way through some fairly nasty territory to get back to where he was used to, and along the way anything could have happened."

"Crap," Ray Dean said. Somebody else would have said, "Shit." He just couldn't. There was a difference that being from his kind of people made in the way you behaved that nobody up here had managed to call him on yet.

Shelley came all the way into the room and closed the

door behind her. "The thing is," she said, sitting down on the edge of Ray Dean's desk, "we don't want anything to happen to him."

"Of course we don't."

"I mean, for more than the usual reasons. You know and I know that if Sherman isn't around to carry on with that lawsuit, Drew Harrigan's people are going to paste that whole sorry drug mess on him and Drew Harrigan is going to end up walking off scot-free."

"They're going to try to do that even if he is around to carry on with the lawsuit."

"I know that. But it won't be the same, will it? Sherman might win the lawsuit and that would leave Drew Harrigan in a lot more trouble than he would be otherwise, or Sherman might lose it and then they'd want to put him in jail and you know as well as I do that they couldn't put Sherman in jail without putting Drew Harrigan in too, at least for a while. Think how it would look otherwise. Think of the political fallout."

"So?"

"So there's good reason for us to take a little extra time tonight and try to find him and bring him to safety. If he doesn't want to live at the SRO—and I don't blame him, those places are hellholes—maybe we could bring him back here and let him sleep in the storeroom. He wouldn't be any trouble to anybody and he'd be warm."

"He'd end up pissing on the printer paper."

"No, he wouldn't. Or maybe he would. We can always buy printer paper. What's it worth to you to get Drew Harrigan off the air?"

Ray Dean looked at his radio, propped up on a shelf in front of the collected works of Ernest Hemingway. "I listened to the replacement guy tonight. He was hopeless."

"Right," Shelley said. "That means he was ineffective, which is definitely what we're looking for, isn't it? Think of it. No more hour-long rants about how it's all their own fault. They made their bed and they should have to lie in it. Decent citizens shouldn't be taxed to pay for bums who have no respect for themselves. No more letter-writing campaigns to the mayor of Philadelphia demanding to get the homeless off the streets and put them in jail, for God's sake. What do these people want, a return to the days when we arrested people for being poor?"

"Did we ever have days when we arrested people for being poor?"

"We had poorhouses," Shelley said, "and we put people in jail for debt. Or at least they did in England. It was in that book you gave me."

"*David Copperfield.*"

"That's the one. They want to go back to that. I mean the Dickens thing. They want to punish poor people for being poor."

"Sherman Markey's principal problem isn't that he's poor."

"I know that."

"Poor is easy to fix," Ray Dean said. "There's a problem you can solve by throwing money at it."

"We really don't want Sherman Markey to disappear. Not now. We should have one of the vans go actively looking for him. Yes, even in this weather and even though we have a lot of people to bring in. It's just a matter of letting one of the drivers know and giving him some idea of what to look for. He can pick up other people on the way."

Ray Dean rubbed the sides of his face with the palms of his hands and thought about it. It wasn't just Sherman Markey they should be looking for. In fact, under most circumstances, Sherman Markey was well down on the list of people they should be worried about, because Sherman was an alcoholic, not a paranoid schizophrenic. Unless he was too drunk to see, he knew he could die of cold and he had nothing against spending the night in a shelter if he could find a bed. Nobody ever had to corner Sherman at the end of a dead-end street and hope to hell he didn't have a knife under the folds of his too-big clothes and the will and the delusory vision to use it.

"There's another thing," Shelley said.

Ray Dean looked up.

"There's Drew Harrigan's people," Shelley said. "Don't you know as well as I do that they want Sherman dead? It wouldn't take much. They could hire some street kid for a couple of thousand dollars and that would be the last you'd see of Sherman Markey."

"Oh, for God's sake," Ray Dean said. It wasn't just "shit" he couldn't say. He couldn't say "for Christ's sake" either. You didn't want to be caught doing that in an area of the country where a church could have ten thousand people show up for Wednesday evening prayer services.

"I know you think I'm exaggerating—"

"—I think you're behaving like a loon. What's wrong with people? Do you honestly think that Drew Harrigan, who, no matter what else he is, is a major force in American media, who meets with congressmen and presidents, who does commercials for everything from shaving cream to fast food, do you honestly think a man in that position would go out and hire some coked-up street kid to stick it to a mess of a homeless man who's going to lose his lawsuit anyway because he's not going to be able to remember whatever it was he was supposed to testify to when he gets to the witness stand? Do you really believe that?"

"To save himself a few years in a federal penitentiary? Yes. I believe that."

"Then I give up," Ray Dean said. "I really do. There used to be a world where we all gave our fellow citizens the benefit of the doubt. We didn't think they were out to get us. We didn't think that perfectly sane people went out and committed murders, hired hit men, I don't know what. We didn't suspect they were doing God only knows what behind closed doors and always to—to—I don't know—I don't know what to think anymore."

"It wouldn't be that much trouble to have the drivers actively looking for Sherman. It really wouldn't. And he'd be easier to find than you think. He's got a red hat."

"A red hat?"

"Chickie told me. They bought him new clothes, and one

of the things they bought him was a red hat. It was in the store where they took him shopping and he liked it, so they bought it for him. One of those watchman's hats, you know, except instead of navy blue or black, it's in bright red. You'd probably be able to see him across the street. He'd be no problem to pick out in a line of people waiting for dinner at a soup kitchen."

"Okay."

"Okay?"

"Okay," Ray Dean said. "Get the address of the SRO, find out whose route goes by there, have him reconfigure his night a little to check the area. Tell the rest of them to look for Sherman if they know him or the red hat if they don't. We might as well keep an eye out."

"Excellent," Shelley said. "I thought you were going to say no. I thought you were going to stand on principle. You spend a lot of time standing on principle. It drives me nuts."

"This *climate* drives me nuts," Ray Dean said. "I mean, what's wrong with people? When did we all start suspecting each other? When did we all start being afraid of each other?"

"When Reagan was elected," Shelley said promptly. "It's the Republicans' fault."

Ray Dean kept his mouth shut as she jumped off the desk and flounced out the door, the very picture of a University of Pennsylvania undergraduate with a Serious Interest in Social Justice.

That was among a number of good damned reasons why Ray Dean had never told anybody here that he was a registered Republican.

8

This was the kind of weather that made Alison Standish think she really wanted to own a car more substantial than the Cooper Mini she'd picked up only a year and a half ago. She'd told her friends and colleagues that she'd bought it for the fuel efficiency. Cooper Minis were the hot car across the campus of the University of Pennsylvania this year. They really were fuel-efficient, and if you had to park on crowded city streets, or in university parking lots where half the students owned SUVs that didn't quite fit within the lines of demarcated parking spaces, there was no better vehicle. The problem was, Alison already knew the Mini didn't do all that well in heavy snow. There had been a fair amount of heavy snow last winter, right after she'd bought it, and she'd found it was far too easy to get stuck in the snow dunes the DOT piled up or to spin out on black ice when you weren't paying attention. Of course, even SUVs spun out on black ice, and the real solution to the snow dune problem was a DOT that took its job seriously and cleared the streets instead of just pushing muck from one side of them to the other, but somehow none of that seemed to matter when she was stranded in the road and the people who rescued her were clucking their heads about her stupidity in buying such a small car for a city with such bad weather.

The other problem was that she hadn't bought the Cooper Mini for its fuel efficiency, or even for its ease of parking. She'd bought it because she'd seen it in *The Italian Job*. The people in the Women's Studies Department could say anything they wanted about being oppressed by media images, but the fact was that Alison liked the idea of herself zipping around town like Charlize Theron—of even looking like Charlize Theron. Not that she was all that bad-looking, really. She was tall and thin, which helped. She had good bones in her face, and thick darkish-blond hair that didn't look as if it were going to be in need of Rogaine anytime soon. It was just that, working at the university, there was a tendency to let yourself go, to skip the makeup, to pull your hair back in something sensible instead of having it cut and colored properly. At the moment, her dirty-blond hair was more than a little gray. She was fifty-two years old, and although she didn't quite look it—thank *God* for whatever genetic blessing she'd gotten that had made her face so slow to wrinkle—she felt it more and more often these days. She wasn't tired in the physical sense. She had always been very

physically vigorous, and she was still. She was exhausted to
the point of collapse in the psychological sense, and that
was—that was—. She couldn't think of what that was. She
had noun disease. The names of things escaped her. She
only wished that the names of people would escape her, but
she had no such luck.

On the car radio, turned up far too high for her to concen-
trate on the road, *The Drew Harrigan Show* was just going
off the air. The host wasn't Drew Harrigan this time, because
he was blessedly in rehab. The replacement was a jokey-
sounding Southerner who had nothing like Drew Harrigan's
sense of comic timing, or delivery. He also had nothing like
Drew Harrigan's scope of content in commentary, which
was nothing if not a relief. Alison had listened to the whole
last hour of the program, and there hadn't been a word about
her in it. There hadn't been a word about her in the rest of
the program, either, any of the three other hours of it, because if there had been, somebody would have shown up at
her office door to tell her about it.

She peered through the windshield at the road ahead of
her, full of cars moving not very fast under streetlights that
needed to be brighter. She did not look down at the piles of
folders and papers next to her on the front passenger seat.
Some of them were student papers, assignments to correct
from the courses she taught in Intellectual History of the
High Middle Ages and Christian Theology and Jewish
Scholarship in the Period of the Crusades. Some of them
were forms and proposals related to the attempt to establish
Medieval Studies as an interdisciplinary minor. Some of
them were just housekeeping: forms to sign for her advisees,
forms to file about failures and excessive absences, forms to
file for the faculty health plan and the faculty Senate Committee on the Curriculum and the university search committee for a new dean of the College of Arts and Sciences. The
ones she didn't want to look at were the ones related to her
Drew Harrigan problem.

Out on the street, traffic lights went from red to green
without much happening. Policemen parked at the curb in

squad cars that were like taxis with their off-duty lights on, not available for business. Homeless people walked carefully close to the walls of buildings, like nuns in medieval convents, taught that walking in the open was a sign of arrogance and pride. Alison wondered just how cold it was out there. Minus something, she was sure, because she'd been hearing about it all day. She wondered how many of the homeless people she saw would still be alive in the morning, and then she wondered at herself, and all the other drivers on this road, including the policemen in their parked car. They all knew what happened in weather like this. They all knew they were looking at people who were scheduled to die, just as surely as anybody had ever been scheduled to die in the death chamber. Alison was sure that a good number of these people would write letters of protest, or even show up and carry signs, if someone was about to be executed. Out here they did nothing except turn off whatever part of their brain actually saw these people they were looking at. They were the same way with the lines of people at the soup kitchen doors and out in front of the Goodwill before it opened. She was, too. It was all well and good to label people bleeding heart liberals, but she didn't think anybody whose heart was bleeding could be so . . . oblivious to what was going on out here.

There was a little break in the gridlock and she inched the car forward, through the intersection, before coming to a near stop again. Whoever had programmed the traffic lights in this part of town either hadn't known what he was doing or had done it so long ago that the traffic patterns he had worked to control had no relations to the ones that existed now. She had only another two blocks to go before she got to her turn, and then another block and a half before she got to her building. It wasn't as if she had to go far. It was just that, trapped in the car like this, she found it too hard not to think.

She was, she thought, the last person at the university who should be having a Drew Harrigan problem. Jig Tyler, yes, of course—as far as she was concerned, Jig Tyler should be having a problem with all sane people, the ones who weren't living in a fantasy of global revolution resulting in a golden age led by Plato's philosopher-kings. She'd once spent five minutes contemplating what life would be like under the rule of Jig's philosopher-kings, and the vision had been so acute she'd wanted to lie down on the couch and do nothing but watch Miss Marple movies for a month. Of course, there weren't that many Miss Marple movies. She would have had to watch the same ones over and over again. There were only so many times she could stand to contemplate Margaret Rutherford's marriage of convenience to Stringer Davis. For some reason she had never been able to understand, she was unable to see a large, fat woman with a small, thin man without imagining them naked and together, as if there was a glitch in her brain that needed to work out the logistics of something that was none of her business. Most of the time she found it impossible to imagine people together. When people had dragged her along to porn movies or erotica, if they were the expensive kind—she'd just gone unfocused when those parts came on the screen, and ended up not remembering anything at all.

I'm insane, she thought now. *I'm truly and irrevocably insane.* The light at the next intersection was suddenly green, and the traffic was suddenly sparse. She sailed through both—okay, with the second one bleeding through the yellow into the red a little, but she couldn't help herself—and turned onto her street. On the side streets like this, there were not so many homeless people, or not so many lights illuminating them.

There was a space at the curb, the perfect space for a Mini. There was an SUV in the space behind the open one and an SUV in the space in front, and both of them were over their limits. Alison pulled in between them and asked herself if she was absolutely sure that the automobile insurance she had would replace the car if one of the SUVs ran over it trying to get out in the morning. The reason she shouldn't be having a Drew Harrigan problem was simple. She wasn't in the Women's Studies Department, which he hated. She didn't even like the Women's Studies Department, and the people who taught there didn't like her. She wasn't a socialist. She wasn't a Communist. She wasn't even a Democrat. She always registered Independent, which in her case meant she had no idea what side she was on, and didn't want to think about it. She wasn't any of the things Drew Harrigan hated except, maybe, a professor in a field he probably thought was "useless," meaning medieval literature. It made no sense to her that she would have ended up in the mess she had ended up in, and all because of a vendetta that had no foundation in anything she could think of, ever.

She looked at the pile of papers on the passenger seat and decided to skip them. She got her big shoulder bag from the floor and unwound herself from behind the wheel onto the street. It was ridiculously cold out there, and the wind was making it worse. She thought about the homeless people she had seen on the pavements as she'd driven home, and then she ran around the front of the car, across the sidewalk, and up the front steps to her building. It was a beautiful building, really. Once a long time ago it had been somebody's very elegant town house. Now it was four very elegant apartments. She let herself into the vestibule with her key, found Carrie Youngman's buzzer on the board, and leaned against it as if she were announcing a fire.

"What the hell?" Carrie said through the intercom.

"It's me. I need Irish coffee."

"In or out?"

"In. You don't want to go out. You've got no idea what it's like out there. Can I come on up?"

"Sure."

Alison didn't need Carrie to buzz her in. She used her key again and then went running up the long flights of stairs. There was an elevator here, in the back, useful for just two people, but she never used it. It saved a lot of trouble and hassle with dieting if she just ran up the stairs.

Carrie was on the second floor, just below her own apartment, which she didn't want to see at the moment. There would be messages on her answering machine and more calls coming through on the phone. That would happen because she'd just, accidentally sort of, left her cell phone in her desk at the university.

Carrie had the door open by the time Alison got to the top of the stairs. Carrie was wearing a long nightgown made of knitted cotton with an enormous T-shirt pulled over it. The T-shirt said: THIS IS WHAT A FEMINIST LOOKS LIKE.

"Apparently," Alison said, "a feminist looks like a slattern having a bad hair day. What did you do to your hair?"

"It's what I didn't do to it. Brush it."

"Okay."

"Well, I only look this way around the house. I promise you if I wear it outside I'll do it when I'm done up respectably. I had a deadline to meet."

"And that means you didn't get dressed or brush your hair?"

"No time."

"I had a friend in college who wanted to be a writer, and she made a point of always getting up and getting dressed just as if she were going into any other kind of office."

"Your friend was mentally ill. Or maybe it was just more of that crap with Wellesley. So what's been so terrible about your day?"

Alison moved into the apartment and sat down on the couch. It was a very nice couch, but the white of its upholstery was no longer really white, and it was covered with copies of *The Weekly World News*.

"This what you were writing for today?"

"I couldn't if I wanted to. I don't have the imagination. What's been so terrible about your day?"

"They scheduled the inquiry this morning."

"Are you serious?"

"Yes, Carrie, of course I'm serious. And don't tell me you don't believe it, because I can't believe it, either."

"But I don't get it," Carrie said. "What are they going to inquire about? I mean, Drew Harrigan says this student came to him and complained that you gave worse grades to conservatives and Christians than you gave to liberals, okay, he said that—"

"About five hundred times over the course of three weeks."

"Yes, I know, but still. He never gave the name of the student. There may not even be any student. He could have made the whole thing up. How could anybody possibly know? What's the university going to investigate?"

"They're going to investigate me," Alison said. "They're going to make an inquiry into my classroom practices and my grading practices. They've asked for my grade books for the last five years, so they can go over them assignment by assignment, and they've put out a call for testimony to the university community. They'll mail notices to my former students through the alumni records. So that my students and my former students can come in and testify to, you know, how I behave."

"But that's all right, isn't it? You don't really give poorer grades to conservative students because they're conservatives, do you?"

"Oh, for God's sake," Alison said. "I don't even know what most of them are, politically. I mean, I don't teach a political subject. I teach medieval literature and medieval philosophy and that kind of thing. We talk about Thomas Aquinas and bringing Aristotle back into the tradition of Western thought, and Chaucer and the rise of vernacular poetry. I suppose you could make those things political. The Women's Studies Department probably does make those things political. But I talk about poetic forms and the enthronement of logical analysis in the medieval European university."

"So," Carrie said, coming over to the couch with a cup, a saucer, a bottle of Irish whiskey, and a big electric coffee percolator with its cord hanging down behind like a bridal veil, "there's nothing to worry about, is there? You're not guilty."

"I'm a professor at an Ivy League university. My students are the result of a long culling process that turns competition into the be-all and end-all of life itself. You know and I know that there are people I've given grades to who weren't very happy with them, people who wanted A's and didn't get

them, people who want to blame anybody but themselves for
their own records."

"And these people will all be conservatives?"

"No," Alison said. "These people will turn this inquiry
into an auto-da-fé. It'll be a chance to get their own back,
and they will. There are times I want to slaughter every water buffalo on the planet."

Carrie was putting together the Irish coffee. The cup was
larger than an ordinary coffee cup, and the percentage of
whiskey to coffee was larger than in most Irish coffees. Alison reached forward and took a long swig. It was straight alcohol with essence of coffee bean.

"Water buffalo," Carrie said.

"Oh, it was something that happened a few years ago
with the speech code. We've got a speech code. It's completely asinine. It's the modern university's equivalent of an
old Catholic formulation on free speech—error has no
rights. Whatever. There was an incident where this kid who
was brought up in Israel or somewhere shouted out his window at a bunch of girls whooping it up in the quad and said
they sounded like a bunch of water buffalo, which happens
to be an exact English translation of some common light in-
sult in Hebrew, and they were black and took it as a racist re-
mark, so the university tried to prosecute him under the
speech code, and he got outside lawyers and whatnot interested and it was a huge scandal, mostly making the university look bad. Which it should have, because free speech
isn't about speech you like but about speech you don't. Anyway, that's why they feel they have to investigate every time
somebody like Drew Harrigan makes accusations like this.
Just in case. Because they don't want this student to prove
his case in an outside court of law and make the university
look bad again."

"But there may be no student," Carrie said.

"I know."

"And you've got tenure."

"I know." Alison took another long swig of coffee. Alcohol, alcohol, alcohol. Alcohol could be very good to you if

you treated it right. Unfortunately, the next morning it made you feel as if you'd been run through a food processor with a bunch of sand. "Tenure doesn't fix everything," she said finally.

"And?"

Alison shrugged. "I don't know. I keep telling myself I don't need to worry, I haven't done what Drew Harrigan's been accusing me of. They can't find evidence of something that isn't there. But I know university inquiries. You don't have the same due process protections you have in a court of law. I may end up having to sue the university to clear my record. I may end up ostracized, although I admit that doesn't seem to be happening at the moment. And all I can think about is the fact that if Drew Harrigan would only spend an extra, oh, six months in rehab, this whole thing would probably die down. Because the administration doesn't want to pursue it any more than I want them to. They just want to cover their asses."

"Maybe the cops will be waiting for him at the door of the clinic when he walks out, and he'll be so wrapped up in legal troubles he won't have time to bother about you."

"It's a nice thought, but I talked to a guy over in the law school about that. Apparently, probably not. They're going to shift most of the blame onto this guy who was supposed to be supplying him with the pills."

"The homeless guy?"

"Yeah. And then, you know, Drew Harrigan is a victim, and he gets ordered to therapy, and that's that. My guy at the law school said it was practically a done deal."

"I think it's disgusting the way celebrities get treated by the law."

"I think everybody thinks it's disgusting the way celebrities get treated by the law," Alison said. "But they do, and here we are. I just wish I knew what started all of this. It's the one thing that makes me think there might really be a student out there somewhere complaining that I gave him a bad grade because he's a conservative. I mean, how else did Drew Harrigan get my name? I'm not an academic media star. I don't teach in a sensitive department. This came out of nowhere, and I have no idea why."

"Get absolutely stinking drunk and sleep it off and then get up and go on with what you've got to do," Carrie said. "That's how I handle it. It's like a catharsis. Once I'm through it, I can do anything I have to do."

"I keep thinking that maybe that homeless person will just disappear. Isn't that awful? I just can't help thinking that if he wasn't around to be the convenient scapegoat, Drew Harrigan would be in a lot more trouble than he's in, and I'd be in a lot less."

"He's filed a lawsuit, hasn't he?" Carrie said. "Maybe he'll win."

"Maybe he will," Alison said, but she didn't believe that. In at least one case, the socialists weren't entirely crazy. There really were disparities of power in the world, and there was no disparity greater than the one between a homeless drunk and a media powerhouse. This homeless person would take the fall for Drew Harrigan, and Drew Harrigan would go on giving lectures about how all drug addicts should be locked away in penitentiaries for fifteen years every time they got caught with a half ounce of marijuana in their pockets, and the university inquiry into the allegations of bias on the part of Professor Alison Elizabeth Standish would proceed as planned, delivering ruin to somebody, because that was what it was designed to do.

Alison took another long swig of the Irish coffee, and decided that getting blind drunk was not that stupid an idea after all.

9

It was just turning midnight, and Sister Maria Beata of the Incarnation thought she could not read another page of *Ascent of Mount Carmel* without going completely, utterly, and irrevocably insane. Beata had come to Carmel because she loved and admired Carmelite spirituality, by which she meant the works of St. Teresa of Avila and St. Edith Stein.

She'd never read anything by St. John of the Cross before entering the novitiate, and she had only grazed that silly book by St. Thérèse of Lisieux, *The Journey of a Soul*. It hadn't occurred to her that there might be good reason why Thérèse's book had sold more than any other work of Catholic piety in hundreds of years, and why a modern Carmel might want to build on that popularity to keep its sisters dedicated to the contemplative life. Quite frankly, if Beata had to read much more of this overwrought mysticism and sexually charged ecstatic transportation into the presence of God, she thought she might quit Carmel for a life with the Dominicans as a mistress of the Inquisition.

Except, of course, there was no Inquisition anymore, not in fact or in name. There was the Congregation of the Doctrine of the Faith, which used to be called the Holy Office, which used to be called the Holy and Roman Inquisition, but that was the wrong Inquisition for her purposes, not the one in Spain but the one in Rome. Of course, she didn't really know what her purposes were. She had come to Carmel wanting only to find silence, and she had found that, even though the silence wasn't silent enough.

At the moment, the silence was being broken by the sound of the monastery bell ringing the hour. It was the ordinary bell marking ordinary time, not the one that rang for prayer. She was tired. She should lie down on the cot for a rest, as she was supposed to do, but it had been a restless day. The one time she'd tried, she'd ended by staring up into the dark that obscured the high ceiling. It had seemed a better idea to get up and read. That way, when it came to tomorrow night, when she was not on duty, she would lie down at nine when the lights went off and have no trouble at all dropping off.

It was hardly possible that she had lived in this monastery for years, and her body still hadn't adjusted to the schedule. But it hadn't.

There was a knock on the door. For a second, Beata thought it was nothing. There was a lot of wind out there. Maybe a branch had been knocked against the side of the building. Then the sound came again, and she got up to look through the eyehole at who was standing on the front steps.

She'd had a roommate in college once who'd called those eyeholes Judas holes. She had no idea what had made her think of that. One of the homeless men was standing on the doorstep, his arms wrapped around him, without a hat. She was not supposed to let anyone in when she was here alone at night, but she couldn't imagine keeping this man waiting outside like that, in that weather. She pulled the door back and pulled him in.

"You're going to freeze to death," she said. "You shouldn't be out in the wind without a hat."

"They stole his hat," the man said.

"Whose hat?"

"They stole his hat," the man said again. He smelled of beer and vomit. They all smelled of vomit. It permeated their clothes, even when the clothes were newly washed. "The dead man. They stole his hat."

Beata tried to process this. "There's somebody dead," she said. "Out in the barn."

"They stole his hat."

"Yes, I see. They stole his hat. And he's dead. Are you sure he's dead? Are you sure he isn't just passed out?"

"He's not breathing," the man said. "And they stole his hat. I didn't think that was right. Even if he's dead. It was a good hat. Red."

Beata paused. She remembered the man in the red hat, waiting to get into the barn, when she was coming back tonight to tell Reverend Mother about the property. She shut the door to keep the wind out and tried to think.

"Let me get a sister," she said, "and we'll go see. Then we'll know if we should call the ambulance."

"I can tell you who stole the hat," the man said. "I saw them do it. I tried to stop them. But nobody listens to me."

"It's all right about the hat," Beata said. "Let me get a sister, and let's see what we've got to do now. Is he just lying out there, in the barn?"

"He's on the floor," the man said. "He had a cot, but when

they took his hat they rolled him off on the floor, and they've got the cot now. It wasn't right about the hat."

"No," Beata said. "No, of course it wasn't."

She looked hard into the face of this man, but it just blurred. As soon as she blinked, she could no longer remember what he looked like. She thought of the man in the red hat, and decided she had never really known what he looked like, beyond noticing that his clothes were cleaner than the clothes of the other men in line. If civilization was the process of learning to see our fellow human beings clearly and plainly, in their blood and skin and bone and brain, as vitally a part of us—Beata didn't think she was yet very civilized.

She went to the portress's desk and picked up the phone to get Reverend Mother out of bed.

You came to Carmel to look for answers, and all you ever got was the silence and the darkness and the long line of men and women who had come before you, who had wanted to look into the face of God without falling down dead. Some of them thought they had seen what they were looking for, and some of them were sure they had not, but in the end it all came down to the man in the red hat whose face was nothing but a blur and a shadow, and the man standing in front of you whom you couldn't make real no matter how hard you tried.

Reverend Mother was not going to be happy to be woken at midnight, and the ambulance men were going to be even less happy to come by to pick up the body of somebody who was not only already dead, but of no damn use to anybody at all.

PART ONE

Monday, February 10
High 3F, Low −14F

To fall in love is to create a religion that has a falli-
ble god.

—JORGE LUIS BORGES

The world condemns liars who do nothing but lie,
even about the most trivial things, and it rewards
poets, who lie about the greatest things.

—UMBERTO ECO

ONE

I

There were times when Gregor Demarkian forgot where he was, not in space—it was impossible to forget you were on Cavanaugh Street when you were on it—but in time, so that he turned over in bed and expected to see Elizabeth sleeping next to him, or opened the top drawer of his dresser to look for the laminated ID card he'd carried his last five years in the FBI. He would have felt better about it if it had only happened to him when he was asleep, or just waking. He knew enough about dreams to have lost all tendency to feel guilty about the content of them. He had been thinking about Elizabeth a lot lately, and about the FBI, although he had to admit that he was more than happy to be retired, given the way things were going at the moment. He had come to the Bureau when it was still run by J. Edgar Hoover, a psychopath with sexual problems and a driving obsession to redefine normality for the rest of the universe. He had quietly celebrated on the evening of Hoover's funeral, because he'd known that only death would exorcise that man from the Bureau's soul. Then he'd had his own life to worry about, and his own problems, and now he was here, no longer concerned with serial killers or office politics. He could not imagine what he would have done if he had been one of the people responsible for ignoring the evidence that could have stopped the 9/11 attacks. He could not imagine a Bureau culture where so few people had been fired in the event. He had no idea what he was doing thinking about 9/11 now, so long after the fact, but for some reason it had been on his mind for weeks.

The truth is, he thought, *I've got too much time to myself.* It was true. There had been nothing in the way of a consulting job coming through the door for some time now. Since he made a point of never going out to solicit them, that meant there had been nothing in the way of crime to think about for some time now, either. Watching true crime on Court TV and A&E didn't quite make it. Then there was the problem of the apartments, plural. The new church was finished, or as finished as any church ever got, what with committees to worry about carpets and pews and better glass for the windows, and Tibor had moved back into an apartment of his own, with a new little courtyard and a new set of hyacinth bushes behind it. Bennis was on tour, the first one she'd agreed to in five years. On an intellectual level, Gregor knew that this was a professional necessity. Authors didn't go out on tours just for the hell of it, since they were apparently very confused and confusing things. Wires got crossed, bookstores didn't get their copies of the books on time, hotels had the wrong reservations, airplane tickets turned out to be for the wrong days to the wrong places. On an emotional level, he was—he didn't know what. It would have helped if he had understood what was going on in his relationship with Bennis these days, but Bennis was not like Elizabeth. If Elizabeth was mad at you, she shouted at you until you surrendered. If she was happy with you, she did little things around the house for you and made your favorite foods for dinner several times during the week. Beyond that Elizabeth did not get too complicated, at least when it came to their marriage. There was mad and happy and sexy on at least a few nights a month. That was it, until the cancer got her, and things got very complicated indeed. But dying was complicated, Gregor thought. You couldn't blame a woman for becoming complex and hard to unravel when she was dying.

Bennis was complicated as a matter of principle. She was complicated about her morning coffee. She was complicated about her shoes, none of which she liked, except for the clogs, which didn't go with anything. Most of all, she was complicated about their relationship to each other, which had none of the clean obviousness of what Gregor was used to in something "settled." Maybe it was just that Bennis did not consider them settled, while Gregor did. Gregor had tried to fix that by asking her to marry him, but she'd gotten complicated about that, too, and now she was off in the Midwest somewhere, signing copies of a book called *Summer of Zedalia, Winter of Zed.* Gregor had tried to read one of her books while she was away, but he couldn't do it. They were filled with fairies and trolls and elves and unicorns, and in spite of the fact that they were very well written—even he could tell they were very well written—he couldn't get into them. They were of different generations. Maybe that was where all the complications came from. At any rate, his generation wanted realism, not fantasy. His generation didn't believe in ghosts or angels or the supernatural. His generation wanted the solidity that came from the laws of nature rather than the laws of Nature's God. He wanted to chalk it up to the fact that his generation had fought a war, but Bennis's generation had fought one too. They'd just gone about it oddly.

His hair was wet, and all the rubbing he was doing with the towel wasn't making it any drier. The heat was on full blast, as if it needed to be to guard against the ridiculous cold they'd been having week after week for a month now. He had left his clothes over the top of the hamper: boxer shorts, trousers, undershirt, good white shirt. His socks and shoes were in the bedroom. His ties were hanging from tie holders in the closet. There was a sweater laid out on the bed. He was working very hard not to put on a tie for a day when he was doing nothing but hanging around Cavanaugh Street.

"Didn't you ever wonder about Ozzie Nelson?" Bennis had asked him once. "I mean, he never went out of the house, and there he was wearing a tie to sit in the living room reading the paper while the television was on."

He put on the boxer shorts and the undershirt and the trousers and the shirt. He went into his bedroom and got the clean socks he'd left on his night table. The message light was blinking on his answering machine. Someone must have called while he was in the shower. It was Bennis's idea to have the answering machine in the bedroom. Gregor thought it was completely nuts. What was the point of an answering machine if it didn't let you sleep through calls in the middle of the night?

Maybe that was the problem. Maybe they shouldn't have tried living together, even temporarily. It had seemed like a good idea at the time. It had even seemed necessary. Tibor was out of his apartment, since the place wasn't structurally sound after the church was bombed. He could take Bennis's apartment while Bennis stayed with Gregor, which she did most of the time anyway. But there was a real difference between staying the night almost every single night and actually moving in. There was a difference in the way you felt about the way things were done and the places things were put.

He pulled on his socks, then reached onto the bed for his sweater, a good three-ply cashmere one from Brooks Brothers, Bennis's idea of a Christmas present. He sat down on the edge of the bed and pushed the play button to hear the message. If it was Tibor saying he wasn't up to going to the Ararat for breakfast, Gregor thought he would smash something.

"Mr. Demarkian?"

Gregor frowned. The voice was, sort of, familiar, but he couldn't place it.

"Mr. Demarkian, I know it's only six thirty in the morning, but I remember from when we met before that it's best to get you early. I hope I haven't woken you up. I don't know if you remember me. My name is Edmund George. Chickie. People call me Chickie. We met a couple of years ago when you were consulting with the Philadelphia Police about the, you know, the murders connected to the gay stuff. I'm sorry, it's early in the morning and I haven't had my shower yet. Anyway, that's who I am."

Gregor actually did remember him, and now he knew what it was that was odd about the voice. The Chickie he had met had been a "flaming queen," as John Henry Newman Jackman had put it, but not the kind who came by it naturally. It was as if he needed to exaggerate an effeminacy he didn't really have, as if it wasn't enough to be "gay," or even to be "out," if you didn't throw it in everyone's face in a way that they couldn't possibly ignore it. The voice on the answering machine was not effeminate in any way. If he hadn't known something about Chickie already, he would not have automatically assumed that the man wasn't straight, or anything else but another guy with a Philadelphia tinge to his accent, the Italian street kind of Philadelphia twinge. Gregor wondered what Chickie was doing now.

"Anyway," Chickie was saying, "I don't want to run out your machine and get cut off, or anything, but I've got a problem. Actually, the organization I volunteer with has a problem. And I was thinking, you're probably the best person in the city to ask about it. So I was wondering if it would be okay if I came over and talked to you. I can come over right this minute, if you want me to. I'm just going to step in the shower and wake myself up, but after that I could be at your place in twenty minutes. I'm not all that far away. It's the Justice Project I volunteer for, by the way, and it really is important. You can call me back and leave a message on my machine if you want to see me right now, or call later or whatever. At your convenience. I'm at 555-4720. Thanks."

Gregor sat on the edge of the bed for a moment, thinking. The Justice Project. He'd heard a lot about the Justice Project recently, because of . . . that was it, the Drew Harrigan drug thing. Gregor hadn't paid much attention to it. He didn't like men like Drew Harrigan, no matter which side of the political divide they inhabited. Drew Harrigan, Rush Limbaugh, Al Franken, Michael Moore: here was another way his generation was not like Bennis's, and not like this

Chickie's, either. He had no idea when politics had become this angry, and this ugly, but he hated it instinctively. These days, he didn't follow debates and he didn't read editorials. He figured out which of the available candidates came closest to his preferred political identification of "a little common sense, please," and voted for that.

He wondered why he was spending so much time thinking about "generations." He wasn't aware of feeling particularly geriatric. He *wasn't* particularly geriatric. Maybe Bennis was making him as complicated as she was herself. Maybe he'd start finding it impossible to choose between the brown socks and the gray ones and have to resort to an investigation of the psychic foundations of his attitudes toward color. He wasn't being fair. He wanted Bennis to come back and start acting like herself again, meaning like the self she'd been acting like before they had all gone to Massachusetts.

His bedroom windows were rattling in the wind. It was going to be another bad day in a string of bad days. He'd gotten to the point of thinking of twenty degrees as "warmer." Whatever else was going on with him, he was undoubtedly bored. It wouldn't hurt to take his mind off whatever it was it was on. It was significant that he didn't know what it was on. He needed coffee. He needed Bennis at home, where he could have a screaming fight with her and get it all over with.

He picked up the phone and dialed 555-4720. The voice on the answering machine tape not only had no trace of effeminacy in it, it could have belonged to a Chief Justice of the United States Supreme Court. That was a gift, Gregor thought. It had to be very useful to be able to turn your voice into that wide a range of effects.

The screaming beep went off. Gregor said, "Mr. George? Yes, I remember you. If you're really in that much of a hurry, I'm going to be having breakfast at the Ararat restaurant on Cavanaugh Street from about seven thirty to eight thirty. Come on by and talk to me. I'll see you there."

He hung up and stared at the phone. Then he reached for his shoes on the floor and put them on. Bennis was always telling him he had to do something about his shoes, because they were too formal. He couldn't imagine himself in a pair of running shoes, or whatever they called them these days. He used to call them sneakers.

One of the first things they taught new agents at Quantico was to pick their spots. Don't fight every battle. Don't answer every challenge. Don't follow every lead. Maybe he needed to go back for retraining at Quantico. It was too bad they wouldn't have him, and he wouldn't last a day without kicking somebody's ass.

2

It was cold. It was worse than cold. The temperature with the windchill was supposed to be something like minus twenty-five, and the windchill was no joke, because the wind was no joke. By the time Gregor was standing on the steps in front of Fr. Tibor Kasparian's front door, his fingers felt cold enough to fall off, and he had them stuck into the pockets of his coat. His head was bare, so the skin on his face felt as if it had *already* fallen off. At least, it had no feeling in it. His ears were entirely numb. He rang the doorbell and heard a cascade of excited yips coming from the other side. This was new. It sounded like a dog. As far as Gregor knew, Tibor didn't have a dog.

Tibor came to the door and opened up, and right there, running around his legs, there was indeed a dog. It was a very small dog—Gregor didn't know anything about dogs, but he knew what a puppy was when he saw one—and it was completely, happily berserk, bouncing around on the vestibule carpet as if it had pogo sticks for legs, chasing first up Tibor's legs and then up Gregor's, wagging its tail so hard Gregor thought the thing was going to fly off. He came all the way into the apartment and closed the door behind him. The cold was getting in. The dog took off for the living room on a run, barked happily a little longer, and then came running back.

"When did you get a dog? Gregor asked. "You didn't say anything about a dog."

"It's Grace who got the dog, Krekor," Tibor said. "She's a chocolate Labrador retriever named Godiva. Grace got the dog and then she had to go play in New York, so I'm keeping the dog for the week. She's a very nice dog."

"A chocolate Lab named Godiva."

"Yes, well, Krekor, what can I say? I didn't name the dog. She really is a very nice dog, very intelligent and very affectionate. And small, so she isn't hard to keep. I rigged up a kind of Kitty Litter box in the back air lock—"

"Kitty Litter for a dog?"

"Sand, Krekor, sand. You can't ask a small animal like this to go out in the cold to do its business. I keep it in the air lock and it doesn't bother me. Come into the living room. If you sit on the couch, she'll sit on your lap."

Gregor decided to sit on the chair, because although Godiva really was a very nice dog, he didn't want dog hair all over his trousers. He even had an excuse for that, since Chickie was coming. He looked at the books on Tibor's coffee table, which as usual was so covered that nobody could put a cup of coffee on it without threatening either Aristotle or Jackie Collins. Today there were a few new arrivals: a novel called *Baudolino* by Umberto Eco; another novel called *Blindness* by José Saramago; *Harry Potter and the Goblet of Fire.* Tibor must be having a fiction week.

"The thing is," Tibor said, coming back to the living room from the kitchen, "I can't take the dog into the Ararat. The Melajians don't mind, but apparently the city of Philadelphia does, and you can't take dogs into restaurants unless they're Seeing Eye dogs. I'd try to pass Godiva off as a Seeing Eye dog, but she's too small and she's, uh—"

"A little too active?"

"Something like that, yes, Krekor. It's really too bad, because Linda Melajian is very fond of her. But I think she would end up running all over the place and overturning tables and things if she got out of hand."

"You can leave her here, can't you? She can stay in the apartment for an hour."

"She can stay, yes, Krekor, but she's a Labrador retriever.

She's a very affectionate dog. She needs company. That's why Grace didn't leave her in her apartment and have me just come by and walk her and feed her a few times a day. They get depressed if they don't have company, this kind of dog. So she's staying here with me, and we sit together to watch television, and then at night she comes in and sleeps on the bed."

"Don't Labs get to be really big dogs? I mean, how is Grace going to feel about that sleeping on the bed stuff when the dog is fully grown and weighs a hundred pounds?"

"By then she will have gone to obedience school, Krekor. It will be all right. Give me a minute. I've forgotten where I put my wallet."

"Look in the medicine cabinet," Gregor said. "That's where you usually leave it."

"You're perhaps not as respectful as you could be, Krekor, where a priest is concerned."

Gregor liked to think he was unfailingly polite to everyone, which might or might not be true.

3

There had been a small problem with the dog, who had wanted to come with them until she dashed into the courtyard and realized how cold it was. Then she'd dashed back inside and begun crying pitifully to get them to come back in with her. Gregor thought she probably thought they were insane to be going out in this weather, and she was probably right. Tibor had compensated by spending a few minutes kneeling on the ground at the door and speaking to her in a cooing voice Gregor thought was usually reserved for babies in distress. He couldn't believe Tibor hadn't frozen his kneecaps to the slate tiles in the process. Then they had gone out through the courtyard and around the side of the church to Cavanaugh Street itself, and Tibor had had to stop and look inside.

"They really did a very wonderful job," Tibor said. "And we don't have the iconostasis anymore, which was only there because we took this over from a Greek Orthodox congregation, and isn't really the Armenian way. And we have held off Hannah Krekorian and Sheila Kashinian, and there is no stained glass in the windows with pictures of St. George slaying the dragon on them. Sheila has no sense of place or time, do you understand that? And Hannah just goes along with her. I know that it's too much to ask that American schools should teach the history of the Armenian Church, but the Armenian Church should teach it. What did you all learn in religion lessons when you were growing up?"

"Not much," Gregor said. "The priest taught them himself and he only spoke Armenian, and most of us barely did. Also, he smelled, and he was a nasty man."

"I think Sheila Kashinian secretly wants to be a Roman Catholic. I don't mean as a matter of what they believe. I don't think she knows what they believe. I don't think she knows what we believe, or why there's a difference. I think she wants to be Roman Catholic so she can sit in a Gothic church with stained glass windows and imagine herself becoming a nun."

"Only if there's an order that gets its habits through Nieman Marcus," Gregor said.

"We need to be nicer, Krekor. Howard gave us ten thousand dollars for the new church."

"Bennis gave more, and she doesn't even believe in God."

"I know, Krekor, but Bennis has more. Howard gave the ten thousand dollars and between that and the money Bennis gave, and all the smaller things, we have a new church that looks like it belongs to the Middle Ages, when people really gave money to churches. Of course, we have the kneelers, which is not traditional, but I think it was the right decision. People aren't what they were. You can't get them to kneel on the floor anymore. Even the pews are an innovation, really. In the early days, people didn't sit in church. They either stood or kneeled and the floors they kneeled on were made of stone."

"I'm surprised anybody ever came to liturgy."

"If they didn't, they were fined. Yes, I know, Krekor,

don't say it. Things have changed and they've changed for the better. I wish the elections were all over. Since I came to this country, since I first received citizenship, I've been the most conscientious voter on the entire continent. But I'm tired of them already, this year."

"The conventions haven't even happened yet."

"It doesn't matter. It will all be anger and craziness. When I first came to America, people weren't angry like this all the time, Krekor. People were passionate about politics and, yes, there were some idiots in the New Left, what they were thinking I don't know, but most people were not angry like this. It is not one side or the other now. It is both of them. And it doesn't matter what the issue is. If you don't like the tax cuts, you are a traitor who wants to sell out the country to Islamic fundamentalists. If you don't like abortion, you are a fascist murderer who wants to enslave women as breeding machines with no right to a life of their own. It's not that there isn't any center anymore. It's that there isn't any sense. First the Republicans accuse President Clinton of paying for a hit man to murder his friend. Then the Democrats accuse the Republicans of allowing the 9/11 attacks to happen on purpose, if not causing them themselves. It doesn't matter who gets elected in November, it will be the same thing all over again, and do you know why? It's because it's not about politics. It's not about are we going to have a welfare state or a laissez-faire one. It's not about should there be public schools or private schools that get vouchers. It's not about politics. It's about religion."

"It is? Are the Democrats pushing religion?"

"Tcha," Tibor said. "You're too limited in your scholarship. There is real religion, which is about our relationship to God, which is important. But there is another kind of religion, and that is the religion that is about identity. It is about banding together in a group and defending ourselves against what we fear, when what we fear is each other. It is about not wanting to live in a world where we are in a minority, because it is uncomfortable to be a minority. That kind of religion talks about God sometimes, but it doesn't have to. It can call itself Christian or Muslim or Hindu or Communist or Libertarian or Green. I like real religion, Krekor. It's been of enormous importance and value in my life. This other stuff, I look at it and I fear for the survival of civilization."

"That's quite a lecture for five minutes to seven on a Monday morning."

"Don't be flippant, Krekor, it matters. I'm more American than most Americans. From the day of my naturalization, I've kept a flag in my house; now I keep it in my kitchen. I have little lapel pins with the flag on them. I have a red, white, and blue baseball cap. I embarrass the people who were born here with my enthusiasm. I think this is the greatest experiment in the history of the world, the story of the Tower of Babel falsified. But lately I am not so sure it is going to survive. Not in any form in which I recognize it."

"I think it will survive," Gregor said. "I think it's just one of those times, like during the Civil War—"

"This you think is a comforting analogy, Krekor?"

"I didn't mean I think we're going to have a civil war. I mean it's one of those times that we go through where we reinvent ourselves. The Civil War was the worst of it, but there have been other times. Franklin Delano Roosevelt and the Great Depression, for instance."

"Tcha. I like Roosevelt. I like both Roosevelts, though the first one was perhaps a little overenergetic."

"I'm just saying that we get angry and we get upset and some of us even get nuts, but we don't fall apart. We didn't even fall apart when we fell apart, so to speak. And now I'm talking like a descendant of Ralph Waldo Emerson, instead of the son of two immigrants from Armenia. Would you go back to Armenia, if you could? It's free of the Soviet Union now."

"No, Krekor, I would not go back, not even with the craziness here. And it's more than just a matter of central heating, although that's certainly a factor. It's odd to think, isn't it, that people can be born out of place and out of time? You'd think that the force of culture alone, of upbringing, would suit you more for the place you were raised than some other place, but it doesn't always work like that. It didn't work like that for me."

They had arrived at the Ararat, and Linda Melajian was just unlocking the plate glass front door. "Come on in," she said. "I know it's five minutes early, but I'm as ready as I'm ever going to be and you can't stay outside in that cold. I keep thinking about that phrase everybody uses. When Hell freezes over. I think it did."

"That would be interesting in a story," Tibor said. "A science fiction story, a kind of disaster movie. What happens to the world when Hell freezes over."

Gregor gave a little shove to the back of Tibor's coat and propelled him inside to the warm. Along with having apocalyptic thoughts about politics, Tibor seemed to be having a problem getting through doors this morning. Gregor went to the window booth with its long low cushions and slipped inside.

"I'll get you coffee in a minute," Linda said. "I've got to put out a few more sugar racks before I can say I'm ready."

Through the big windows that made up the outside wall of the booth, Gregor could see people beginning to appear on the street, wrapped up in coats with the collars pulled high and their faces out of sight under scarves. Most of them had had the sense to wear hats and gloves. All of them were heading for the Ararat, although a few of them stopped to buy the papers at Ohanian's first. Gregor tried to count up how many mornings he had spent having breakfast in this same booth in the Ararat, but it wasn't the kind of calculation he was good at. It suddenly occurred to him what was making him so nervous at home: the building was deserted. Grace was away in New York giving concerts with the group she played harpsichord for. Bennis was away on her book tour. Old George Tekemanian was out on the Main Line staying with Martin and Angela, who thought he'd do better if they could be sure he wasn't going out in this cold at his age, which he would be if he stayed here, because he'd come to breakfast. The building was deserted, and he was surrounded by silence.

"Krekor?" Tibor said. "Are you all right? Linda brought the coffee and you didn't even say thank you."

"I'm fine," Gregor said. Linda had certainly brought the coffee. It was sitting right there in front of him. "I was just thinking. I got a phone call this morning."

"From Bennis?"

"No, not from Bennis. And don't nag. She doesn't call much. And I have no idea if that's normal or not. This is the first time she's been away for any significant amount of time since, ah, you know."

"Yes, Krekor, I know. What was the phone call?"

Gregor took an enormous sip of coffee and looked out the window one more time, just as Lida Arkmanian came out of the front door of her town house to meet Sheila and Hannah on the street. Lida and Sheila had fur coats. Hannah had a cloth coat in red so bright it almost seemed to be pulsing like the bubble on top of a police car. A few doors closer, the Very Old Ladies came out of their building in a tight little knot. They were older than Old George, but they weren't about to miss their morning at Neighborhood Gossip Central.

"Let me tell you about Chickie George," Gregor said.

TWO

I

It was exactly seven thirty-one when Chickie George walked through the door of the Ararat, and Gregor Demarkian didn't recognize him. That was odder than it seemed. Very few people came into the Ararat from out of the neighborhood during breakfast hours. Cavanaugh Street was reasonably central in the sense that it was easy to get from it to where most people had to work, without being actually central, meaning in the middle of the city. People who came from outside the neighborhood to eat at the Ararat almost always came because of restaurant reviews in the *Inquirer* or profiles of Gregor Demarkian, who had once been caught eating there by a reporter from CNN. The profiles had to be constructed from available sources, since Gregor never gave interviews. Consulting for police departments was the kind of work that was likely to dry up if you spent too much time in front of the cameras. Having worked in the FBI of J. Edgar Hoover, Gregor was used to letting other people get credit for what he had done. On a lot of levels, he even preferred it. There was something to be said for living outside the modern unholy circle of fuss.

Gregor did pay attention when the man he didn't recognize walked into the Ararat, because a stranger at seven thirty-one was a phenomenon. Then he went back to listening to Tibor moaning on again about politics, or the lack of civility in politics, or something. The stranger in the doorway looked like a partner at one of Philadelphia's better law firms. He was wearing a black coat over a black suit. Gregor could tell because the coat was open. Tibor was complaining about same-sex marriage.

"Both sides are being very dishonest," he was saying. "If the side that says it only cares that not every state be required to honor gay marriages, all it needs to do is call for a constitutional amendment saying that no state has to recognize any other state's same-sex marriages, and that gets rid of the problem with the full faith and credit clause."

Gregor was only vaguely aware of what the full faith and credit clause was, and then because Tibor had explained it to him. Tibor sometimes made him feel as if he should have gone to law school instead of business school. He'd joined the FBI in the days when every special agent was required to be either a lawyer or a CPA, and he'd thought he was better with numbers than he was ever going to be at the law. He was also fairly sure that the law in all its intricacy would bore him to tears. He understood crime and criminals. He didn't understand the fascination with the kind of thing Tibor was now railing on about, waving the butter knife in the air while he did it.

"Then there is the side that favors gay marriage," Tibor said. "They say they are only pursuing a civil rights issue and they don't want to tell anybody else how to live, but that isn't true, either. If it was, *they'd* be in favor of the amendment I mentioned, and of course they're not. Everybody is looking to change the culture, Krekor, that's what the problem is. The issue isn't politics, really, it's about who the culture will look like and who will feel at home in it. And it's exacerbated by the fact that the ordinary American doesn't seem to understand the difference between a state law and a federal law."

"The oddest young man just walked through the door," Gregor said. If the coat was open, the man must have been walking around in the cold wind with it open. Gregor had had enough trouble just going without a hat. The man didn't have a hat, either, although he did have good black leather gloves.

"Pay attention, Krekor," Tibor said. "The world is going to hell around you and you don't pay attention. People really don't know the difference between a state law and a federal law. They think of all law as federal, most of them, or they think that if something happens in one state it has to happen with another. They're not aware that the states have their own constitutions. When they hear Constitution, they think of the federal one. The ignorance is breathtaking. It makes it impossible to have a decent conversation about anything."

"Is that what this is about?" Gregor asked him. "Did you go spend the evening with that religious group you belong to—"

"The Philadelphia Coalition of Churches," Tibor said. "Tcha, Krekor, you're impossible. It's not a religious group. It's a discussion group made up of pastors and rabbis. It used to be interesting. Now it's all fighting, and the Evangelical pastors are talking about leaving, because the rest of us are liberal pilot fish for the Antichrist. Do you know what pilot fish are, Krekor? I had to go look it up."

The man in the black coat was looking carefully around the restaurant, pausing a little at almost every table and then moving on. He got to the window booth and stopped, nodding a little to himself. Then he started to walk over. Gregor was still vaguely fascinated with the idea that the man must be close to freezing to death, if he'd come any distance at all. Then the man got closer, and held out his hand.

"Mr. Demarkian? I don't know if you recognize me. I'm Edmund George. Chickie."

Gregor was struggling to get up from the booth. It was always a struggle to get up from that booth, because it was built low to the ground, so that you had the impression that you were sitting on the floor, the way they really would in Armenia. The young man he was looking at was extremely good-looking, more like an actor than a citizen on the street, but not like any actor Gregor had ever seen. He took the hand and shook it.

Chickie George smiled slightly. "I know. I don't look the same. Everybody says so. It's amazing that an act like that can so change people's perceptions of what you're like *physically*. But the act had to go. It didn't feel right somehow. And the University of Pennsylvania Law School was not going to be happy with it."

"You're looking to go to law school?" Gregor said.

"I'm in law school, second year. I started after all that mess with St. Anselm's and St. Stephen's. And Margaret Mary went to New York to be a nun. So."

Gregor was completely lost. He remembered Chickie George, if only slightly. He remembered St. Anselm's and St. Stephen's. He didn't remember Margaret Mary at all. He would have thought she was Chickie's girlfriend if he didn't know better. What she was instead, he couldn't say.

He waved at the booth, and Chickie said, "Thank you," sliding in next to Father Tibor.

"Tell me," Father Tibor said. "Do you favor same-sex marriage or oppose it?"

Chickie looked nonplused. "I suppose I favor it. I know I'm supposed to. I'm gay. But mostly, I don't think about it."

"There," Tibor said. "You see? An ordinary citizen off the street, and what does he say? He says he doesn't think about it. This is the way it is with most citizens off the street. They don't think about it. This is my point, Krekor. This issue is not politics. It is not what people want to hear, or want resolved, or want to have discussed. This is two fanatics shouting at each other, and taking up all the air."

Gregor slid back into the booth. "This is Father Tibor Kasparian. He's a little worked up this morning."

"About same-sex marriage?" Chickie said.

"About politics, I think," Gregor told him.

"I am not worked up about politics," Tibor said. "I am depressed about them, which is different. I do not like the way the world is going. I do not like the issues that are being brought forward for discussion. I do not like the Democrats, and I do not like the Republicans. I do not like Ralph Nader, either."

"Maybe you ought to throw in Harry Browne and Ross Perot," Chickie said.

Tibor took a piece of toast off the stack in the middle of the table and started to butter it.

Gregor waved to Linda Melajian. "Let's get you a cup of coffee or something. You must be freezing. You had your coat open when you walked in here."

"I only had to get from the door of the cab to the door of the restaurant," Chickie said, as Linda materialized. "Coffee would be fine, though, thank you. I'm moving at warp speed this morning. I've got a contracts class to prep for and then an hour at the Justice Project this evening, and classes in between. Law school sounded like a great idea when I first had it, but it really can be a drain."

"I'm surprised you find time to volunteer at the Justice Project."

"I had to volunteer at something," Chickie said. "I was going crazy. I've got nothing against rich people. I don't even have anything against rich pricks as a matter of principle. It's just that you wouldn't believe how many people go to law school with the ambition to make the world safe for corporate polluters."

"Ah," Tibor said. "You're a liberal. Or a Green."

"That one would be mostly Green, I think," Chickie said. "But what I am is a skeptical libertarian."

Linda was back with the coffee. Chickie said thank you as she put it down in front of him and then shrugged off his coat. The black suit was a very good black suit, Gregor noticed. He couldn't remember if Chickie had been well dressed when he'd met him at the church.

"Well," Chickie said. "Thank you for seeing me this early in the morning. I'm sorry to be in such a rush. I know your schedule must be packed."

"My schedule is clear," Gregor said, "and it's rarely packed. The Justice Project has something to do with the drug case that Drew Harrigan is involved in, right?"

"Right," Chickie said, "but not on the side of Drew Harrigan. He's got his own lawyers for that, and expensive ones, too. And he's got the ACLU, which ought to embarrass him but doesn't. Or at least it doesn't seem to. Nobody's seen him for a month."

"He's disappeared."

"He's in rehab," Tibor said. "Tcha, Krekor, at least watch the television news."

"I do watch the television news," Gregor said. "I don't pay attention to celebrity gossip. I mean, if the man's in rehab, what business is it of mine?"

"That's the important thing," Tibor said. "Learning to mind your own business. Nobody can mind their own business anymore."

Chickie looked amused. "We represent Sherman Markey," he said. "Sherman did some handyman work around Harrigan's apartment for a while. I've never been able to pin down what. At any rate, when Harrigan was caught carrying a ton of prescription drug medication, all obtained illegally, he fingered Sherman as the guy who got the drugs for him. You know, not a regular supplier, not a dealer, but the person he'd send out to the pharmacy or over to a new doctor's office or something when he couldn't go himself because he'd be too obvious. Most people know Harrigan on sight, or a lot of them do. So he needed a blind, and he said Sherman was it."

"And you don't think Mr. Markey was the one?"

Chickie shifted slightly in his seat. "Actually, as far as the Justice Project is concerned, that's sort of beside the point. The reason we got involved in the beginning was because of the way the case unfolded. They picked up Harrigan. Harrigan fingered Sherman. They arrested Sherman. And then the whole thing sort of exploded. They got Sherman a public defender who was completely useless, but that's par for the course. What wasn't par was that Sherman didn't do what he was supposed to and come right out and confess. He flat out refused. And one day he was being taken back to jail after being questioned for the umpteenth time, and there was a reporter from WB-17 standing out near the sergeant's desk, and Sherman fell on her and started wailing that they were torturing him to get him to confess to something he didn't do. And all hell broke loose."

"I can imagine."

"So we stepped in," Chickie said. "We would defend him if he was guilty or not, that isn't the issue. The issue is competent representation. So we got him out on bail, cleaned him up, got him a room at an SRO—I know, we should have done better, but it was all we could afford—and then we filed a lawsuit for him against Drew Harrigan for defamation. Kate Daniel suggested it about the same time she suggested she come down here and handle this herself. It was a smart move."

"Kate Daniel is here?" Gregor said. "Handling your defense of Markey?"

"Handling the lawsuit, mostly," Chickie said. "It really was a smart move. It meant we could be playing offense, which is damned hard to do when your client is a homeless alcoholic and the opposition is a national media star. Anyway, that's where we were as of two weeks ago. Harrigan was incommunicado in rehab. Sherman was suing. Kate was making life hell for everybody in the office. And then Sherman disappeared."

"Disappeared," Gregor repeated. "You mean he took off? He made bail and decided not to hang around and see if he was going to go to jail?"

"You see, that's it," Chickie said. "With somebody else, that would have been the first thing I thought of, too. But Sherman isn't somebody else. You asked me if I thought he was innocent. Well, I do. You'd have to meet him to understand. It's six of one, half dozen of the other that he's got the start of cirrhosis of the liver. He can't think straight from one moment to the next. He forgets things. Hell, he forgets where he is, sometimes. He's got one thing on his mind and that's getting enough alcohol to keep himself anesthetized. I can't see him working out a schedule of pharmacies to go to to make sure he didn't go to any one so often that he'd be suspected of being an OxyContin addict. And even if you say Harrigan worked out the schedule himself and just sent

Sherman, I can't see the pharmacies serving him. This is not your poster boy for the homeless problem. He drinks, and he not only drinks, he smells. He doesn't bathe. He doesn't brush his teeth. He doesn't use deodorant. It would cost money he'd rather spend on wine.

"You hear all that stuff about the hard-core homeless. Sherman is it. We put him up in an SRO, but we knew he wouldn't stay. He won't stay more than a single night in the shelters, either. Those places have rules. They have to. Sherman doesn't like the rules, because they always mean he can't drink on the premises. I can't see Sherman remembering which pharmacy Harrigan told him to go to, not for ten minutes. I can't see him taking cash—that's what Harrigan claims, that he gave Sherman cash—and going to a pharmacy and buying drugs. He'd get distracted by a liquor store. I can't imagine the pharmacist selling him OxyContin, and I can't imagine a doctor prescribing it for him. The whole scenario is completely bogus. And so is the idea that he would deliberately skip town to avoid the legal hassles. Mr. Demarkian, ten minutes after we got him out of jail, he didn't remember he had legal hassles. He's not that mentally coherent."

Tibor was listening now. "And this person is left to roam the streets?" He seemed stunned.

Chickie George shrugged. "Involuntary commitment is a form of incarceration. You can't just run around committing people for their own good. There are all kinds of issues involved there."

"Let's not worry about false imprisonment at the moment," Gregor said. "You say he's missing. Since when?"

"The morning of January twenty-eighth, at least. It might have been earlier, but we went looking for him on the morning of January twenty-eighth, and he was nowhere to be found."

"Where did you look?"

"We checked his SRO. We should have found him a better place. He might have stayed. But we didn't have the money, and he'd probably have ended up getting evicted anyway. He can get pretty damned odd on alcohol."

"Where else did you look?"

"We checked the homeless shelters," Chickie said. "Actually, those got checked twice. Ray Dean Ballard had his people looking out for Sherman the night before. That would have been the twenty-seventh. They weren't making a systematic search, though. They were just keeping an eye out for him. We'd just bought him these new, clean clothes and gotten him spruced up a little because of the case. He had a bright red hat. We thought he'd be easy to spot."

"Who's Ray Dean Ballard?"

"He's the guy who runs Philadelphia Sleeps. They're a homeless service. They run a few shelters, but mostly they run vans to try to get people to go into shelters, especially in this weather. Same thing with soup kitchens, getting social services, getting legal help. They had vans out that night because it was lethally cold, and they had their people looking out for Sherman. And they didn't find him."

"Did that bother you at the time, that they couldn't find him?"

"Not really, no," Chickie said. "Sherman is Sherman. He really could just wander off and forget where he was, forget what he was doing, forget where he was supposed to be. For the first few days, I wasn't worried at all. I just thought— well, you know. Sherman is Sherman. He probably got hold of a few big bottles of wine and he's off drinking them. Either that, or he lost the hat, so nobody knows what they're looking for anymore. There's an odd thing with homeless people. Nobody remembers their faces. They remember the clothes, you know, and the shtick, if there is one, but they don't remember the faces. Not even most of the people who work with the homeless full-time."

"Would you recognize Sherman Markey's face?"

"I think so," Chickie said. "But I'm not claiming to be a saint. I really don't know. He'd be wearing the clothes we gave him, though. I'd recognize those."

"You gave him only one set of clothes?"

"No, but he left the others in the SRO. We bought him a big royal blue parka. We were trying to make him stand out as much as possible. Ray Dean had a fit about that, because he says that makes them targets, especially the winos, because they're unconscious so much of the time. So it may be he's out there and he's lost the parka and the hat and he's just wearing a khaki shirt and new blue jeans. Or maybe not."

"Exactly," Gregor said. "I take it you've considered the possibility that he's dead."

Chickie looked away, out the window, onto Cavanaugh Street. It was coming on to eight o'clock, and the solid gray of the sky seemed faintly backlit. It was officially morning. "I haven't just considered it," Chickie said, "I'm assuming it. He froze to death. Or he got rolled and murdered for whatever he had on him, which wouldn't have been much. Or he just died. He wasn't in the best of physical shape. If Drew Harrigan were out and about instead of telling his troubles to group therapy in rehab, I'd even have my suspicions that Harrigan murdered him."

"Why?"

"Because Sherman was more useful to him dead than alive. Because with Sherman alive, it's too easy to see the holes in Harrigan's story, for one thing. And because with Sherman alive and in trouble with the law, it's harder for Harrigan to get let out on probation instead of doing some prison time. If this was an Agatha Christie story, I could think of thirty people who might want Sherman dead."

"But you don't think any of them killed him?"

"No," Chickie said. "You don't go to the bother of murdering people like Sherman, not unless you're a street mugger who can't think past the next wallet. I think we can rule out one of those cases where you get to appear on the front page of the *Inquirer* as the Armenian-American Hercule Poirot. But I still need to find Sherman, and I was wondering if you'd be willing to help."

"I'm not exactly the world's best bloodhound," Gregor said. "Especially not these days."

"Oh, I wouldn't ask you to go physically track him down," Chickie said. "We've already tried that, really, and we had a better shot at succeeding than a professional would have anyway, because we know how homeless people think and we know how Sherman thinks. It's not that. It's just that I've spent the last week trying to get the Philadelphia Police to take us seriously, and I haven't gotten anywhere yet. I thought you might put in a good word for us, or a fire up their asses, or whatever you think might work."

"So that they'll go out and search for Sherman Markey?"

"No," Chickie said, "so that they'll do a morgue check for the fingerprints. Sherman was fingerprinted when he was arrested. They could use those and check them against the bodies that have come into the morgue in the last couple of weeks. According to the paper this morning, half a dozen homeless people have died in the last two weeks of exposure to the cold. I know that others have died for other reasons. All those people are sitting in the morgues, waiting for the coroner to have a stray minute to get around to doing their autopsies, and those have been fingerprinted, too. I think if we ran a morgue check, we might find Sherman."

"And if you do, then what?"

"I don't know," Chickie said. "It will probably depend on how he died. But I'd like to know that he died, and not have to be sitting here wondering if he's wandering around somewhere, getting frostbite because he can't remember he's got a perfectly good room in an SRO. Well, it wasn't a perfectly good room. But you know what I mean. It was clean, and it had heat."

"And you think I have influence with the Philadelphia Police?"

"Don't you?"

"At the moment," Gregor said, "I don't know."

2

An hour later, Gregor Demarkian was lying on the couch in his own living room. His shoes were under the coffee table, where they tended to fall when he kicked them off without thinking. His cell phone was lying squarely in the middle of his chest, on top of the sweater, two presents from Bennis, melding. He had no idea why he was feeling so restless. Chickie George was a nice man. He had a simple problem, and the favor he'd asked for had been neither out of line nor incomprehensible. It was more sensible than not to do a morgue check under the circumstances. It was not so sensible that the police were being recalcitrant about doing one. He ran it around and around in his mind. Sherman Markey was a homeless alcoholic, and therefore low priority. Sherman Markey was a principal defendant in a high-profile celebrity drug case, and therefore high priority. The second should trump the first. Either somebody in the PD was being close to criminally stupid, or there was something else going on here. Gregor was willing to bet that there was something else going on here. The questions were, what and for whom? Either Chickie George was withholding information from him, or the police were withholding information from Chickie George. About one thing, though, he and Chickie were in complete accord. If Sherman Markey was dead, it wasn't likely that Drew Harrigan had murdered him, in person or by proxy. If he had, there was something odder happening here than he dared to imagine.

The thing was, it wasn't so simple these days, deciding if he had "influence" with the Philadelphia Police. A year ago, it would have been no problem. Now it was an election year, and as in all election years, people were watching their backs. He had always been apolitical. Even when politics had been what he thought of as "nice," he had been apolitical. Now it just felt like something that existed to muck up his life.

Not more than a few months ago, he had promised himself to stay out of crime in the city of Philadelphia until at least the start of 2005. It didn't mean much that Chickie George wasn't actually asking him to investigate a crime, or even anything that was necessarily connected to a crime. He needed the Philadelphia Police, and he knew without asking that the Philadelphia Police were not going to be happy to hear from him, especially concerning a case that could have some serious media traction if it was played right. The mayor's office wasn't going to be happy to hear from him, either. And all that, in spite of the fact that he had always had extremely cordial relations with the government of the city of Philadelphia during all the years he had been living on Cavanaugh Street, right up until the minute before last.

He sat up and put the cell phone on the coffee table. He stared at it for a minute—he hadn't wanted a cell phone; that had been Bennis's idea, part of her campaign to bring him into the twenty-first century—and then picked it up and flipped it open. The buttons were so small, he always thought he should punch them with the tip of a chopstick, or maybe a toothpick. He punched them with his fingers, and waited while the phone rang. Then somebody at the other end picked up, and he heard the deep-throated, cheerful hum of Angela Wallaby's gospel choir–trained African-American South Philadelphia accent saying, "You've reached the offices of John Henry Newman Jackman at the headquarters of Jackman for Mayor: a new vision and a new future for the city of Philadelphia. How can I help you?"

Well, Gregor thought, *you could talk John out of challenging the sitting mayor of Philadelphia to a goddamned primary run.*

Since Angela wasn't likely to agree to anything like that, Gregor said, "Hey, Angela, it's Gregor Demarkian. Tell the next mayor of the city of Philadelphia that I have something of a problem."

THREE

I

Neil Elliot Savage did not get into the office before nine o'clock unless there was a reason for him to be there, and in his experience there almost never was. The mania for workaholism was, in his opinion, much like the mania for downscale Southern accents, country music, and stock car racing, a corruption of everything that was vital and important in culture, a surrender to the forces of populism and vulgarity. It was better to spend the morning at home, with Beethoven coming out of the Bose sound system he'd installed in the kitchen only two years ago Christmas and Henry James propped up on the little wooden reading stand he kept on the kitchen table next to the blond rush mat he used to mark his place. When he'd been married—and there was something he didn't like to think about, even for a minute—it was Katherine who had set up the place mat every morning and laid out a linen napkin next to a setting from her everyday silver. It was Katherine who had poured his juice and made his coffee. It was Katherine who had put his toast out next to pots of creamed butter and ginger preserve. The whole scene had been like a fantasy from those very same Henry James novels, except that throughout the project Katherine had been livid and steaming. That was what Neil remembered most about Katherine—the anger that was both wide and deep, that covered everything.

"I didn't spend three years at the Harvard Law School to pour orange juice for you in the morning," she would say, when the anger went beyond the point where striking attitudes was enough for her. "And you didn't get Parkinson's disease at Phillips Exeter. You can pour your own damned coffee."

In the years since—and there were many years—Neil had wondered why she hadn't walked out on him long before, but of course that was the times. You didn't walk out on a perfectly good husband in 1963. You especially didn't file for divorce because he wanted you to pour his orange juice in the morning, and you thought you were too busy and important to do it. Eventually, he'd gotten her a maid, and that was when the real trouble started. That was when he realized that she wasn't really angry about the orange juice. She didn't care about making beds. She didn't care about making toast. What she cared about was the fact that she was one of only two women in her graduating class at Harvard Law, she'd had to be twice as intelligent and twice as determined as any of the men there to make it at all, and now she was married in Philadelphia and had nothing in particular to do.

Well, Neil thought, she had something in particular to do now. He hadn't mentioned it at the office when the subject had first come up, but he was going to have to, soon. The men in the firm who remembered his marriage were largely long gone. Partners did that. They got worn-out by age and time. The ones who did remember probably didn't realize that this Kate was that Kate. She wasn't using Savage as a last name, and she'd never used her maiden name when she'd come to firm parties or paid her respects to the managing partner's wife at Christmas. She also wasn't from Philadelphia, so not so many people knew her family as might have if the firm had been located in Boston or New York. She hadn't even called herself Kate. When Neil thought of the two of them married, she was always Katherine to him, as she had been Katherine at Vassar when he'd first met her, and she'd first explained how and why she intended to go to law school, and what she intended to do with the degree once she got it.

Of course, she wasn't doing, now, what she had intended to do with the degree when she'd first started at Harvard, and he'd first decided to indulge her by not insisting that they get married right away, as soon as he graduated from law school himself. The truth of it was, he'd been afraid to press her. He'd been afraid she'd turn him down. He'd been able to sense the ferocity in her even then. Then, of course, the "women's movement" had come along, and that had been the impetus she needed—no, Katherine never needed impetus. She had that all on her own. The "women's movement" had been the *narrative* she needed, as they would have said when Neil was in college, and the narrative had taken her out of his life forever, and to New York. She would have gone anyway. It would only have taken her longer. She needed someplace to be that would let her be a lawyer, and Philadelphia at that time and in that era was not it.

Of all the vulgarities in a vulgar age, Neil thought that the "women's movement" was the very worst. It made ugly what had the right to be beautiful, and harsh what had the right to be gentle. It wasn't that he begrudged women the right to be lawyers if they wanted to be. It was that he begrudged the loss of grace in the world that had come about when women began to shriek. Maybe he just begrudged the loss of Katherine, who had not only walked out on his life and let him arrange the divorce in any way he wanted to, without so much as a backward glance at the property settlements, but had never bothered to send him a Christmas card in all the years since. He sent Christmas cards to her, when he knew where she was, which was less often than he liked. He kept the photograph album of their wedding that she had left behind.

Right now, he kept only the orange juice. The rest of the food—toast, coffee, ginger preserve, butter—he put away or threw away. None of it appealed to him. It was one thing to say he didn't like to get into the office before nine. It was an-

other thing to waltz into the office after nine. Even Grayson
Barden didn't do that. The fact was, he'd been sitting here at
this table for an hour and a half, thinking not about work, not
about getting ready to get going, not about Drew Harrigan
and his problems, but about Kate, and the fact of Kate was
making it impossible for him to move. He should have married again. He should have abandoned his principles and
found some nice Philadelphia debutante who wanted nothing more than to spend her days arranging charity functions
and playing tennis at a country club, and married her, and
done what all partners do, put up with it. If it had felt too
sordid, he wouldn't have had to have a mistress on the side.
He just couldn't seem to make himself care, one way or the
other, about the sort of woman who would be interested in
marrying him. The divorcées and widows his own age were
the least attractive of all. They were not only not-Kate, they
had hardened in their tastes and attitudes. They already
knew all they wanted to know.

It was already eight forty-five, and if he hadn't wanted to
see Kate again he should have told someone at the firm what
the situation was, and asked to be taken off Drew Harrigan's
account. He should have done that in any case, because he
truly hated Drew Harrigan and everything he stood for, and
the attitude was plain on his face every time the man's name
was mentioned. The problem was, the rest of the firm felt the
same way. Even the secretaries were Old Philadelphia
enough to consider Mr. Harrigan something of an embarrassment to the name of Barden, Savage & Deal.

It was eight forty-five and he had to get out of the house.
He had to get his car, or find a cab, and go into the office. He
had to sit behind his desk and behave as if nothing important
was happening, because nothing important was. Kate would
not be embarrassed to see him, and he knew it. She would
not be intimidated by the idea of negotiating with her ex-
husband, and he knew that too. She would not be shy about
letting everybody in the room know that they had a long
shared past that she didn't look back on with fondness. She
would not let any of this get in the way of the work she was

supposed to do, and that was the final straw. Neil would be sitting there barely able to get any work done at all, and Kate would be on the other side of the conference table—she had insisted on either a conference room or a meeting in her own office at the Justice Project, which nobody at the firm was going to agree to—as cool and focused as if she were in her own living room with nobody else in sight.

He was sweating, and the meeting wasn't until noon. He had the whole morning to get through without throwing up or doubling over in pain from the cramps that kept spasming through him like labor pains. He had no idea why it was this bad, or why Beethoven did nothing to cure it, as Beethoven always had in the past. He just wished it was all over with, and he could go back to worrying about Drew Harrigan's escrow arrangements, which mattered far more than Sherman Markey at this point, and would matter far more in the future. It would be different if there was any possibility that Drew Harrigan had killed him, but there was no evidence that the homeless old man was dead, and Drew was more securely locked up than he would have been in jail.

Not for the first time, Neil Elliot Savage thought that he might really like to see Drew Harrigan in jail.

2

The nine o'clock show was just about to go on, and not for the first time, Marla Hildebrande felt guilty. She felt especially guilty because it was clear that Frank Sheehy didn't feel guilty at all.

"It isn't like we murdered the man," Frank said, stretched out on the couch in her office again like he was beached there. "We don't even know he's dead. He's just disappeared."

"For two weeks in weather like this," Marla said. "You know as well as I do he must have frozen to death somewhere. And we were wishing for it."

"We weren't wishing for it. We were just hoping for something to come up that would make it politically feasible for the DA to go for a pretrial diversion program or probation or whatever the hell would get Drew back in front of a mike as soon as possible. And here we are."

"Assuming he isn't found. And I'm hoping he'll be found."

"So am I, because it doesn't matter if he's found," Frank said. "The disappearing act is going to make him look bad, which will make Drew look better. Really. That's all we need. We don't need anybody dead. We don't need apocalypse and destruction. We just need Drew."

Marla sighed. She switched on the speaker next to her on the desk. They were keeping Drew's big opening. It was still *The Drew Harrigan Show,* after all. The hokey announcer's voice came on, riding a crest of horn music. "It's Drew Harrigan, the man with his heart in the *right* place, coming to you from Philadelphia." She shut the speaker off.

"After this, you don't want to know."

"That bad?"

"I told you. None of them are bad. They're just bland. And they lack fire. Have you given any thought whatsoever to what I said to you about finding other talent? Even if Drew comes back from rehab and we don't have to worry about another hiatus, we still need a more diversified list. We can't go on like this letting one person hold us hostage."

"So, go looking. Didn't I tell you you could go looking?"

"Yes," Marla said. She hesitated a little and opened the long center drawer of her desk. "I have gone looking. Or listening, as the case may be. I've been listening to satellite pickup of little stations all over the West."

"Why the West?"

"Because you need the accent," Marla said. "God forbid anybody should sound like they came from New York or New England. It's guaranteed to brand them as an intellectual snob. But I don't like the Southern ones. It's overkill."

"And under brains," Frank said. "Why is it that a Southern accent always makes people sound twenty IQ points stupider than anybody else?"

"You don't think Ray Dean Ballard sounds twenty IQ points stupider than anybody else."

"It's not the same kind of Southern accent. Did you know his name isn't really Ray Dean?"

"What did he change it from, Joe Bob?"

"Aldous."

"Like Huxley."

"It's his mother's maiden name."

"Whatever," Marla said. She was fiddling with the tape. It was a very good tape, even though she'd made it off the satellite hookup, which made everything sound like a cat pissing. She got it into the tape machine and hit the rewind button, because she'd listened to it last night, and it was obvious from the way the thing looked that she'd forgotten to rewind it. She always forgot to rewind things. She wondered why that was.

"I like this one," she said, "not only because I like the guy, but because I like the content. I know politics sells, but I think we're coming to the end of that on a lot of levels. There's too much rancor, too much anger."

"I thought you said that was the point. That our listeners are angry."

"They are. But they're angry about a lot of things, not just 'liberals.' And they've got a couple of dozen angry white guy talk radio hosts to listen to."

"So, this is what, a shock jock?"

"No. We've got FCC problems," Marla said. "The FCC is suddenly forcing all the 'obscenity' off the air. It's enough to make you crazy. Also, I don't really get the shock jock thing. I don't have an ear for it. No, this is something else. His name is Mike Barbarossa, and he's from Seattle."

"Uh-oh," Frank said. "Seattle, the home of Starbucks, computer programmers, and the lowest citizen church attendance of any part of the country."

"Wanna move?"

"Let me hear the tape," Frank said.

Marla heard the hard chunk that meant the tape had stopped rewinding and pushed the play button. At first there was nothing but fuzz. Marla thought she needed to learn how to burn a CD off the satellite feed. It might be clearer. Then there was some tinny music that sounded as if it were being run through yet another not very good tape machine.

"Ignore the technical level," Marla said. "This is a small station, they probably don't have the money or expertise. We could fix that."

The tinny music stopped and a mildly twangy voice said, "It's five o'clock in the city of Seattle and this is Mike Barbarossa coming to you with sanity, common sense, and an uncorrupted crap detector. We ought to apply the crap detector to the commercials, but we never do. Give a listen to this message from our sponsors and I'll be right back, with the day's first winner in the Just How Stupid Can You Get contest."

Frank Sheehy frowned. "We couldn't let him do that to the commercials, could we?"

"Sure we could. People know the commercials are propaganda. They know they're crap. And the sponsors don't give a damn as long as they have the captive audience, which they will have, in the car with nowhere to hide. Seriously. Listen to this."

"Okay," Mike Barbarossa said. "We're back from that fantasy land where a new car can get you a love life and a new cake recipe can bring you closer to God. It's time for Mike's How Stupid Can You Get roundup, the way we start the day with news that makes you think the human race should have been extinct long ago. Let's start with Mr. Tim Mayfield of Marden, Oklahoma, who cut off his own penis in order to blame the 'crime' on a woman who came home with him from a bar and then refused to sleep with him. After he'd cut his penis off and thrown it across the parking lot of the trailer park where he lived, he called the police and blamed the whole thing on Shirley, resulting in a manhunt lasting three days—maybe I should say womanhunt for our feminist listeners—that left police more and more suspicious that something was wrong with Mr. Mayfield's story. Mayfield finally confessed, and he's being charged with making a false crime report. It turns out that it's not illegal to cut off your own penis in Oklahoma."

"What the hell?" Frank said.

Marla was ecstatic. "Don't you love it? It's like the Darwin Awards for radio. Sometimes he does stuff from the Darwin Awards, and then he gives them credit. Oh, and plugs their books and their Web site—www.darwinawards. com."

"The whole show is this?"

"No." Marla turned the tape off for a moment. "This is the opening bit, where he collects stories of people being stupid from all over the country and then reads them. There's a section later in the show where he takes phone calls, but that's not the best part. At the end of the show, every once in a while, probably when he has material, he does stories on local charlatans. Psychics. Alternative medicine scams. Faith healers."

"He goes after religion?"

"Calm down." Marla said. "It's not as bad as you think. He doesn't go after regular religion, churches, things like that. He goes after these guys who get people to come and pay them money so they can pray over them and declare them well, except the people never are well. You know what I mean."

"I know that shows like that get absolutely no money and have absolutely no audience," Frank said. "For Christ's sake, Marla, what are you thinking? That group up in New York, what's their names, CSICOP, those people, they've been trying to get into radio or television for years, and it's always bombed flat. People like their illusions. They don't want to hear that their favorite psychic is an alcoholic fraud who's using their money to take vacations in Barbados."

"Listen," Marla said. "The problem with CSICOP's stuff is that it's always too serious. I like CSICOP a lot, I really do, but they're always dead serious and full of references to I don't know what, scientific protocols and things. Most people get bored with that stuff and won't follow it, and a lot of people can't follow it. But that isn't what Mike Barbarossa does. What he really is is debunking for the same audience that listens to Drew Harrigan, well, some of them, plus a lot of guys in the same situation who can't stand Harrigan. The guys we've never been able to reach before. What Mike Barbarossa does is to make those guys feel smarter than the idiots around them *and* smarter than the kind of PhD that falls for this sort of nonsense. It's perfect. And Mike Barbarossa is perfect. Listen to that voice."

Marla pushed the play button again.

Mike Barbarossa said, "Now we come to the case of Mr. James Burns, of Alamo, Michigan, where they have one of those little liberal arts colleges you can never figure out why anybody goes to them. Mr. Burns was trying to fix his truck one night. He'd been hearing a niggling little noise, and he couldn't figure out what it was. So what Mr. Burns did was to get a friend of his to drive the truck out to the Interstate while he hung on underneath it and listened. They found his body wrapped around the drive shaft."

"Oof," Frank said.

Marla turned the tape off again. "It's good stuff, Frank, and it will work. At least let me call this guy and ask him if he'll send me an audition tape. It won't cost us anything, it won't cost him any more than a FedEx package, we'll have better quality sound. We can have him on the network in a month and on the syndication list in three. It won't matter if Drew Harrigan has to go to jail for life. We'll have a backup. And a good one. Listen to me, Frank. I think this is the coming thing."

Frank actually did appear to be listening. Marla had to give him that. Just to make the case stronger, she turned on the speaker and let the voice of Drew Harrigan's stand-in host flow through the room. Except that the voice didn't actually flow. It sort of dripped. It sounded like the man had sucked on a helium balloon.

"Turn it off," Frank said. "You've made your point."

"I can call him?"

"Go right ahead."

"I can tell him we're looking for a headliner?"

"Isn't that pushing it?"

"Maybe, but I'm going to tell him. Trust me, Frank, this will work. And we'll all feel better about it. You don't like

Drew Harrigan anyway. He's a pompous windbag and a pain in the ass to work with. I don't like Drew Harrigan. He's a walking threat of a sexual harassment suit, if nothing else. And the techies don't like Drew Harrigan. You'd think these people would realize that you just shouldn't piss off the staff, but they never do. I'm going to go make a phone call to Seattle."

"I'm going to go have some more coffee," Frank said. "Do you remember when you hired Drew Harrigan? I told you at the time that we'd come to regret it."

Actually, what Frank had told her at the time was that he wanted to be protected from ever having to be in the same room with Drew unless there was somebody else present; but it didn't matter. Frank walked out the door, and Marla went flipping through her Rolodex to find the card she'd written Mike Barbarossa's contact information on. She gave a passing thought to Sherman Markey, and then she just let it go. She couldn't go on feeling guilty forever, and it wasn't like she'd killed the man, or forced him to sleep in the streets on a night when it was cold enough to freeze a man's balls into ice cubes.

She had a schedule to fill, and now that she had a chance in hell of filling it, without Mr. Drew Harrigan, she was feeling better than she had in months.

3

At the Monastery of Our Lady of Mount Carmel, Sister Maria Beata of the Incarnation was just finishing up her duty in the kitchen and getting ready to go out to man the front desk. The reading in refectory had been even more of St. John of the Cross, and the reading in *schola* this afternoon would be the same: the monastery was going through a positive orgy of the works of St. John. Beata thought she could stand it if only somebody besides herself would say the obvious: that the man was a sexual hysteric; that his ecstatic visions were sexual to the point of being embarrassing; that the fact that St. John had been named a doctor of the Church centuries before St. Teresa had been allowed to carry the title was embarrassing for its bad taste as well as its sexism. Nobody else would say the obvious, though, so she would have to. And then she would be in trouble again.

She put the last dish away in the cupboard, wiped her hands on her wide white apron, then untied the apron behind her neck and waist and took it off. She hung it on one of the hooks that had been hammered into the kitchen wall just for aprons—they shared aprons; whoever needed one took whichever one was available; they didn't have aprons of their own—and went out of the kitchen, across the refectory, and into the hall. The Angelus bell started ringing just as she reached the grille, and she fell into the prayer without thinking much about it.

"*Angelus Domini nuntiavit Mariae*," a voice came from above her head.

"*Et concepit de Spiritu Sancto*," she answered, and then she was at the grille and the door with its careful locks, leading to the vestibule.

She let herself out of the cloister and nodded to Sister Immaculata at the desk. The rule was that the front desk had to be manned at all times by an extern sister, in case anyone came to the monastery in need of prayer or assistance. In Beata's experience, not much of anybody did.

"Good morning, Sister. Did we have any visitors while we were listening to Annunciata drone endlessly on about the Bridegroom at breakfast?"

Immaculata frowned, to let Beata know that she did not approve of this kind of conversation, which criticized the good faith efforts of other sisters, and solemnly vowed sisters at that. Beata ignored her.

Immaculata leaned over and rummaged through the drawer in the desk. "As a matter of fact, we did. An old man, one of the men from the barn, came in to give you this."

"This" was a bright red watch cap. Beata blinked.

"He said to tell the 'other nun,' which I presume is you, that he was wrong about the hat. They must not have stolen the hat after all, because he found it last night under one of the beds in the back of the barn. Do you understand any of that?"

"Of course. It was that man who died here, a couple of weeks ago. Don't you remember?"

"I remember that a man died."

"Yes," Beata said, "well. He had on a hat, a brand-new watch hat, this one. I remember seeing him wearing it, standing in line waiting to get into the barn when I came back from the lawyers' that day. When he died, this other man came to the door to tell me that he was dead and that some other men had stolen the hat. Except either they didn't, or they stole it and then lost it, because here it is."

"I'm not comfortable with this idea of giving over the barn to homeless people," Immaculata said. "It's not— they're not just homeless, these men. They're troubled. Some of them are mentally ill. Some of them are violent. We don't have anybody here who knows how to treat them professionally. And that wasn't the first one who died."

"Yes, well, Sister, homeless people will die in weather like this. We might as well do what we can to alleviate the situation. I wonder what I ought to do with the hat."

"Give it to the coroner, I suppose," Immaculata said. "Or to the police generally. Isn't that what's supposed to happen when somebody dies a pauper and his body is taken off wherever they take things like that, by the authorities?"

There were times when Beata wondered if Immaculata lived in a time warp, so that the world she saw looked a lot more like the one Dickens had seen than the one Beata did, but in this case, she supposed the woman was right.

Who else would they give the hat to, if not the police?

FOUR

I

There were people who had told John Henry Newman Jackman that he ought to quit his job as commissioner of police of the city of Philadelphia while he tried to unseat the present mayor in a primary challenge for the Democratic nomination, but none of those people were his friends, and none of them were his fellow police officers, and besides, he wouldn't have listened to that kind of advice in any case. In Gregor Demarkian's experience, Mr. Jackman rarely listened to advice of any kind, from anyone, on any matter. They'd first met when Gregor had come to Philadelphia as the FBI officer on a kidnapping case. If there was one thing Gregor was happy never to have to do again, it was to work kidnapping detail as a special agent of the FBI, complete with unmarked brown sedans parked on the side streets of nearly abandoned city districts, cold coffee in Styrofoam cups, and a partner who couldn't stop whining about the way his wife treated his dog. There was a memory from the past, coming out of nowhere. Gregor didn't think he'd thought of Steve Lillianfield in twenty years. And good riddance.

John Jackman, on the other hand, he'd thought of. Almost from the moment Gregor had resettled himself on Cavanaugh Street after the death of his wife and his retirement from the Bureau, he'd been watching John Jackman's slow but steady rise up through a spider's web of increasingly more important jobs to the place where he was now. Gregor couldn't say it had never occurred to him that John might want to run for elective office. It had, but the office in question was, perhaps, president of the United States. That would suit him. The idea of John Jackman as mayor of Philadelphia was nearly . . . something.

Gregor knew, without having been told, that if he was going to talk to John after nine, he'd have to talk to him down at police headquarters. John was on a crusade to prove that he could run for everything—possibly even for the presidency, although he hadn't mentioned it—while still being completely focused on his regular duties and completely effective as a commissioner of police. Gregor had no idea when he was going to campaign, or had been campaigning. John was nearly lunatic on the subject of making "personal" calls from his office. The history of police commissioners in Philadelphia wasn't a pretty one. There had been a lot of corruption over the years. John had swept into that job promising to change all that, and he'd been behaving like a cross between Joan of Arc and Savonarola ever since. Still, he must have been campaigning sometimes, but that was political news Gregor did keep up with. The primary challenge was going very well. It was going so very well, the present mayor was not expected to survive it.

The cab pulled up in front of the tall, blank building that now served as police headquarters, and Gregor got out his wallet to pay the man. The cab hadn't quite made it to the curb, which was solidly packed with parked cars. That meant that all the cars behind them were blocked from going forward until Gregor got his act together and his business done.

Gregor hurried. It was still cold, but not quite as cold as it had been this morning. He should have worn a hat anyway. He just wasn't used to wearing one. He threw the cabdriver a small wad of bills that included a more generous tip than he might have given if he'd had time to think about it, and made the door in a run. The homeless people that he knew would be here later in the day were not here yet. He wondered where they had gone. The people walking up and down the sidewalks all had their coat collars turned up and their hands in their pockets. A sign on a store across the street said both 9:27 a.m. and 2 degrees F.

In the building, he stopped at the security desk and gave his name and destination. The guard looked through the notes on his clipboard and said, "Oh, yes, Mr. Demarkian. You're going to Mr. Jackman's office. Take the elevator."

Gregor had no idea how else he could get to John's office. He supposed there were stairs, but he'd never actually seen any. He got onto the elevator with two women, both African-American and both dressed in serious business suits. It was generally agreed that John had brought needed formality into the building and an end to what had become ritual complaints about the lack of African Americans on the police force and its support staff. The women were pretty, but not as pretty as John's receptionist, who looked like she ought to take over for Naomi Campbell if Campbell ever decided to retire.

Gregor got out of the elevator on John's floor and presented himself to the Ms. Campbell in training, whose name was actually Shoshona Washington. She looked at him as if she'd never seen him before—which she had, so many times that he could have been a member of her family—and then checked her book for his name. Only then did she deign to call in to John's office and announce that he was there.

It wasn't John, but John's assistant Olivia who came out to get him. Olivia was the latest embodiment of John's theory of hiring assistants, as opposed to hiring receptionists.

"With receptionists, you hire pretty," John had told him, when he'd first staffed this office. "With receptionists, you're looking to hit people in the eye, and besides, they don't do much anyway. But with assistants, you need brains, you need common sense, and you need organization. With assistants, you need church women."

"Doesn't this violate the separation of church and state somehow?" Gregor had asked him, imagining for a moment an entire Gospel choir taking up the space just outside John's office door.

John looked disgusted. "It's not about their religion. I don't care if they strangle chickens and worship the devil. It's about their entire mind-set. I mean, look at these women. They keep their churches running. They do the books. They schedule the pastor's time. They clean the places out. They issues the press releases when they have to be issued. They run the Sunday School and the choir and all the projects. You get a bunch of them together on the bus, they can make a kid with a boom box turn the sound off by just staring at him. Church women."

Olivia was a tall, heavy, dignified woman in her fifties. Gregor had always thought she could get a kid with a boom box to turn the sound off by staring at him all on her own. She held out her hand to him, and he took it.

"Good morning, Mr. Demarkian. It's good to see you."

"It's good to see you, too, Mrs. Hall." It had taken him a moment to remember her last name, because John always called her Olivia. But it also hadn't seemed right for him to call her Olivia himself.

She was leading the way back to John's office. "He's very excited to see you. I don't know what it is you have for him, but it must be more interesting than what we've got around here at the moment. Isn't it a terrible thing, what happens in the winter? I've got no use for people who drug and drink and waste the only life the Lord is going to give them, but I don't see leaving them to freeze to death in the street, either."

"Maybe the campaign is getting him down."

Olivia Hall turned to give him a long, cool stare. "We don't talk about the campaign on police premises," she said. "We don't mix the campaign with the work here."

"Of course not."

She turned away again, and knocked on John's door. "It's the homeless people who are getting him down, and all this cold. Every precinct in the city has had at least one homeless death so far this season, and it's going to get worse before it gets better. It depressed him. He's the kind that wants to make everything right, and this is something nobody is going to make right anytime soon."

"Of course," Gregor said. He still felt like a third grader who had been scolded by the teacher in front of the entire class, in spite of the fact that there was nobody around who could have heard Olivia's rebuke to him. Mrs. Hall, he reminded himself.

Olivia Hall opened John's door and shooed him in. "I'll hold the calls for twenty minutes," she said, without being asked. "But you know that's the best I can do, under the circumstances. It's not my fault we're under siege."

"Why are you under siege?" Gregor asked, coming in and sitting down.

John sighed. "It's the mayor's office. They keep trying to get proof that I'm slacking off. They have somebody calling every minute or two to ask trivial questions and give even more trivial orders that I'm not going to follow and don't have to, but the idea is to catch me not here, or something. They even phone me at lunch. It's insane."

"According to Mrs. Hall, we don't talk about the campaign here."

"Right. Well, you know. The idea is to never mention it to employees and staff, because that way the people over there can't say I'm campaigning while at work, or forcing people to support me, or something. He's an asshole, you do know that, don't you, Gregor? The mayor, I mean. He's an asshole, and I deserve to win."

"You apparently are winning."

"Yeah, I am. But that's because I'm not the only one who thinks he's an asshole. The party thinks he's an asshole. And that one's between you and me."

"The party is backing your primary challenge."

"Exactly."

"I was wondering about that," Gregor said. What he'd really been wondering was why John would want to upset the party brass by challenging an incumbent. It made much more sense if no upset was going to be involved. "Thank you. It seemed like an odd bit of timing, your running right now."

"It's not. Look, he can't get re-elected. You know that and I know that. He was a complete mess on the Catholic Church scandal thing. He's in the Cardinal's pocket, or at least looks like he is. It was either somebody chucking him off the ticket, or letting the opposition have the mayor's office. And you know we never let the opposition have anything."

"Too dangerous," Gregor said.

"You don't really give a damn, do you?" John said.

"I don't really give a damn about politics," Gregor said, "which is getting to be a liability, since it's all anybody seems to be able to talk about anymore. I do give a damn about whether you get to be mayor. I'd like to see that."

"Well, that's good."

"I fully intend to vote for you for senator, when you run for that."

"That's a bit down the line at the moment," John said. "You want to see what Olivia dug up for you on your problem?"

"Sure."

There was a stack of papers sitting squarely in the middle of John Jackman's desk. He picked them up and handed them over. "I didn't want to say it when you called me over at the campaign, because I wasn't positive, but it turns out I was right. We already *have* run a fingerprint check for Sherman Markey. In fact, we've run two, and not just on the corpses in the morgue. We've run it through recent arrests, too."

"And?"

"Not a thing. Nothing even close. Every once in a while you get some ambiguous stuff; we don't even have that."

"What about deaths?" Gregor asked. "Homeless people have died in the city these last two weeks, right?"

"Yes." John sighed.

"And?"

"And, what can I tell you? It's been a brutal winter. It's supposed to get worse over the next week or so. It isn't going to get better anytime soon. If I knew what to do about this stuff, Gregor, I'd do it. The legal people say we're not allowed to arrest them unless they've actually committed a crime. We can't arrest them for vagrancy anymore because vagrancy laws are unconstitutional. We can arrest them for public drunkenness if they get rowdy enough, but most of the ones we're most worried about don't get rowdy. We can't commit them to a mental institution unless they're a clear and present danger to themselves or others, which they aren't, because falling asleep in subzero temperatures so that they accidentally freeze to death in the night isn't considered being a danger to themselves. That's meant to mean only active suicide. And a lot of them won't go into what shelters are available, even for the night.

"I mean, seriously, Gregor, seriously. What other evidence do we need that somebody is mentally ill besides the fact that he absolutely refuses to accept a warm bed on a night with subzero temperatures and chooses—*chooses,* I'm not making this up—to sleep on a park bench instead? Ed Koch had the right idea. When the temperature goes below a certain level, you round them up involuntarily and you get them inside whether they want to go or not."

"Koch got into a lot of trouble for that."

"He was still right," John said. "The law makes assumptions that aren't valid. The law makes assumptions about the intentions of the people who want these guys to go into shelters that are not valid. The law makes assumptions about these people themselves that are not valid."

"The law is responding to the fact that for decades, a husband who didn't want his wife to divorce him or a city administration that didn't like poor people could get them involuntarily committed on nothing much better than a say-so," Gregor said. "And you know it. The law is what it is today because of how it was abused in the past."

"And that still leaves us with a city full of homeless people, mostly alcoholic and drug-addicted old men, who aren't in their right minds because their minds were eaten away by rotgut years ago, or were paranoid schizophrenic to begin with. I'm sorry, Gregor. I know the history. I really do. But I hate this time of winter."

"It's an unusual winter," Gregor said. "Coldest on record in, what, fifty years?"

"Something like that," John said. "But we get at least a couple of days of extreme cold every year, and that means every year we get a couple of nights of people freezing to death. The only compensation, and it isn't much of a compensation, is that most street crime goes way down. Your ordinary street criminal isn't much interested in freezing his patootie off just to get your wallet. Even convenience store and gas station holdups go down. Somehow it figures, you know? They've got no discipline, these people, and no ambition. Shove a little hardship their way, and they just fold."

"Right," Gregor said. He looked around the office. It was spare, to the point of being denuded. Obviously, Olivia Hall didn't decorate, and John didn't have a girlfriend at the moment. Gregor thought about asking John about the marriage thing—weren't successful politicians usually expected to have wives?—and decided against it.

"I think what Chickie was getting at," he said, "was that it's just possible something got missed. We're dealing with a homeless person here. People don't always notice them in the way they notice other people."

"We're dealing with fingerprints here," Jackman said.

"Even so."

"Even so nothing," Jackman said. "Look, I'm going to send you over to the district attorney, who's the one you want to talk to if you want to know everything there is to know about this; but the facts are simple. We did not one, but two searches, and we got nothing. We checked out every corpse of every homeless person who came into the morgue from break of day on January twenty-seventh until midnight February nine, and we didn't get a thing. Which doesn't mean he isn't dead, mind you. People die in abandoned buildings and back alleys and we don't find them for weeks or months. So anything could have happened. But if he came into our system, we would have found him. Because we were careful. We were very, very careful."

"Because the Justice Project asked about him?"

"Because this is Drew Harrigan and his people that we're dealing with," John said. "This is a guy who's forced congressmen out of office and gotten superintendents of large school districts fired. He's coming out of rehab in a couple of weeks, and when he does, he's going to be loaded for bear, and the bear he's going to be loaded for is us. We arrested him. We're going ahead with the prosecution. The DA isn't backing down. The police aren't backing down. And I've got a mayor who's suddenly making noises like he's a Harrigan fan and who wants my ass more than he wants to win the lottery. What do you say?"

"I'd say you were probably very careful."

"Right," John said. "We were all very careful. But on the assumption that it never hurts to be more careful, and because it's you that's asking, I'm going to call over and get them to run one more check. Who knows, maybe Markey showed up on a slab in the last day or two and nobody caught it going in, although they're supposed to check. But I want you to go down and talk to the DA and let him outline exactly what's going on here. Drew Harrigan didn't get where he was without knowing how to win a street fight better than most other people, and he isn't going to go down without taking a hell of a lot of people with him."

"Is he going to go down?" Gregor asked.

Jackman nodded. "I think so. Harrigan's people, hell, practically everybody, thinks we want to back away from a trial, but we don't. The DA is in a state of world-class piss-off. He's being portrayed in the press as a corrupt little shit who just wants to persecute a pathetic homeless man so he can let the rich guy off the hook, which is about as realistic as saying that the NRA is really in favor of gun control. There have been rumors around town for weeks that we had Sherman Markey killed because that way we could let Harrigan off with probation because people wouldn't be upset about how we're treating the homeless guy —"

"Wait a minute," Gregor said. "Doesn't that contradict the other thing?"

"Of course it contradicts the other thing. Do you think anybody cares?" Jackman was out of his seat and pacing. "The whole thing is getting to be more and more of a mess

by the minute, and if there's anything I want, truly and really, it's to find Sherman Markey under conditions that will
not support the claim that we killed him. Which doesn't
mean that people won't say that anyway. I've made an appointment for you to see Rob in an hour. He's clearing his
desk so that he can talk to you. Be on time."

"I'm always on time," Gregor said.

"Yeah, okay, you are, I'm sorry." Jackman sat down
again.

Gregor looked toward the office door. "This Mrs. Hall,"
he said. "Is she efficient?"

"If Olivia Hall were running the Defense Department,"
Jackman said, "its budget would be half what it is now, we'd
have twice as much in the way of hardware and three times
as many soldiers, and the food would be good. I'm trying to
get her to run for City Council. Don't tell me I'm not an honorable man. The day she wins a seat and leaves me, I'm going to cut my throat, but I'm encouraging it anyway. Go see
Rob. He'll give you what you need to know."

2

Downstairs on the street again, with his coat collar pulled up
and his hands in his pockets like everybody else, Gregor
considered the fact that an hour was a long time to have to
go not very far to a place he could reach on foot. He looked
around the neighborhood. He had been in this part of town
more often than he liked to remember, but he usually arrived
in a cab and left in a cab. He didn't know much about what
was here. It looked prosperous enough. Ordinary precinct
houses often seemed to have been built on the worst street in
the vicinity, or to have become such as people moved out not
to be threatened by the parade of felons that went in and out
the doors. Maybe not so many felons went in and out here.
He walked up to the intersection—he ought to find a place to
get some coffee, and there was one; he'd remember it for
later—and looked in both directions without finding what he
wanted. He went another block and looked down that inter-

section, and there it was: an outpost of Barnes & Noble. He gave a mental nod to Bennis's lecture about always using independent bookstores and went on down to it. If there was another bookstore in this neighborhood, he didn't know where it was, and he wasn't going to take a cab back to Cavanaugh Street to find one now.

He went into the Barnes & Noble and looked around. He didn't do much shopping in bookstores. Either Bennis or Tibor tended to pick up his books for him, or he bought them from Amazon because they were easy to find. He looked at the big central display right inside the door and didn't see what he was looking for, or anything like it. He moved a little farther into the store and promptly got lost. There was a big section of something called "Bargain Books" that seemed to consist entirely of oversized volumes on various artists and their works, and oversized cookbooks. He had a crazy urge to see if he could find something called *Picasso's Guide to Spanish Cooking.*

A young woman in good gray flannel slacks and a bright red sweater walked up to him. "Could I help you with something? You look confused."

"I'm looking for something I'm not sure exists."

"If it's a kind of book, it probably exists," she said reassuringly. "And there's a good chance we have it. We carry over twenty thousand titles in this store."

Twenty thousand titles sounded good. The store didn't look big enough. "Do you know a talk radio host named Drew Harrigan?"

The woman looked wary. "Of course I know him. Well, know of him. We've never met. I mean, I don't think he shops in this part of Philadelphia."

"Has he written a book?"

Now the woman looked more than wary. "Um, well, yes. Of course he's written a book. He's written three. The newest one is a *New York Times* bestseller." She looked at him more closely. "Do you really mean to say you didn't know that?"

"I don't listen to a lot of radio," Gregor said. "Except, you know, *All Things Considered* and this oldies station where they do a lot of Jan and Dean. And I don't like politics."

"You don't like politics and you want a book by Drew Harrigan?"

"I want to know what all the fuss is about."

"Are you, well, you know, conservative?"

"Conservative how?" Gregor asked.

"Conservative," the young woman said. "You know, like, Republican."

"I think I'm registered as an Independent," Gregor said. "Does that matter?"

"Does that matter how?" she asked.

Gregor was beginning to feel as if he had landed in the middle of a *Monty Python* skit. Then the woman started, and leaned closer to get a better look at him.

"Oh," she said. "I know you. You're that man. The Argentinian-American Hercule Poirot."

"Armenian," Gregor said, automatically. "I'm Gregor Demarkian, yes. And I just want to know—I don't know—how the man thinks, maybe. What he says. What gets people so upset about him."

The young woman nodded. "The *New York Times* bestsellers are right over here. We give those thirty percent off in hardcover, and the latest book is in hardcover, if that's the one you want. It's called *Heart on the Right Side*. That's true, you know. He has some genetic condition, and all his internal organs are backwards, so his heart is on the right side of his chest instead of the left."

"I had heard that," Gregor said.

"It makes it all the more easy to understand how his head got up his ass," the young woman said. "And if you tell anybody I said that, I'll deny it. I could get fired."

"I won't tell anyone."

"God, you don't know how it embarrasses me. That he's from Philadelphia, I mean. That he works out of here. I mean, at least Rush Limbaugh moved to Washington, or wherever."

"I take it you don't like Mr. Limbaugh much either?"

"At the moment, I like Dean," the young woman said, "but I don't really care. I'll vote for a hamster if that's the only choice I've got. Here's the book. Over at Boardman's, they've got this thing on display in a trash basket. That's what I'd like to do. They're independent, though."

"Why don't I just buy this?" Gregor said.

"You wouldn't believe how many people do buy it," she said. "Some of them buy six or seven copies at a time. It's eerie."

"Maybe they're buying for friends."

The young woman gave Gregor a long, pitying look. "Maybe he's sending people out to get the numbers up," she said. "Maybe the conservative organizations are sending people out to get the numbers up. You'd be amazed at what people do to get on that bestseller list. This is going to cost you twenty-five ninety-five. You're going to be upset you spent the money."

FIVE

I

Jig Tyler always had his classes scheduled as early in the day as possible. He had the eight to ten graduate seminar hour sewn up, and nobody who wanted to teach graduate students in mathematics could schedule simultaneously without risking having no students at all. It wasn't that students came to do their doctorates in mathematics at Penn because of Jig—although most of them did—but the simple fact that Jig was also one of the most effective teachers in the history of the field. In an academic area known for its eccentrics but not oversupplied with media stars, Jig was not only a familiar face on television but blessed with a teaching style more Barnum than scholastic. He would have been charismatic even if nobody had ever given him a Fields Medal and two Nobel prizes.

This morning, he was charismatic but dead on his feet. He had had a long, unrestful night, in the worst sense in which he experienced such nights, and now his head was pounding as if it was going to explode. He had taken an ibuprofen at breakfast, but it hadn't helped. He had tried lying down flat on his back on the floor of his office and transferring the pain to the sky blue Chinese vase he kept on top of his old metal filing cabinet, but that hadn't worked either.

He didn't really believe in the silly "natural medicine" reme-
dies he accepted from researchers he met at conferences and
symposiums, but it was only polite to accept them, and there
was no reason not to give them a try. In the end he had had to
admit that he was going to have to take something serious to
get rid of the ache, and that had put him in a bad mood for
the entire last hour of the seminar. It didn't help that his
Monday seminar was his worst, full of students he thought
of as rank idiots. Of course, he thought of most students as
rank idiots, and a good proportion of professionals in every
field he'd ever worked in, too, but that was a natural hazard
of being who and what he was. He knew there were people
like him who were not like him, so to speak. That is, he
knew there were people who could do what he could do in-
tellectually without being so alienated from everybody and
everything else around them. He'd even been careful to read
books by one of the more famous examples, Richard Feyn-
man. He still hadn't been able to get it. The Monday seminar
was not full of the usual idiots. The Monday seminar was
full of the kind of people who questioned the very legiti-
macy of education, never mind of high literacy. Jig had
never understood why so many people in mathematics and
the sciences found it impossible to understand why people
read Shakespeare or listened to Bach.

And then, of course, there was Delmore Krantz. Delmore
Krantz was in the Monday seminar. Delmore Krantz could
give a lecture on "elitism" that lasted for several days and
never come up for breath. Every once in a while, Jig wanted
to take Delmore by the shoulders and tell him that everybody who was worth anything was an elitist of some kind.

At least Delmore hadn't said anything this morning about
hegemonic discourse. Not even once. Jig thought he ought to
be thankful for small favors. He made his way down the hall
toward his office, the mass of students trailing behind him
like germs behind a man with pneumonia. None of them
wanted to approach him for fear he'd shout at them. If they
did approach him, he would shout at them. He got to his of-

fice, unlocked the door—there was something; when he'd first come to Penn, in the 1960s, nobody ever locked their doors, or thought they had to—and got his bottle of Percocet out of the top drawer of the filing cabinet. He remembered when that cabinet held files. Now it held Percocet, Darvocet, Darvon, and Demerol, plus a lot of sports equipment he never used.

Delmore was standing in the doorway, hesitating. Unlike the others, he wouldn't go away unless he was sent away. Jig had had one of those nights with the dreams, and he knew it would be impossible to explain them to Delmore. He didn't know if he could ever explain them to anyone. That old fear that he wasn't really human, that the aliens had put him down here on his own for some reason he would never be able to guess, and then disappeared, murdered by a mob of terrified townspeople. That old conviction that people didn't actually hear him when he spoke. Words came out of his mouth, and he heard them, but to other people they were just breaths of air, without significance. He couldn't remember how old he had been when he first realized that it really was him, not them. He was really the one who was so different from everybody else that he was unrecognizable as human.

Headache or not, he wanted a cup of coffee. After the worst of those nights, he never felt like eating, and that was on top of the fact that he rarely felt like eating anyway. He needed a cup of Fair Trade coffee and something not too impossible in the way of breakfast food, like toast.

Delmore Krantz cleared his throat. Jig gave one last desperate foray into speculating about what it was that Delmore wanted from him, and turned around.

"I feel like hell," he said. "I'm going to go over to the Green Food place and get some coffee and whatever."

"I'll come with you to the Green Food place," Delmore said. "I support the Green Food place. We need more progressive options for eating out in Philadelphia."

Jig thought they needed more decent steak houses for eating out in Philadelphia, but he wasn't ready to go three rounds with Delmore over food and capitalist hegemonic discourse, so he let it go. He grabbed his pea coat from the coatrack he'd set up in a corner and shrugged it on. Come to think of it, maybe it was the last girl who had set up the coatrack in the corner. He couldn't even remember who the last girl was. He did remember his ex-wife, and his children, in spite of the fact that that had all been long ago, but the girls just came and went. Sometimes, Jig suspected they were using him as a handy alternative to that Nobel Prize sperm bank.

There, Jig thought. *Somebody in this nation must want smart people. There was the Nobel Prize sperm bank.*

"Dr. Tyler?"

"Sorry. I was thinking about the Nobel Prize sperm bank."

"Excuse me?"

"The Nobel Prize sperm bank. You know. Some guy out in California had a sperm bank where the contributions were limited to Nobel Prize winners and people with IQs above—"

"The Repository for Germinal Choice," Delmore said. "It closed in 1999."

"Lack of interest?"

"I think there was a public outcry against designer children," Delmore said. "But you can see that it's going to happen again. It has to. This is the direction capitalism is going in, has always been going in, except now without the restraints of religion or the liberal regulatory state there are no boundaries. Designer children. Intelligence is just one of a list of desirable traits parents will be able to choose for their children. Height, for instance. There will be no more short children in the American upper class."

"Do you really think the, what did you call it, Repository, that it served the American upper class?"

"It wasn't cheap."

"How many times do I have to tell you that class isn't chiefly about money," Jig said, but he said it without rancor, because his headache was receding. It was the lack of sleep, that's what it was. He still didn't sleep nearly as much as most people. Five hours was about the limit, before he felt groggy and tired the entire day. Still, he wasn't a graduate student anymore. He had to have at least three uninterrupted hours. If he didn't get them, he got mornings like this one.

He went over to his desk and looked at the answering machine blinking away at him. There was something else that had changed. In the old days, secretaries had taken messages in the department office, written them down on small square white sheets of paper, and then brought them in and put them under the paperweight on the desk. He didn't know if he missed that or not.

He turned on the answering machine and listened. There were three messages, all from students in his Tuesday-Thursday seminar who were going to hand their papers in late. He let the message tape switch off.

"I'd complain about late papers," he said, "except that all my papers in graduate school were late, too. Are you coming with me or not?"

"Of course I am. I said I was."

"I was hoping I'd get a message from Ms. Daniel. I don't suppose she'll be staying long, now that Mr. Markey seems to have disappeared, but you never know. I would have liked to have met her."

"Haven't you already?" Delmore looked confused. "We called her. Didn't you talk to her when we called her?"

"Of course I did, but on the phone. I meant it would have been nice to meet her. It doesn't matter. We're still blessedly free of Mr. Harrigan's noise, if only for another twenty-something days or so. Things have been quiet around here."

"Yes, they have," Delmore said darkly. "You have to wonder why that's the case, don't you? Things shouldn't be quiet around here. There should be protests. And stuff."

"Protests about what?"

"Protests about the war," Delmore said. Then he seemed to flounder.

Jig took pity on him. It was never a pretty sight, Delmore floundering around, trying to remember what the point of the conversation was. "I've told you and told you," he said. "It's the tuitions. You want to know why it costs more to go to college these days than people in the bottom fifth of the income stream make in a year, so that students will have huge loans they have to pay off when they get out? And why is that? Because students with huge loans to pay off have to worry about where they're going to get a job that will pay enough to pay the loans off. Social work won't pay that kind of money. The arts won't pay that kind of money. They're forced to get jobs in banking and industry, and if they want jobs in banking and industry—"

"They have to keep their records clean," Delmore said, looking triumphant. "I remember, yes. No antiwar demonstrations, because they might get arrested, or get a reputation as a troublemaker, and that would make them unemployable. I don't understand how people can live like this, I really don't. What are loans, after all? They're not going to throw you in jail for not paying loans. Just don't pay them and do what you want with your life. In a decent society, university education would be free anyway."

Jig was going to say something about capitalist hegemonic discourse, but then he didn't. His headache wasn't that far in the past, and he was feeling so much better that he could barely remember what the pain had been like. Besides, it was true, Drew Harrigan was not on the air today, and wouldn't be tomorrow.

"Come on," he said. "Let's go. Maybe I'll pick up the papers. I couldn't read mine at home. We can watch the mayoralty campaign and you can complain about John Jackman."

"He puts a black face on reactionary politics," Delmore said piously.

Jig was about to launch himself at that one, too, but finally he just led the way out of the office, waited until Delmore followed him into the hall, and locked up. It was Monday. He had no other classes, and he could take his laptop to the student union to work on the article he had to have finished by Friday. He could pipe classical music in his ears and tap away on the subject of media brainwashing and the public blackout of dissent. He could work on an equation that had been bothering him for two years, but that he wasn't likely to be able to solve now, at his age.

He just wished he had heard from Kate Daniel, although he had no idea what he wanted her to say to him, or what he'd do if she called.

He just felt a little . . . uneasy . . . not knowing what was going on with all things Drew Harrigan.

2

Ellen Harrigan was rarely faced with the truth about her life as Drew Harrigan's wife, and when she was, she responded to the information by going shopping. That was what she was doing today, in spite of the cold and the wind that made even the lobby of her own apartment building feel uninhabitable. It wasn't that the lobby was cold. The lobby was never cold. It was the sound of the wind rattling the doors that caused the problem, which was that sitting there in one of the chairs arranged for visitors, waiting for her car to show up, she felt as if she were in a house with a ghost in it. Ellen Harrigan believed in ghosts. She believed in angels, too, and in a God whose personality was very like that of Fred Rogers, although she didn't like Fred Rogers or his neighborhood at all. PBS was bad. She knew that. She'd known it even before she'd married Drew. PBS was taxpayer-supported television for rich people, and not rich people like her.

The truth about Ellen Harrigan's life was this: she knew absolutely nobody anymore. The friends she had had before she married Drew had all melted away. They weren't comfortable in the big apartment, and they couldn't follow her to the kind of department stores where she now did her shopping. They were elementary school teachers and nurses and typists, just the way she had been before she'd been married. She'd grown up with most of them, gone through Brownies and Girl Scouts with them before the Girl Scouts became the latest outpost of lesbian feminism, taken First Holy Communion with them in white dresses and white veils and white patent leather shoes with cultured pearls on the toes. They watched *Touched by an Angel* every week, without fail. They went to the movies when there was something good on, like *Titanic*. They had dinner out every month at a Chili's or a TGI Friday's. They weren't comfortable in her living room, with the pictures on the walls of herself and Drew with President Bush at the inaugural ball, with Newt Gingrich at the launch of his new book, with Senator Santorum at some party somewhere where Ellen had had to wear a ball gown made of shimmering blue silk. Ellen wasn't really comfortable with all that either, but she found she couldn't go back to TGI Friday's. She was out of place, and she had no idea how it had happened.

The problem was, there was nobody from this life, either, to take up her time. The women she met, even the women on their own side, were all like Martha and Danielle. They had degrees from big-name colleges like Yale and Vassar. They talked about federalism in family policy and reconfiguring the tax code to favor traditional family forms and entrepreneurship. They were always writing books. In spite of the time they spent defending "stay-at-home moms" from the evils of elitist liberal feminism, Ellen didn't think a single one of them would opt to be a stay-at-home mom herself, and none of them had any time during the day to do things like go to a movie or have lunch. They all had jobs, and the kinds of jobs that ate up ninety hours in the work week.

The car was here, and Ellen got up to let the driver hold the front door for her and then hold the car door for her, because she was supposed to do that. When he got into the front seat, she tapped on the glass and leaned forward.

"Not downtown right away," she said. "I want to go to Christopher's."

"You have an appointment at the hairdresser?"

He sounded hesitant, because if she'd had an appointment at the hairdresser he should have known about it. Her scheduler should have said something.

"I don't have an appointment, no," she said. "I just want to stop there and check something."

It didn't matter if she had an appointment or not. They'd take her. There was something good about being married to Drew.

Christopher's was not very far away. It was only a matter of a couple of intersections. On another day, she might have walked the distance, although she had to be careful with that. Most people didn't know who she was, or who she was married to, and wouldn't recognize her if their lives depended on it, but the true Drew-haters—and there were more of those than you'd think—were relentless. She'd been cornered on the street on several occasions, as if she could do anything about the way Drew talked about Social Security or Head Start on the air.

It was after ten o'clock. When they pulled up to Christopher's, the driver double-parked next to a Volvo and a Saab and started to get out to open her door for her.

"You don't have to do that," she said quickly, popping the door herself.

The door buzzed open, and Ellen pushed it in. The receptionist was on her feet with her hand out.

"Mrs. Harrigan," she said. "Am I supposed to have you down for an appointment? I don't remember you in the book."

"No, no," Ellen said. "I just, I was wondering, if Hermoine had a minute, do you know? It's just. Things."

The receptionist made no gesture that indicated she had understood what Ellen was talking about, or cared. She went back behind her desk and picked up the phone. She must have talked to Hermoine. Ellen didn't hear her. She was staring at the photographs on the walls as if she'd never seen them before.

A moment later, Hermoine came in, a sensible-looking middle-aged woman in flat rubber-soled shoes and hair she had let go naturally gray. If Hermoine cared about looking as young as she felt, nobody knew.

"Mrs. Harrigan?" she said.

"Oh," Ellen said. "Well."

"Come on back," Hermoine said.

There wasn't much to the back. Christopher's wasn't a big place. They never scheduled more than ten or twelve hair appointments a day, and maybe as many manicures. They just charged enough for each so that they didn't have to do more.

Hermoine's office was a little closetlike space near the door that led to the back alley where the garbage was taken out. Hermoine went in first, and sat behind her desk. She waved Ellen to a chair.

"If you have an emergency, we can do something for you, of course," she said. "But it really helps if you know beforehand. I know that's not always possible—"

Ellen hadn't taken the chair. "It isn't that kind of an emergency. It's just. Things."

Hermoine licked her lips. If Ellen hadn't known it was impossible, she'd have said the woman was annoyed. Hermoine was never annoyed. "What things?" Hermoine said.

It was, Ellen thought, the sound of the human voice she needed. It didn't matter if it was annoyed or not. "Things," she said. "I was sitting in the apartment. I was showered and dressed and all done up and that was it. The whole place felt like it was pressing in on me. I don't think I've been out much at all since Drew went into rehab, and it's more than twenty days before he comes back, and I thought I was going crazy."

"Ah."

"And I felt—wrong. Do you know what I mean?"

"No."

"I felt bad. Guilty, I guess. Because except for the loneliness, I hate to say this, but except for the loneliness it's been better with him gone than with him here. It's not him, you understand. I like having him around. It's all the stuff that goes on. The people who shout at him. The people who call. You wouldn't believe the people who call. I can't answer my own phone. They call and swear at me."

"At you?"

"About Drew," Ellen said. "They don't really care about me. It's all about Drew. It really is. The ones who stop me on the street are the same way. And of course I don't know what they're talking about, and then they get mad at me and call me names, and half the names I don't know either. It's not Drew himself, you know. It's the show."

"It must have calmed down some, then, since Mr. Harrigan has been . . . away."

"Not really," Ellen said. There was the chair, empty. Hermoine expected her to sit in it. Ellen usually tried to do what was expected of her, because it was easier, and it meant that fewer people got mad at her. She sat. "They come up to me and talk to me about the rehab now. They call him a hypocrite. They call me a hypocrite, although I don't get that. How do they know what I believe in to know that I'm a hypocrite? I never say anything about anything in public. I just wear a dress and smile. And then there are the people from his office. They're always trying to tell me things. They're trying to tell me Drew is going to go to jail, except now they say that he won't."

"Now?" Hermoine sounded puzzled. Ellen was glad that she no longer sounded annoyed. "Why now?"

"Because that man has disappeared," Ellen said. "That awful homeless man. I never get his name straight. The one who got Drew the drugs. The one who was suing him. Can you imagine that? He got Drew the drugs and he was suing Drew for ruining his life or something, and the lawyers were all taking it seriously. It's like Drew says. The courts are out of control. They're run by a bunch of liberal idiots who want to destroy the country and turn it over to the UN to run."

"Ah," Hermoine said.

Ellen shifted in the chair. It was a terrible chair. She had never been in Hermoine's office before. She thought it was not outfitted in the expectation that Hermoine would have visitors. Or, at least, not visitors from among her clients, who were used to comfortable chairs.

"Anyway," Ellen said, "he's disappeared, or something. Do you want to know what woke me up this morning? My cell phone rang. The number is supposed to be a secret. It's not under my name. The only people who know what it is are Drew and a few of his assistants at the office. But somebody got it. And it rang."

"And?"

"And whoever it was accused me of having that terrible man killed," Ellen said, and suddenly she was so near tears she couldn't keep them back. It made no sense. She hadn't felt like crying when the call had come this morning. She hadn't felt like crying at any time since. At first, she'd merely been angry. Then she'd been afraid. Then she'd been—claustrophobic, that was the word. "They said Drew had had it done, had hired a hit man, from rehab. Can you imagine? He's not even allowed to talk to me from rehab, and he's supposed to be hiring hit men to chase homeless people around and have them killed. It was awful. You wouldn't believe how awful it was. And I was afraid he'd call back. So I put the cell phone down the garbage disposal."

"What?"

"I know, I know," Ellen said. "It wasn't the most sensible thing. I know it wasn't. But I couldn't help myself. Whoever it was had an awful voice, and he just went on and on. About how he knew we'd had that man killed, and how he was going to tell the police about it, and how Drew was going to die from lethal injection and that's what ought to happen to somebody who's such a big supporter of the death penalty. Except he didn't say supporter. He said, I remember, cheerleader. Such a big cheerleader for the death penalty."

"And when all this happened you put the cell phone in the garbage disposal?"

"That's right," Ellen said. "And then I called for the car, because I wanted to get out of the apartment. I thought he might have the number for the regular phone, too. I mean, those calls get screened, but things get through. You wouldn't believe it. People leave messages on the answering machine. I didn't want to be in the apartment anymore, just in case, and it was so quiet. I had to get out. I thought I'd go shopping."

"Instead you came here."

"Yes, well. I didn't want to start talking about all this in a department store somewhere where everybody could hear me. You have to be careful with things like that. You say things and you don't think there's anybody around to listen, and then everything you've said shows up on the front page of the *National Enquirer* the very next Monday. Drew's been on the front page of the *Enquirer* enough. And to think I used to actually like that newspaper."

Hermoine sighed. "It would have been easier if you'd called ahead," she said, "but we'll manage something. How about a manicure and some new color for your nails? That will give you time to rest and think about things. All I ask is that you consider calling the police when you leave us this morning."

"Calling the police? Why? The police are the ones who are persecuting Drew."

"Maybe. But that phone call sounds like a threat, or something close to it. You have no idea who made it. Somebody may be looking to do you harm."

"Just because I'm married to Drew?"

"There are a lot of crazy people in the world."

"I know there are a lot of crazy people in the world," Ellen said, "but they're all liberals. Aren't they? Wasn't this man a liberal?"

"I think it should be enough that he was threatening your husband with death, even if it was death by execution," Hermoine said. "You shouldn't take threats lightly. And you shouldn't ignore them. And I think your husband would say the same if he were here."

"I wish he was here," Ellen said. "I hate rehab. You have no idea how I hate rehab."

Hermoine didn't say anything to that. She just stood up, and Ellen automatically stood with her. It was true, though. She really did hate rehab, and she hated even more all the things that were connected to rehab. She was sure, though, that Drew would never order anybody killed.

"It just doesn't make any sense," she said, as Hermoine led her from the room in the direction of the manicurist. "Why would Drew want to murder some stupid old man who wasn't worth anything to anybody? If he was going to murder somebody, he'd murder somebody who mattered."

3

Ray Dean Ballard understood that the term "out" had come to cover a lot of other things besides being gay. There were people who said they were "out" as shopaholics, for instance, and people who said they were "out" as liberal Democrats, especially if they lived in the South. There was an entire movement to convince atheists to "come out," and Ray Dean could never hear the term without thinking of young women in white dresses making deep curtseys in the middle of a ballroom floor. There was no movement anywhere to help people like Ray Dean Ballard to come out, and he didn't expect there to be one soon. He kept wondering how long he was going to get away with it. For now, people wrote off what they thought of as his "eccentricities" by saying he came from the South, and you could never tell what people from the South would do. There was nobody in this office who had gone to Vanderbilt with him, or even to Emory or SMU, where they might have known someone in his family. There was nobody here who could expose him for who and what he was, except Kate, and he didn't count her. She wouldn't expose him for the same reason he wouldn't expose her. He had no idea why he was thinking about this now, on this particular morning, when what he was supposed to be worrying about was what had happened to Sherman Markey. He wondered why it was that so many people who did the kind of work he did found it necessary to hate all things graceful, and elegant, and true.

That "true" there. That was going to get him into trouble.

Shelley Balducci was standing in his office door, waiting. She'd been there for quite some time. Ray Dean didn't think he'd have much trouble with her if she knew the whole truth about him, but you could never tell. The Shelley Balduccis of this world were a complete mystery to him.

"I don't see what you can do," she was saying. "Chickie

went to see Gregor Demarkian. Mr. Demarkian will go to see whoever he knows on the police department. That should at least get people moving again."

"Doesn't it bother you that he could be dead out there, in a morgue someplace, maybe not even in a morgue? Would you like that to happen to you if you were dead?"

"But it wouldn't happen to me," Shelley said sensibly. "I've got a huge family. Somebody would be looking for me."

"We're looking for Sherman. It's not doing a lot of good."

"I know. But the morgue people, they look at Sherman and they can tell right off he's a homeless person. Forget the clothes. It doesn't matter how new the clothes are. Homeless people have new clothes sometimes. They get them from Goodwill."

"There was the bath, too," Ray Dean said. "They didn't just get him new clothes. They got him cleaned up."

"I know," Shelley said, "but they couldn't fix the rest of it. The state of his teeth. The shape his body was in. You could tell he was a homeless person just by looking at him."

"And people would know you weren't just by looking at you?"

"Of course. There's a difference, don't you see? I can't believe you don't think there's a difference."

"I didn't say I didn't think there was a difference. I said—" But there seemed no point in saying it again. What Shelley was saying was true. Sherman Markey did look like a homeless person, and in a way no clean change of clothes, or bath, or haircut could change. Something happened to people who lived out on the street that left an indelible mark. He wished he knew what it was.

"Besides," Shelley was saying, "there's nothing you can do about it, is there? It's not your fault. We had people looking all over for him that night. We had vans out. If he was anywhere within our area, we would have found him."

"If he was still alive."

"Okay," Shelley said. "If he was still alive. But you know, you can't blame yourself for that. It's not up to you. People are what they are. It doesn't matter if Sherman was on the street because he had a disease or because he had no damned luck at all or because he behaved like an idiot and a jerk and brought it all down on his own head. He was a homeless person. They die a lot in the bad weather. Nobody noticed him because nobody notices homeless people. You have to go from there."

"To where?"

"What's that supposed to mean?"

"Nothing," Ray Dean said. "Nothing at all. Never mind. You're right. I'm going to make a few phone calls and then I'll okay the van schedules for tonight. Ask C. J. to come see me in about half an hour, will you? We've got a donor willing to supply the Station Street soup kitchen for seven straight days in return for a public announcement on my part. I'm happy to comply. Okay?"

"You don't look good," Shelley said.

"I'm fine," Ray Dean said.

She hesitated some more, and then walked away, down the hall, out of sight. He watched her go. He wasn't fine. He didn't begin to be fine. It bothered him no end that people were willing to give to charity if they got a nice big announcement in the papers about it, or something else to make them feel important. He couldn't count the number of dinners he had to have with big donors who demanded personal attention in exchange for the food they gave and the checks they wrote. He needed those people. He knew he needed them. He couldn't supply the organization himself. He couldn't begin to cover the needs of the people who lived "rough," as their one Aussie put it. He just didn't understand why every single person in the city of Philadelphia didn't rise up and demand that something be done about these people who couldn't feed or house themselves, who died in the cold, who died in spit and blood and vomit.

He wanted to believe that people would be different if they were brought up differently, that it was just a matter of training and education. He knew that wasn't true. There was no solution for human nature, and no answer to the deepest of his questions about right and wrong. It was bad enough that some people were born rich and others were born poor. It was worse that some were born well and some were born mentally or physically ill. What did you do about a life that could never escape the confines of biochemistry?

You did something better than this, Ray Dean told himself. But this was all he knew how to do, so he was going to go on doing it.

He picked up the phone and punched in the number Kate Daniel had given him the last time he talked to her. Maybe he could ask her why he was depressed the way he was.

SIX

I

The district attorney of the city of Philadelphia was a man named Robert Benedetti, and the only thing Gregor Demarkian knew about him for sure was that he hated to be called "Bob."

"It's the alliteration," John Jackman had said, six months ago, when they'd first discussed the man. "It's the BB. He hates it."

Gregor couldn't remember why it had come up. Benedetti was new in the job. His predecessor had dropped dead of a heart attack in the middle of a mob-based murder trial, and for about a week there had been speculation across the country that he'd really been the victim of a contract hit. The problem was, nobody knew of a contract killer who could make heart attacks happen so realistically that they looked like nothing else to four pathologists in a row. The man had been overweight, underexercised, and addicted to both cigarettes and coffee. He worked too hard and too long. His blood pressure would have looked better as one of those thermometer indicators that let the public know if the local fire department has raised enough money in donations to buy a new lounge set for the firehouse. Robert Benedetti had been appointed to fill out the rest of his term, and here he was, coming up on a general municipal election in November, and not a known quantity.

Gregor gave his name to the receptionist and sat down in the waiting area. It was not an unfamiliar place. He'd been to see various district attorneys since he'd started consulting with police departments, and none of them ever seemed to do anything to change the waiting room's ambience. The carpet was clean but a little worn, and determinedly bland. The pictures on the walls were of nothing that could offend anybody, ever, mostly because they were either of flowers or so abstract as to be indistinguishable from confusion. Gregor knew better than to do that thing about modern art that marked anyone who engaged in it as a provincial idiot—he wasn't about to start talking about how all the paintings like that looked like something that could be done by a five-year-old child—but in the most private recesses of his brain, he still wondered why anybody bothered. And why, exactly, was good representational work no longer really "art"? He should have paid more attention to his Humanities courses when he was at Penn. He wasn't sure he'd paid much attention to anything while he was at Penn, besides making damned sure that his grades were as close to perfect as he could get them, to make equally sure that an Ivy League school would take him for his graduate work. Gregor couldn't even remember having had a strong ambition in any one direction. He hadn't been considering the FBI while he was in college, traveling by public transportation every day from a Cavanaugh Street that was still poor tenements to the University of Pennsylvania of the late fifties, full of preppies and debutantes, and not all that dedicated to educating the kinds of people who needed scholarships to survive. Now he thought that his only ambition back then might have been to *make it out.* Making it out was different from making it. Making it meant having a lot of money and your picture in *People* magazine. Making it out meant just . . . never having to go back where you'd come from.

And here he was, back where he'd come from. Did it matter that where he'd come from didn't really exist now any more than the Gregor Demarkian of that period of time existed now? It mattered that Cavanaugh Street was town houses and expensive condominiums and not tenements and railroad flats.

He was up on his feet and walking around the room, looking at the pictures on the walls the way he'd look at pictures in a museum, when somebody cleared his throat behind him. Gregor turned and found a short, wiry, intense young man in a gray suit that didn't look like it fit him, because no suit anywhere would ever look like it fit him. His body was the wrong shape for suits. *This is a man who ought to be a boxer,* Gregor thought. But the man was holding out his hand, so Gregor held out his hand, too.

"It's Mr. Demarkian," the man said. "I recognize you from your pictures. I'm Rob Benedetti."

"Ah," Gregor said.

"Ah?"

"I was wondering what you used for a nickname," Gregor said. "I've heard from several people that you don't like to be called Bob."

"Right," Benedetti said. He seemed to be at a loss for where to take the conversation next, for which Gregor didn't blame him. He threw an odd look at the pictures on the wall and at Gregor standing to look at them and said, "Why don't you come into the office and we can talk. John said you were going to help the Justice Project in the search for Sherman Markey."

Gregor followed Benedetti's retreating back, wondering if he should bother to go into any long explanation of his present relationship to the case. It didn't help that he didn't know if he had any relationship to the case, or even if there was a case.

He was explaining about the visit he'd had from Chickie George when he really noticed the room he'd been led into, and then he stopped. It was the most remarkable place he'd ever seen. If there was a paperless office in the United States, this wasn't it. There were stacks of file folders full of paper everywhere: on the desk, on the floor, on the bookcases in piles obscuring the books, on the seat of the chair Gregor was supposed to sit in. It was like one of those paintings that got titled *Schizophrenic's Hallucination* or *Paranoid's Dream*. It was beyond a mess. It was a threatening mess.

"Excuse me," Rob Benedetti said. He reached over and took the files off the chair Gregor was supposed to sit in. Then he held them in his hands for a moment, wondering what he was supposed to do with them. Then he dumped them on the pile on his desk. Given how much was there, a few more probably wouldn't make a difference.

"Are you spring-cleaning or something?" Gregor asked.

Rob Benedetti went around the desk and took a few file folders off the seat he was supposed to sit in himself. "I've been trying to get Carson's stuff straightened out," he said. "Carson was, I don't know. Not exactly caught up. Not that I blame him, mind you. He must have been sick for months before he fell over. My wife is always trying to make me go to the doctor, and like that, because she says this is a job that kills people, but I think that's going too far. Anyway, Carson must have been sick for a while, because here we are, and there's a lot of back stuff that needs to be taken care of, and I've been going through it piece by piece so that I can figure out what's going on."

"How's it going?"

"You can see how it's going," Rob Benedetti said. "Never mind. We'll get to it or not. I'll get elected in November or not. In the meantime, we've got a Drew Harrigan problem."

"I don't," Gregor said.

"Yes, you do, whether you realize it or not," Benedetti said. "How much do you know about Drew Harrigan?"

Gregor had been carrying his coat over his arm when he came into the office and laid it down over the back of the chair when he'd sat down. Now he stood up, rummaged around in it, and pulled out the book he'd bought at Barnes & Noble.

"I've got this," he said. "I know he's very successful. I've never heard him on the radio."

"Did you look at the book?"

"A little."

"And?"

Gregor hesitated. "It doesn't seem fair to criticize when I've barely read anything but a line here or there, but the lines I've read have seemed a little ham-handed and simplistic. Simplistic to the point of being inaccurate sometimes."

"It's okay. You can call him an idiot in this office if you want to."

"I don't know that he is an idiot," Gregor said. "I've got a tendency to feel that people who become great successes at legitimate endeavors, and even some of the ones who become great successes at illegitimate ones, are probably bright enough. Competition is tough. It's not easy to make something of yourself, especially not a big something."

"Maybe," Benedetti said. "Maybe the truth is that he got to be a big something by pandering to the idiots in his audience. He's got a lot of idiots in his audience, and you're hearing that from a man who's probably closer to Harrigan politically than he is to John Jackman. I'm nobody's liberal. But."

"But?"

"But if the man isn't an idiot, he's a liar," Benedetti said. "He has to know that the stuff he says is wrong. He's got a staff. They call here every once in a while to check things, and we try to be good about providing them with information. We try to be good about providing everybody with information. With Harrigan, it doesn't make any difference. If it isn't what he wants to hear, he doesn't hear it. All I can say is thank God he's going after the national audience and not just the one here, or we'd all be dead as doornails from the misinformation."

"I still don't see how that makes him my problem," Gregor said.

Benedetti sighed. "How much do you know about the case so far?"

Gregor gave a rundown that included the traffic stop that had revealed a pile of illegal pills on the front passenger seat of Drew Harrigan's car, the arrest, and Harrigan's fingering of Sherman Markey.

"Right," Benedetti said. "Now, you got to understand something. The cops that pulled Harrigan over didn't know it was Harrigan when they pulled him over. It was just some guy in an expensive car, driving like he'd had about twenty martinis. But within maybe a minute, they did know, because Harrigan wouldn't shut up about it. I'm going to send you down to talk to them later, and they'll tell you about it. The pills were there. They had to take the guy in. Harrigan acted like, because it was him, they could just let him ride."

"Is that possible?" Gregor asked. "Are there police in this city who would have let him ride?"

"I don't know," Benedetti said. "There are police who are big fans. Harrigan is very pro-cop, at least superficially. He's in favor of the death penalty. He's in favor of stiffer sentences. He doesn't like *Miranda* much—"

"I thought the cops had gotten used to *Miranda*."

"They have," Benedetti said. "What they don't like is how easily a conviction can be overturned because of *Miranda* violations, or alleged *Miranda* violations. I don't like that either. Anyway, Harrigan is good with that stuff, so there are fans on the force. I don't know if any of them would have, or has, let him loose after finding him driving around in that state of mind with pills in the vehicle. But he went ballistic, and that gives me a feeling I don't like."

"Meaning you think that a cop did let him off in similar circumstances at least one other time," Gregor said.

"Meaning I think it's possible," Benedetti said. "I don't want to go labeling the beat officers before I know for sure. But if you talk to the two men who arrested him that night, Dane Marbury and Mike Giametti, they'll tell you what they told me, and that's that Harrigan went completely berserk when they insisted on arresting him. He got *physically* violent."

"He doesn't look like somebody who could do much damage getting physically violent."

"Nah, he didn't. He's out of shape as hell. He's practically as bad as Carson. Rush Limbaugh went on a diet. Drew Harrigan never bothered. But anybody can get physically violent. Harrigan pushed the officers, kicked them, bit one of them on the hand—"

"—Bit him?"

"He was flying," Benedetti said. "God only knows what he had in him at the time, because once his lawyer got into it he wasn't about to take a drug test, but the likelihood is Oxy-Contin at least."

"OxyContin doesn't make you violent, though, does it?" Gregor said. "It's a tranquilizer, or something like that."

"It's a pain reliever. It's most similar in effect to narcotics."

"Just as I said, not the sort of thing to make you violent."

"No," Benedetti said, "but you've got to remember a few things. First, it wasn't the only thing he was taking. There were a lot of different pills on the seat, including three different kinds of prescription diet pills, which are amphetamines. Second, he didn't get violent until Marbury and Giametti tried to arrest him. And third, people react differently to the same kinds of pills. That he was flying was a pretty good bet. You can see the police reports and the stuff from the station house, where he apparently behaved like a loon. Including singing."

"He was singing in the station house?"

"He was singing 'Do Wah Diddy Diddy,' or whatever it's called."

Gregor looked down at the picture on the back of *Heart in the Right Place*. "That must have been something to see. But you know, you still haven't told me why I have a Drew Harrigan problem. I was brought into this to help find Sherman Markey. Granted, nobody would be looking for Markey if it weren't for Harrigan, I still don't see why I need to deal with Harrigan to find Markey. In fact, I'm not even sure I'm supposed to find Markey. All I was asked to do was to get you people to—"

"Do another morgue check, I know. It's been done. John Jackman called it in an hour ago. But you've got to understand what the thing is with Drew Harrigan."

"What is it?"

"Harrigan named Markey as his contact for the drugs,"

Benedetti said, "something that everybody knew as soon as they saw him couldn't be true. John said you hadn't met Markey yet?"

"That's right."

"He's an old alkie, a really old alkie. He's been pickled for decades. Like a lot of these guys, he's spaced. He's almost like an Alzheimer's patient, except that he can focus on one thing, and that's getting another drink if there isn't one sitting in front of him. Harrigan didn't just say Markey got him the drugs, which I wouldn't have believed anyway. Harrigan said he sent Markey to pharmacies, doctors' offices—"

"Jackman told me."

"Okay," Benedetti said. "So Harrigan comes in, gets booked, calls his lawyer, and tells us all about Markey, right? We go get Markey, which isn't hard, because he hangs out in only a couple of places and ends up at the same shelter when it gets too cold. We get Markey. We bring him in. It's pretty obvious that whoever got Harrigan the drugs, Markey wasn't it. So then I decided to do something, and I think it was probably a mistake."

"What did you decide to do?"

"Charge Markey."

"Even though you knew he couldn't be guilty."

"Yeah," Benedetti said. "Look, Mr. Demarkian. This is the thing. Harrigan is behaving like a celebrity jerk. From off, his attitude has been that we can't touch him and we won't because he's such an important person. He was that way to the officers in the car, he's been that way to everybody he's talked to since. He seems to think it's *automatic* that because he's a big celebrity we won't bring any serious charges against him and we won't insist on jail time. This is the guy who goes on the air four times a week and tells the world that the district attorneys of practically everywhere are complete wusses because they don't send more white drug addicts to jail. That's his solution to the difference in incarceration rates for drug crimes by race. Put more white drug addicts in jail, and if we don't, we're full of shit when we say we're serious about the drug war. Sorry."

"That's all right," Gregor said.

"Charging Markey got me two things," Benedetti said. "The first thing it got me was an excuse not to drop charges or make a deal with Harrigan. I couldn't do that and charge Markey at the same time because it would look like favoritism. It would look like I was going after a poor homeless man and letting the rich guy off the hook. Not that that isn't done every day, because it is, but it gave me cover with Harrigan's attorney. The second thing it got me was something of a lever to try to find out who was really getting Harrigan those drugs. Because you know and I know that somebody was, and that that somebody isn't some pathetic old alkie living on the street. And I want him."

Gregor thought about it. "I can't see that you did anything unethical. Your reasoning makes sense. Is Drew Harrigan going to get some kind of celebrity free ride?"

"Probably." Benedetti sighed. "In the long run. Oh, we'll put him away for a few months, but it'll be a token thing. He'd be at too much risk in the general prison population, and there's no real point in jailing him anyway. If you ask me, there's no real point in jailing most of the people we jail. Violent offenders, yes. People who defraud over and over and over again. Okay. But why is it exactly that we put away some kid for smoking dope and keep him in jail for a year, or five? Why is that sensible? Or embezzlers, or people who kite checks? I can think of a million better ways to handle those things than jail."

"Are you going to say those things in the election?"

"Not on your life."

"So you have your answer," Gregor said. "You still haven't told me, why do I have a Drew Harrigan problem?"

Rob Benedetti stared at the ceiling, then at the floor, then out the small square window that seemed to have a view of nothing but blank gray walls. Then he turned back to Gregor. "The word's been out on the street for the last three days," he said, "that Sherman Markey is dead, and Drew Harrigan killed him."

"Drew Harrigan is in rehab."

"Drew Harrigan's accomplice killed him, then," Rob said.

"Jackman said something about this," Gregor said. "He said people were speculating. So what?"

"It actually goes a little farther than that," Benedetti said. "The night Sherman Markey disappeared, he was wearing a new set of clothes the people at the Justice Project bought him, including a bright red watch hat. On the morning of Tuesday, January twenty-eighth, a homeless man walked into the precinct station on Hardscrabble Road and tried to report a theft. He said a man he knew had died in a homeless shelter the night before, and some of the other men had stolen his hat. His bright red hat. He wanted to report the theft on behalf of the dead man."

"And the police let him file a report?"

"No," Benedetti said. "They sloughed him off, and that would have been that, because nobody would have remembered it. However, today, because you've been around asking questions and John Jackman is a friend of yours, we've had people double-checking things. And then we got lucky, and there was a coincidence."

"What coincidence was that?"

"One of the extern sisters at Our Lady of Mount Carmel walked into the Hardscrabble Road precinct station with the hat and the old guy who'd tried to file the report the first time," Benedetti said. "Just before you walked into this office, I got on the phone to everybody in creation and started the wheels rolling. There was a death at Our Lady of Mount Carmel that night; we're trying to find out what happened to the body. I want to send Marbury and Giametti out to the monastery—do you know about that, it's nuns, but it's still called a monastery?"

"You can get that from EWTN and Mother Angelica."

"Right. Okay. Anyway, here we are. We have the hat, and granted there are a lot of watch hats and a lot of them are red, the coincidences are piling up beyond what seems sensible. What scares me, what I really can't get out of my brain, is that this might be my fault. I thought I was being clever. I got Sherman Markey killed."

"Do you really think that's likely?" Gregor asked.

"I don't know," Benedetti said. "It's that kind of thing. I don't know Drew Harrigan well enough to know what he'd go for, and I don't know who his accomplice is at all. I haven't got a clue as to what's likely in this case. I just know I've got a hat, and no Markey, and that when Harrigan walks out of rehab, I want to be standing there personally with the handcuffs. There's celebrity free ride for you. I got an experiment for you to do sometime. Go find some black kid off the street, up for possession for the first time. Offer to pay his way to some fancy total immersion rehab place. See if you get anywhere with the judge."

"Who was the judge?"

"Bruce Williamson."

"Oh, God."

"Exactly. I'm going to get you a car, take you over to see the guys, okay? It's better that than have you wasting time looking for taxis when it's nearly lunch hour. They said you didn't drive."

Gregor didn't drive, but it wasn't the kind of thing he wanted to go into at length, so he just stood up, got his coat, and got moving.

2

A few moments later, sitting in the back of a plain black un-marked sedan—where did they find the cars they bought for police departments and city governments?—Gregor Demarkian found himself turning Drew Harrigan's book over and over in his hands. He didn't like the man's face. It was too round, too smooth, too well taken care of, too smug, although he didn't like to make judgments like that about photographs. You couldn't tell if somebody was smug or not from a photograph, just as you couldn't really tell if a defendant was remorseful by the fact that he didn't show any emotion while he was in the courtroom. Gregor hated people who came up with entire screenplays' worth of motivation and character development from a few quick glimpses of a person under extreme emotional distress. Not everybody cries when told that the person they love most is dead. Some people can't break down in public, and wait to do it until they're alone. Not everybody looks guilty and haunted when he feels guilty and haunted. Some people go numb with guilt and look like they're made of stone. This was why Gregor had never really been happy with the idea of trial by jury. It was made worse by the fact that attorneys deliberately attempted to seat the least educated and least literate jurors they could find, on the assumption that the stupid are more easily influenced than the bright, and not by facts and evidence.

Gregor opened the book at random. The paragraphs were short. There was a lot of white space at the top and the bottom and the margins. Obviously, Drew Harrigan didn't expect his average reader to have a doctorate in literature from Yale.

> *You know what really gets me about liberals? Liberals never met a criminal they didn't like. Doesn't matter what he's done. Doesn't matter that he's just slaughtered thirty people in a bank he's been robbing. Doesn't matter he's spent his entire life ripping people off and beating people up and being good for nothing, you arrest him and some liberal will come running to say it's all society's fault. You know whose fault that is? Yours. It's your fault if this piece of scum kills thirty people in a bank. You get up every morning. You go to work. You put in your time. You pay your bills. You stay out of trouble. And it's your fault, this guy tried to rob a bank, and instead of putting him in jail we should give him an income twice as much as what you've got and send him to therapy to talk about his childhood.*

Gregor sucked in air. That was—what? Trite. The sort of thing that had been around for twenty years or more. He

wondered if Drew Harrigan's audience was young enough
not to realize that Harrigan was just repeating things that had
been said a hundred times before by a hundred other people.
It was disturbing to think they might be older, and looking to
hear the same things they'd been hearing for as long as they
could remember. Gregor flipped through a few more pages.

> *All this year's field of Democratic presidential
> candidates is pretty pathetic, but the winner of
> the National Loser Party Award for Biggest
> Loser in the Bunch has to be John Kerry. I
> mean, come on, people. It's not enough that
> Democrats are traitors to America in fact, that
> any one of them would rather be living in
> Moscow, Russia, than Moscow, Idaho, they're
> going to go for a guy who looks so French he
> could be Brigitte Bardot's evil twin?*

Gregor blinked. John Kerry looked French? John Kerry
looked so New England, he could have been Cotton
Mather's evil twin. And wouldn't somebody like Drew Harrigan think Brigitte Bardot, who was a big activist in the animal rights movement, evil enough on her own, so that if she
had an evil twin, he'd have to be good?

His head was swimming. He'd left home this morning expecting to do nothing more than spend an hour with John
Jackman and get a promise of another morgue check. He'd
been muddled and depressed, thinking about Bennis, thinking about himself. He'd wanted something to take his mind
off the narcissistic and uncontrollable.

He wasn't sure he'd meant something like this.

SEVEN

I

Alison Standish felt that if the university was attempting to conduct its investigation into her teaching in a way that did not leave it open to charges of responding to Drew Harrigan's programs, it was doing a very bad job. As a matter of fact, as of this morning, it was doing a very bad job of investigating, and as the days went by it only seemed to be getting worse. In the first place, there was the secrecy. The investigation was secret in a way that would make a grand jury fan salivate. Nobody involved in it was allowed to tell anybody else what they had told the committee, nor what anybody else had told the committee, not even a lawyer. Alison was sure that couldn't be legal. For another thing, nobody was allowed to confront the witnesses, not even Alison herself. If a former student came forward to say that he had had to sit through a lecture praising Marxism in Alison's class, Alison couldn't ask him about it, and couldn't even know who he was. It was like an interrogation from the Holy and Roman Inquisition—not the Spanish one, which came later, but the one the Vatican ran in Rome, which had called Thomas Aquinas down for questioning and forced him to take the long trip by horse that killed him. Alison didn't expect to die. She didn't even expect to have her classes suspended.

She was beginning to think she needed to find somebody outside the situation to help her, and stop assuming that the university was the community of scholars it had been set up to be in the Middle Ages.

Hell, that one hadn't even worked in the Middle Ages.

She sat at her desk and looked, without reading, at the document in front of her. She wasn't reading it because she'd already read it, about four times, since she'd first picked it up in her mailbox an hour ago. These were supposed to be her office hours, but it didn't matter. Students almost never came, and none had come today. She was free to obsess as long as she wanted to about this piece off . . . this piece of . . . She didn't know what it was a piece of. She didn't know how to respond to it. It didn't matter that she knew it was untrue, and that Roger Hollman, the dean, must also know it was untrue. The idea was obviously to act *as if* it were true, and worse, to presume the truth of it unless the falsity was proved. Who was it who said you couldn't prove a negative? Somebody from the Middle Ages, probably. Alison was having a hard time remembering the Middle Ages at the moment. What she was remembering, for no reason at all, was her marriage. That had all been so long ago it might as well have happened to somebody else, but there you were. She had been married, to a professor of history at Temple who had eventually moved on first to New York University and then to Tufts. She had had a child, named Simon, who had died at the age of seven after many long years with leukemia. There was a time there, just for a moment, when she might have been somebody else than who she was: David's wife, Simon's mother, a woman who "kept her hand in" by reading other people's books on scholastic theology and the art of the icon but otherwise had nothing to do with this at all. She didn't know if she would have been happier if her life had turned out that way. She did know she would have been happier if Simon had lived. It occurred to her that she had gone past the time when having another child was feasible, and maybe she shouldn't have left it so late.

That's ridiculous, she thought. She didn't want another

child. If she'd ever had one, she would have been scared to death of it. She would have examined it for symptoms of leukemia daily, and then examined it some more, home medical encyclopedia in hand, hoping to cover all the fatal illnesses possible in children, miserable because she'd know that she could never cover them all. It was odd the way people turned out. It was odder what they wanted in times of crisis.

The thing was, even though the proceedings were secret, the testimony was only secret up to a point. She didn't receive names, or dates, or the time periods when a student may have been in her classes, but she did receive the accusations themselves. Up to now, most of them had been trivial and embarrassing. Someone had complained that she showed far too much approval of feudalism, because it implied that she opposed "the legitimate aspirations of poor people and people of color." Someone had complained that she called on men with their hands raised more often than she called on women—who could possibly know if that was true or not? Had there been a student in one of her classes counting the other students who were called on to speak and writing it all down in a notebook in preparation for a time like now? That wasn't the kind of thing the university would take seriously, and it wasn't the kind of thing Drew Harrigan had been complaining of. This, however, was:

> *The entire thrust of Professor Standish's course in Church and State in the Europe of the High Middle Ages was to insult Christian students and call them evil and stupid. She spent some time in almost every class talking about how the Middle Ages proved that Christians should not be in charge of governments and Christianity would also produce tyranny and torture if it got any power. She compared the situation in the Middle Ages to the political work of the Religious Right now, saying that the Religious Right was the same as the witchburners and Inquisi-*

*tionists who had killed hundreds of people for
their beliefs in the twelfth century. She referred
to the President of the United States as somebody who thought he was on a Crusade. When
students protested her bias, she told them they
either agreed with her or were too stupid to see
the parallels.*

There was more, but the more there was, the more ridiculous
it got. At one point, the writer complained that Alison did
not "respect" his belief that witches were real and consorted
with Satan, but tried to push her "secular humanism" on him
and every other student in the class. As if she were supposed
to just nod and make encouraging noises when students
claimed to see ghosts or experience levitation. Maybe she
was. Maybe that was what the New University was all about.
Hammered by the left and the right, they weren't supposed
to teach any longer, and they surely weren't supposed to up-
hold the traditions of high literacy and the Western Enlight-
enment. Civilization as they knew it was over. Everything
really was political now.

I'm going insane, Alison told herself. Then she picked up
the two-page "testimony," held it carefully with the thumb
and index finger of her right hand, as if it were contami-
nated, and got up to go down the hall to the chairman's office. Alison knew better than to start with Roger Hollman.
He had a secretary who could keep her out. She'd start with
Chris McCall, and he could deal with it.

Chris's office was an office like any other. The door was
open when he was willing to see students, but Alison knew
he was there even when the door was shut, working away on
his latest paper on Icons of Individualism in Twentieth-
Century American Popular Culture. The door was shut. She
turned the knob and walked right in.

"What the hell?" Chris said.

Alison closed the door behind her. "I would have knocked,
but you'd have pretended you weren't here. We have to talk."

Chris was an athletic, middle-aged man with a ponytail,

an atavism, really, a throwback to the days when middle-aged men actually believed they looked younger if they never saw a barber. Alison threw the "testimony" down on his desk and sat down herself.

"Look at that."

Chris didn't. He just looked uncomfortable. "I have looked at it. They sent me a copy."

"Well?"

"How do I know?" Chris said. "It's important to give the students a safe place to express their opinions. That's what the investigating committee is doing. It's important to hear them out and respect—"

"Respect what, Chris? Whoever this is thinks witches are real. Not Wiccan-practicing modern witches, but the kind that ride on broomsticks and have sex with Satan."

"Yes, well. Evangelical students, the ones who take the Bible literally."

"What, Chris? They're supposed to come here and never get that idea challenged? Should we shut down the entire Religious Studies Department? We might as well shut down History, Archeology, Geology, and Biology while we're at it."

"That's not the point," Chris said. "The point is whether you called this student stupid for being a Christian believer. I mean, for God's sake, Alison. You know what it's been like around here since the water buffalo mess. We can barely breathe in the direction of conservative students without the administration having a complete fit."

"The kid in the water buffalo case wasn't a conservative student," Alison said, "and the trouble we had over it was over the secrecy of the proceedings, which is what is going on here. This is like a Star Chamber, Chris. It's absurd. At the very least, I have the right to due process, to be able to confront the witnesses against me, to advice of counsel—"

"—Due process doesn't apply to university committees," Chris said quickly. "They aren't adversary proceedings. You don't have enemies you have to protect yourself against."

"No? Did what's his name in the water buffalo incident have enemies he had to protect himself against?"

"That went wrong," Chris said. "It got out of hand."

"This is about to."

Chris licked his lips. Alison didn't think she'd ever realized, before, how soft and weak and self-protective he was, and yet she should have. She'd known him for years. She had a sudden vision of that alternative lifetime again—Simon alive, herself as a housewife in suburban Boston—and then snapped herself back to the present. She was angry. She had been afraid, but now she was angry.

"Let's not go into how I feel about being investigated because an idiot like Drew Harrigan made charges against me on a radio program targeted to the kind of illiterate asshole who never made it past high school, if that," she said. "Let's just go with what we've got. I came to you instead of Roger because you were easier to get to. You'd better go tell Roger if you know what's good for you."

"Roger isn't going to just drop the investigation," Chris said. "He couldn't. He's got a responsibility—"

"When I leave this office, I'm going to hire a lawyer," Alison said. "There's a woman in town I went to college with. She's an attorney who works on high-profile media cases. She'll know one locally who'll suit my purposes. I'm going to hire a lawyer, and I'm going to give a press conference. And I swear to God, I'll make the water buffalo case look like a day at the beach in comparison."

"If you go to an outside source, the committee can suspend you from teaching."

"Let them try it." Alison leaned forward and took the two-page "testimony" off Chris's desk. "The first thing we're going to look into is this. Because you know what, Chris?"

"You can't blame a student for having an opinion."

"No, I can't. But I can blame a nonstudent for claiming he was a student. Or she. Because my classes are small. The one mentioned, Church and State in the Europe of the High Middle Ages, never has more than ten people in it. Don't you think I would have noticed if a student in my class believed in the devil or any of the rest of this nonsense?"

"If you really were that dismissive, the student may not

have felt it was safe to speak up. He might have kept it all inside."

"Bullshit," Alison said. "Go talk to Roger, Chris. I've had enough."

It was one of those times when what Alison really wanted was to see Chris's face after she'd left the room, but even the medieval necromancers had never figured out how to manage that one.

It was too bad.

2

Kate Daniel couldn't decide how she felt about the call she'd just had from Alison Standish. She would have liked to say bemused, but she'd never been sure what the word "bemused" meant. It was a little like finding out that her ex-husband was representing Drew Harrigan in a case in which they might have to have something to do with each other. It wasn't that she minded hearing from people in her past, exactly. It was that she didn't know how to respond to them. She had the feeling they all remembered the Kate Daniel who had always been called Katherine. She thought they'd expect to see her in A-line skirts from Villager and matching crew-necked sweaters and a circle pin. She couldn't really remember what she'd worn in college, or as Neil Elliot Savage's wife. What she remembered most of the time was being afraid. She was afraid of the girls she went to school with. She was afraid of Neil. She was afraid of herself. God only knew how she'd gotten the guts to get herself to law school, or out of her marriage, but here she was, and she didn't want to go back.

To be fair, nobody seemed to be interested in seeing her go back. Surely Alison hadn't. Kate was a little sorry that she couldn't help Alison herself, because the case sounded absolutely perfect, right down to the false accusations from a conservative source, but there it was. Alison wasn't homeless. She had good degrees and a tenured faculty position. Sherman Markey was homeless, or dead, and he had nothing at all. It was, Kate thought, time for her to find somebody to sleep with. She wasn't looking for a relationship with depth. She was looking for sex. Sex cleared her head.

Lots of things cleared her head. Chickie George made it . . . well, there was that "bemused" again. Chickie was standing in the door to the office she had taken over, holding a file folder and looking dejected. The office was so clean it looked as if it were in pain.

"He said he'd get them to check," Chickie was saying, "and that's the best I could hope for, really. I don't know. Maybe we're wrong. Maybe he isn't dead."

"We can always hope," Kate said, "but if he isn't dead, where is he?"

Chickie shrugged. "He's an addled old man. Everybody keeps saying that. Maybe he got his hands on some serious booze and went on a bender."

"For two weeks? If he went on a bender for two weeks, he would be dead."

"People go on benders for longer than that," Chickie said. "No, I know what you mean. Not people in Sherman's kind of shape. I don't know. Maybe he fuzzed out and can't remember who he is or where he's supposed to be. Maybe he's just wandering around someplace."

"In the open? Then why hasn't anybody seen him?"

"I don't know," Chickie said. "Never mind. I know. He's probably dead. And maybe they'll do another check and find a corpse they overlooked. The whole thing is just getting so . . . odd. If you know what I mean."

"Sure," Kate said. "There's another possibility, you know. He could be dead, but not in a morgue. He could have died in some abandoned building somewhere and they just haven't found the body yet. It's cold. As long as it's cold, there's no smell. You'd be amazed at how many bodies they find in vacant lots once the spring thaws come."

"From the smell?"

"Exactly."

"That's pleasant to contemplate."

"Pleasant or not, that's the way things work," Kate said.

"This time, though, we need them to look. I'm not sure we can go on with the case with Sherman missing, and I think we need to go on with the case. It's important. Harrigan will be out in, what, twenty or so days? We don't want him to walk. We do have to find Sherman."

"Can we go on with the case if we find him and he's dead?"

"I don't know," Kate said. "I'll look into it. And don't say we should never have reported him missing. We had to, under the circumstances. We probably had to under any circumstances. Have you talked to Harrigan's lawyers yet?"

"No, I thought you had."

"I have," Kate said. Then she decided to let that one pass. "Never mind. It's all under control. Go back to doing whatever you normally do and I'll leave you alone until I get something definite going on."

"I'm supposed to be going to class," Chickie said. "I haven't been doing a lot of that lately. Are you sure you want me to go on? You always seem to have so much to do."

"Most of it has nothing to do with this," Kate said. "You go."

Chickie hesitated in the doorway. Then he turned around and walked off, looking like something Central Casting had sent in to play a lawyer. Kate wondered what would happen to him once he passed the bar. A lot of kids said they wanted to go into public interest law, or work with the people who ordinarily wouldn't have representation, but those big-firm salaries were waiting, and they were bigger and more outside the scale of ordinary experience every day. Penn was a good degree. It wasn't as good as Yale or Harvard, but it was still a good degree. Somebody like Chickie would have offers.

Kate knew herself well enough to understand that she couldn't say, for sure, that she would be doing the kind of work she was doing if there had been anything like an alternative when she was first looking for a job. In the end, she was glad she'd chosen the work she had. She'd seen enough of the women who came in the law school classes after hers, who had had offers, not to envy them. If she put in a one-hundred-hour week, it was because she was working on something she believed in, something she honestly thought would make the world better. It wasn't in order to save Exxon from being sued by the Alaskan fishermen whose livelihoods it had ruined by hiring a tanker captain who couldn't hold his liquor, or to keep Enron executives out of jail and with their personal fortunes intact after they'd trashed the retirement savings of hundreds of their workers. Neil would probably say she was an idiot, or a Communist, but she was neither. She just didn't see the point of spending her life, the only one she would ever have, making the rich richer and behaving as if the poor didn't exist.

Of course, there were dangers in the other direction. She had promised herself long ago that if she ever heard herself talking about "the transgressive hermeneutics of grammar" or describing her case as a "struggle against oppression," she'd stop whatever she was doing, walk right out the door, and go to work for the Morgan Bank.

Right now, she just thought she needed a vacation. She'd come straight out here after settling a case in New York for the Coalition for the Homeless, which had been very good work but a long haul, dealing with city lawyers whose only purpose in life was to get her to run out of money and out of steam, and she was exhausted. She could use an island with lots of sunshine, lots of sand, and lots of liquor.

Here was something else she thought was important—she never, ever denied that she was who she was. Her idea of what to do about equality was to make the poor richer, not chuck herself into penury or play the martyr by buying her clothes at Kmart when she was able to shop at Saks. She was not a martyr, or a saint. She was just doing work she loved to do.

The phone on her desk buzzed. She picked up and the receptionist said, "Ms. Daniel? It's Mr. Ballard on line three."

Speaking of somebody who was trying to be a martyr or a saint, Kate thought. She picked up and said something noncommittal into the phone. Ray Dean Ballard always made her a little nuts. The fact that he insisted on calling himself Ray Dean made her nutser. If that was a word.

"Don't be pissy," he said. "I've got some news."

"That's good," Kate said, "because we're not much with news here this morning at all. What have you got?"

"The body, maybe."

Kate sat up. "Are you serious? Where is it? How long has he been dead?"

"Calm down," Ray Dean said. "It's not that far gone yet. I got a call from my guy in the District Attorney's Office. Demarkian's been in to see Benedetti."

"That's not news. We knew he was going to do something like that. That's why Chickie went to see him."

"True enough, but now the two of them have gone out to the Hardscrabble Road precinct house. They're stopping somewhere on the way, to get the guys who arrested Harrigan. But the thing is—"

"What's Hardscrabble Road?"

"It's about as close to the absolute edge of the city limits as you can get," Ray Dean said. "You'd practically think it wasn't part of the city at all. There's a convent out there. Monastery. Carmelite nuns."

"Benedictines," Kate said automatically. "Sherman Markey was supposed to be a regular at some homeless shelter run by Benedictines."

"Yes, I know that place, this isn't that. This is way out. They don't have a homeless shelter so much as they've got a barn they let people sleep in when the weather gets cold. The city would have a fit about the fact that there's only one bathroom and no real beds, except everybody is scared to death we're going to have a really big haul of people freezing to death this winter. Anyway, they found the hat. The red hat Sherman was wearing the last night anybody saw him alive. It turns out that somebody died out there on the night of the twenty-seventh."

"And they didn't tell anybody?"

"Of course they told somebody," Ray Dean said. "They called an ambulance, the whole magilla. But at the time the hat was missing, or something. Anyway, the hat was left behind. The body is at the morgue somewhere, they're going to try to go find it. But this is going to be Sherman. It all fits."

"The place doesn't fit," Kate said slowly, "does it? You say it's way out on the edge of the city? How would he have gotten there?"

"How do they ever get anywhere?" Ray Dean said. "We can work that out later. You should be ready for news, though. It's coming this afternoon. And it's going to be more interesting than you think."

"Why?"

"Because you know the monastery I'm talking about. Our Lady of Mount Carmel. It's the one that owns the land you guys had the lien put on, the land Drew Harrigan gave to the nuns after you guys sued him on Sherman's behalf. The one where Drew Harrigan's sister is the Abbess."

"Jesus Christ," Kate said.

"Exactly. Hold on tight. This is going to be a wild ride. I'll call you back later. I've got a bunch of stuff to do. I just wanted to make sure you were warned."

"Right," Kate said. Then she put down the phone and stared at it.

It wasn't the clients who got to her. It wasn't the plaintiffs. It wasn't the defendants. It wasn't even the other lawyers and judges. It was just this, the stuff that came out of the walls when you weren't expecting it.

3

The order to run fingerprint checks on any and all corpses that had been delivered to the morgue since January 27 had come down more than two hours ago, and everybody in the facility had been ignoring it ever since. It wasn't that they didn't want to be helpful, Dr. Ramarcharadan thought. It was just that there was so much to do that nobody could handle their real workload, never mind all these calls for fingerprint checks. Dr. Ramarcharadan was from the Punjab. He'd been in America a total of fifty-two months. He was the most conscientious of men, but there was only so much he could do with a facility that was short-staffed in the best of times, and now—with this cold and the people dying from it—so outclassed that it might as well have been doing nothing at all.

Except that that wasn't true, and Dr. Ramarcharadan knew it. He was managing six autopsies a day these days. He was beginning to see corpses in his sleep. In India, he had not been a pathologist, and hadn't expected to be. Here, he'd had no other choice. In a few years, he might be able to get all his certifications in order and be allowed to perform surgery again, which was what he was trained for.

At the moment, he was all suited up and ready to go on one more corpse. His back hurt, his legs hurt, his feet hurt, and everything in his head was humming. He'd been at it since six o'clock this morning. He thought his wrists were about to fall off.

The good thing about pathology was that you didn't have to worry about finesse. Unless there was some overriding reason, and he couldn't think of what one might be, you could just go ahead and do what you did without worrying about the patient's feelings. This patient was on the chart as a homeless man picked up on one of those nights when just taking out the garbage could give a man frostbite. Dr. Ramarcharadan didn't think there was much to be preferred in the Punjab over the United States, but the weather was definitely something. He tapped into the chest bone, made a long cut, and began to peel away the skin. They were getting to them far too late these days. They always left the homeless ones for last, because nobody was waiting to take possession of them. They should get at them right away. There was something wrong about leaving them here for so long, even frozen, even knowing they could not deteriorate.

Dr. Ramarcharadan's wife sometimes said she didn't like him to touch her when he came home, because she knew he'd had his hands on dead bodies, and that was the work of untouchables—but he didn't believe that. She was not a religious woman, any more than he was a religious man, and she didn't approve of the caste system either. He thought it was an excuse, the way other women might get a headache. Ah, well. She'd borne him three sons in four years, all American citizens. Maybe she was just tired.

If he hadn't been thinking about the sons—good sons, too, strong and healthy, and intelligent—he would have noticed sooner. As it was, he was peeling back bone before it struck him, and for a long moment he didn't understand what he was seeing. It was the intestines he noticed first. What were the chances of that? He should have seen the obvious, but he hadn't.

He took a deep breath and told himself to calm down. He thought about the newspaper headlines and the television news stories and the editorials in magazines over the last few weeks. He tried to remember what he did and didn't know about how the law worked in the United States of America. The problem was, he mostly didn't know. He wasn't even sure that this would not, somehow, turn out to be his fault.

He looked at the intestines again, just to make sure. They were still twisting in the wrong direction. Then he looked up the torso and checked that, too. It had not miraculously become something it was not.

He stepped back away from the table and motioned to the nurse. When they were both outside the swinging doors in the waiting area he said, "We must call the police now, right away. We must not touch this body again until they come. Do you understand that?"

She nodded frantically and then took off at a run.

Dr. Ramarcharadan didn't remind her that there was a phone on the wall not fifteen feet away.

He didn't blame her for her panic.

EIGHT

I

For the Philadelphia Police Department, the real problem with the cold was that engines wouldn't start. There had been some talk about constructing a heated garage for police and emergency vehicles, and the ambulances were parked in underground hospital garages that were never allowed to get cold enough to stall them, but in the end fiscal responsibility won out over common sense and shared history. Besides, it was an election year, and in an election year it never did anybody any good to suggest something that might require raising taxes. It did do whoever suggested it some good to propose new products and services, but this wasn't 1957 anymore. If you suggested the service, your opponent would bring up the taxes.

"I don't think anybody knows what they're talking about when they're talking about taxes," Rob Benedetti said, as he put Gregor into the car that would take him to Detectives Marbury and Giametti. "I mean, what do they think? They're going to pay for the police department with air?"

The only thing Gregor Demarkian knew about taxes was that he paid them, and he didn't even know much about that, since Bennis's accountant figured them for him and all he did was write checks. He got into the car, glad it was running and glad it had the heater on.

"Let me tell you what people think about taxes," Benedetti said. "They think that the government is spending a gazillion dollars on crap. Programs to bring Bolivian folk music to public schools. Programs to support the Daughters of the War of 1812 in their drive to mount an opera on the war to tour American high schools. Programs to establish an Institute of Broccoli Studies in northwest Tennessee."

Gregor couldn't help himself. "Is Tennessee a big broccoli-growing state?"

"How am I supposed to know?" Benedetti said. "That's not the point. The point is that people think there are millions of these programs and they take up most of the budget, so all we have to do is get rid of the silly programs and we can have all the police and fire protection we want, and it isn't true. There are programs, but they only take up a little money compared to the rest. When you cut taxes to the point where my own nieces and nephews could afford to pay them out of their allowances—and, believe me, my sister doesn't hand out Rockefeller-sized allowances—anyway, you see what I mean. It's completely insane. You should tell John Jackman it's completely insane."

"I'll try," Gregor said.

"We've got six vehicles that wouldn't start this morning in this precinct alone," Rob Benedetti said. "That's six right here around my office. Plus I don't remember how many state cars that won't go. We need heated parking spaces. It's winter, for God's sake. It's cold enough to turn rabbit turds into icicles. What do they want from us?"

What Gregor wanted was to get the car moving and out of the way. He had no idea what had started Rob Benedetti on taxes, but just in case it was something he'd said, he wanted to be sure he wouldn't be able to say it again. He made noncommittal noises—yes, of course it seemed sensible to pay enough in taxes to get the police protection you needed; no, of course it didn't make sense to think that we could do away with taxes altogether and still have a city worth living in—and thought that politics in an election year was like Armenian Lent. Whether you wanted to take part in it or not, it chased you until it hunted you down.

Which reminded him: Lent was coming up soon. Cavanaugh Street would be full of women cooking lentils in oil. The Ararat would serve him eggs with sausages for breakfast, but Linda Melajian would look disappointed in him when she put the plate on the table, and Tibor would sigh a lot. It wouldn't do him any good to remind them all that Armenian Lent was one of the things he had wanted so desperately to escape when he left Philadelphia for graduate school.

Finally, the car was on the road and moving, and Gregor went back to feeling as if he were in a road trip movie. He thought he'd done more traveling in cars today than he ordinarily did in any given week, and all to get from one place to the other in a mostly confined area. The activity felt pointless. He wasn't really all that emotionally involved in finding Sherman Markey, or in anything Drew Harrigan might think he wanted to do. On the other hand, the activity had done what he'd started out hoping it would do. He'd spent most of the day not thinking of Bennis Hannaford at all.

I'm too old, he thought, *to have the kind of relationship with a woman that requires me to work hard at not thinking about her.*

Marbury and Giametti worked out of a precinct not very far from the District Attorney's Office. It was their car that wouldn't start, which was why Gregor was going to them. It was afternoon now, and there were more people on the street, many of them aimless. In spite of the cold, though, Gregor thought it was better in February than in December, because in December it got dark in the middle of the afternoon.

One of the men was waiting at the curb when the car drove up. He was tall and thin and shaggy in a way policemen usually aren't. In Gregor's experience, men who joined the police force liked to think of themselves as being in the military. They went in for buzz cuts and too many hours spent working out with weights.

The car drew to a stop and the tall man opened the door at

Gregor's side. He really did not look military at all. His hair came down over the back of his collar. His fingers were so long, they could have been caricatures out of a cartoon about a skeleton. The effect was thrown off by the short police jacket, standard uniform issue. It had been made for a compact, bulky man who loved his G.I. Joe dolls. The skeleton put a hand out to help him from the car.

"Mr. Demarkian?" he said. "I'm Dane Marbury. We've given up on the car. Mike's gone to get us a new one. And we'd both like to thank you very much."

"For what?" Gregor was out and closing the car door behind him. The cold was still wicked. The wind was still stiff.

"For giving us something to do on a long, boring day," Marbury said. "Don't mind us. This is the least exciting precinct in the city. We've got rich guys. We've got hookers. Don't let anybody ever tell you that rich guys only like high-priced call girls. You wouldn't believe how many of them like to pick up hookers off the street, skanky hookers, too—"

"Dane, for Christ's sake. He used to be with the FBI."

The person who said this was the bulky, compact man Gregor had been imagining in a police uniform jacket, and he came equipped even with the buzz cut. Dane Marbury turned around and shrugged.

"So he was with the FBI," he said. "What does the FBI know? They're clueless on the street and you know it."

"The FBI knows from rich guys being blackmailed by cheap hookers. How do you do, Mr. Demarkian. I'm Mike Giametti."

"How do you do," Gregor said.

It really was cold out here. Neither of the young men seemed to notice it.

"I still say we ought to thank him," Dane Marbury said. "He's got us out of here for the afternoon, and I'm more than happy to go. I'm not all that interested in rich guys and I'm not all that interested in hookers."

"No, I'm glad to get out of here, too," Giametti said. I've got us a ride. The nuns are going to be waiting."

"And it's cold," Gregor said.

The two younger men looked at him, seemed confused, and blinked.

2

The precinct that included the Monastery of Our Lady of Mount Carmel was supposed to be "not central," or "out of the way," but Gregor had never imagined it might actually be out in the country. He kept trying to get his bearings and couldn't. They were in the city, then the city petered out, then there were miles of strip malls and fast-food restaurants, then there was grass, or as much of it as you could see under the heavy coating of snow that had not disappeared this far out into the country. Except that they couldn't be in the country, Gregor thought, because they were still within the city limits. If they hadn't been, then the police who covered Hardscrabble Road would belong to a township, and not Philadelphia.

Mike Giametti looked just as confused as Gregor was. "If the map didn't fit, I'd think we were lost. You sure this is where we're supposed to go?"

Dane Marbury nodded. "I checked the maps back at the precinct. This is where we're supposed to go. You wouldn't think it was part of the city, would you?"

"I don't think it's part of the city," Giametti said. "I think we're lost."

"Next intersection should be Colcannon Street," Marbury said.

All three of them held their breath as the next intersection came up, but it was Colcannon Street. The problem was that there didn't seem to be much of anything on Colcannon Street. There were a few low buildings: a hardware store, a pharmacy, a pawnshop, a Laundromat. There were a few vacant lots. The area didn't look depressed as much as it looked never developed, and Gregor didn't think there was anywhere in the city of Philadelphia, or even in the greater Metro area, that hadn't been developed.

"Next intersection is Gwane Street," Marbury said.

The next intersection was Gwane Street. There was nobody walking around on the pavements at all. The whole
thing could have been a stage set for a *Twilight Zone*
episode. Still, Gregor thought, there was that pawnshop.
Pawnshops meant poor people, or at least people living close
enough to the edge that they needed extra money fast and
had no choice but to part with the things they loved to get it.
It wasn't impossible that an area with a pawnshop would
also be an area with homeless people.

"I know why it looks so wrong," Gregor said suddenly.
"There aren't any adult bookstores."

"There aren't any adult bookstores in most of the neighborhoods of Philadelphia," Dane Marbury said. "What do
you take us for?"

"In neighborhoods with pawnshops, there are adult bookstores," Gregor said. "Except here, there aren't."

"Maybe they're afraid of the nuns," Mike Giametti said.

Gregor shifted uncomfortably in the backseat. This was a
squad car, so he was in the compartment usually reserved for
people who had been arrested for something or the other.
"Tell me about Drew Harrigan," he said. "Rob Benedetti
said—"

"Yeah," Marbury said. "It's our big claim to fame. If we'd
realized who it was—no, that's not true. He was behaving
like a jerk. In a car. Just what you need on a city street, with
cars and pedestrians everywhere."

"The car was weaving?"

"The car was doing weird things with speeding up and
slowing down," Giametti said. "It would, like, rev up and go
for a few feet and then he'd hit the brake and when he started
up again, he'd inch forward. The street wasn't packed but
there were other cars, and they were getting pretty upset.
You couldn't tell what he was going to do next."

"Yeah, and then he hit the gas pedal for serious," Marbury said, "and just sort of shot off, right through a red light,
and we decided we'd had enough. So we stopped him."

"And then it started getting weird," Giametti said.

"I didn't know who he was," Marbury said. "I mean, I

know he's famous, he does commercials, but what can I say? I'd never seen him. And I don't listen to his radio show."

"He expected us to recognize him, though," Giametti said. "And he did look sort of familiar to me right from the beginning, but he was flying. I mean, he was absolutely off the wall. He was singing."

"Benedetti said he was singing when you got him back to the precinct station," Gregor said.

"Oh, he was singing there, too," Marbury said. "But he was singing right off in the car, between bouts of calling us stuff I'm not supposed to say in uniform except on a witness stand. He kept saying, 'You know how important I am? You know how important I am? John Cleese is going to play me in the movie.'"

"Not John Cleese," Giametti said. "John Goodman. You know, the guy who played Roseanne's husband on TV."

"Whatever," Marbury said. "We hauled him out of the car, and that was when he really started screaming at us. He kept saying, 'You can't arrest me. You can't arrest me. I've got a deal with the city. I've got a deal.'"

"He said that?" Gregor said. "That he had a deal?"

"Yeah," Giametti said. "Over and over again. Thing is, I think we'd have heard about it. I mean, our precinct is in this guy's own neighborhood. If he'd cut some kind of deal with some of the beat cops, we'd have heard about it."

"Somebody would at least have tried to warn us off him," Marbury said.

"So what we thought was, maybe there's some guys who just let him go when they find him because they feel sorry for him, or because they're fans. There are a lot of conservatives on the police force. We figured he'd been stopped for behaving like an idiot a couple of times and the cop who stopped him gave him a break and let it pass. It happens, even for people who aren't celebrities."

"But anyway," Marbury said, "we figured we weren't obliged to do the same, and we didn't want to see him on the road for another goddamned minute, so we took him out of the car, and that's when we saw the Tupperware thing on the front passenger seat. It was weird because I recognized the thing. The container. My wife's sister sells Tupperware. We have a container just like it at home. And it was full of pills."

"The whole front of the car was full of pills," Giametti said. "He'd been speeding up and hitting the brakes, and some of the pills had gotten loose and spilled on the floor and the seat and everywhere. Everything you could think of. Oxy-Contin. Percocet. Darvocet. Percodan. Benzphetamine. Phentermine. Uppers, downers, you name it. All prescription."

"There's this thing they do on the street," Marbury said, "called a rainbow cocktail. You take a whole bunch of pills and you pick 'em by the color, and then you down the whole thing with Scotch. That's what we thought he'd been doing. We asked him to take a Breathalyzer test and he refused. So we handcuffed him and put him in the squad car."

"We got the handcuffs on before he knew what we were doing," Giametti said. "Getting him into the car wasn't so easy. He went berserk. He kicked. He bit. He body-blocked. You wouldn't think it to look at him, but he can manage one hell of a body block. He's a big guy. He should have played football. I thought we were going to have to call for backup, but we got him in the car, and then we got back to the station as fast as we could."

"We were hoping the drive would calm him down," Marbury said, "and it did some. I mean, he just sat back there singing and calling us motherwhatevers every few seconds, and he wasn't jumping around. So we got him back to the station, we start to take him out of the car, and wham, there he goes again. He slammed into me from the side with his hip hooked out and I fell on my ass, and then he started to run, and Mike had to go after him, and by that time I was calling for backup, so about thirty guys showed up just as Mike grabbed him."

"And we've got all these guys surrounding him, guns drawn, and what does he do?" Giametti said. "First he starts screaming that they can't shoot him, because don't they know who he is?"

"By then we all did," Marbury said. "A couple of the guys

with the guns even said so out loud: 'Oh, my God. We've arrested Drew Harrigan.' "

"But just when I thought we were going to have to put him in a straitjacket," Giametti said, "he started singing again. And that was it. That was all he did for the rest of the night. Sing. He sang every oldies song I've ever heard of and a few I haven't. 'Do Wah Diddy Diddy.' 'Peggy Sue.' 'Great Balls of Fire.' "

"And we get him in the station," Marbury said, "and we book him, and we fingerprint him, and we photograph him, and he's still singing. He won't shut up. He won't answer questions. Forget it. He's still singing. So we slam him in a room and tell him he either starts behaving himself or we'll lock him up for the night, and he demands to see his lawyer. And that was that."

"That was that?" Gregor asked. "You just let him go?"

Giametti laughed. "He got Neil Savage down here. You know Neil Savage? From Barden, Savage & Deal?"

"I know Barden, Savage & Deal," Gregor said. "But they're not a criminal firm, are they? They don't handle this kind of thing."

"They handle whatever their clients want them to handle," Giametti said, "and they've got the advantage of being the firm that represents the Republican Party in Pennsylvania. Plus, of course, a whole truckload of Republican bigwigs and semi-Republican bigwigs."

"What do you mean semi?"

"Well," Marbury said, "you can't really blame Drew Harrigan on the entire Republican Party, can you? I mean, they didn't hire him. They don't pay him. He's on his own."

"He's just on his own and he only likes Republican politicians," Giametti said, "but, yeah, Dane has a point. It's just that Barden, Savage & Deal represent a lot of the big noises in conservative politics in this state. All the pro-life groups, for one thing."

"I'm pro-life," Marbury said.

"That has nothing to do with anything," Giametti said. "Anyway, Neil Savage himself came down to the precinct station, told Harrigan to shut up—which he didn't really do, since he went on singing—got on the phone, and within half an hour we had a hearing before a judge and the judge had set bail. Fastest thing I've ever seen in my life. You wouldn't have believed it. Then Savage got Harrigan out the door, and that was the last we saw of him. The next morning, we got word that Harrigan had entered a total immersion rehab program and would be incommunicado for the next sixty days, the whole thing had already been cleared with the judge. And then there was a statement, which Savage read at a press conference. It was the statement that accused Sherman Markey of being the go-between for all the drugs."

"This was Bruce Williamson who was the judge?"

"That's the one." Marbury sniggered.

"Marvelous," Gregor said.

"This is going to be it," Marbury said, leaning closer to the windshield to get a better look at the small sign by the side of the road. "God, it's deserted around here. You've got to wonder how they stand it. Sherman Markey didn't get him the drugs. Did we tell you that?"

"Everybody keeps telling me that," Gregor said.

"It's the truth," Marbury said. "You should have seen Sherman when he was alive. He couldn't think straight enough to remember he was on his way to the men's room when he needed to take a piss. And neither one of us believes that crap about Sherman doing work around Drew Harrigan's apartment for spare change. Sherman couldn't do any work beyond whatever it took to get the cork out of the wine bottle, and he saved himself the trouble of that most of the time by buying the kind of wine that has a screw top. Assuming he bought any at all and didn't just finish open bottles people left on the street."

"That's a driveway," Giametti said. "Look at it."

"That's not a driveway, that's an alley," Marbury said.

He pulled the squad car up to the curb. There were almost no cars parked anywhere on this street. There were still no people. Gregor started buttoning his coat again, in anticipation of the wind. It was only anticipation, because he couldn't let himself out. There was no way to open the doors back here from the inside.

"I'm glad Rob isn't interested in letting him off," Giametti said. "I'm sick of these guys who piss and moan about everybody else, who want the police to act like the Spanish Inquisition, then they get into some trouble and they expect to walk right out of it. We ought to stick more of these guys in jail sometime. That would do more than anything else I can think of to improve the level of public discourse."

"Mike reads heavy magazines," Marbury said solemnly.

Then they both got out onto the street and opened up for Gregor at once. The two open doors created a wind tunnel that sent cold air slamming against Gregor's face as if he'd just stepped up to a working fan.

"Damn," he said, and got out himself.

3

Gregor Demarkian saw the nun as soon as he walked through the precinct house door, because she was a vision from another time and another place: a nun in a habit, a real habit, that went all the way down to the floor, that completely covered her head. The only difference in the picture he was imagining was on the forehead. She had no white band of cloth on the forehead. Instead, her black veil was draped over a white headdress that ended at her hairline. Black veil, white wimple, brown habit. Gregor wasn't sure he'd ever met a Carmelite before. Then he looked down at her feet and realized she was wearing only socks and sandals, not real shoes.

She was up near the counter, pacing up and down in front of the sergeant on duty as if nothing on the planet could convince her to stay still. She was very young, and very pretty, tall and slender and erect. Except for Audrey Hepburn, she was the only person Gregor had ever seen who looked too thin in a traditional nun's habit. He wondered what it was about the shoes.

"You just can't keep questioning him over and over

again," she was saying. "He's not well. He doesn't have any answers. What do you think you're doing?"

"If he wants a lawyer, he can ask for one."

"I *am* a lawyer," the nun said. "If you want my credentials, I'll call the monastery and have Sister Immaculata bring them in for me. He's a tired, sick old man and his only crime was to find that hat and bring it to my attention. I should never have told you who he was. This is completely ridiculous."

Gregor, Giametti, and Marbury had reached the counter, and the young nun turned to look at the three of them. She seemed surprised to see them there—which said something, Gregor thought, about the level of traffic this precinct had had here so far today.

"How can you be a lawyer?" the sergeant asked. "You're a nun."

"I'm a lawyer because I went to law school and passed the bar before I ever became a nun," the nun said, "and besides, I'm not a nun, I'm a religious sister. And if you don't let him out of that room and get those two detectives off him, I'm going to get him to declare me his counsel and I'm going to sue the department back to the Stone Age. You really can't do this. It doesn't make any sense, and it isn't right, and you know it."

"What's the difference between a nun and a religious sister?" Gregor asked.

The religious sister wheeled around to look at him. "Excuse me?" she said.

"My name is Gregor Demarkian," Gregor said.

She hesitated, then brightened. "Gregor Demarkian. The Armenian-American Hercule Poirot. Are you here about this? Do you actually think that poor homeless man murdered Sherman Markey? Because if you do, I have to say I don't think much of—"

"What's the difference between a nun and a religious sister?" Gregor asked again.

"A nun takes solemn vows," the religious sister said. "She's usually cloistered, in papal enclosure, although there are some exceptions. A religious sister takes simple vows and works in the world. Most of the people you call nuns aren't really nuns, technically. You know, the teaching sisters and the nursing sisters and that kind of thing. They're religious sisters."

"I thought the sisters at Our Lady of Mount Carmel were cloistered," Gregor said.

"Oh, they are," the sister said. "Most of them. But I'm not, and Sister Immaculata is not. We're extern sisters. Cloistered nuns have to have extern sisters to go out into the world and do what needs to be done on a practical level. Like coming here with the hat. And getting involved in all this idiocy with treating that poor man like he's some kind of criminal, when all he tried to do was the right thing. What do we teach people when we punish them for doing the right thing?"

"Nobody is punishing anybody for anything," the sergeant behind the counter said. "Not yet. And nobody is arresting your guy."

"Who knows who's doing what to him?" the sister demanded. "You've had him in that room for half an hour, completely cut off from me or any other possible help, and don't tell me he waived the right to an attorney. You know as well as I do that he isn't competent to make a decision like that. Now, you're going to go and get him, and let me talk to him, and leave him alone, or I'm going to find a judge and make you release him. And if you don't think I can do that, you don't begin to understand where I'm coming from."

"Mr. Demarkian," the sergeant said, leaning across the counter to hold out his hand, "don't mind Sister here. We aren't giving the old guy the third degree. We're just trying to find out what happened on the night this Sherman Markey guy died."

"Are we sure it was Sherman Markey in the hat, then?" Gregor said.

"Not officially, no," the sergeant said, "but Detective Willis told me to tell you that it's just a matter of time. We know where the body is. They've just got to get to the pathologist and make him move it. So much for fingerprint databases, but that's just me. Give us a few seconds here and Detective Willis will be right out."

"Tell Detective Willis that if he isn't out a lot sooner than that, I'll have his balls," the sister said.

The sergeant frowned. "Nuns didn't talk like that when I was in school."

"You weren't holding sick old men against their wills when you were in school."

A woman appeared from one of the doors behind the counter and called, "Is there a Detective Marbury here? There's a call for you from the District Attorney's Office."

"That'll be confirmation," Marbury said.

He walked back to where the woman was waiting for him, and Gregor went back to contemplating the religious sister. He had no doubt at all that she would make good on her threat. She had the look of someone who was used to being taken seriously. The sergeant was ignoring her. Gregor didn't think that would go on for long.

"Sister?" he said.

"Oh, excuse me," the sister said. "I haven't introduced myself. I'm Sister Maria Beata of the Incarnation. No, never mind all that. We never use all that except in official documents. In a way, I'm glad you're here. Maybe you can bring some sanity to these proceedings."

"Maybe," Gregor said. "Did you see the man who died? The person we think is Sherman Markey?"

"Not really," Beata said. "Oh, I saw him in passing. He was waiting at the door for the barn to open when I came back to the monastery from doing some business downtown. And I saw him after he was dead. I can't give you much information about him."

"Would any of the other sisters have seen him?"

"Most of the sisters don't actually leave the enclosure to visit the barn," Beata said. "They're not supposed to see outsiders at all, except from behind the grille. It's only Immaculata and me who go out there while the men are there. The monastery used to keep cows, you know, in the old days. Before the city got so built up. It would be against the law now, I suppose."

Gregor was about to suppose the same thing, when the door at the back swung open again, and Dane Marbury came out, looking sick.

"Listen," he said, coming up to them. "We've got to get out of here. Mr. Demarkian is wanted at the morgue."

"They found the body?" Giametti said.

"Sort of."

"What does that mean?"

Marbury looked at the floor, and the ceiling, and then at his hands. "They found a body," he said. "But it isn't Sherman Markey's body. They're pretty sure that what they've got is the great Drew Harrigan himself."

PART TWO

Tuesday, February 11
High 4F, Low −9F

Ours is an era of mass-starvation, deportation and the taking of hostages.

—GEORGE STEINER

It seems clear to me that the will must in some way be united to God's will. But it is in the effects and deeds following afterward that one discerns the true value of prayer....

—ST. TERESA OF AVILA

And it came to pass that in time the Great God Om spake unto Brutha, the Chosen One: "Psst!"

—TERRY PRATCHETT

ONE

I

In dreams the people who should be present are absent, and the people who should be absent . . . something. The words wouldn't come. Gregor Demarkian thought that might be because he didn't have any words. He had a big bag full of something, but it all seemed to be marshmallow Peeps, in every possible color, including purple. He looked out over the vast audience in front of them and realized they were all *cynocephali,* men with dogs' heads. He wouldn't have known what to call them if he hadn't been talking about it to Tibor just a day or two ago. Maybe some of them were women with dogs' heads. He didn't know how to tell, since they all seemed to be wearing identical sky blue jumpsuits. They were all carrying parachutes, too. He knew he couldn't stop talking, because if he did, one of them would stand up to speak, and assuming he could translate the barks—did *cynocephali* bark? Tibor hadn't said anything about that— all he would hear would be another lecture about politics, and it wouldn't matter whose side the *cynocephali* were on. Maybe one of them was running for something, mayor, president, dogcatcher. Maybe they had an ideology that told them that if the other side got into office, the world as we know it would be destroyed, all good would be defiled and outlawed, all evil would be installed and mandated. Maybe they were awaiting the end of civilization and the rise of a fascist state, where dogs would be forced to wear collars and jailed if they were caught without them, where they would have no freedom of religion to refuse vaccinations, where they would be required to live with a master or be marked for judicial death.

It was cold in the room, so cold Gregor thought his hands were turning into icicles. He wanted to touch his hair to make sure it was in place. Maybe if he did that he would be able to remember the words. Maybe he had never had the words. He didn't want to give a speech. He didn't want to talk to *cynocephali*, either. He didn't think he had a lot in common with them. He didn't think he had much to say even to people he did have a lot in common with.

It was cold because the window was partially open. He could see the crack at the base of the sill. There was a bit of paper stuck there, waving in the wind that was coming through. He tried to sit up and realized he was lying flat on his face. A moment later, he saw that his face was on his pillow, the window that was open was in his own bedroom, and the *cynocephali* were nowhere but in his imagination, planted there by Tibor discussing the travel narratives that had circulated throughout Europe in the twelfth century, in the wake of the Crusades.

Gregor turned over on his back, sat up, and looked around. The room was ridiculously dark, in spite of the fact that there was a streetlight right outside his window, which usually made it unnecessary for him to turn on a light when he wanted to go to the bathroom in the night. He switched on the lamp on the night table on what he had come to think of as "his" side of the bed. Then he looked over to the other side and wondered how he'd managed to sleep for as long as he had—he had no idea how long that was—without disturbing it. Maybe it had something to do with the fact that he had gone to sleep without turning down the covers, getting himself undressed, or in any way preparing himself for what was supposed to be a long period of quiet. He had a feeling he had had no quiet at all, and it wasn't just the *cynocephali.*

He hadn't taken his shoes off, either. They were still on his feet, hard-edged penny loafers Bennis thought would look better on him than his old wingtips. He got himself upright and his legs off the side of the bed. He kicked his shoes off and then bent over to take off his socks. The clock on the bedside table said 4:46. He presumed that was a.m. Surely, if he'd slept through breakfast at the Ararat and then missed his ten o'clock appointment with John Jackman, somebody would have come looking for him. It really was cold in here. It was freezing. Could he have turned the heat off in a daze when he'd wandered in a couple of hours ago?

He got up, shrugged off his jacket, but didn't bother to undress any farther. He went out of the bedroom and down the dark hall to the thermostat. The thermostat said sixty-eight degrees, but it didn't feel like sixty-eight degrees. He jacked it up to seventy-eight, because he could always turn the heat down again if he needed to. Then he went the rest of the way down the hall to the bathroom. If he'd told Bennis about feeling cold like this, she'd say he was coming down with something, and maybe he was. He'd just spent several hours standing around in a morgue refrigerated to a point where even somebody who'd spent days exposed to this February chill would think somebody was overdoing it, and in the end he had gotten absolutely nowhere on any front he considered important.

He hesitated in the bathroom doorway, realized what he'd forgotten, and went back to the bedroom. He got boxer shorts, an undershirt, a robe, and a pair of sweatpants out of his drawers and went back to the bathroom again. He wasn't operating on all eight cylinders, as Tommy Moradanyan Donahue would say, and yet he'd be willing to bet that Tommy had no idea what "all eight cylinders" meant, having never encountered a car with more than six. Or maybe he had.

I'm losing my mind, Gregor thought. He shut the bath-

room door, turned on the shower as hot as he could make it
without scalding himself, and then began to strip off his
clothes and throw them in the various hampers Bennis had
set out to contain them: whites here, darks there, dry cleaning in a third place. He was sure he'd had a sweater when
he'd gone to see John first thing yesterday morning, but he
had no sweater now, and he had no idea what had happened
to it. Steam was rising out of the shower stall in great white
billows. He opened the stall door and stepped in under the
water, instantly warmed. He was tired, that was all that was
the matter with him. He hadn't come in until one thirty, and
then he'd fallen asleep in his clothes, and now it was not
very many hours later, and he knew he wasn't going back to
sleep. He didn't think he'd be able to go back to sleep even
if the mayor hadn't come down to the morgue and virtually
threatened him with death.

Actually, literally, what the mayor had threatened him
with was jail.

The water was too hot. If he was fully conscious, he
would be worried about being burned. Now he wasn't. He let
the water fall over his head in cascading sheets and found
himself happy for the warmth of it. He wanted everything in
his life to be warm. He wanted to move to someplace like
Orlando, or Palm Springs, where it was never cold at all unless you walked into a meat locker, and then you had a temperature gauge to play with if you wanted that to change.

What he really wanted was to know where Bennis was,
and what she wanted from him. Here was why he didn't like
to go without sleep, and why he didn't like to spend much
time in this apartment by himself. When he did either, he
found himself thinking obsessively about Bennis's mood the
last time they had really talked, and all the times since then,
when conversation had seemed impossible. He tried to remember if he had ever had the experience of a love affair
gone wrong, or come apart, and he didn't think he had. The
only woman he had ever loved before Bennis had been his
wife. He had loved her and married her and then stayed by
her while she died, but there had never been any suggestion,

even during the worst of his days on kidnapping detail, that there could be a divorce. Of course, Bennis hadn't suggested anything like divorce, either, and couldn't, since they weren't married. There had to be a word for what happened when a relationship broke in the absence of matrimony. If there wasn't, somebody should invent one.

He didn't really know if the relationship was broken. It wasn't from his side, or he didn't think it was. It might be from hers, but if it was he didn't know why it was, and she wouldn't tell him. Sometimes he understood the people who wanted desperately to return to the fifties, when rules were more rigid than they were now and there were fewer choices to make and fewer confusions to get lost in. When he got saner, he realized that that had to be an illusion. It could not have been so wonderful in the middle of Red Scares, McCarthy witch-hunts, and illegal abortions staged in back alley "clinics" where the "doctor" drank nonstop and nobody ever cleaned the floors.

He'd sounded like Bennis just then. It was the kind of thing she'd say. He'd tell her she was simplifying, and she was. It would all be good-natured, except that nothing had been good-natured those last few weeks before she'd left. The tension had been so thick it had been as if the air between them in the room had turned into mayonnaise. And he still had no idea why.

Right now, he just wanted her to come home. What bothered him—what had been bothering him for days—was the possibility that she wouldn't, or at least not really. She'd call from Seattle and say she'd decided to move out West. She'd ask Donna Moradanyan to box up her things and send them up. She'd come back only to pack a suitcase for a four-month trip to India and the Far East. She'd call one night and talk to him, but it would be as if what had been between them had never happened. She'd talk to him the way she talked to Donna, or Tibor—or, worse, to the people she didn't know very well, the ones she was friendly with because not to be friendly would be to be rude, but to whom she never revealed anything important.

Of course, Gregor thought, you could say she had never revealed anything important even to him, because she was like that. There was always something about Bennis that was just one step away, inviolate. Men were supposed to like that in women. He didn't know if he liked that in her. Men were supposed to have women figured out by the time they were thirty. He didn't have this one figured out at all, and to prove it he could stand here under this streaming hot water and not know whether she was angry at him or not, in love with him or not, missing him or not. He didn't even know where she was on this book tour.

What he did know was that the water in the shower seemed to be getting hotter, and if he didn't get out from under it he was going to look as red as Dilbert in that episode from the television show. He had no idea what had made him remember the Dilbert television show, but there it was.

He had no idea what had made him fall in love with Bennis, either, or whether he still was in love with her.

He not only didn't have women figured out by the time he was thirty, he hadn't done a very good job on himself.

2

Forty-five minutes later, Gregor was standing on Fr. Tibor Kasparian's doorstep, ringing the bell and stamping one foot and then the other the way he'd seen people do in old movies when they were supposed to be cold. He really was cold. No matter how bad the apartment had felt, it had been as nothing compared to the real weather on the outside, and he found himself again wishing he'd bought a hat, or earmuffs, or something. Then he thought he couldn't imagine himself with earmuffs, and Bennis probably couldn't, either, since she'd never bought him a pair. On the other side of the door, Tibor was fumbling with locks and other things. Gregor thought he heard something fall over. The door shuddered on its frame and then pulled inward. Tibor was standing there in good slacks and two sweaters, but no shoes.

From behind him, there was a small cascade of pattering,

and the dark brown puppy poked her nose into the outside air. She didn't like it, and retreated immediately in the direction of the living room. Gregor saw what had fallen. It was a stack of Tibor's books, one of the paperback stacks he kept against the walls all over the house. This stack included Dennis Lehane's *Mystic River,* Karin Slaugher's *A Faint Cold Fear,* and John Stuart Mill's *On Liberty.* At least there was nothing in Latin, Greek, Hebrew, or Assyrian. Father Tibor was the only person Gregor knew who had gone to see Mel Gibson's *The Passion of the Christ* and not needed to read the subtitles to know what the actors were saying.

Tibor closed the door behind him and waved him toward the living room. "I still say you could have waited half an hour, Krekor. I would have been awake naturally in half an hour."

"Sorry."

"No, never mind. I would have been awake but not dressed and showered, so maybe it wouldn't have mattered that much. I saw you on television yesterday evening. You should have stopped in when you got home. There will be a hundred people at the Ararat this morning wanting a full report."

"They'll have to wait. I've got to meet John for breakfast, and then I have to go downtown to get yelled at by the mayor."

"Why does the mayor want to yell at you?"

"Because he thinks I'm 'identified' with John, and he thinks John is only calling me in on this one to look good to the electorate, and the whole thing is a stunt to get John to win the primary. I don't know. Did I tell you I hate politics?"

"Several times."

Tibor was out of the room to the back now, in the kitchen. Gregor took a seat in the living room and looked around. One of the changes they had made to this apartment when it had been rebuilt after the bombing was to install forced hot air heating and cooling systems, because that meant that Tibor could have central air-conditioning in the summer. It also meant that there were no more baseboards running along the walls to give heat, and Tibor could stack up books at all sides, everywhere. The living room now looked as if it were made of books. Every single one of the stacks looked as if it were about to fall down.

Tibor came back with two coffees. Gregor took his and sipped it very slowly. He knew from experience that Tibor's coffee was either very bad, or Armenian, meaning strong enough to qualify as a controlled substance.

Tibor sat down on the couch and the dog jumped up to sit down with him. Gregor wondered if Grace allowed that, or if she would come home to find that her dog now believed it was a dog's God-given right to ruin the furniture.

"So," he said. "This man was famous, and now he is dead. If the mayor was smart, Krekor, he would call you in himself."

"Would he? I don't know. I've been trying to figure out what to think of all this for hours, and I haven't come up with anything. Oh. I brought you something." He stood up and went looking through the pockets of his coat. "Here it is," he said, coming up with the book. He tossed it over. "Drew Harrigan wrote a book. I want to know what you think."

"You have read this book, Krekor?"

"No, of course not," Gregor said. "I've read bits and pieces of it, here and there. I only bought it yesterday, to see what all the fuss was about. I still don't know. You read more than I do, and you keep up with all that stuff. I thought you might tell me what it means."

"It means that Mr. Harrigan was a gentleman of the right wing," Tibor said solemnly. "If you had brought me *Lies and the Lying Liars Who Tell Them*, I would have told you that it meant that Mr. Franken was a gentleman of the left wing, and also that he knows how to use pronouns correctly. It's a political book, Krekor. What's it supposed to mean?"

"I don't know," Gregor said. "If I knew the answers to things like that, I wouldn't be wishing I'd been in Los Angeles when this case came up. I think I should leave the country every time there's an election year. I mean it. People don't make any sense. They get angry at each other over things that don't make any sense. Everybody yells nonstop for months and in the end, where are you? Back where you started, with another election coming in a couple of years."

"Voting is an important obligation of citizenship," Tibor said gravely.

"Paying taxes is a more important obligation of citizenship, and I do that," Gregor said. "But I don't like this stuff. I don't like all the yelling. I don't like the business of making the other guy look like a cross between Lucifer and Hitler. And I especially don't like being told by the mayor of the city of Philadelphia that I'm a stealth contributor to John Jackman's primary campaign. I don't give money to candidates. I'm not that stupid."

Tibor shrugged. "It will get worked out, Krekor. The mayor can't be seen to be obstructing a police investigation into the murder of a famous man. It is murder, isn't it? They know that for sure?"

"Yes," Gregor said. "It definitely is murder. Poison was what the pathologist decided last night, and not very sophisticated poison. Straight arsenic, and lots of it. They found the bag with his personal things in it. There was a big bag of pills. They're analyzing those, now. I seem to be running into a lot of arsenic-laced pills lately. That's odd for a coincidence."

"It seems to me like a fairly sensible way to commit a murder," Tibor said. "Not that murder is ever sensible, you understand, but that lacing somebody's medication with arsenic is a sensible way to go about it if you can be sure that nobody else will take the pills. That was the case here?"

"Absolutely. Harrigan was a pill addict. Nobody else was going to get near his pills. The thing is, we almost didn't find him. He'd been in the morgue for two weeks without anybody knowing it was him, and the doctor who did the autopsy pulled the corpse out to work on thinking it was a homeless man who'd died at Our Lady of Mount Carmel out on Hardscrabble Road. If it wasn't for the situs inversus, it would have been weeks before we found the body, if ever. It would at least have been until he was supposed to reappear from rehab, which wouldn't be for another twenty-something days."

"Situs inversus," Tibor said. "The site is inverted?"

"It's a medical condition," Gregor said. "All your organs are on the wrong side and your intestines curve in the wrong direction. Your heart is on your right instead of your left, for instance. That's what the book title means. He made a big deal about it. His heart was on the right side, literally. On the right side of his chest. And that's how the pathologist figured it out, or rather suspected it. He opened up the body and the heart was on the right side, and he remembered the ads for Harrigan's program, which always mentioned the fact, and there we were. He called the police, told them what he had and what he suspected, and they ran a fingerprint check. Which was funny, really, because they'd run at least three other fingerprint checks on that body in as many days, and come up blank. Of course, it wasn't Drew Harrigan's fingerprints they were looking for. It was Sherman Markey's."

"And this is a case the mayor does not want you involved in?" Tibor said. "It sounds like just your kind of thing. It is complicated. It is absurd. It is making a lot of noise. It was on every news station last night, Krekor, and I did listen, but I must have missed the part about the situs inversus."

"Or maybe they never mentioned it. I don't know what the reporters know about how the body was found. The problem is, here is the body, and we don't begin to have any idea how it ended up where it ended up, and dead at the same time. The one thing that we went over and over and over yesterday was where it was found, and were they sure this was the particular body that had been found. And the answer is, yes, there's no question whatsoever. He died in the barn at Our Lady of Mount Carmel on the night of January twenty-seventh or the early morning of January twenty-eight. And the ambulance came out and got the body. It was tagged and filed in a morgue drawer. It's been there ever since. Which leaves us with a number of very interesting questions, starting with why a man like Drew Harrigan would pretend to be homeless and go sleep for the night in a barn full of homeless people. I mean, this isn't just some rich guy. This is a man who gave every indication of absolutely loathing homeless people. He called them crazy. He called them lazy bums. He said at one point that the police should round them all up, put them on a boat, and dump them on one of those islands they use for landfills."

"Oh, tcha," Tibor said. "There is no point in reading this man's book."

"No, do it, please. For me. Because I can't read it. And you've got to understand he was speaking on his radio program, and that program has an audience with a distinct ideological skew."

"Dumping the homeless in a landfill is not an ideological skew," Tibor said. "It's a sin. It is the essence of an anti-Christian perspective."

"Interestingly enough," Gregor said, "I don't think Harrigan had much to say about religion. Anyway. We have to figure out what he was doing in that barn, wearing Sherman Markey's hat or one exactly like it—"

"He had the hat of the man you were looking for?"

"Well," Gregor said, "don't get too worked up yet. It was a red wool watch cap. There are thousands of them for sale in the city. They cost maybe thirty dollars. It could just be a coincidence. But, for now, yes, he was wearing a hat identical to the one Sherman Markey was wearing the last time anybody remembers seeing him. And Sherman Markey is still missing. And Harrigan was supposed to be in rehab, but if he's been dead for two weeks, why hasn't the rehab place gotten in touch with the judge to report Harrigan AWOL? The more you try to think it through, the worse it gets, and the worse it gets, the more keeps landing on you. We all sat around last night in John's office—me, John, Rob Benedetti who's the district attorney, the two cops who had the original Harrigan drug bust—we all sat around talking about it, and the more we talked the more it sounded like an Agatha Christie novel. We were making timetables. It was insane."

"Timetables of what?"

"Of who had seen who where. The last time anybody had seen Drew Harrigan. The last time anybody had seen Sherman Markey. Hats. You name it. By the time we all got through at the morgue it was the middle of the night and nobody wanted to talk to us, including Neil Savage, Harrigan's attorney. And Judge Williamson isn't talking to anybody."

"There's a judge who is a suspect?"

"There's a judge who signed off on Harrigan's rehab, and what all of us want to know is what kind of paper he got to ensure that Harrigan was actually going into rehab and staying there. We all want to know a lot of things, but like I said, it was late, and we couldn't get anybody to talk to us, or they couldn't get anybody to talk to them, and then the mayor called and had a fit about me. This was at, oh, I don't know. Midnight. I hung around a little while longer and then came home. And I'm very tired, and very fed up, and I know I'm going to have to go out there today and listen to John and the mayor both blithering about the primary and the general election and the world going to hell in a handbasket, and all I want to do is take a couple of weeks in Bermuda. It's warm this time of year in Bermuda, isn't it?"

"Warmer than here," Tibor said.

Godiva nuzzled deeper into Tibor's lap, and Tibor petted her absently. Gregor thought that if Grace was away for long, she'd come back to find that dog so devoted to Tibor that she wouldn't want to come back home.

Gregor finished his coffee and checked his watch. If he had to get up in the middle of the night to work on something he wasn't even sure he was being hired to work on, everybody else should get up in the middle of the night to keep him company.

He wasn't sure that was the best policy for a politician to follow, but he felt himself justified in being smug that he was not now, and would not ever be, a politician.

3

At seven o'clock, Gregor was out on Cavanaugh Street, waiting for the cab he'd very carefully called for from Tibor's apartment. It shouldn't have been difficult to get a cab at this hour of the morning, but nothing ever worked the way it was supposed to, and he was taking no chances. Tibor came out to the street to wait beside him, since he had to go that way to get to the Ararat for breakfast anyway, and when the cab pulled up, they were discussing Bennis's book tour. Or not discussing it, as the case might be. Gregor found it difficult to understand why so many people had so much trouble talking about Bennis as if she were an ordinary human being, instead of this fantasy that had dropped out of heaven onto their heads and might go back there at any moment, for any reason.

"I think it is a matter of professional obligation," Tibor was saying as the cab was stopped at the light only two intersections away. "I think you arc wrong to believe that it has anything to do with you. I think that if Bennis were angry with you, she would tell you. Bennis is like that."

Gregor was about to say that he had no idea what Bennis was like, but the cab was suddenly there, pulling in so close to the cars parked at the curb that it threatened to scrape the paint from a green Volvo and a yellow Ford Escape. Gregor gave one small thought to who on Cavanaugh Street wanted to pay for the gas on an SUV when he was living in a city where the hills were few and the snow removal was good, and then got into the cab's backseat.

"Never in her life has Bennis ever made any sense to me," he told Tibor, through the still-open door, "and she doesn't make much sense to me now. All I know is, she's upset about something, she's been upset for months, she won't tell me what's going on, and now she's disappeared. And I don't care if you call it a book tour or a professional obligation, it's still a vanishing act. I'm too old for this, Tibor."

"You're never too old for love," Tibor said.

The problem was, this situation had nothing to do with love, and Gregor knew Tibor knew it. He slammed the door shut and told the driver to go down to John Jackman's office. Here was one early morning John wouldn't be spending at his campaign headquarters. The cab pulled out and down Cavanaugh Street far more quickly than it had advanced from the stoplight to pick Gregor up, and they were suddenly in a built-up section of the city, full of office buildings and hole-in-the-wall restaurants with plate glass windows. The sky was already light, with that sharp edge to it that meant the air was extremely cold.

The first thing Gregor caught sight of that his mind fixed on was a dispenser full of copies of the *Philadelphia Inquirer,* its headline glued to the Drew Harrigan story but properly vague, as it would have to be given the time limitations of going to press while the investigation was still stumbling around in confusion. The next thing he saw was a homeless woman wearing a thick bulky coat, stockings that fell down her legs, and bedroom slippers. It was the image of a moment, connected to nothing, indicative of nothing, and before he had really absorbed it the light changed and the cab shot off and away, onto other streets. Gregor found himself thinking of something the nun had said last night, while they had both been sitting in the police precinct's waiting room for the second time.

"The trick about the homeless problem," she said, "is getting anybody to realize there's a homeless problem at all. We notice homeless people when they scare us. When they don't scare us, it's as if they're ghosts. We look right through them. We don't see them at all."

The homeless person Gregor Demarkian was not seeing at the moment was Sherman Markey, and it made him very, very worried.

TWO

I

For Ellen Harrigan, the worst thing the night before had not been being taken to the morgue to look at the dead body. The worst part of yesterday had been coming back to the apartment and realizing she had no idea of what she was supposed to do. She tried to remember how her mother had been when her father died, but that didn't work. When Ellen's father had died, Ellen's mother had been immediately surrounded by Ellen's aunts on both sides of the family. Nearly a dozen women had crowded into their house and brought casseroles, cleaning buckets, Mass cards, and gossip. They had arranged for the funeral, catered the wake, and called Father Henfrey about having a novena said for the repose of Ellen's father's soul. Ellen had no idea who was going to do all that now. There would have to be a funeral, but Ellen didn't know how to arrange one, and didn't want to know. She didn't know if Drew should be buried from the Catholic Church or not. He never went to church unless he was out on the road touring, and then he went because his fans went, or lots of them did. It had been forever since Ellen went to church, too. You got away from things like that when you no longer lived where you were supposed to. She did still believe in God, because it was stupid not to, and the only people who didn't were liberals and secular humanists, who were even worse than liberals. Still, she couldn't just sit in the apartment day after day now that Drew was gone. She was going to have to do something.

She didn't know when she had decided that she ought to go into Drew's office, but as soon as she arrived at the office doors, she knew it had been the right thing to do. Drew's offices were on the fifteenth floor of a tall building in the center of the city, a self-contained suite with big double glass doors with the words DREW HARRIGAN: HEART ON THE RIGHT SIDE stenciled onto them. Ellen shuddered at the sight of them. She'd always hated that thing about Drew's organs being all on the wrong side of his body, and she still resented the fact that there was a right side for them to be on.

She pushed through the double doors and walked into the lobby. Nobody was at the receptionist's desk, but that made sense. It was far too early.

Her head hurt, just a little. Somebody had given her a sedative last night, but it hadn't put her to sleep. It hadn't done anything for her that she could tell. She was cold in this office, in a way she hadn't been outside, although it was freezing outside. She looked at the walls. They were covered with big, outsized pictures of Drew. They were posters for books and the radio show and the television show, which hadn't gone over too well.

She had no idea what she was going to do next—she had imagined herself walking in and meeting the receptionist, or something; maybe she had just imagined herself walking in to find the staff all assembled and ready to listen to her—but while she was working it out, Martha Iles came into view, realized she was there, and stopped.

"Ellen?"

Ellen Harrigan hated that voice. She truly hated it. It had everything in it she had learned to fear, early. Wellesley. Harvard and the Kennedy School of Government. Girls sitting at the front of the class in the desks right in front of the teacher's own, their hands always in the air. It mattered only a little that Martha was so plain she might as well have been a chipmunk.

"Ellen, what are you doing here?" she said.

"I've got a right to be here," Ellen said. "This was Drew's office. It's going to be mine, now. It's going to be mine because he's dead."

"Yes," Martha said, sounding exasperated. "We know he's dead, Ellen, it's been on the news all night. But we have work to do. Drew wasn't just a person, he was an enterprise, and dead or not we've got obligations we've got to fulfill."

Danielle Underwood came out from behind the partition that led to the offices in the back. She was prettier than Martha, and her accent wasn't anywhere near as awful, but Ellen knew that she was much the same. All these women were alike, really, all these women with careers, thinking they were better than everybody else, thinking they were special. Ellen took great satisfaction in remembering that these days, when you called somebody "special," you weren't talking about how bright they were.

It was hot in here now, hot-cold, hot-cold, hot-cold. Ellen unbuttoned her coat. "I don't think you should make decisions without talking to me," she said. "I'm going to be in charge here now. I don't want you doing things that are going to be blamed on Drew if I don't know about them first."

"But that's ridiculous," Martha said. "You have no idea what goes on in this office. You have no idea what it is we do. You can't give orders about something you know nothing about."

"I can give orders about something I own," Ellen said. "And I own this. Whatever it is, now that Drew isn't here."

"You don't own this yet," Martha said. "The will will have to be probated. In the meantime, I'm going to keep this office running the way it ought to be run, the way Drew wanted it run, the way I ran it for him. And if you don't like it, you can see the lawyers."

"Martha," Danielle said.

"Don't shush me," Martha said. "This is ridiculous. She

doesn't know the first thing about the work Drew was doing. She doesn't even know what he did besides be on the radio, and she only knows that because she's got her radio dial turned to his program. She's a walking clothes rack, that's all she is. He married her because she looks good in photographs."

Ellen smiled slightly. That might very well be true, at least up to a point. She thought Drew might also have married her because she made him feel comfortable. Unlike Martha, or Danielle, or the "right-wing blondes" who had taken over television lately, she didn't have that Seven Sisters–Ivy League accent, and she hadn't grown up taking summer vacations on Martha's Vineyard.

She suppressed a sudden, almost irresistible urge to tell Martha Iles exactly what Drew Harrigan liked to do in bed. She went all the way back to Drew's office, let herself in, and looked around. It was neat. There were no papers on the desk. There were photographs, mostly of her. She thought they should have had children. Then she changed her mind. To be left with children to bring up after their father had died young was not a good thing. She'd had an aunt that had happened to. Both the children had grown up wild, and one of them had landed in jail for shoplifting when she was only twenty-two.

Martha Iles was hovering at the office door. Danielle Underwood was hovering right behind her. Ellen went over to Drew's desk, pulled out the swivel chair, and sat down. It was an enormous desk, like the ones executives had in movies from the 1950s. Ellen hated movies from the 1950s. She hated movies from the 1940s, too. She hated all things from back in history. It was all too long ago, and the people never made any sense. She did like this desk, though. This desk made her feel invincible.

Martha Iles came a little farther into the room. "I don't know what you think you're doing," she said. "I don't know what you think you can accomplish. You can sit behind a desk, anybody can, but that doesn't mean you can do the work that comes across it."

"It means I can fire you," Ellen said.

"Not today, you can't," Martha said.

"Then I'll wait," Ellen said. "I'll call the lawyers this afternoon and we'll see what happens, won't we? No, I'll call them now, here, from the desk. I've got Neil Savage's home number. I'll bet I can get him over here right this minute. Don't you think so?"

"I think you've lost your mind," Martha said.

Ellen thought that this was something she hadn't considered. With Drew gone, she was both rich and powerful, if only powerful in this little sphere here, in the office. She could grow to like this, and when she had destroyed it, when she had fired them all and sold whatever needed to be sold and settled whatever needed to be settled, she could go back home and never have to worry about anything again. She knew that people were supposed to have a lot of trouble coming back home when they had been away for a long time, but that was because they became accustomed to the way things were done in the places they'd gone. Ellen had never been accustomed to any of it. She could slip back into life at home as easily as if she'd done nothing more radical than take a day shopping at Wal-Mart. She was even looking forward to shopping at Wal-Mart again.

Drew had wanted to live in this world, but Ellen had never understood why.

2

Sister Maria Beata of the Incarnation was having a bad morning. The only consolation for it was the fact that it wasn't her usual bad morning. There had been no reading from St. John of the Cross or, even as bad, St. Thérèse of Lisieux at refectory. She thought that if she had to hear all that treacly nonsense about the Bride and the Bridegroom one more time, she'd spit in the soup. The reading this morning had been from St. Teresa of Avila herself, and it had been deliberately bland and unconnected to "the world." The last thing Reverend Mother wanted was for her nuns to think too long and hard about what had happened to Drew Harrigan, of all people, in their own barn. They'd never been happy about letting people into that barn in the first place. Of course, they had said prayers at Mass this morning and at Office for the repose of Mr. Harrigan's soul, but they'd said those before, the night he died. They just hadn't known his name then. It wasn't the Mass or the Office that was bothering Beata, or the readings at refectory, or how crazy she sometimes got in the long silences that were the background music of all that went on in Carmel. She was not listening for the voice of God this morning, and she wasn't distressed at the fact that she wasn't hearing anything. It was still true that she might have made a mistake, coming here, but she didn't have time to think about it now. She knew in her bones that there were aspects to this situation Reverend Mother hadn't considered, and she wasn't looking forward to the fact that she was the only one here who would be able to warn her.

Sometimes, in periods of enormous stress, she thought about the life she had had before coming to Carmel, and about the fact that Reverend Mother had been reluctant to receive her because of it. In the long months when she was discussing her vocation through the grille a couple of times a week, she had sometimes thought that she would have had an easier time being accepted if she'd been a drug addict and felon instead of Susan Titus Alderman, graduate of Bryn Mawr and the Yale Law School, Rhodes Scholar, Harkness Distinguished Fellow in History.

"It's not the intelligence," Reverend Mother had said, when she first came to Carmel. "The intelligence is an asset. It's the ambition. You're a very ambitious woman."

"I don't think I am," Beata had said at the time, and by now she had decided that she had been telling the truth. She had not been ambitious. The constant struggle had made her tired and annoyed, even though she engaged in it and even though she was good at it. She looked back on all of that as a kind of delirium, implanted in her by a father for whom competition was an end in itself. You played to win no matter what you played. You made sure always to be among the first in any group you might enter. If she had joined a street gang, she would have been the leader of it in six months flat. As it was, she was president of her class twice during her years at Exeter, head of the yearbook committee, star of the Branch-Soule Debating Society, most active member of the Broadside. She was the kind of student schools featured in their recruiting catalogues and highlighted in their alumni newsletters. She was organized, efficient, intelligent, and relentless. And by the time she came to Carmel, she was sick of the whole thing.

No, she thought again, it wasn't the ambition that was the problem. It was the alienation she felt at the way so many of the men and women who had built this order saw God. She did not want to experience an ecstatic union, not even on St. Teresa's terms, and St. Teresa was as levelheaded as they came. She didn't want to be a Bride to anybody's Bridegroom, not even when the Bridegroom was Jesus Christ himself. The imagery alone made something deep inside her shut right off. It seemed to her that it ought to be possible to approach God as a mind instead of a heart, to approach Him in the clear light of the reasoning He'd endowed human beings with to begin with. Maybe she should have been a Benedictine, or a Dominican. If the Jesuits had admitted women, they might have been her best bet.

This morning, her best bet would be to ditch her habit and escape the monastery, but she knew she wouldn't do that, and not only because she didn't want to leave, unhappy as she was at times lately. Along with the need to win, her father had implanted in her the need to take responsibility, so here she was.

Here Reverend Mother was, too, pacing back and forth in front of her desk. Beata came in and bowed as she had been taught to do. Everything at this Carmel was elaborately formal. It was the kind of thing you couldn't know about a cloister until you were already inside it.

"I'm sorry for your loss, Reverend Mother."

"What?" Reverend Mother said. "Oh, you mean Drew. I suppose I should feel loss, but I don't. I'd like to think that was because I was being perfected in my vocation. We're supposed to be detached from the people and things we knew in the world. But it isn't that. Drew and I never really got along very well. We haven't spoken much in years."

"Yes, Reverend Mother. It's still a loss, though, isn't it? I'm sorry to be so obtuse, but I don't have any brothers or sisters."

"I had only Drew. We weren't even close as children. Never mind. You wanted to see me? Immaculata is getting a little mulish about the amount of time you're spending away from the desk. And yes, I know it's hardly your fault, but she is what she is."

Beata let that go. Immaculata most certainly was what she was, and what she was was a woman who had entered the convent because she'd had no other place to go. Beata had known nuns like that growing up—well, all right, religious sisters—and the breed always made her nervous. There was an undertone of anger and resentment in them that could break out at any time.

Reverend Mother motioned to the chair. Beata sat down. "I'm sorry to bother you," Beata said, "but it occurred to me that nobody may have told you what's coming. And you'd have no reason to know. So I thought I'd better warn you."

"About what? Do you mean what's coming about Drew?"

"Yes, Reverend Mother. I know you don't listen to the television very often, but you must have heard by now that the police are treating this as a case of murder. And that's going to mean certain things."

"I suppose it will," Reverend Mother said. "Do you mean you think they'll treat me as a suspect? Because he was my brother, I mean, and he died in the barn."

"There's that, yes," Beata said, "but it really isn't the most difficult thing. I doubt if they'll seriously consider you a suspect. You had no reason to murder him, not even in regard to the property, because the property will still be held in escrow even with your brother gone. I will say, though, that they're going to have a fit—"

"—Sister."

"Sorry, Reverend Mother, but there's almost no other word for it. They're going to be very upset when they find out about the property and your connection to Drew, and they're going to want to know why I didn't say anything about either last night. And we can't very well say I didn't know, because I saw Neil Savage on behalf of the convent just a couple of weeks ago."

"They'll think we're hiding something," Reverend Mother said.

"I doubt it, Reverend Mother, although they'll say they do. The thing is, they're going to want to search the monastery."

"You mean search the barn?"

"No, Reverend Mother, I mean search the monastery. The whole thing. Including the enclosure."

"But they can't search the enclosure," Reverend Mother said. "Lay people aren't allowed in the enclosure."

"I wouldn't really want to be the one who tried to sell that to a judge in Philadelphia at the moment," Beata said. "Reverend Mother, you've got to understand that everybody is going to be acting under constraint. There was just a huge priest pedophilia scandal in this city, not that long ago. The police department and the mayor's office both got hit with accusations that they'd given the Catholic Church special treatment and that as a result of that, many more children were harmed than would have been otherwise. They can't be seen to be giving us special treatment in this case."

"But we're not talking about special treatment," Reverend Mother said. "Drew wasn't killed in the monastery, he was killed in the barn. The barn is out there. There's a big wall around the monastery and the barn is on the other side of it."

"So is the monastery's front door," Beata said. "You must

realize that police procedure would demand they search the premises here, all of them, if this wasn't a monastery. There'd be no question, and no trouble getting a judge to sign the warrant. And you have to understand that the Cardinal isn't likely to be much help. He was brought in here to fix things after the scandal. He's not going to want to cause another scandal by insisting that the monastery enclosure not be violated."

"But the police make exceptions for religion all the time," Reverend Mother said. "I mean, well, think of it—"

"Here's a reason to watch the news more often, Reverend Mother. The last district attorney wanted to end the practice of excusing priests from testifying to what they'd heard in confession. It's a new world out there. At the very least, they're going to have to insist on searching your office and your cell, because you will be a suspect. In the end, they're going to have to insist on searching everything. There's no way around it. If you did kill your brother—"

"Sister."

"If you did, you could have hidden any number of things in this building, anywhere in it. You have free run of the place. You've got more than that. You've got control of the place. You could have concealed pills, poison, anything, anywhere around here."

"Did they say where they thought I'd have gotten the poison in the first place?"

"They didn't say anything about you and poison. I'm just telling you the way they're going to think. And the poison they were talking about yesterday was arsenic. It's easy enough to get. It's what's in rat poison. I think we have dozens of boxes of the stuff in the cellar."

"I don't think we have dozens of boxes of anything in the cellar," Reverend Mother said, "but I take your point. You do realize what this means, don't you? They'll break the enclosure. The monastery will have to be reconsecrated."

"It can be done."

"Oh, of course it can," Reverend Mother said, "but it's

an enormous problem. And then, what about the nuns? We'll have to send them off someplace, or their own vows will—"

"No," Beata said. "I don't think so. It will look like—"

"You must be joking."

"I'm not," Beata said. "It will look like you're sending them away for a reason, because one of them knows something, or because one of them is the murderer. I'm sorry, Reverend Mother, but we're just going to have to put up with it. It won't be for long, and I doubt if anybody will be required to testify at the trial, if there is one, except me, since I was the one who saw the body and called the ambulance. I know it's a problem, and a pain in the neck. And we can certainly talk to the Cardinal and see if he's willing to mount a rearguard action. But in the long run, he'll lose, and you'll look guilty. I think it's better just to get it over with."

Reverend Mother licked her lips. "You said there was an old district attorney. Does that mean there's a new one now?"

"That's right. The other one died suddenly, and this one was appointed."

"Is this one . . . friendly to the Catholic Church?"

"I don't know," Beata said. "He isn't somebody I knew when I was practicing law. He's got an Italian name. He might have been brought up Catholic."

"Which could be good or bad," Reverend Mother said. "I don't know. I'd better call the Cardinal this morning, I suppose, and talk it out with him. He's going to do that thing where he doesn't shout, but it's worse."

"I know," Beata said.

What she didn't say was that if the new district attorney was an anti-Catholic fanatic, the Reverend Mother could find herself arrested, and it wouldn't matter at all that there wasn't going to be evidence enough to bring her to trial. It was the kind of thing she should have been thinking yesterday, when she didn't come forward with the information that the convent was intimately connected to Drew Harrigan and all his works, and not just because he'd died in the barn.

It was the kind of thing she would have thought of automatically if she had still been practicing law, and it bothered her that she hadn't thought of it when it really mattered.

THREE

I

John Jackman's office was not really a neutral venue, although that was what he had declared it was when he decided, the night before, that they would all meet there in the morning. Gregor didn't really blame him. John was brilliant and young and African-American in a city and state where being all three could propel him into the Governor's Mansion, someday, and Gregor thought he wanted to get there sooner rather than later. After that, he probably wanted to install himself in the White House, although Gregor tried not to think about that. He could hate politics all he wanted, but he knew that if John ever ran for governor, or president, he'd be doing some speeches in front of the kind of crowd that looked on A&E true crime specials the way other people looked at the front page of the newspaper. At the moment, John wanted to install himself in the mayor's office, and to do that he had to be perceived as a man who could handle all the crime the city of Philadelphia threw up. He didn't need a high-profile celebrity murder case in the headlines every day for weeks, or even months. He didn't need the perception that he was unable to stand up to rich people when they got in trouble; but that perception was inevitable in cases like this one, because rich people had good lawyers who knew the rules of the game. He especially didn't need to give the present mayor an opportunity to complain about him on the six o'clock news. He now had all these things, and with them the memory of the fact that he had been a first-rate homicide detective. He was on a tear.

He could have used being married, though, Gregor thought, getting out of his cab in front of John's building. Just up the block, Rob Benedetti was getting out of another cab, looking very unhappy. Gregor decided that he wouldn't say anything to John about being married, because John would scream and yell, and because the worst of what could be done to him politically probably wouldn't be given his reputation. Gregor had a hard time imagining anybody convincing the general public that John Henry Newman Jackman was gay. There was another thought that made Gregor wish he never had to think about politics again. It was only in election years that he remembered that a good chunk of his fellow citizens wouldn't vote for someone who happened to be gay, and a bigger chunk wouldn't vote for someone who didn't believe in God, and a yet bigger chunk than that wouldn't vote for someone who used four-letter Anglo-Saxon words, even on occasion. Of course, all politicians did that last thing, so it was just a question of never getting caught at it in public, but still. Or maybe because. It didn't matter. He didn't think this was what the founders had envisaged when they established a nation where citizens could vote.

"Mind their own business," he said, out loud, into the cold air, and Rob Benedetti, coming up the block to join him, blinked.

"What was that?"

"Nothing," Gregor said. "I was just thinking out loud. Do you like politics?"

"Like them? I don't know. I suppose I do. I'm running for district attorney."

"Wouldn't you rather be appointed district attorney?"

"We don't appoint district attorneys in Philadelphia," Rob Benedetti said. "We elect them. Except in circumstances like mine, you know, where a DA has to leave and there's a few months before the next election. Are you all right?"

Gregor was fine. "I just wish it were next year instead of this one," he said, "when nobody is running for anything."

"Somebody is always running for something in Philadelphia," Rob Benedetti said. "We have elections for something pretty much every year."

"Not elections I hear about," Gregor said. "That would be enough."

There was a security guard waiting at the door of the building, sitting on a folding chair and reading the sports pages. He dropped the paper as Gregor and Rob Benedetti came up, recognized Rob immediately, and opened up.

"Sorry," he said. "We've got a bomb threat. And there's a huge fire down on Curzon Street."

"You've got the building locked up because there's a fire on Curzon Street?" Gregor asked. "That's a mile away from here."

"It's making everybody jumpy," the guard said. "It's the homeless people, you know what I mean? Some of them started a fire in a waste bin out behind an abandoned building and the building caught fire, and now half the block has gone up. I'm surprised you didn't hear the sirens, even if you weren't exactly close. I heard the sirens when I was coming in this morning."

"I heard sirens about an hour and a half ago," Rob Benedetti said. "I didn't think anything of it. There are always sirens in town."

"There's another thing," Gregor said, as they moved off toward the elevators. "Homeless people. There's a problem, it's a real one. What to do about the homeless people. Some of them you can give homes to, but some of them you can't. They won't go to homes. They're mentally ill, or they're addicted to drugs or alcohol, and they just won't go. But they're around. They starve and they freeze to death. They get sick and spread their sicknesses. They upset pedestrians and tourists. You'd think there would be something that could be done for them, for them, not to them, and I've never yet heard a politician in this city even mention them. Not even once."

"I have," Rob Benedetti said. "Old Ellery Dreen used to go on about them all the time. Round 'em up and put 'em in workhouses or send them to jail. Whatever."

"Ellery Dreen wasn't a serious politician," Gregor said, "and I didn't say do something to them, I said do something *for* them. John isn't talking about homeless people in his campaign. I know because I've read his stuff. The mayor isn't talking about them. But they're out there, and we've got the worst cold we've seen in thirty years, and they're freezing to death, or causing fires, which could kill firefighters, and here we are. That's what's wrong with politics, you see. They yell at each other about family values and gay rights and whether you approve of teaching evolution in the public schools, but nobody talks about anything that's actually happening that it would make sense for a government to do something about. And then everybody gets angry, and calls each other the spawn of Satan, and the whole process becomes nothing but a way for people who were already very angry to begin with to be angry in public."

"I don't think I've ever called anybody the spawn of Satan," Rob Benedetti said, amused.

"Metaphorically," Gregor said morosely. The elevator was here. The doors slid open. He and Rob Benedetti got on it and watched the doors close in their faces. Gregor wondered why people did that, so automatically—got on the elevator, turned to face the doors. He thought he was either going insane or in need of about forty continuous hours of sleep.

The elevator reached their floor, stopped with a bump, shuddered, and then sank a little. Gregor tried to put the image of them plunging several stories to the basement right out of his head. The doors opened. He didn't dash for the solidity of the floor.

"You might consider," Rob Benedetti said, "the possibility that they're angry all the time. It isn't just politics that makes them angry. They're just angry."

"At what?"

"I don't know," Rob Benedetti said. "I haven't got that far. But I've been thinking about it. I've thought about it a lot. Because I think it's true. Not everybody, you know, but a lot of people are just plain angry. All the time. I don't think they know what they're angry about themselves. Sometimes I think they're just disappointed about the way their lives turned out, as if they were owed something better, but they don't know what. I'm probably not making a lot of sense."

"I'm going to kill that woman," John Jackman said. "I'm going to kill both those women and then I'm going to shit on a shingle."

The voice floated out over the heads, down the corridor, into the air. John was in his office. They couldn't see him.

"When John swears," Rob Benedetti said, "the world must be coming to an end. I guess we ought to go down and see what he's doing."

2

What John Jackman was doing was pacing around his desk, around and around, as if he was circling it the way a bird of prey circled an object of his desire. Olivia Hall was standing just inside the door, her arms folded across her chest, looking like she wasn't having any.

"If you're going to cuss, I'm going to go sit at my desk," she said. "If you're going to blaspheme, I'm going to go home."

"I apologized. Didn't I? I apologized."

"You apologized for swearing," Olivia Hall said. "You didn't apologize for threatening to kill a couple of nuns."

"Oh for Christ's sake."

"Home," Olivia said.

"I'm sorry," John Jackman said. "And I didn't mean I was going to actually kill the nuns. It was an expression. And I've got reason to be upset, Olivia, I do. I've got reason."

"I didn't say you didn't have reason," she said.

"What's going on?" Gregor said.

"I'll let you and these two gentlemen talk," Olivia said. "I'll send the officers in as soon as they get here. You calm down, John. Lose your temper, lose the argument."

"This isn't an argument. This is a murder investigation."

"You're not going to win any murder investigation swearing and taking the Lord's name in vain," Olivia said. "I'll be right outside, getting some real work done."

She left the room and closed the door behind her. All three of the men stared at the closed door as if they expected it to open again, revealing Olivia with wings. Then John Jackman coughed, and that broke the spell.

"Remarkable woman," he said, sitting down behind his desk. "I don't even know if she's going to vote for me in the primary, never mind in November. I don't even know if she's a member of a political party. But I'll bet she votes."

Gregor didn't want to get back on the subject of voting, or politics. He paced around the room as if he had never been in it before. John didn't go in for a lot of extraneous decoration. The walls had his degrees on them, and the awards he'd won, and a picture of him with President Bill Clinton, at the start of some federal anticrime initiative.

"So," Gregor said. "What made you start making death threats against nuns?"

"We got a call this morning," John said. "That nun from yesterday, what's her name—"

"Sister Maria Beata," Benedetti said.

"That sounds right," John said. "Anyway, she walked back into the precinct house this morning and explained, calm as you please, that there was something she hadn't mentioned yesterday, and that's that the Mother Superior of this convent is—"

"Abbess of this monastery," Gregor corrected.

John looked at the ceiling. "I don't have time for this. I really don't have time for this. The Abbess of this monastery happens to be Drew Harrigan's sister."

Rob Benedetti sat up a little straighter. "Really?"

John blew a raspberry. "Do you honestly think I'd be making this up? Things aren't bad enough, I now have nuns for suspects. Half the Catholics in the city already hate us for the way we prosecuted the pedophilia cases—no, that's not true. All the Catholics do. Half of them think we didn't do enough and half of them think we did too much. And now I've got nuns, and you know as well as I do that by the end of business we're going to have editorials and television pundits screaming that we let them get away because we're too deferential to the Catholic Church, and the Catholic press is going to be screaming that we have no respect for freedom of religion, and the whole thing is going to end up as a *Lifetime* movie."

"Calm down," Gregor said. "It's not enough that the Abbess is Harrigan's sister. She'd have to have a motive for killing him. Did she have one?"

"I don't know," John said. "We've got an appointment to go out there this morning as soon as Marbury and Giametti show up, and you can ask her then. I won't be able to go along, of course. It's not my job. But the three of you can handle it and report back. And I have a terrible feeling that the answer is going to be yes."

"Why?" Rob Benedetti asked.

"Because," John Jackman said. "Because. And don't tell me hunches are crap, because I don't believe that. If it turns out a nun actually killed Drew Harrigan, this really is going to be a *Lifetime* movie."

"If it turns out a nun really killed Drew Harrigan," Gregor said, "this is going to be a major production with Julia Roberts in the starring role. Before you send me out to interrogate somebody, don't you think we ought to clarify my position with the mayor's office? He was threatening to arrest me last night."

"He isn't going to arrest you," John said. "He was just saying that for the television cameras."

"You'll come say that to the judge if I end up in jail on obstruction charges," Gregor said.

"Don't worry about obstruction charges," Rob Benedetti

said. "I'm the one gets to decide whether anybody hits you with obstruction charges or not, and I'm not going to charge you."

"You may not be here after November," Gregor said.

There was a lot of noise from outside. The door swung open, and Olivia Hall walked in, looking both dignified and disapproving. "The detectives are here," she said.

A moment later, Marbury and Giametti came in, holding their coats over their arms and looking as if they would do anything, anything at all, not to have this woman looking at them anymore. They waited, standing, while Olivia took another look around the room. They didn't relax until she was gone and the door had been shut behind her.

"That was scary," Dane Marbury said. "That's always scary. I think that woman could control a prison without bothering to resort to weapons."

"Never mind that," John Jackman said. "Did you do what I asked you to do? Did you find anything."

"Absolutely," Giametti said. He reached into the pocket of his trousers and came up with a small, folded piece of paper: "334, 335, and 336 Albemarle Street. Those are lots, one of them vacant, the other two with abandoned buildings on them. They're not in a great location, but they're not in an absolutely impossible one, either. Drew Harrigan deeded them to Our Lady of Mount Carmel Monastery after Sherman Markey filed his lawsuit for defamation. After, the timing is important. On January twenty-fifth, two days before the last time anybody saw Harrigan alive, the Justice Project went into court on behalf of Markey and had the properties liened so that the monastery couldn't sell them, which it thought it needed to do because the monastery looked like it was going to sell them, since it had found a buyer."

"You got all these people out of bed?" John said. "I'm impressed."

"We didn't need to get them out of bed," Dane Marbury said. "We did a Google search and found some back stuff in the *Inquirer*. I don't know how accurate it all is, but we can recheck when we question. The thing that got us, though, was the timing."

"Right," Giametti said. "Harrigan deeded the property *after* the Justice Project filed their defamation suit."

"Which means he did it after he'd already gone into rehab," Marbury said. "Where supposedly he couldn't get in touch with anybody, because he was in a total immersion, absolute isolation program for sixty days."

Jackman looked carefully from one to the other of them. "Was that even possible?"

Gregor stirred. "It depends," he said. "The best guess is that Harrigan was never in rehab at all, but if that's the case, there has to be some collusion on the part of the judge. That's Williamson?"

"Yeah," Marbury said.

"Okay," Gregor said. "That's not impossible. The other possibility is that Harrigan's lawyer has power of attorney and did this under his own steam. But the attorney is Neil Savage, right? One of the more conservative attorneys in the city, conservative in the sense of not liking to go in for legal oddities. So I can't see him deciding on his own to deed the property over to the nuns in order to shield it from the defamation suit, but I can't see Harrigan having made provision for what to do in the case of a defamation suit, since they're not automatic or even usual. Never mind the fact that Sherman Markey, being a homeless man without any assets, probably didn't look like somebody who was going to end up with heavyweight legal representation."

"Boy, they got that wrong," Giametti said.

"Yes," Gregor said. "Well, there's also one more possibility, although it's not the one you want to hear."

"You don't even have to mention it," John said. "It could be a put-up job. The nuns could have colluded with Drew Harrigan to shield the property, the sale could be some kind of legal maneuver to return the property to Harrigan himself in a way that Markey couldn't touch it, we could be looking at financial fraud charges as well as murder charges, and the entire Catholic population of Philadelphia could end up waiting in the street for me so they can beat me up. I don't care what Olivia says. I really am going to kill those nuns."

"I don't think you have to go that far just yet," Gregor said. "I'd guess the collusion scenario is unlikely. They could have a good explanation for all of this."

"So go and ask them about it," John said. "They're the ones who had the body. Ask them about that, too."

3

If it had been up to Gregor, they wouldn't have all taken one car. He understood that Hardscrabble Road was on the edge of the city, and that it might be difficult to find a cab that wanted to go there, but that inconvenience would be more than made up for by the fact that, with separate cars, any of them could leave at any time. He didn't know why, but he had an urgent need to be able to walk out on this at will. The only consolation he had for the fact that that would not be possible was the further fact that he would not be required to sit in the backseat of a squad car again. Knowing that they would be shepherding both the district attorney and the Armenian-American Hercule Poirot, Marbury and Giametti had acquired an "unmarked," meaning a car not painted to look like a police car, but otherwise so ridiculously stolid and neutral nobody but a cop would have been willing to drive it. This one was tan, with tan seats. It was some kind of sedan, and so boxy and slow-looking it could have used a pair of really big tail fins. Gregor thought he would always be disappointed that he had missed the fad for tail fins in cars. He would have bought a car like that, if one had been available to drive. He would have let Bennis drive it, since he almost never drove himself, and when he tried he tended to drive into things.

Why had Drew Harrigan been in a barn full of homeless men at a cloistered monastery at the edge of the city? Even assuming he needed to get around without being recognized, the barn seemed like an extraneous detail—an exaggerated gesture that didn't look as if it was necessary for anything. Gregor Demarkian did not believe in murderers who did elaborate things for the sake of doing elaborate things, or of being clever. Murderers were not clever. Most of them were barely even conscious. They got liquored up and started a fight in a bar. They got high on speed or cocaine and started imagining that the neighbor was sending his cat over to poison their supply of beer. They got fired or blew a tire or lost some money on the races and then just lost it themselves. The ones who tried to be clever were the least clever of all. They always forgot things. Most of all, they forgot that the detective story cliché that said all cops were stupid was just that, a cliché, and not reality.

"Are you okay?" Rob Benedetti asked him, as they began to move into an area of small, triple-decker houses.

"I was thinking about Charles Stuart."

"Who's Charles Stuart?"

"It was a murder case in Boston a few years ago," Gregor said. "This guy was driving through a poor neighborhood with his wife when he stopped at a stoplight or something. I don't remember why they stopped. But then, according to him, they were attacked by a large black guy, armed. Then they were kidnapped and driven to Mission Hill by force. The guy killed the wife and shot Stuart himself in the stomach."

"Ack," Marbury said. "I remember that one. It wasn't a black guy, right? It was—"

"Stuart himself," Gregor said. "Yes, exactly. Stuart killed his wife and shot himself in the stomach so that he could claim they were attacked. Which was pretty interesting, since most murderers wouldn't take a chance like that. He could have killed himself."

"Maybe he just didn't realize how dangerous it was to do what he was doing to himself," Rob Benedetti said. "I mean, most of these guys aren't rocket scientists."

"No, they're not," Gregor said, "and he probably wasn't either, although he was a successful man. He wasn't entirely stupid. But the reason that I was thinking about it was that the answer was the simplest one. Wife is dead, husband killed her. That's the way it works ninety-nine percent of the time. The simplest explanation is usually the right one."

"Occam's razor," Giametti said solemnly.

"Try applying Occam's razor in this case," Gregor said. "What was Drew Harrigan doing in a barn full of homeless men on the edge of the city—I mean, *look* at this route; it's not like we're right next door to the Liberty Bell—what was he doing there? Do you know what the simplest explanation is?"

"That he went there to visit his sister for some reason," Rob Benedetti said.

"Exactly," Gregor said. "And that he was dressed as a homeless person and pretending to be one so that he didn't get spotted, because, let's face it, he's an unusual-looking person. Was. Big and fat and florid. Got his picture on a million things, including a book that's in the stores now. That's the simplest explanation here, except for one thing."

"What's that?" Marbury asked.

"Why bother with the barn?" Gregor said. "If he wanted to see his sister, why didn't he just go right up to the monastery and ask to see her? Under most circumstances, the simplest explanation would be that he didn't want anyone to know he was seeing her, but that doesn't make sense, either. He's dressed as a homeless person. Nobody is going to know it's him to begin with. He doesn't gain anything by sleeping in the barn, assuming that's what he was doing. Turn it around. Maybe it was the Reverend Mother who insisted on the barn. Maybe she's the one who didn't want to be seen talking to her brother, or even to a homeless man. But there's no reason for that, either. She's his sister. Why shouldn't she talk to him? Especially since he's in trouble and she's a nun."

"Do you really think it's going to turn out to be something like this, something this simple?" Rob Benedetti asked. "Do you really think we're going to end up arresting a nun?"

"I don't know," Gregor said.

"We'd like to avoid it," Rob Benedetti said. "Not because we're soft on the Catholic Church, but because it's always bad news when we arrest a little old lady. A little old lady in a habit is going to be worse."

"And they're going to be really impressive habits," Giametti said. "I didn't think nuns wore habits like that anymore, all the way down to the floor."

"The nuns on EWTN do," Marbury said.

They were getting farther and farther out now, into the areas Gregor had already decided weren't really in the state of Pennsylvania at all. They could have been anywhere, the remnants of an industrial city that had long since lost both its industry and its claim to civilization.

"Every once in a while," he said, "you do get cases where the simplest explanation isn't the right one, but when you do, it's almost always because there's a perpetrator in the picture who feels the need to star in his own movie. Somebody who has to devise patterns, make plots, see the world as a functioning whole without a single element out of place. And that's worrisome."

"Because they tend to get away with it?" Rob Benedetti said.

"Oh, no," Gregor said. "They're the last kind of murderer to get away with it. The ones who get away with it are the ones who act on impulse and just disappear. That was the whole point of Murder Incorporated. It's hard to catch a murderer who just walks up, gets it over with, and has no other connection to the victim. No, what's worrisome about the murderer who does the not-simplest thing is that he, or she, is almost always a fanatic."

FOUR

I

Where were you on the night of January 27? That was the basis of a play Marla Hildebrande had read when she was in high school, and now it struck her as odd, that she was sitting here in her office trying her best to answer it. The play was by Ayn Rand, she was sure. She'd read it during her only period of "political engagement," except that nobody is ever really politically engaged with Ayn Rand, except maybe Alan Greenspan. If politics was something like Ayn Rand envisaged it, Marla could get herself interested in it. It wasn't the particulars of Randian politics that had intrigued her, though, it was the tone. High moral drama, intensely personal statements of commitment and conviction, conspicuous heroism conspicuously observed—it would be like being in the kind of movie whose television ads involved a lot of trumpets. When she wasn't happy being what she was, Marla could see herself starring in one of those, something with Russell Crowe in it, and boats, something with an execution scene at the end, so that she could brave death and give a speech in the most affecting possible circumstances. Anne Boleyn. Sir Thomas More. Mary, Queen of Scots. Marla could see herself playing all of them on the scaffold, as long as she didn't have to be on a scaffold herself.

She was going insane. That was the problem. She had been sitting in the office since seven, and not one single practical thing was done. The network wasn't going to run itself. The contracts weren't going to get signed. The talk show hosts and disc jockeys weren't going to get monitored—and you had to monitor them. The network ran mostly conservatives, so there wasn't usually a problem with the FCC on obscenity, but there was always the danger that one of these guys would commit slander on the air or challenge a sitting United States general to a duel at high noon. That would be funny, except that a guy named Charlie Little had done it once, and the general in question had shown up at the studio loaded for bear. Frank was probably right. The general probably wouldn't have done anything. It would have ruined his career. Still.

In the end, Marla always did come back to liking herself as she was. There was a lot of satisfaction in it. She wasn't a Genius, so she didn't have to prove her depth and originality at every moment. She wasn't a Creative, so she didn't have to show her disdain for society by wearing silly clothes and swearing a lot. She wasn't a Titan of the Industry, so she didn't have to win every battle she fought and only be seen in cars that cost more than most people made in the course of two years. She wasn't beautiful, so she didn't have to rush around to plastic surgeons to stem the tide of time with Botox and lifts. She had nothing to prove, and that made it far easier to do her work, do it well, and stay employed.

Even in high school, when everybody had been working so hard to be cool and popular, she had known better than to try to be either. If you just went your way, if you just did what you were supposed to do when you were supposed to do it—well, then, everything would be all right. You would get where you were going. You would have what you wanted. You would be who you wanted to be in the end.

The problem was, she didn't remember what she had been doing on the night of January 27. The chances were good that she had been here, talking to Frank about something, but she didn't actually know if she had, or what they'd been talking about. And the police would ask. She knew they would. They would look into her life, too, and although they would find nothing there, nothing she had to be ashamed of, nothing that could be construed as damaging—well, they might not find anything like that, but they were bound to search the building. They were bound to check into the fires she had put out over the years. They were bound to do a lot of things. It wasn't as easy as it seemed it ought to be to display your innocence in a murder investigation.

She got up, went over to her filing cabinet, and then remembered she needed her key. The computer was supposed to usher in the new paperless office and make furniture like the filing cabinet completely obsolete, but Marla didn't know any large office anywhere without a few of these cabinets. She wondered what other people kept in them. She kept files, but then the cabinets had been built to hold files.

She got the key out of her purse and the top drawer of the cabinet opened up. She took out the entire stack of folders inside. They were ordinary manila folders, legal sized, color-coded with stick-on tabs. One of them held the documentation in a hit-and-run case in Palm Harbor, Florida. Fortunately, the kid who'd been hit hadn't died, and hadn't been permanently injured. He'd just been thrown from his bike and stuck in the hospital for six weeks in traction, because he broke both his legs and his collarbone in the fall. One of them held the documentation in a shoplifting case in Fort Wayne, Indiana. That one had been a little stickier. There were photographs of three gold cigarette lighters, two Rolex diamond watches, and a woman's turquoise and onyx necklace making their way into pockets and out the door. Marla couldn't remember how many times she had told her people only to shop in the very best stores. If they were overtaken by a fit of kleptomania in a place like that, well, the store would be used to it, and used to covering it up. One of them held the documentation in a stalking case in Enid, Oklahoma. That had been the easiest of them all, because it had just been a question of transferring the idiot out of Oklahoma to somewhere he wouldn't have access to the girl, which meant Portland, Maine. There hadn't been another girl, for which Marla was grateful. She was less grateful that the girl in Enid, Oklahoma, had been fifteen years old, and that the disc jockey in question had been arrested for the third and definitive time when he'd gotten himself completely tanked on Stolichnaya, stripped to the skin, and stationed himself in her backyard beneath her bedroom window. When the police picked him up, he'd been baying at the moon, or something.

There were always things like this. They happened. Radio was an odd medium. It was full of people who had little or no self-control. She was expected to deal with the emergencies and put out the fires. She did it.

The folder that really worried her was the one with the red label on it, red for deal with this now, this is an emergency. She pulled it closer to her and opened it. Yes, all right, there were the drug incidents, dozens of drug incidents. Ever since Drew was arrested, the papers had been full of shocked editorials and even more shocked quotes from friends. Nobody had suspected. He'd managed to get away with it for so long. All that was bullshit, and Marla didn't mind using the word that fit. Anybody who didn't know Drew Harrigan had a drug problem didn't know Drew Harrigan. Anybody who thought that Drew Harrigan was successfully hiding the drug problem he had wasn't on the inside of Drew Harrigan's operation, or on any of the police forces in the Philadelphia ADI. Drew not only got out of control, he traveled. He drove everywhere. Marla had begun to truly hate that damned Mercedes car, because before Drew had it he had been more than satisfied with being driven around.

By the end, it was only Ellen who was being driven around. Drew was out on the road and out on his own. He liked to stop into places and see if people recognized him, too, and being who he was, being Drew and not NPR, that meant going into the kind of bars with neon signs in their windows advertising Miller beer. If there was one thing Marla had told her people more often than she'd told them only to shoplift in the very best stores, it was to stay out of places where men got drunk on the cheap. There was always some guy who'd decide he hated you just for the sake of giving himself an excuse to beat you up. There was always a bartender with a hot line straight to the local police station. There was always a guy hiding out in a booth in the back who wanted nothing more than to get the *National Enquirer* a tip they would use on their front page. These were not the incidents Marla was most proud of, because these were not the incidents she had been able to cover up completely. Drew had landed on the cover of the *Enquirer* on and off. He told people, on the radio and off, that it was a form of persecution. He was just an innocent bystander, dropping into a place for a beer, and this is what the liberals did to him.

Marla always thought that if liberals ever attacked Drew Harrigan, he wouldn't know what to do about it. They'd beat on him with copies of the collected works of John Dewey, and he'd be reduced to calling in the cops the way he'd once been reduced to calling in the teachers when the bigger kids at school took his lunch money and locked him into his locker.

Marla wondered how much of Drew Harrigan could be explained by the fact that he'd spent grade school as a fat, soft, cringing victim of a little kid, and that by the time he got to be six feet four and four hundred pounds, it was too late to do in the kids he still hated for making his life miserable.

The interesting pieces of paper in this folder did not have to do with Drew's transgressions per se. Transgressions were part of the game. The interesting pieces of paper in this folder had to do with bribes. That wasn't what they called them. Neither Drew nor Frank would have said they were bribing half the police departments in Pennsylvania to keep Drew out of trouble. Still, bribes were what they were, and Marla had known, from the first time they paid one, that she had to have a record of what they had given to whom and when. Yes, it was illegal activity and yes, they shouldn't have done it, but they had done it, and not to keep a record of it was to let the police departments in question completely off the hook. Marla had bank receipts, Internet wire transfers, receipts for SUVs donated to one police department and computers donated to another. She had withdrawals clearly marked "for the Upper Merion PD" and "for Lehigh PD re disorderly stop." The notes were clear enough so that they could be read by a judge or a district attorney or a jury without having to be translated by her. There was a paper trail a million miles long, which she had planted carefully and deliberately, and with Frank's full knowledge, as the only way they had to cover their asses in the event of the kind of meltdown they had been subjected to when Drew got arrested for drugs . . . but the problem was no longer that Drew was arrested for drugs. It was that Drew was dead, almost certainly murdered, and the big question was going to be who had murdered him and why. This file was almost certainly evidence of a motive. Hell, she could go to jail for nothing but what she admitted to in it. Frank could go to jail, too. And to keep themselves out of jail they might have done whatever it was the murderer had done to get Drew out of the way.

Filled his pills full of arsenic, Marla thought. She'd heard that this morning on the radio as she was coming in to work. She'd heard it on NPR, as a matter of fact. She did listen to their own stations most of the time, but in the car she wanted news, and for that she wanted NPR. The one thing they did badly on this network was news.

The problem was, she could go to jail for getting rid of this folder, too. There were laws against destroying evidence. She could always tuck it into her tote bag and bring it home, but then she'd have to find a way to get rid of it there, and she didn't keep a shredder in her spare bedroom. Besides, shredders weren't foolproof. She'd seen movies where the police reconstructed shredded documents. Getting rid of a big, fat file folder full of documents was as hard as getting rid of a body, and she didn't have the first idea of how to get rid of a body. She'd always counted on the fact that the police would be no more interested in bringing this evidence forward than she would be herself, but that was because she hadn't expected Drew to be arrested by two cops who weren't in on the deal and weren't interested in being in on it, or prosecuted by a new district attorney who knew nothing about the kind of arrangements that had been put in place by the old one. If she shredded the folder here, somebody would see her shredding it. Even if she waited until after hours, there was always the chance that somebody would be around late, or that a cleaning woman would see. Besides, this was radio, people were around late all the time. If she didn't shred it and just took it out and threw it somewhere, in a garbage can, in the water, somebody would find it and fish it out and sell it to the highest bidder. Marla Hildebrande had watched enough true crime to know that murderers were fools to think they could hide what they didn't want anybody to see.

The problem was, the folder wasn't going to go away by itself, and she didn't think the police were going to take more than a day or two to get around to searching the place.

2

There were times when Ray Dean Ballard needed to stop being Ray Dean Ballard and become Aldous Ballard again, himself. He used the Ray Dean the way an actor used a costume. It was necessary in his line of work, but he never mistook it for reality. That made his life difficult sometimes. It seemed to him that he shouldn't have to worry about it so much, or for so long. He'd been working with homeless people now for over a decade. He'd been living on the salary they paid him, in the kind of apartment a salary like that could afford, in the clothes a salary like that could afford. He should have proved his sincerity by now. Sometimes he thought there was never any way to prove your sincerity in a situation like this. He was one of them until he became suspect, and he didn't want to become suspect.

This morning, he also didn't want to play Ray Dean Ballard. He didn't think that had anything to do with Drew Harrigan's death per se. After all, he barely knew the man, and what he knew he didn't like. Still, the news was all over television and the radio. *Morning Edition* had it. The newspapers piled in stacks in front of newsstands had it. Everybody had it. If he'd owned a television, he could have done nothing for the next several hours but listen to reports about when Drew Harrigan died, how and where his body was found, who and what was going to be in trouble now. He didn't have a television, and didn't want one, and when he passed one in the window of an electronics store he paused only for a minute before moving on down the street. He did not look like the Ray Dean Ballard they were used to at the office, now. He was wearing a better coat, for one thing. The real difference was that his demeanor was almost completely changed. He was fed up, and restless, and he wanted to do something with the morning.

The first thing he did was to stop at a pay phone and tell them he wouldn't be in until later. He'd left his cell phone at home, because he didn't want to be interrupted, and he didn't bother to tell them why he wouldn't be in or where he'd be instead. That was one of the perks of being the boss. You didn't owe anybody any explanations. The second thing he did was to stop at an ATM machine and get some money. Usually, he was careful not to carry too much around with him in cash. Nothing got people's attention as much as a big wad of bills in a wallet. He checked the limits he was allowed and opted for five hundred dollars. It came out at him in tens and twenties, as if he had just committed a bank heist.

Out on the street again, he looked around at what was really a very prosperous neighborhood. The stores were good, selling things people needed at prices far above what people needed to pay. In another part of town, you could get a watch. In this part of town, you could get a Swiss Army watch, or a Rolex. He had never really understood Rolexes. If he wanted to spend $17,000 on something, he'd buy himself a car. Except that he didn't understand cars, either.

He turned first left, then right, then left again, reaching each intersection at increasing speed, feeling more and more reluctant to slow down for pedestrians or traffic. Now that he'd decided to do this, he wanted to get it done. He saw only one homeless man on his way. The man was young and completely a mess. He was filthy. His trousers were literally in rags, in strips that hung down from his knees like abstract expressionist curtains. In spite of the wind and the cold and the time of day, he had his member out, waving in the wind. He was pissing on the tires of every car parked at the curb.

This is the truth, Ray Dean told himself. *I am not able to solve the homeless problem. Nobody is able to solve the homeless problem. The homeless are not a problem. They are a fact of life.*

He made one more turn, and then there it was, the one building in Philadelphia he was usually careful to avoid: the Markwell Ballard Bank. It was not the kind of bank people used to open checking accounts or savings accounts or nip into to get a little money. It had no tellers, no customer lines, no little bank of deposit slips next to the door. In fact, the door wasn't a commercial door, open to the public. It was locked, and to get in you had to ring a bell and be admitted by a doorman.

Ray Dean rang the bell. The doorman peered out the plate glass of the window and then opened up.

"Mr. Aldy," he said. "It's been a long time. I hope you're doing well."

"I'm doing fine, Fitz. Is Cameron up there waiting for me?"

"Mr. Reed has been in his office for an hour," Fitz said. "Everybody still hopes you'll come into the business, you do know that, don't you? We're all waiting for you."

"If you go on waiting, you'll get like Rip Van Winkle," Ray Dean said. "I'll go on up. I hope you have an unexciting day."

"Every day is unexciting except the ones where the president comes to visit or the protestors camp out on the street, but there isn't going to be that kind of thing today. I bought myself pepper spray if the protestors come back."

Ray Dean half ran to the stairs and started up, four flights, he didn't care. He really was restless today. He made it up all three flights in record time, and without becoming breathless. All that running he did was obviously paying off. He went through the fire doors into the fourth-floor lobby and saw Cameron Reed pacing back and forth in front of the receptionist's desk, as if he had nothing at all else to do. The receptionist didn't look pleased.

"Aldy," Cameron said. "I dropped everything. What's the emergency?"

Ray Dean had half a mind to say "murder" right here where everybody could hear it, but he didn't. He knew what Cameron was really worried about.

"It's just something I need," he said, edging Cameron toward his office door. "Let's go into your office and be private. Really private. Turn off the intercom."

"Margaret knows everything, Aldy, you know that. I don't keep anything from Margaret."

"Turn off the intercom," Ray Dean said again. "I mean it, Cameron, this is private."

Cameron looked anything but pleased, but Ray Dean hadn't expected him to be pleased, so he didn't worry about it. They went into the office and shut the door behind them. Cameron went over to the bank of buttons on his desk and flipped one up. He told Margaret that he was going to be "off-line" for a few minutes. Then he flipped the switch the other way again.

"The other one, too," Ray Dean said.

"I don't know—"

"The other one too," Ray Dean insisted. "Come on, Cam, don't do this. I grew up in offices like this. Granted, not the Philadelphia ones, but they're all alike. My father is a paranoid nutcase."

"Your father is a great man."

"The two things aren't mutually exclusive. Flip off the other one."

Cameron looked away for a long moment, then pulled out a drawer and fiddled with another set of buttons.

"Of course," Ray Dean said, "I don't put it past the old lunatic to have had this whole place bugged like the Moscow embassy, but that will have to do in the way of precautions. Let me ease your mind and tell you that I still have no interest in coming into the family business. You're welcome to be heir apparent to my father's endless obsession with all things financial, except that I really appreciate it when you send me the dividend checks. Okay?"

Cameron visibly relaxed. "Okay," he said.

"It should have occurred to you that if I'd changed my mind about that, I'd have talked to my father first. We do talk, you know. We talk a lot. If he gets bored, don't be surprised if he decides to solve the homeless problem all by his own self. I want you to do something for me. I want you to run a financial check. Not the kind the credit card companies run before they give somebody a card; a real one. The kind you'd give to somebody the bank was thinking of loaning a couple of hundred million dollars."

"We wouldn't expose ourselves to that extent on a single loan."

"You know what I mean."

"Yeah," Cameron said. "Yeah, I do. You got a reason for this? You're not thinking of asking us to loan a pile of cash to a friend of yours or anything, are you? That doesn't sound like you. Are we invading this person's privacy for a reason?"

"I don't know if you can invade the privacy of the dead," Ray Dean said. "And the last thing I'd want is for the bank to loan this guy any money. Although, Lord, I'd give something to be a fly on the wall if my father and this man ever met. You know who Drew Harrigan is?"

"Of course I know who he is. He's a buffoon."

"He may be a buffoon, but he's a very influential buffoon, and at the moment he's dead. Murdered, according to the Philadelphia Police."

"I did hear that he was dead. Are you saying you're a suspect in his murder?"

"I suppose half of Philadelphia is a suspect in his murder," Ray Dean said. "Maybe half the country. I think I can honestly say that Drew Harrigan gave five new people reasons to kill him every time he opened his mouth on the air, and he was on the air four hours a day six days a week for years. I want to know who was bankrolling him."

"You just said he was on the air four hours a day six days

a week. He was a popular radio host. Maybe he didn't need anybody bankrolling him."

"He might not need them now, but he would have in the beginning," Ray Dean said. "I've been looking into it. His whole shtick depends on research, on knowing things that nobody else knows. And in order to do that, he's got to develop sources, he's got to have equipment, he's got to have money, and he didn't have it when he started. I want to know who's bankrolling him. And don't tell me maybe somebody started off doing it and isn't now, because you know that's not how those people work. Scaife. Olin. Whoever it was, they like to get control and keep it."

"It wouldn't be Olin," Cameron said. "And I'm pretty sure it wouldn't be Scaife, although he provides the money for a lot of this kind of thing. Why do you want to know who was bankrolling him? Do you think his backers killed him?"

"No. I think his drug supplier killed him, but there may be more of a connection there than you'd think. That's not it, though. It's just that it's been bugging me. My guy is still missing. As far as I know, it's still safest to assume he's dead."

"Your guy?"

"Sherman Markey. The homeless man Drew Harrigan—"

"Never mind," Cameron said. "I remember. You think that if you find out who was bankrolling him, you'll find your homeless guy?"

"No, I think I'll find out what the point was," Ray Dean said. "I made a list of Harrigan's targets last night. A couple of professors at Penn, one of them being Jig Tyler."

"The man is a Stalinist asshole," Cameron said.

"I'm not disagreeing. But, look, there are those two. Jig Tyler for being a Stalinist asshole, as you put it. The other, a woman, for being a 'lunatic feminist.' Then there's two Democratic congressmen, one from Massachusetts, one from Oregon. The one from Massachusetts is in favor of same-sex marriage. The one from Oregon is in favor of assisted suicide. Then there's a Democratic senator from Illinois and the problem there seems to be that the guy is in favor of some provision in some trade act that is opposed to the spirit of NAFTA, or something. I couldn't figure that one out, and I'll bet most of his listeners couldn't, either. It doesn't make any sense. There's nothing coherent about it. There's no point."

"What makes you think there's going to be a point?"

"There always is a point," Ray Dean said, "and you know it. I want to know what the point is. I want to know who was backing him. I want to follow the money. Could you do that for me?"

"Sure," Cameron said. "It'll take a couple of days, maybe. Or maybe not. It depends on how secretive they're being, and how good they are at keeping secrets."

"If it was us, would you tell me?"

"No."

"Is it us?"

"Don't be an ass," Cameron said. "You know how your father feels about people like Drew Harrigan. Or Reagan Democrats in general. Or the guys in the pickup trucks with the Confederate flags, as Mr. Howard Dean put it."

"My father never let his personal feelings get in the way of business. I don't think he's starting now."

"He's not," Cameron said, "but he's bankrolling the other side, so I think we can safely say that you can be more certain than you might have been otherwise that he's not the force behind Drew Harrigan. Why don't you just let the police do their job? They'll look into the finances."

"They won't begin to know how to look into the finances," Ray Dean said, "and you know it. Besides, I'm not necessarily interested in telling the police anything. I'm just interested in knowing. As soon as possible."

"Your father will be pleased to know you're taking an interest in the business."

"My father is writing a book on the moral responsibilities of global capitalism. All he ever talks to me about is how he's convinced I'm going to get killed, just like what's his name, who was teaching in Harlem."

"You can't blame him. You work with some very crazy people. Violent people."

"So does he," Ray Dean said. "They just dress it up in fancier clothes. You've got my office number. Call me there. Ask for Ray Dean. Nobody knows who Aldy is."

"Are you at least using Ballard?"

"Of course I'm using Ballard. Be good for me, Cam, okay? This is making me nuts. And I've got a feeling we're going to hear nothing but bad news for the foreseeable future. I think my guy is going to show up dead, and I think the police are going to land on me with both feet. I was the one who sent vans out to search for a red watch cap on the night Drew Harrigan was murdered, wearing a red watch cap. Crap."

FIVE

I

Gregor Demarkian didn't know what he thought a Carmelite monastery was going to look like. Maybe he imagined a castlelike building with Gothic spires and a moat. Whatever it was, it wasn't this blank front of a building that faced on the pavement like all the other buildings in the neighborhood, only the wooden door at the side indicating there was more to its property than to those of its neighbors. The wooden door shielded a driveway that led to the barn. Gregor could just see the other building at the back of the narrow space through which cars would have to drive if they wanted to park back there. He wondered if the monastery had cars, and if it did have them, what they were used for. The nuns were supposed to be cloistered. They wouldn't be running around the city looking for the nearest McDonald's drive-through.

They parked at the curb without difficulty. There weren't a lot of cars here jockeying for spaces, which was odd. Even in the worst neighborhoods it was usually difficult to find a space. Marbury and Giametti put their police marker in the front window and got out. Gregor and Rob Benedetti got out, too. Gregor went up to the wooden door and rattled it.

"This would be how the homeless men got to the barn, wouldn't it? Do they unlock it in the evenings?"

"I don't know," Benedetti said. "You can ask the nuns. Come inside."

Gregor let himself be led around to the front door again. It was a very plain front door, distinguished only by the crucifix squarely in the middle of it, Christ in agony, dying on the Cross. Rob Benedetti rang the bell. They all stood on the doorstep, waiting in the cold. It was cold, too, as cold as it had been these past few weeks, and maybe worse. Gregor was beginning to think there was something wrong with him that he never remembered to bring a hat.

The door was opened by a nun Gregor didn't know, in the same long, full habit Sister Beata had been wearing at the precinct station. She nodded to them without speaking and then gestured them inside. She didn't ask to see anybody's badge or identification, although Marbury had been getting his out of his coat pocket all the time. They trooped into the foyer and got their first surprise. The first way in which this monastery was different from the buildings around it would most certainly be the ceilings, which were more than high. Old buildings tended to have high ceilings, but Gregor didn't think a neighborhood like this would have that kind of old building in it. He wondered what this building had been before the nuns took it over, and what renovations they had made before they turned it into a convent.

The nun led them through the small foyer into what seemed to be a waiting room, and Sister Beata rose from behind the desk there to greet them. Gregor was more than a little proud of himself for being able to recognize her. Nuns in full habit were like homeless people. You tended to look over them, rather than at them.

Sister Beata gestured to them to follow her, and they all trooped down a narrow hall to a pair of frosted-glass double doors. Beata opened them, gestured them all inside, and then came in herself, closing the doors behind her. Gregor looked around at what was obviously supposed to be a sitting room of some kind. The pictures on the wall were all determinedly religious, and not remarkable for anything but their indulgence in Catholic kitsch. There was Christ with the Sacred Heart coming out of his chest, a lick of flame at the top of it, as if it were a specialty candle. There was Christ surrounded by sheep and holding a lamb. There was the Virgin Mary holding out her arms, with light coming out of her fingertips. Beata caught him staring at the pictures and smiled.

"Yes, Mr. Demarkian. The art is awful. But it, like everything else in this room, including the paint job on the walls, was donated to us by the Sodality Friends of Carmel, and we appreciate their concern and support for our life lived within these walls. Would you all sit down please? We've got a few problems I need to discuss."

The men all remained standing. Beata looked even more amused, then made an elaborate show of sitting down herself. The men all sat.

"I thought that sort of thing went out with my mother's generation," she said.

"It's," Giametti said. "Ah. It's—"

"It's the habit, Officer Giametti, I know," Beata said. "It's ironic, really, because this habit marks me as an extern sister, and as an extern sister I'm the lowliest creature in a cloistered community. I am, however, able to be here with you. Nuns who have taken solemn vows are not able to be here with you. They live in strict enclosure. They never leave the confines of the consecrated area of the monastery. They don't see people face-to-face. If you want to visit with them, you must talk to them in the conversation room while they remain behind the grille. Reverend Mother Constanzia is in fact a cloistered nun."

Rob Benedetti stirred in his seat. "You know, that's not going to work," he said. "We're going to have to talk to the Reverend Mother, if she's the one who is Drew Harrigan's sister—"

"She's the one," Beata said.

Rob Benedetti plowed determinedly on. "And we're going to have to do it face-to-face, not behind a grille. We do try to make accommodations for religious convictions, but—"

"It's quite all right, Mr. Benedetti. The Reverend Mother and I discussed that this morning. It's a little more complicated than you realize, but we've asked permission from the Cardinal for Reverend Mother to break enclosure in this matter and for the community to abandon enclosure so that the police may search where they like."

"The barn," Marbury said quickly.

"The barn is not within the enclosure," Beata said. "You'll see when you get back there. There's a wall separating it from the enclosure. We used to use it for a garage before we gave up the cars, and we needed a place mechanics could get to when they broke down. They were a nuisance, really, and you don't need cars in the city, and we don't go anywhere anyway. But here's the thing. We are arranging it, but it hasn't been arranged yet. Before you can see Reverend Mother anywhere but through the grille, before you can search the monastery proper, we've got to have permission from the Cardinal. I'm sure he'll give it. The problem is, he hasn't given it yet. He's in Rome."

"And you want us to wait until he gets back from Rome?" Marbury said.

"Hardly," Beata said. "We've got a call in. The thing is, we don't have permission now, and we may not get it while you're here this time, and that may mean—"

"That we'll have to come back," Rob Benedetti said.

"I know it's a long way," Beata said, "and I do apologize, but we didn't think. We should have, of course. I remembered it almost as soon as I tried to get to sleep. Things were confused."

"I'm sure they were," Gregor said. "But we can talk to you now, can't we, Sister?"

"Of course," Sister Beata said.

"You said before that you didn't go anywhere anyway, but that isn't strictly true, is it?" Gregor asked. "You yourself do go places, and I'd expect you're not the only one. That's why you're an extern sister."

"True," Beata said. "There's me, Sister Immaculata, and

Sister Marie Bernadette. We are all allowed to go out into the world and do what the community needs us to do. The shopping, for instance."

"Do you go out often?" Gregor asked.

"Almost every day."

"What about the post office?" Gregor asked. "Do you go to the post office?"

"Once a week, on Friday," Beata said. "There's almost always something. We need stamps. Or we need to send packages. That used to be easier. They used to pick those up at the door. Now with all the Homeland Security initiatives, they want us to bring the packages in personally. So I do."

"What kind of packages do you send?" Rob Benedetti asked.

"We send copies of the works of St. Teresa of Avila, our foundress, to people interested in Carmelite spirituality," Beata said. "Also the works of St. John of the Cross, St. Thérèse of Lisieux, and St. Edith Stein, all Carmelites, all writers. We send holy cards, especially the one with the Blessed Virgin giving the scapular to St. Simon Stock—"

"What?" Marbury said.

"St. Simon Stock was the original founder of the Carmelite Order," Beata said. "St. Teresa of Avila only reformed the order and established this branch of it. Legend says that the Virgin appeared to St. Simon Stock and gave him the brown scapular we all wear, and told him that anyone wearing this scapular at the moment of death will not fail to make a good one."

"A good death?" Marbury said.

"That's right," Beata said. "There's a concern, isn't there, with a good death? With a death that leaves us reconciled to God."

"What's a scapular?" Gregor asked.

Beata picked up the long piece of material hanging down in front of her dress. "This is. It goes all the way down behind, too. Lay people wear a symbolic representation of it, two square pieces of wool cloth on a pair of strings that hang front and back across your shoulders under your clothes. We have a lot of those, too, and we send them out. It's not so much what we send, you know, as that people need to feel that we're listening. That somebody is listening. It always surprises me how many people there are who are lonely and isolated in this world."

"Why surprise?" Gregor asked.

"I suppose because it seems nonsensical," Beata said. "If there are so many lonely people out there, why can't they get together with each other? I'm a very practical person, really, the last sort of person you'd think would be attracted to Carmel in some ways. And it makes me impatient. Fortunately, I'm not asked to deal with souls in trouble. The only responsibility I have for the mail is delivering it to the post office when there's too much of it to be mailed directly from here. And buying stamps."

"Tell me about the night Drew Harrigan died," Gregor said. "For the moment, I'm going to assume it was Drew Harrigan here that night and that he died here that night. Forensics could change that. When did you first notice him?"

"Do you mean, when did I first notice the man in the red hat?" Beata said. "Because that's all I noticed. Just a man, generic, in a red hat. I didn't recognize Drew Harrigan."

"Would you have?" Gregor asked.

"Under the circumstances?" Beata said. "Probably not. He was in clean enough clothes, and the hat was clean, but one of the first things I noticed about him was that he was unkempt and his face was dirty. And besides, I'd never seen Drew Harrigan in person, and I hadn't seen him very often even in the media. He was on the air before I came to Carmel, but he was nowhere near as big as he is now, and I doubt if I'd seen half a dozen pictures of him in my life. So no, it isn't odd that I didn't recognize him any of the times I saw him that night."

"Any of the times?" Gregor said. "How many times were there?"

"Well, there was the first one," Beata said. "That was when we came home, Immaculata and I, from meeting with the lawyers."

"Which lawyers?" Benedetti said.

"Drew Harrigan's lawyers," Beata said.

Every one of them sat up a little straighter in their chairs.

"Why ever would you be meeting with Drew Harrigan's lawyers?" Gregor asked.

"Well," Beata said, "let's start with this. I am a lawyer, so Reverend Mother thought it would be better to send me than to rely entirely on the lawyers from the Archdiocese."

"You're a lawyer," Rob Benedetti said. "Have you ever practiced in Philadelphia?"

"Of course."

"Where?" Benedetti asked.

"At the firm of Coatley, Amis," Sister Beata said. "I was a week away from taking up a partnership when I decided to come to Carmel. They were not pleased with me."

"The only person who ever left Coatley in the lurch on a partnership was this woman, this Alderman woman, who did the Racicot Barrelson case "

"That's right," Beata said.

"You're Alderman?" Benedetti asked.

"Susan Titus Alderman. I was. Needless to say, my family isn't really in love with the idea of Carmel, either. Especially since it meant I had to have converted to Catholicism to come. We still think Catholicism is a little tacky in my part of Pennsylvania."

"The Racicot-Barrelson thing was brilliant," Benedetti said.

"Thank you."

"Could we get back to why it was you were meeting with Drew Harrigan's lawyers?" Gregor said.

Beata nodded. "Mr. Harrigan had deeded a few parcels of property to us a couple of weeks before. And don't ask. Yes, it was definitely after Sherman Markey decided to sue him for defamation, although if he was trying to shield property, he should have done it a good time before. I'd worry more about the civil forfeiture laws than I would about a homeless man with help from the Justice Project."

"And you were meeting with Drew Harrigan's lawyers in regard to this deed?" Gregor asked.

"No," Beata said. "The deed was finalized. The problem was that we wanted to sell the properties, because we had a bank loan—still have it, actually—a very substantial one, that we'd taken on as a balloon payment, and the payment was coming due. And, of course, since this is Carmel, we didn't have the money. So we wanted to sell the properties. But Sherman Markey's lawyers had gone into court and had liens placed on them, saying that Mr. Harrigan had only deeded them to us in order to shield them from any judgment that might arise from Mr. Markey's defamation suit. So I was meeting with Mr. Harrigan's lawyers to find out what the situation was exactly. I'm a little out of the loop here, if you can believe it."

"When is the balloon payment due?" Gregor asked.

"It was due and passed," Beata said. "The bank agreed to roll it over into a conventional second mortgage. We told the Cardinal about it and he had one of his patented ice-cold glaring hissy fits."

"This was two weeks ago?" Gregor said. "Did you really expect to have the properties sold in two weeks?"

"We had a buyer," Beata said.

"Who?" Rob Benedetti asked.

"We don't know," Beata said.

"How can you not know?" Benedetti asked.

"The offer was made anonymously, about four days after Drew Harrigan deeded the property to us," Beata said. "We took it seriously, because it was made through the Markwell Ballard Bank."

"That's interesting," Gregor said.

"I thought so, too," Beata said. "You really do have to take it seriously. There had to be a buyer out there who was both willing and able to buy the property, or Markwell Ballard wouldn't have handled the negotiations. They don't need anybody's business. They've thrown clients out for far less than making bogus buy offers. The thing is, they also don't take in any guy off the street with twenty dollars in his pocket. When I was still in the world—that's what we call not being in the convent, being in the world—the minimum you needed to open an account at Markwell Ballard was two million dollars. And that just got you an appointment. If they didn't like your face, that was all there was to it. Drew Harrigan didn't have an account at Markwell Ballard."

"You know that for sure?" Gregor asked.

"Yes," Beata said. "Neil Savage mentioned it. It was so odd of him to have said it that I would have thought he was deliberately throwing me misinformation except for the fact that he was so incredibly, triumphantly *satisfied* about it."

"Mr. Savage is Mr. Harrigan's attorney?" Gregor said.

"That's right."

"Mr. Harrigan has an attorney who hates him?" Gregor said.

"Apparently."

"This is getting odder all the time," Gregor said. "So you went to see Mr. Savage, and you came back, and you saw Drew Harrigan, where?"

"To be accurate, I saw a man in a red watch cap," Beata said. "And it was just as I was getting out of the cab with Sister Immaculata. The door was open, the one that leads to the barn, and the men were already lining up to get in to sleep. It was dark, but it wasn't time for us to open up yet. And I saw a man in the line with a bright red hat, and it was the hat I noticed."

"Did he look well, or sick, or drugged?" Gregor asked.

"I didn't get close enough to tell," Beata said. "I was standing on the sidewalk. He was down near the barn door. It might have been anybody at all in that watch hat. But I saw the watch hat."

"Did you see him again?" Gregor asked.

"When he was dead," Beata said. "One of the other men came to me in the night and said that the man in the red hat was dead, and some of the other men were stealing his clothes. They'd already stolen the hat."

"So when you went to see him the second time, he wasn't wearing the hat?" Gregor asked.

"No," Beata said. "And I know what you're going to say. It could have been somebody else in the hat the first time. Yes, it could have been. But the man who came to see me, he's called Whizbang Joe—"

"Is that supposed to mean something?" Gregor asked.

"Probably," Beata said, "but I don't really want to know what. Anyway, Joe came in to see me and he seemed to think it was the same person who'd had the cap all along. I know homeless people aren't the best witnesses, usually, and Joe is as addled as the rest of them, but he was very certain, and very upset because of the theft. So I tend to think he knew what he was talking about. Anyway, I went out with him and looked at the body and made sure it was really dead and not just passed out or in a coma—"

"And you didn't recognize him as Drew Harrigan then?" Benedetti asked.

"No," Beata said. "But he really was a mess, a big one by then. He had vomit all over him. He was, I don't know, the way they get when they die like that. We've never done this with the barn before. It was the Cardinal's idea this year. But we had two deaths before this one anyway. They die—I don't know how to explain it—they die bereft of humanity."

"How did you decide he was dead?" Gregor asked.

"I put my head on his chest to hear if I could hear his heart beating, and then I tried to take a pulse. When those didn't work, I took the back of my crucifix and held it up to his nose. To see if his breath clouded it."

"Then what did you do?" Gregor asked.

"I asked Joe to stay with the body. I came back into the monastery, told Reverend Mother what had happened, and we called the ambulance. Then I went back to the barn to wait next to the body until the ambulance men came. They came pretty quickly, actually. They don't usually, for homeless cases. Not when the person is already dead."

"And the ambulance men came and took the body away," Gregor said.

"That's right."

"And then what?" Gregor asked.

"And then nothing," Beata said. "It's as I said, we'd had a couple of others. We send them to the morgue and we pray for them, but after that, we don't have anything else we can do for them."

"But you must have heard the news reports, about the disappearance of Sherman Markey," Gregor said.

"No," Beata said.

Gregor raised his eyebrows. "It was all over the news, Sister. It was a major story for at least a couple of days."

"Mr. Demarkian," Beata said, "you don't understand what an enclosure is. We don't have a television here—oh, we have one. It's in a storeroom on the second floor and Reverend Mother would take it out if the president were assassinated or there was a nuclear attack. It came out after 9/11 for a couple of days. But mostly it just stays in the storeroom. We don't watch it. We don't get newspapers. We don't get magazines. We are on the Internet."

"Somehow, that figures," Marbury said.

"But we're not really on it, the way most people are. We have a Web portal and a Web site and we answer mail. Or, rather, I do, because as an extern sister I have the right to be 'outside.' But for a piece of news to penetrate here, it's got to be a lot more important than the report of the disappearance of a homeless man in Philadelphia. Even one connected to Drew Harrigan and his drug problems. I did notice that Ben had broken up with J. Lo. Or vice versa."

"I think she walked out on him," Giametti said helpfully.

Gregor was about to ask if the monastery had had any contact with the physical body after the ambulance had taken it away, if any of them had been asked to try to identify it, for instance, when the sister who had let them in came to the door and tapped lightly.

"I'm sorry to interrupt," she said, "but there's a person here, a woman here, saying she's come to find Mr. Demarkian. I—she's uh, a little upset, I suppose. She's very insistent. And I did say you were all busy, but—"

"You can't just keep me *standing* here," somebody said, and the voice was such a high, wailing shriek, Gregor winced. "Don't you know who I am? You can't just keep me *standing* here like I'm not anybody and you can jerk me around."

They all turned in the direction of the voice, because it was coming closer. Gregor could hear the sound of needle-sharp heels clacking into the hardwood floor.

"You can't just keep me *standing* here," the voice said again, and then she was there, right in front of them, like a bad joke.

2

Whoever she was, she wasn't very steady on those high heels. Gregor looked down and saw the ankle straps straining against ankles that weren't steady enough to wear them gracefully, and then those heels, at least three and a half inches high, and so thin they looked like toothpicks. The rest of the woman seemed to be of a piece. Her hair was improbably blond and improbably enormous. It was the kind of thing women went in for when they were competing to be Miss Mississippi. The earrings were real, though. There was no substitute for emer-alds that looked so perfectly like emeralds as those did, espe-cially at that size. The dress and the coat were just odd. They were both conspicuously expensive, but neither of them fit right. The coat was much too large, its heavy, ostentatious fur slipping off her shoulders every time she moved. The dress was much too small, making her hips look larger than they might have and forcing her breasts to strain against the fabric. She reminded Gregor of Marilyn Monroe, except that Mon-roe was a woman who commanded attention because of her very presence, and this was a woman who commanded atten-tion because she was decked out so freakishly she made her audience uneasy about what she would do next.

Rob Benedetti was on his feet. They were all on their feet, even Sister Beata. Sister Beata looked as if she were about to be asked to throw the woman out, or as if she wanted to.

Rob Benedetti said, "It's Mrs. Harrigan, isn't it? What are you doing here?"

"Looking for Mr. Demarkian," Ellen Harrigan said. "Mr. Armenian-American Hercule Poirot. I called his place and there wasn't anybody there. So then I called Commissioner Jackman. You wouldn't believe how much it took me to find out he was here. You probably think I'm stupid. Everybody thinks I'm stupid. But I'm here."

"Is there something in particular you want to see me about?" Gregor asked.

Ellen Harrigan turned to face him, looking him up and down. Gregor was interested to note that the looking over didn't bother him at all. This woman really had no force of personality at all. She was like a gigantic doll. Even her rampages made little or no impression.

She dropped the coat off her shoulders, onto the floor. Gregor got the impression that she made a habit of dropping her clothes on the floor, the sort of thing that Bennis, who had been born and raised rich as sin, would never do. This one not only dropped her coat, she stepped on it. Shades of Barbra Streisand's first television special.

"I've brought a list," she said. "That bitch at the office said you think I'm a suspect, so I brought a list."

"A list of what?" Gregor asked.

"A list of all the people who wanted Drew dead," Ellen Harrigan said. "There are a lot of them. Liberals. Communists, some of them. Traitors. You wouldn't believe it. They all wanted him dead."

"Your husband was a public man," Gregor said carefully, "but at least the way this stands right now, there really isn't the likelihood that the perpetrator will turn out to be somebody who only knew your husband through his radio program. It's more likely, you see—"

"I'm not talking about people who knew Drew only through his radio program," Ellen Harrigan said. "I'm talking about people who hated him. His syndicators, for one thing. And Jig fucking Tyler. The smartest man in the world. Smarter than all the rest of us. And that woman who works with him who has a Communist cell and makes all her students join it. And that Southern freak over at the homeless people. They all wanted him dead. All of them. You're not going to make me a suspect just because I'm not politically correct."

Gregor Demarkian no longer had the faintest idea what this woman was talking about, but he did know one thing.

She was dead drunk.

SIX

I

Alison Standish saw the interoffice envelope on her desk and the man sitting in the chair near the bookcases at the same time, and for a moment she thought the sight of the man was stranger than the sight of the envelope. She was in her coat and had a cup of coffee in her hand. She'd picked it up at a place a few streets away that didn't use branded cardboard cups to put their take-out coffee in, because she'd learned long ago that she was useless at figuring out what was and was not an acceptable place to buy coffee. Starbucks was out, because it was a large corporation, and it didn't matter that it hadn't been a large corporation twenty years ago. Other places were out because they were just too downscale. It wasn't all right to buy a cup of something nameless from a local deli. Still other places were out because they served "Free Trade" rather than "Fair Trade" coffee, which mattered to people, although Alison couldn't straighten out why. Coffee tasted like coffee to her. She was sure there were special kinds, with hidden subtleties of flavor, that she could have if she was willing to spend a lot more money than she wanted to to get her caffeine fix in the morning. She was equally sure that the politics of coffee were intricate and nuanced, that many coffee growers in

South America treated their workers as no better than slaves, that coffee-growing co-operatives were ready and able to sell her coffee if she was ready and able to pay the extra price it would cost to pay people decently. Hell, she was even ready and able to pay the extra price it would cost to pay people decently. The problem was, she could never keep the brand names straight. She ended up walking down the long halls to her office carrying something that blazed out her lack of sensitivity, her lack of awareness, her lack of political commitment. At least that last part was true. The only thing Alison Standish was politically committed to was Pope Leo IV, and he had died in 855 CE.

The man was vaguely familiar, Alison wasn't really sure why. She wasn't paying much attention, because it had suddenly struck her that the envelope was very odd indeed. Interoffice mail came to her mailbox, not her desk. And the last thing the departmental secretaries had any interest in doing was delivering mail to the offices of individual professors.

She went to the desk and picked it up. It was from "the office of the chairman," as if the chairman had an office. God, but Roger could be so damned *pretentious*. It only got worse when he wrote his articles, which tended to be heavy on the "transformative experience" of "trangressive texts." The fad for postmodernism and deconstruction was waning, and Alison thought it couldn't come too soon. She'd spent enough of her life listening to literature professors spout gibberish.

She looked at the envelope and frowned. She wanted to open it, but the man was still sitting there in her visitor's chair, saying nothing, looking expectant. She put the envelope down again.

"I'm sorry," she said. "You are—? Did we have an appointment?"

"Oh, no," the man said. "I just—I looked you up on the system. These are your office hours. So I decided to come over. Under the circumstances."

"Are there circumstances?" Alison asked. There was the envelope, waiting for her. She couldn't have been fired. Getting a tenured professor fired was damned near impossible. Other things could have happened to her, though. She could have been censured, or suspended. She could have been put on monitoring, which would mean that a representative of the university would sit in on all her classes to make sure she didn't say something she shouldn't. She'd never heard of that happening at Penn, but it had happened other places. On the other hand, it was usually the diversity co-ordinator or somebody like that who did the monitoring, and those people were more concerned with professors who hated left-wing students than the ones who hated right-wing students. Maybe the right-wing students had their own monitor who could be brought in if the occasion demanded it. Alison didn't hate left-wing students *or* right-wing students. Mostly, she didn't even know which were which.

"You can open that if you want," the man said. "I don't mind."

"No, no," Alison said. "It's all right. I'm sorry to be so rude. I'm afraid I don't remember you."

"We've never met. I'm Jig Tyler."

"Oh," Alison said, and thought: *Good grief, the great man himself, two Nobel prizes, the Fields Medal, five best-selling books.* She put the envelope down again and held out her hand. "I'm sorry I didn't recognize you. I mean, I did, a little; you looked familiar but I couldn't place you. I'm Alison Standish. I'm very happy to meet you."

Jig Tyler had stood up and taken her hand. He gave it a good quick shake and let go. "You'd better sit down and read that letter. You'll feel better or worse depending on whether you've heard the news."

Alison picked the letter back up again and opened it. No matter how thrilled she was to meet Dr. Tyler, she really wanted to know what was in this letter, and she wanted to know it now, not later. She sat down behind her desk and ripped it open. Roger was pretentious, but not ridiculous. The letter started *Alison,* and she immediately relaxed.

I'm glad to be able to tell you that the commit-
tee has looked into the allegations of the stu-
dent in question and found them without
foundation.

Alison wanted to fix the syntax—you didn't use "found" and
"foundation" in a single sentence with only two words separating them—but instead she chucked the letter onto her
desk and looked up at Dr. Tyler in his chair.

"Relieved?" Jig Tyler said.

"Very," Alison said. "Did you know what it was about?"

"About an allegation that you systematically discriminate
against students with conservative views, brought out by a
few broadcasts by Drew Harrigan. It's all over campus that
the department launched an inquiry and it's been all over
campus since this morning that they were going to abandon
it. I take it you're relieved."

"Very. I know you've been in trouble like that a dozen
times, but I don't have two Nobels to fall back on."

"I take it you haven't heard the news," Jig Tyler said.

"If you mean the news that Harrigan is dead, yes, I've
heard it," Alison said. "It's a terrible thing."

"Boot up your computer and get online. You need to see
something."

Alison swiveled her chair to the side and tapped at the
keyboard, sending the screen saver, a picture of the cathedral at Rheims, shuddering. The desktop appeared and she
clicked on the Internet connection, which came up immediately, since the university was on a cable system and not on
dial up anymore. She rather missed the sound of dial up, the
way she rather missed the sound printers used to make before they got the silent ones.

"Go to CNN," Jig Tyler said. "That ought to work."

Alison hesitated, and then went. The window came up
with a picture of Drew Harrigan in the middle of it, and for
just one moment Alison thought it was nothing but another
story about the murder. Then she saw the inset picture of a
vapid-looking blonde holding up what seemed to be a piece

of legal-sized typing paper, and the words: HARRIGAN WIDOW NAMES NAMES.

"What's this?" Alison said.

"That's Mrs. Drew Harrigan, the fair Ellen," Jig Tyler said. "Have you met her?"

"I've never even seen a picture of her before. Who's she naming the names of?"

"Well, there's you, for one. And me."

Alison looked up. "Me? Why? I don't even know her."

"I do, although only in passing. Believe it or not, the Harrigans and I get invited to some of the same fund-raisers. You'd be amazed at the people I'm willing to put up with for charity. The names she's naming are the list of people she believes had motive, opportunity, and blind unreasoning hatred to kill her husband."

Alison blinked. "But that makes no sense," she said. "Why would I want to kill her husband?"

Jig Tyler pointed to the envelope on the desk. "That. Drew Harrigan is dead and the inquiry is over."

"But it doesn't have anything to do with that," Alison said. "It can't have. I threatened to sue the department back to the Stone Age. That's what happened."

"That's not what it's going to look like."

"But this is ridiculous," Alison said. "The police can't be taking this seriously."

"Well," Jig Tyler said, "if my sources are to be believed, and they usually are, she took it to the police first. Actually to Gregor Demarkian. Tracked him down at that convent where the body was found this morning and gave the list to him. Then she seems not to have believed that he was taking it seriously, so she came back here and called a press conference. That was at about ten thirty. It's now just about noon, and that story is on every wire service on the planet. The police are going to have to take it seriously."

"Good God," Alison said.

"Assuming God exists, I doubt if he's good. But mostly I assume he doesn't exist. Do you believe in God?"

"No, not really, I suppose. I don't think about it much."

"For what it's worth, I don't think Drew Harrigan believed in God much, either. He just found God a convenient co-pilot for the show. Have you listened to the show?"

"I tried once. I couldn't get through it."

"It's frightening how many stupid people there are in the world," Jig said. "And the most frightening thing of all is that they know they're stupid. They feel it. That's why they get so hysterical about 'pointy-headed intellectuals' who 'look down on them.' It's projection. They look down on themselves. And it's not just the ones who vote Republican. If you ask me, the Democrats are worse. The liberals are the worst of all. It's a shill. They make people believe things can get better if they just fool around with the system a little, instead of getting rid of the whole thing at once."

"You think that's wrong? That things can never get better by fooling around with the system a little?"

"They can get superficially better," Jig Tyler said. "You can buy people off with a house and a car and enough money for a vacation every summer. They don't notice that the house is a crackerbox in a soulless housing development where all the neighbors' houses are the same, or the car breaks down in five years, or the summer vacation means trekking out to a godforsaken little patch of sand with five thousand other people crowded onto it and staying in the kind of motel that advertises rooms for twenty dollars a night, no cable. They don't notice that the people who are robbing them blind have their own islands in the Caribbean and their own planes with full bedroom and bath facilities and never get crowded anywhere."

"I read one of your books once," Alison said. "*The One Party System,* that one."

"So I'm repeating myself," Jig Tyler said. "I'm sorry. I just get so carried away. It seems so obvious to me. There are many more of us than there are of them. They can't continue to rule unless we allow them to continue to rule. For decades, every time another election came around, I'd expect to see an insurgency. I almost thought I had one in the sixties. The sixties were a sham, and since then we've had nothing but corporate party politics. It's like toothpaste that comes in three different colors. They're all the same. The differences between them are superficial."

"I used to go on those sorts of vacations when I was little," Alison said. "We had a trailer, though. We didn't go to motels. We'd drive down to Cape Hatteras and hook up and spend the week there, and then we'd drive home. It really wasn't awful, you know. I found it very enjoyable. I know my parents did, too."

"They wouldn't have enjoyed it so much if they'd realized what they didn't have. Do you know how I spent my vacations when I was little?"

"No."

"At my father's house in Rome. The first time I had dinner with the Pope, I was six years old."

"I don't think I'd have much liked having dinner with the Pope when I was six," Alison said, "and it has nothing to do with the fact that I wasn't Catholic."

"We weren't Catholic, either. My father was in the diplomatic corps. Which means I grew up around very rich people without being a very rich person myself. They are what they are, you know. They're not stupid. They know they have to pay off at least a little if they want to stay in power, or in business. So they pay off, just a little. But never more than just a little. And they present the suckers with two options: a Democratic Party that's working for them and pretending to be trying to take care of the people they hurt, and a Republican Party that's working for them and pretending to care about people with 'traditional values.' They distract Democratic voters with puny-assed programs that won't even begin to address the problems created by global capitalism, never mind the yawning chasm of inequality it creates. They distract the Republican voters with God, guns, and gays. They despise everybody who doesn't have a bank account the size of Wisconsin and they always win. And the suckers get themselves all worked up about *Roe* v. *Wade* or immigration law, and never even see it happening."

"And you go on CNN and say all these things, do you?"

"Yes, well," Jig Tyler said. "It's good for their image to present at least some opposing views. That way, they can't be accused of censorship. And they always get somebody like me to present them. I'm the sort of person people who aren't rich think of as rich. I've got a cushy job. I'm an Ivy League intellectual. I can be presented as completely out of touch, and nobody they'd really want to listen to, so mostly they don't listen."

"But you do the shows anyway."

"I do, yes," Jig Tyler said. "There's always the chance that there are one or two people ready to hear. They'd think you were rich, too. Do you know that?"

"Yes," Alison said, "I do. My family does, even now. They refer to my time in college as when I went off to that rich kids' school."

Jig Tyler stood up. "I'm sorry to have barged in on you. I just thought you'd better be forewarned. It's going to get fairly nuts before it quiets down. I thought you might not be used to that."

"I'm not."

"If I were you, I'd be careful not to make any statements to the press," Jig said. "Oh, I'm going to, and probably most of the people on that list are going to, but you've never done it before. You've got no idea how to handle reporters' questions. You don't want to say anything that will land you in court on a murder charge when all you've done wrong is mistake the press for people who are willing to listen."

He stood up and looked around, at her bookshelves, at her filing cabinet, at the books stacked on the floor. Alison didn't think she'd ever realized how truly tall and thin he was, cadaverous, like a skeleton in clothes.

"You've got interesting books," he said.

Then he ambled out of the room, as inexplicably, Alison thought, as he'd wandered in. She watched him for as long as she could see him, then turned back to CNN and the story about Ellen Harrigan and her list. She had the kind of uneasy feeling she got when she ate too much dairy at dinner. She wasn't allergic to dairy, exactly, but beyond a certain point it made her queasy and restless. She had the kind of thought she hadn't had in many years, the kind that used to drive her crazy when her parents had it, the kind that had made her early life a long wasteland of waiting to get out of where she was and into a place where people understood books and ideas and everything that went with them.

She wondered what Jig Tyler did for entertainment.

She immediately felt stupid, and awkward, and uneducated. She went back to CNN, and to wondering if Roger had let her off the hook on purpose, because he would have known it would make her look bad.

2

Ellen Harrigan had been in the office since fifteen minutes to ten this morning, and now, when it should have been time for lunch, she was still there, and still shrieking. Neil Savage was beginning to think that Ellen Harrigan couldn't do anything but shriek, the way her husband had been unable to say anything about anything except in that jokey I'm-really-smarter-than-you-no-matter-how-stupid-I-sound tone that all the dim-witted talk jockeys like to affect for use on the radio as well as off. Neil Savage was beginning to lose it, and he knew it. His level of anger was now so high that he couldn't even begin to think about lunch, never mind about getting Ellen out of there, which was what most of his partners wanted him to do. Usually, it was the secretaries who got the hysterics out of the office, but Ellen Harrigan was shrewder than that. She might have the IQ of shredded wheat, but she'd learned not to be fobbed off on secretaries and assistants. She was just going to stand there and have a fit until . . . well, maybe until forever, since at this point nobody knew what she wanted, or what they were supposed to do. Neil thought he did know what she wanted, but he sure as hell wasn't going to give it to her. She wanted to be taken seriously by serious people. She wanted the respect he would have given a Leonard Bernstein or a Saul Bellow without having to do one damned thing to earn it, without having to have even the basic equipment that would have made it possible for her to even attempt to earn it. Neil knew a lot of people like that. They existed especially in business, and among those tacky people who decked themselves out in tatty little bracelets that said, WHAT WOULD JESUS DO? Neil sometimes thought he knew exactly what Jesus would do if he ever met up with them. He'd rip the bracelets off their arms and the MY BOSS IS A JEWISH CARPENTER pins off their shirts and make them all sit down and listen to the entire four hours of Bach's *St. Matthew Passion.*

Ellen Harrigan was still shrieking, and he was still in this mood, when one of the secretaries came in to tell him Kate was here. It took him a few moments to remember that he was supposed to be expecting her. She'd called first thing this morning and asked to come in to see him. He should have arranged to take her out for lunch—but, of course, there was no need to go out for lunch. The firm had a partners' dining room. Only the associates and the help went out for lunch. He didn't dare take Kate down to the dining room now, though. Ellen might show up there, still shrieking, and demand his attention.

The secretary brought Kate in to him just as Ellen Harrigan was getting off another string of curse words, her voice stabbing down the corridor like lightning caught in a box. "Goddamn it you goddamned motherfucking son of a bitch cocksucker—"

If there was more to the sentence, he didn't catch the words. The secretary looked embarrassed. Kate looked amused.

"Who is that?" she asked him. "That doesn't sound like your regular run of client."

"That's Ellen Harrigan, Drew Harrigan's widow. And she isn't the regular run of client; at the moment she isn't a client at all. It's her husband we represented. Although I suppose we'll get stuck with her."

"Why?"

"Because if you're going to do work for the Republican Party, then you've got to accommodate its friends, and Drew Harrigan was a great friend of the Republican Party."

"Drew Harrigan is dead."

"His wife knows how to make herself heard. Listen, Kate, I'm sorry for this. I'm sorry for the noise. I'm sorry for the circumstances. Let me have the dining room send up some lunch and we'll try to talk and avoid the background noise."

"I don't need lunch," Kate said. "But I was thinking. Can the dining room still do tea, real tea, the right way? I could use a pot of Earl Grey tea."

"I can get you that." He flipped on the intercom and asked the assistant to have the dining room send up a large pot of Earl Grey and a club sandwich with mineral water, and then turned back to Kate. It was odd seeing her here, in person. He'd spent decades watching her on the evening news, pro bono defense attorney in this case, head of the Justice Project in that one, a movement lawyer, a Clarence Darrow of the social justice wars. He hadn't expected her to look just the way she had on the day she walked out on him. He knew she no longer wore the good wool tweed suits she used to buy at Lord & Taylor and Bonwit Teller. He knew she hadn't switched to Brooks Brothers like the women who were now partners in his firm. She'd changed her hair. She had a good cut, but none of the elaborate curl and comb that had been de rigueur for the wives of the men who were candidates for partnership when they had both been young. The problem was, she very much looked the way he remembered her looking. She had a remarkable face. On the most elementary level, it didn't change.

"You look good," he said. "You always look younger than I expect you to."

"Well, that's good, I suppose. You look miserable. Is that because of our friend the canary down the hall?"

"Sort of. It's a new world, you know. I don't think I've caught up to it."

"Is Mrs. Harrigan going to continue with her accusations against Sherman Markey?"

"I don't know," Neil said. "I suppose she might. She's desperate to deflect suspicion from herself. That's what today has been about. She gave a press conference. Did you know about that?"

"I saw it."

"We set it up for her." Neil sighed. "We've got to do these things. It's some kind of Faustian bargain—no, whatever is the opposite of a Faustian bargain. Faust got knowledge and wisdom out of his bargain with the devil. We only got power. And it's an attenuated sort of power. It means being completely and utterly helpless when it comes to the most important things."

"It's useful to have, though. Power."

"Of course it is. And I'd rather have the mess we have than be back in the sixties and stuck with the Democrats. Franklin Delano Roosevelt nearly ruined everything that was good about this country. But it's as if we turned a corner somewhere. It's as if there isn't room for civilization anymore. It's all pork rinds and NASCAR and kitsch religion."

"Well, you know the word 'kitsch.' You wouldn't have, thirty years ago."

There was a knock on the door, and Neil yelled for whoever it was to come in. It was the waiter from the dining room, bringing a tray, just like room service in the best kind of hotel. The teapot was made of silver and as large as a samovar. There were no tea bags in sight.

Neil waited until the waiter had set everything out on the desk—his club sandwich, his mineral water—and then positioned the cart near Kate, so that she'd have a place to put her tea. Then he waited while the waiter went out the door and closed it again. He had no idea why he had waited at all. He had nothing to say to Kate that couldn't be heard by everybody in the office, and most people out.

"I always wondered how you were surviving in the new Republican Party," Kate said. "It didn't seem like your kind of thing, really."

"I don't know what being a conservative means if it doesn't mean preserving standards, standing up for classical music against the onslaught of cheap popular noise, standing up for Henry James and Jane Austen against ungrammatical techno-thrillers and children's books about boy wizards who ride broomsticks. It's almost impossible to find a classical music station on the radio anymore, and do you know why? Because of the things we did, because of deregulation. So we spend a lot of energy fending off the people in our own party who want to do away with public broadcasting, because here we are, with conservatives in charge, and without public broadcasting we can't get conservative art and conservative values on the airwaves."

"For goodness sake, Neil. You people have spent two decades telling the whole country that classical music is liberal art and liberal values and everybody who listens to it is a stuck-up snob who wants to destroy the American way of life. What did you expect to happen?"

"I didn't expect to spend two decades telling the country that people who listen to classical music are snobs. Not to put too fine a point on it, I thought that was what liberals did. Think that classical music was for snobs, I mean."

"Well, it's like you said. It's a different world."

"I know it is. I hold out in the hope that there will come a day when we'll have so much power, we'll be so thoroughly entrenched, that we won't have to pander to those people anymore. We'll be able to come right out and be what we are. In the meantime, I'm comforted by the fact that it's still our money. The party strategy people can't go too far in that direction, or we yank the money."

"The question is, are you going to yank the accusation that Sherman Markey supplied Drew Harrigan with those pills?"

"I don't know," Neil said. "I don't know what the canary wants to do, and I don't know how much of what's about to happen we're in control of. The police aren't going to stop looking at Markey just because we're no longer interested in him."

"No, but it's likely they'd stop looking at him if you people stopped contending he'd done the deed. Drew Harrigan's dead, Neil. And you know as well as I do that Sherman

Markey is in no shape to do all the things Harrigan says he did. Or any of them."

"Is? Does that mean you've found him?"

"Sorry," Kate said. "Is or was. No, we haven't found him. And yes, I do know that that means he might be dead. My concern is with what happens if he isn't."

"And what happens?"

"He gets handed a murder charge," Kate said. She looked up from her tea, to the door. "She's an idiot, obviously. And she's tacky, and stupid, and all the other things Republicans like you can't stand. But she's also very well connected, and she's rich, and she's just gone on television and behaved like Joe McCarthy naming names in the United States Senate to take the heat off herself on the subject of the very same murder. I don't trust you. Not any of you. And I don't want Sherman arrested for murder."

"Even if he committed it?"

The cup and saucer they had given Kate for her tea were from the antique Royal Doulton set. The cup was sized for someone who took tea seriously, not as a ladies' modest substitution for coffee. Kate put the cup into the saucer and sat back.

"Have you ever met Sherman Markey?"

"No," Neil said. "I've seen him on the news. I saw him when he was arrested."

"He was probably being walked through a bunch of people with his hands behind his back. I haven't met Sherman Markey either, but my intern has, and he's adamant. The man's hands shake. He's a longtime drunk. His hands might as well have palsy. From everything I've heard on the news, Drew Harrigan was murdered because somebody dumped out the insides of his prescription painkillers and refilled them with arsenic. Never mind the fact that with everything I've heard about Sherman, he'd be incapable of getting little pills like that open and shut again. If he tried to fill them with arsenic, he'd get the stuff all over himself and he'd be dead before he could deliver the load. Sherman Markey didn't kill Drew Harrigan."

"Do you think Ellen Harrigan did?"

"I think that I don't want Ellen Harrigan to get off the hook by plugging it into a sick old homeless man whose only crime so far was to have done a few chores around Drew Harrigan's co-op. I don't want you to use him to help her."

"Do you really think we'd try to pin a murder on an innocent person just to placate someone like Ellen Harrigan?"

"I think that one thing hasn't changed since I walked out on you, Neil. I think that the primary business of this place and all the places like it is to look after the interests of the boys in the club. And the girls. I think you'll do what you need to do to make sure your people are untouched, just the way you always have. Thanks for the tea. It's damned near impossible to get decent tea in the United States. They don't know how to make it."

"Is that what you're going to do? Walk out on me again? I thought we were talking."

"We've said what we need to say," Kate said. "And besides, the canary is shrieking again. Lord, doesn't that woman have a vocal register anywhere within the range of ordinary human hearing?"

Kate was out of her chair. The cup and saucer were back on the cart. She got her briefcase off the floor—*Good God,* Neil thought, *I didn't even see her bring that in*—and leaned over to kiss him on the cheek.

"It really was good to see you, Neil. And it's oddly comforting to realize that you really haven't changed."

Then she was gone, and Neil was sitting by himself in the big, high-ceilinged room, listening to Ellen Harrigan's voice keening and scratching in the distance. If it was up to him, he would get rid of her. He wouldn't even consider taking her on as a client. If it was up to him, he'd get rid of all of them, the business people who'd gotten rich in the last thirty years dealing cars or oil or everything in the world at bargain basement prices, the owners of the chains and the superstores and the fast-food places, the people who never went to college and were proud of it, or who went and had no use for any of the things they were supposed to learn there except maybe for accounting. He'd dump the hard-eyed women with their treacly stories about Good Families and Daily Miracles and Traditional Values. He'd dump the fat, soft pastors from Southern churches who wanted to sue the Library of Congress for carrying copies of Bertrand Russell's *Why I Am Not a Christian,* and their fat, soft wives with their endless tales about the joys of washing dishes and cleaning out closets for the sake of their families. He'd get rid of all the fat people altogether, all of them, every single one of those people who ate too much bad food and covered it up with polyester and rayon from Wal-Mart and J. C. Penney. He'd make white Christian music illegal and *Touched by an Angel* unconstitutional. He'd do something, but he would not represent Ellen Harrigan for any reason at all.

Of course, life being what it was, he would represent Ellen Harrigan, and he'd go down the hall and calm her down himself when he was finally finished with his sandwich.

SEVEN

I

There were now copies of Ellen Harrigan's list everywhere. The media had them, photocopied by Neil Savage's office and distributed at the press conference Gregor thought he ought to have seen coming. The police and the District Attorney's Office had them, photocopied by Rob Benedetti and sent around only after it became clear how far Ellen Harrigan was willing to go. Gregor Demarkian had several, he didn't know why. People kept putting the list into his hands, as if it were desperately important that he, above all people, should know who was on it. The problem was, he didn't know even now that he knew. Some of the names were familiar, like that of Neil Savage himself, an inclusion that made Gregor wonder if Savage had read the damned thing before letting Mrs. Harrigan pass it out to half of creation. Most of the names meant nothing at all to him. Who was Alison Standish? The address and phone number next to her name were of an office on the campus of the University of Pennsylvania, which was going to make the administration over there as happy as that snowball in hell. People kept urging him to look the thing over, but he had. He had. He'd sat in the waiting room outside Rob Benedetti's office now for three hours, studying the list and thinking that the thing he wanted most was to get out and have some lunch. He would have had more autonomy if he was being held on a charge. At least in that case, he would have had the right to an attorney, the right to habeas corpus, and the right to appear before a judge.

What he really wanted was not lunch, but lunch with Tibor, in a quiet place, where they could talk. Tibor might or might not have seen the list—whether he watched the news on any given day depended on what else was going on on that day, and he found a lot of things more interesting than the news—but he would most certainly recognize at least one name on it, and it would interest him. It interested Gregor, too. What did not interest him was sitting in this chair, holding this list, watching television from a set screwed into the waiting room's ceiling, and wondering what the hell Rob Benedetti was doing now.

He rummaged around in his clothes and got out the little cell phone Bennis had given him. There was a large part of his brain that believed that nobody could hear him speak through a phone whose body came down barely to his chin when he held it in his ear, but he persevered. It had always worked before. Tibor picked up on the other end, and Gregor tried to whisper.

"Tibor? What are you doing right now?"

Gregor half expected Tibor to shout and demand that somebody, somewhere, speak, but it didn't happen. Tibor just said, "Krekor. I have been hearing about you on the news. Where are you and what are you doing?"

"I'm at the District Attorney's Office and I'm not doing anything," Gregor said. "It's on Vine Street, do you know where that is? If you're going to take the bus, you can get here on the thirty-two, the thirty-three, and the seventeen. I think there may be more."

"If I'm coming there, I'm going to take a cab. You want me to come to the District Attorney's Office?"

"No. There's a little coffee shop on this block, right across the street from the front door here. I want you to go there and wait for me. Or I'll go there and wait for you. I want you to meet me there."

"Why? This is not a criticism, Krekor, of course I will come. But is there a reason?"

"You've been listening to the news, you said. What did you think of Drew Harrigan's widow?"

"Ah, the blond woman with the screechy voice. Her I did not listen to, Krekor, because she had such a screechy voice, it was impossible to listen. Also, she is one of those people. She is profoundly stupid, so profoundly stupid that she lies when it is not necessary, and if you listen to her you spend all your time trying to figure out where the truth is. There is no point."

"Yes, well. Listen, I'll tell you all about it when you get here. Meet me at that coffee shop as soon as you can. Tell the cabbie to take you to the DA's Office and just walk across the street. I'll be there. And yes, we could have this discussion on the phone, but I need to get out of here before I go crazy. I'll see you as soon as you can get here."

"It will be about half an hour, Krekor. Traffic is like that."

Tibor hung up. Gregor turned off his phone and folded it back into the even smaller shape it had to fit into his pocket. He looked up. The receptionist did not seem to have noticed him making a call, or if she had, she didn't seem to have heard what he said. There was nobody else in the waiting room to hear. He felt a little silly. He wasn't a prisoner. He wasn't making a break for it. It just felt as if he was. Even so, he waited, as patiently as he could, for fifteen minutes before he stood up and went to the receptionist's desk.

"I'm going to run across the street for some lunch," he told her. "If Mr. Benedetti is looking for me, he can find me there. I'll be back as soon as I can."

The receptionist gave him a big smile and wrote it all down on a jumbo-sized Post-it note. Gregor turned his back to her, walked down the hall, and pushed the button for the elevator. Nobody followed him. Rob Benedetti didn't come careening into view, demanding that he sit still and wait until they were off to do whatever it was they were supposed to do. Gregor almost resented the ease with which he was able to get away. He'd only been sitting in that damned waiting room because Rob Benedetti had said it was important.

The elevator hit the ground floor and let him out. He went through the plate glass doors to the street and only then remembered what the day was like. The wind hit broadside, forcing up the hem of his coat until it billowed around him like a cape. He saw a homeless man with his possessions in a shopping cart slip into the narrow alley between two buildings, so narrow he thought the cart wouldn't make it. Then he headed toward the coffee shop at a run. Philadelphia wasn't supposed to be this cold. The New England delegates to the Constitutional Convention had referred to it as a "Southern" city. He wondered where homeless people found the carts they used to carry things around in. The most sensible answer was that they stole them from supermarket parking lots, but there weren't that many supermarkets in downtown Philadelphia, and supermarkets usually marked their carts in one way or the other. He turned into the coffee shop and blessed whoever was to be blessed for the existence of hot air heat.

2

Tibor was five minutes later than he said he would be, and by that time Gregor had managed to drink two cups of coffee and read an entire copy of *USA Today*. He'd have bought the *Inquirer*, but he'd already seen it, or the *New York Times*, but there weren't any left. His only other choice had been the *Wall Street Journal*, and he wasn't ready for that yet. Their editorials gave him headaches. All this coffee was giving him a headache, too. From where he sat, he could see the street and the people going by on it, bent against the wind, wrapped up in coats and hats and gloves. The *Inquirer* this morning had had a little advisory on the front page, warning people that it wasn't safe to go out without every inch of skin covered. Frostbite could happen faster than you thought.

A cab pulled up outside, and the door opened, and a small

man in a long black coat, black gloves, and three different-colored scarves got out. Gregor watched as Tibor paid the cabbie and came across the sidewalk to the coffee shop. If he hadn't known Tibor for so many years, he would never have recognized him now. The scarves were red, yellow, and bright royal blue. The bright royal blue one was pulled up over his mouth and nose, as if he were about to rob a bank.

Tibor came in, looked around, and spotted Gregor in one of the booths at the side. He came down next to the counter with its chrome-accented swivel stools and threw his hat on the empty bench.

"Tcha, Krekor, it's impossible. In weather like this there ought to be an emergency. Business should stop. The city should close down. And then I see there are people on the street, living there in the cold. You did not wait lunch for me, Krekor? I ate hours ago."

Tibor unwound the scarves and put them on the seat, too. Then he took off his coat and hung it on the shiny rack that rose up at the side of the booth. Then he sat down. The waitress was there in a flash. Gregor had the guilty feeling that she had been hovering in the background for a while, watching him take up one of her booths without ordering much of anything. On the other hand, there were plenty of empty booths. Nobody was being prevented from having lunch because he was there.

"Krekor?"

"Nothing," Gregor said. "I'm having an odd day. I keep going into fugues. Could I have a Philly steak big meat with extra cheese and some french fries? And, uh, water, I guess, and more coffee."

"I will have only coffee, please," Tibor said.

The waitress gave them both murderous looks, and stomped off. Gregor shook his head. "I forgot about the cold. I should never have asked you to come out. I was just being held prisoner, or something. Rob Benedetti wants me around even if he has nothing for me to do, and I was tired of waiting until he wanted to move."

"I was getting tired of Hannah and Lida talking to me

about wallpaper for the children's center," Tibor said. "They are good women, Krekor, but they make everything into a production. Buy wallpaper in cheerful colors and make sure you can wash it when children draw on it with crayons, what else do they need to know? But they have to discuss things. So there I was."

"And now here you are. I'm glad you came. I thought you might provide a little insight where I need it. Did you hear any of the news about the screeching woman at all? She came to the police and gave them a list of all the people she thought had motive, means, and opportunity to kill her husband."

"How does she know they had opportunity?"

"Good question. I expect that she's just guessing. But the thing is, there's the list, and she's going on television to announce it, and now we're stuck taking the list seriously. But it's an odd list. And there are a number of very odd people on it."

"Like who?"

Gregor took a folded-up copy of the list from the breast pocket of his jacket and handed it over. "Look at the fourth from the top."

Tibor counted down four, and blinked. Then he counted down four again, although why that mattered, Gregor didn't know. Tibor put the list flat down on the table and sat back.

"Well," he said.

"Exactly," Gregor said.

"Dr. Richard Alden Tyler," Tibor said.

"I think people call him Jig."

Tibor brushed this away. "Tcha, Krekor, what can I say? With some people it might only be a nickname, but with him it is an affectation. Like that man in England, who gave up his title so he could sit in the House of Commons and pretend to be a member of the working classes."

"Tony Benn."

"That's right. Lord Anthony Wedgwood Benn. Or Anthony Wedgwood-Benn, Lord Stansgate. Or something. I am sorry, Krekor, but my memory is fuzzy. In both cases, it is an affectation. In Dr. Tyler's case it is more than an affectation. It is a joke."

"You don't think Jig Tyler really believes the things he says politically?"

"I think that Dr. Tyler believes that the world is full of people so stupid they can be hypnotized by an advertising jingle," Tibor said. "He says he is a socialist, but that is not the case. He is not a socialist. He is a Platonist."

"That's a political party?"

"It's a political attitude," Tibor said. "The world should be ruled by philosopher-kings, because they are so much wiser than the rest of us, and they will make good decisions for us because we cannot make good decisions for ourselves. This is the real political divide in the world, Krekor. It's not between conservatives and liberals or between left and right or between Republican and Democrat or between capitalist and socialist. The real political divide in the world is between the people who think that if you make a decision they think is stupid, you must be too stupid to make decisions, and the people who think that every man has a right to make his own decisions about his own life. The second kind of people understand that we are not free to make decisions unless we are free to make bad ones. It's like seat belts."

The waitress was back with Gregor's sandwich and fries and a coffee cup for Tibor. The sandwich was the size of a small Tiger shark and just as thick. When they said big meat in this place, they meant it. They both sat back while the waitress returned to the counter for the coffeepot. Then Tibor began putting sugar and milk into his coffee. He used a lot of both. Gregor thought he was going to end up with a coffee milk shake, and more milk than coffee.

"Seat belts," Gregor said helpfully.

"Yes," Tibor said. "Seat belts. It is a very stupid thing to ride in a car without seat belts. There is nothing to be said for deciding not to do it that would hold weight with any rational person. This is a fact, yes? But it is also a fact that some people do not like to wear seat belts, and won't wear them. So . . . is it a good thing to pass laws to require you to wear them, or not?"

"We did pass a law to require us to wear them."

"Yes, yes, Krekor, we did. But why? Because those of us who have come to the conclusion that not to wear seat belts is stupid have no respect for the people who came to the opposite conclusion. We don't need to treat them like adults who have a right to make their own decisions. We instead treat them like children who have to be forced for their own good. That's the key, Krekor. Laws should never be passed to save people from themselves. When you begin to do that, you threaten to bring democracy to an end."

"You want to repeal the seat belt laws," Gregor said, not sure he was understanding this.

"The seat belt laws are trivial, Krekor, the principle is not. Democracy rests on the principle that ordinary men and women are fully competent to know their own best interests and make their own decisions about their own affairs. When we pass laws against things people do that hurt only themselves, we say that democracy has failed. It didn't work. Ordinary men and women do not know what's good for them, so we have to have smarter, more rational people force them to live in a sensible way. Seat belt laws. The drug war. Laws against pornography in print and on the screen. Laws against giving birth control to unmarried people. These proposals to tax people who are too fat or who won't exercise or who insist on eating food like that," Tibor looked dubiously at Gregor's sandwich, "rather than green salads with low-fat dressing. And Dr. Richard Alden Tyler, who would legislate those things and a great deal more."

"Well," Gregor said, "we're back to Jig Tyler. But I think you've been surfing the Libertarian Party Web site again."

"No, Krekor, I don't surf the Libertarian Party Web site. I do go to the Reason Foundation, which is run by serious people. The Libertarian Party went off the deep end of ideology long ago. So did Dr. Tyler, only in the opposite direction."

Gregor considered his sandwich, which, apparently, somebody wanted to tax to keep him from eating. Or something. He took an enormous bite off the end of it and thought that Philly steaks were the one thing he had really missed in all those years living in Washington. He missed them every time he went out of town, too, because when people made them other places, they didn't make them absolutely right.

"So," he said. "I thought, since you were the only person I knew who had ever met him, you could tell me whether it made sense to have Jig Tyler's name on this list. If you thought he was capable of murder."

"Most people are capable of murder, Krekor, under the right circumstances."

"The kicker in that one is the 'under the right circumstances.' Most people will kill in self-defense, instinctively. A minority of people will kill under the influence of alcohol or drugs just because they lose all inhibitions. I'm not talking about situations like that. I'm talking about cold-blooded murder. Fill the pills with arsenic. Hand them over. Is he capable of a murder like that?"

Tibor considered it. "Yes," he said. "Under the right circumstances."

Gregor threw up his hands.

Tibor shook his head. "No, Krekor, listen. Not that kind of under the right circumstances. When I met Dr. Tyler, we were on a committee to set up a help service for new immigrants. It was a year and a half ago. The purpose of the committee was to put in place a group of trained professionals who could help new immigrants with their problems with the immigration authorities, with finding a place to learn English, with applying for naturalization, with finding employment, with dealing with regulations if they want to start a business. The committee was put together by Reverend Kim at the Korean Baptist Church. His church was helping many more people than it used to, because there have been many more refugees from North Korea in the last few years. He looked around and saw a need, because many of the immigrants who come here do not come to existing communities and must handle things on their own. He put out a call for help and money; he got lots of help and only a little money. Dr. Tyler put in forty-five thousand dollars."

"Well, that's not to his discredit," Gregor said. "That's very good of him."

"Yes, Krekor, it was very good of him. He is a relatively wealthy man. His books sell well and the Nobel Prize brings about a million dollars with it. But he is like many wealthy men in these enterprises. He gives, but he expects to get in return."

"And what did he expect to get?"

"Our agreement not to attempt to block, or even to protest, legislation that would have made the pastors who practice faith healing liable to criminal prosecution for practicing medicine without a license."

Gregor sat back on his seat. It was, he thought, not all that ridiculous an idea. He could even see a couple of ways around the constitutional problems somebody was bound to bring up, probably the ACLU.

"You'd argue it as a kind of fraud protection," he said. "You'd say there is no evidence that faith healing works, ever—is there?"

"No," Tibor said. "It is my personal opinion that if God wanted to cure all our ills with prayer, He wouldn't have given us the minds to invent modern medicine. I am not saying that God does not sometimes heal us when we ask for healing in prayer. Yes, He does that. I am saying I know of no properly corroborated case of a cure through faith healing. There are stories, of course. People claim things. Some of the things they claim might even be true. But they can't document them, and if they can't document them, then the proper response of rational people is to think it probably did not happen. But here, you see, is the difficulty. Not all people, not even all rational people, have the proper response. They hear the stories, and they find the stories more compelling than the hard evidence. And they go to faith healers anyway. Sometimes they give these people a lot of money they cannot afford to give. Sometimes they do things that make their conditions medically worse. Diabetics throw away their insulin, for instance, and some of the ones who do go into comas and some of the ones who go into comas die."

"I'm surprised nobody has thought of this before, if it's that bad," Gregor said.

"People have thought of it before," Tibor said, "and it's worse than you realize. Jehovah's Witnesses will not have blood transfusions, even to save their lives. Christian Scientists do not consult conventional doctors or use conventional medicine. They use Christian Science practitioners instead. Christian Science practitioners pray with the sick person, but do not use medicines or medical technology. There have been cases involving the death of children—"

"Good God."

"Yes, Krekor, good God. There are states that have passed laws requiring parents to seek conventional medical care for children in spite of their religious beliefs, and those hold up when they are passed, because the child itself is not making the decision and the parent who does make the decision is not hurting only himself. And this is fine with me, Krekor. I have nothing at all against such laws to protect children. But I do have something against such laws to stop the adults involved in these religions from refusing medical care they deem to be sinful or inappropriate. Do I think they're stupid to do this? Yes, dear God, yes. I think they are stupid almost to the point of criminality. But I also think that it must be their choice, and their decision, on their terms, and not mine."

"And Jig Tyler, I take it, didn't feel that way," Gregor said.

"Dr. Tyler expressed the opinion that anybody who could look at the evidence and still think faith healing was a rational choice was not, in fact, rational, and that we do not allow mentally incompetent people to run around making decisions they are unable to make and hurting themselves in the process. If a person is mentally ill, we have hearings and commit him to a mental institution. If people persist in irrational and harmful behavior, we make laws against the irrational and harmful behavior. Like seat belt laws. He brought up the seat belt laws. That's why I was thinking of them."

"And that's why you think he is capable of committing a cold-blooded murder?'

Tibor looked into his coffee cup. It was empty. "Krekor,"

he said. "You have to understand something. Dr. Tyler is a serious person."

"You mean he doesn't have much of a sense of humor?"

"No," Tibor said. "I mean he has, what, *gravitas* is the word, and it isn't English. I'm sorry. He is a great mind, probably the greatest I have ever met. This is not a trick, or a joke. He can do things with his mind I can't even understand, never mind do myself. He is a committed person. Nobody wins two Nobels and a Fields Medal if he isn't. His books are outlandish and overwrought, but they are meticulously researched and meticulously documented. I can only guess how quickly and efficiently his mind works, and on how many levels. When we first met, we talked about the formation of the New Testament, and he quoted St. Ignatius to me, in demotic Greek. I went back and looked up the passage when I got home, and he had it exactly. From memory. From a field he has no professional interest in. In the course of our time on the committee, he quoted from or alluded to everybody from Niels Bohr to Charles Schultz. He's read Dante in the medieval Italian and understood it. He's seen every movie Arnold Schwarzenegger ever made. He speaks six languages and reads ten. He can play both Beethoven and Jerry Lee Lewis on the piano. It's an encyclopedic mind, a comprehensive mind, and the most remarkably detailed memory I've ever encountered in anyone, ever. It's not a 'photographic' memory, it's something better. It's a regular memory, just at four hundred times the effectiveness that most of us can manage. If I'd met him under other circumstances, I might have felt privileged to have some time to talk to him. But."

"I knew there was a but coming," Gregor said.

"If there wasn't a but, you'd have no need to talk to me. There is a but, Krekor, yes. And it is that I think that Dr. Tyler does not think he is human, or does not think the rest of us are."

"You mean, he thinks he's God?"

"No, no, Krekor. He is not trite. I mean that he thinks

there is a difference between us and him, a difference so vast it is not a difference in degree but a difference in kind. He sees us the way we see very intelligent dogs. We can love our dogs, but we don't treat them the way we treat our grandmothers. Dogs do not have rights, because we don't think they would know what to do with them. We put them down, if we think we have to."

"That's trite, though, isn't it?" Gregor said. "The great genius who looks down on lesser mortals. I'd think that is as trite as it comes."

"It may be trite, Krekor, but it's also human nature. If you ask me, the most pernicious idea this world ever came up with, next to the perfectibility of man, which has killed more people than smallpox, the next one is the idea of the genius. Leonardo da Vinci did not think of himself as a genius. He got a lot more work done than most of the people who have thought of themselves as geniuses, and he did it without writing himself out of the human race."

Up at the front of the café, the door opened and a woman came in, looking up one row of tables and down another, as if she was frantic to find somebody, but thought she wouldn't. When she got to Gregor she stopped, nodded slightly, and came forward.

"Mr. Demarkian?" she said.

"That's right," Gregor said.

"My name is Laurie Kohl. I'm an assistant DA in Rob Benedetti's office. He says he wonders if you would mind coming across the street right away, right now, it's urgent. There's been a phone call."

"A phone call about what?"

"I don't know," Laurie Kohl said, "but you're not to go up to the office, you're to wait for him in the lobby, he's on his way down. And there are officers coming. I don't know what's going on. Could you come, please?"

PART THREE

Wed–Thurs, February 11–12
High 11F, Low –2F

Sentences of death, where they are freely chosen,
do not need to be written.

—GEORGE STEINER

But consider, Sisters, that the Devil hasn't forgotten us. He also invents his own honors in monasteries and invents his own laws.

—ST. TERESA OF AVILA

No matter how fast light travels it finds darkness
has gotten there first, and is waiting for it.

—TERRY PRATCHETT

ONE

1

The first thing Gregor Demarkian thought of when he had time to think, nearly an hour later, was that no matter how much he had been complaining of the cold these last few days, he hadn't spent much time outside in it. Now he had no choice.

"Outside and in the back," Rob Benedetti had said, when Gregor met him in the lobby little more than half an hour before.

Tibor had been hanging back on the edges. Benedetti hadn't noticed him. Then a whole line of patrol cars had pulled up, and suddenly everybody was running.

Well, no, Gregor thought, *not quite.* He had felt as if everybody was running, but that had at least as much to do with his age as with the way other people were behaving. Marbury and Giametti had come, and they led the charge out the front door of the building, along the sidewalk, and through the narrow opening of an alley leading behind the buildings. Gregor's stomach lurched as soon as he saw where they were going, and he remembered, as clearly as he remembered his conversation with Tibor, seeing the home-less man pushing a shopping cart through that space. He tried to remember what the homeless man had looked like, but couldn't get anything except the impression of someone tall and thin. He tried to remember what was in the cart, but couldn't get that, either, except that the thing was full. Everybody was right. You didn't really look at homeless people. You didn't notice them in detail, the way you might a "normal" person, although, in Gregor's experience, you didn't notice much about "normal" people either, unless they were somebody you knew or something had called your attention to them. Maybe that was the difference. Maybe you didn't notice much about homeless people *especially* when something called your attention to them. You looked away, the way you would if a friend had just done something to embarrass himself in public.

The backs of the buildings were a maze of fire escapes and garbage cans, stray garbage and discarded needles. Did addicts really huddle out in back of the District Attorney's Office to shoot up? Apparently they did. Maybe they did that even behind police stations. If you were out of sight, you were invisible. The shopping cart was parked right at the end of a long line of metal garbage cans, the big ones the trucks came for three times a week. It might have been one more package destined for removal. Gregor wished he had brought a hat. He wished he had remembered to put on his gloves before his fingers felt so cold they could be broken off like icicles on the ends of his hands. He wished that when Marbury and Giametti got whatever it was out of the cart's big well, it wouldn't turn out to be a tall, thin homeless man in dark clothes.

It wasn't. Marbury reached in and disturbed the rags and papers to find the body. Then he checked for a pulse. When he didn't get one, he got Giametti's help and the two of them began to pry the body loose and into the air.

"They have to do that," Rob Benedetti said to Gregor, coming to stand very close to him as they both watched the extraction. Benedetti didn't have a hat, either, and he'd forgotten the gloves entirely. "Even if they don't get a pulse. Even if they know they're dealing with a corpse. If there aren't maggots coming out of the thing, they have to get it out and check it out again, just in case. The last thing we want is to end up killing somebody by accident, or not getting them help in time when we could have."

"Listen," Gregor said. "I think I saw this cart come in here."

"What?"

"I was crossing the street to get to the coffee shop, and this man, this tall, thin man—no, let me back up. This tall, thin person. I just assumed it was a man. Anyway, he pushed a shopping cart pretty much like this one into the alley that leads back here. There couldn't be two of them, could there?"

"I don't know," Benedetti said.

They both looked at Marbury and Giametti, now working with two other officers. The body came up from the well like an unruly beach ball, and then suddenly it was stretched out between the men, one holding the arms, the other holding the legs, a third officer propping up the torso at the middle of the back. They put the body down on the ground just as the ambulances came up out on the street, their sirens screaming into the cold like needles. They got down on their hands and knees and began to pump at the man, to check him out, to try the impossible. It was remarkable how automatic that was, trying the impossible. Even combatants in war, coming up on the enemy wounded, often tried to save them rather than kill them off.

Gregor moved close to get a better look at the man. It was definitely not the one he had seen on the street. This man was short, and chunky, even though he was thin enough, probably from addictions and malnutrition. His clothes, though, were not as worn as you might expect them to be. They were dirty, but not torn, and not frayed. The man's face was a mass of beard, and that made Gregor stop to think. He saw homeless men on the streets every day. Most of them had stubble, at most. Where did they shave? Or did alcohol make a beard stop growing? It hadn't on this man. His beard was filthy and full of bits of food and dirt, but it was most definitely there. His hair was not. He was close to bald, and he didn't have a hat.

Tibor came up to Gregor's side and pulled on his sleeve. Gregor had had no idea he was still there.

"You should go home," Gregor said. "This is a crime scene, at least presumptively. You can't walk around in it without tainting the forensics."

"I'm not walking around in it, Krekor. I only came because I didn't know where else to go. Do you know who this man is?"

"No, but I've got a guess."

"Your guess is the Sherman Markey person that has been in the papers?"

"Exactly."

"I came to say you shouldn't feel guilty about not noticing," Tibor said. "They look at you and you look away, it's not because you're hard-hearted or don't care what happens to other people. It's because they can't be trusted. So many of them are mentally ill, or on drugs or alcohol, you don't know what they're going to do. You worry that they'll get violent."

"And that's supposed to be better?"

"Tcha, Krekor. Life is what it is. People are what they are. We are called by God to be stewards of the earth and His people, but that doesn't make either the earth or His people suitable for a Disney movie. You're afraid of what will happen if you make eye contact with them. So am I. So are we all. Personal solutions will not work here."

"You'd better go," Gregor said. "That's the ambulance people coming in."

Tibor nodded slightly and walked away, down the alley, toward the street. Gregor knew what Tibor had been trying to tell him, but it didn't make him feel any better. There was something, planted deep inside him by a mother who never turned a tramp away from the door, that said he should be better than that.

The ambulance men were not taking long to decide that the body was just that, a body, and not an emergency. They had pulled back to let the forensics team move in. Gregor didn't remember seeing that team arrive.

"My mother," Gregor said to Benedetti, "used to feed homeless people. They'd come onto the street, back when the street was less upscale than it is now. It was tenements, really. They'd come and she'd be sitting on the stoop with a big basket, she and all the other women, working on things for dinner. Peeling vegetables. Breaking up bread to use in these Armenian dishes, I don't even know what to call them. The men would come by and they would give them food. All the time. Except they didn't call them the homeless, then. They called them tramps."

Benedetti gave Gregor a very odd look. "There are still tramps. And people still feed them. But Mr. Demarkian, this is not a tramp we're dealing with here, and neither are the homeless people you see most of the time on the street. It's not the Great Depression anymore."

"Give me a break," Gregor said. "Do I look that old?"

"It's not the 1950s, either," Benedetti said. "Most of the people you see on the street these days, especially in a city like Philadelphia, aren't just down on their luck. A large proportion of them are mentally ill. You could get yourself killed making contact with them if you don't know how. Another large portion of them are addicted. The alkies won't do you any harm, except to piss on your shoes, but the drug addicts can and do get violent and some of them can and will kill people who look like they have the price of a fix on them. You can't go on some kind of personal crusade to fix things."

"That's what they say about giving them money," Gregor said. "That you shouldn't give them money, because they'll only use it for booze or drugs. That you only encourage them to bother other people."

"I give money to beggars all the time. I don't worry about what they buy with it. If booze and drugs are that important to them, maybe they know something about themselves I don't. And I don't worry about them bothering other people. People could use being bothered more than they are. Do you know what I do worry about? I worry about them following me home, and following me day after day, until I have to have somebody arrest them, or they have a knife."

"Do you really worry that all homeless people are violent?"

"No," Benedetti said. "Almost none of them are. I worry I'm going to get the one in a hundred who is. Give it up, Mr. Demarkian. The homeless problem wouldn't disappear if you were more careful to look these people in the eyes and give them money."

"They've bagged the body," Gregor said.

He and Benedetti both turned to watch the body being lifted up by the edges of the black body bag and carried down the alley to the ambulance waiting at the end. Gregor wondered why they always called an ambulance when they had a dead body, even when they were absolutely positive that the body was dead. It was as if they couldn't bear the idea of someone dying without medical attention, although where any of these men and women would get medical attention, Gregor didn't know. There was Medicaid, but most of these people were too confused to apply for it and too apt to have no address to use when applying. They were paranoid, too. They were afraid of doctors. They were afraid of social workers. Maybe that was the common thread in all their lives. Maybe they were all so afraid of people, and of living, that living like this was better than having to face the demand to communicate on a daily basis.

I'm blithering, Gregor thought. *I no longer know what I'm thinking. If Tibor could hear me, he'd lecture me for an hour.*

"Listen," he told Rob Benedetti. "It's freezing out here. Do we all really have to stand out here in the cold until forensics is through?"

"Nah. We can go back in. I was thinking that myself. Is this the man you saw pushing the cart before?"

"No. This one is short and chunky. Not fat but—"

"Yeah, I know. Some of them are fat, did you know that? It happens more with women than with men. How they get and stay fat, I'll never know."

"Yes," Gregor said, "well, the one I saw was tall and thin. Very thin. I'd say a man, except I don't really know that."

"Because you didn't really look," Rob Benedetti said. "Let's not start that again."

"I wasn't going to. He was tall and thin and wearing dark clothes. That's all I know. We might be able to piece together a few things if we went back inside, though. I told your receptionist I was leaving and where I was going, for instance."

"So?"

"So, she might remember the time," Gregor said. "I told her I was leaving, I came downstairs, and right as I was walking out the building, there this guy was. I saw him pushing the cart along the sidewalk, and then I saw him turn into that alley we came down. The time would be a big help if, as I presume, we think that this is Sherman Markey and the person I saw pushing the cart is the person who killed him."

"And Drew Harrigan," Rob Benedetti said. "We can only hope. Okay, that's good. We'll get the time. I'd be happier if we could get the identification first. We're all just assuming—"

"The woman who came to get me said you had a phone call."

"We did," Rob Benedetti said. "That's part of the reason why we're assuming. Crap. This makes no sense. Assuming this was the guy who killed them both, and this is Markey, dead from I don't know what, why not just leave him wherever he fell? Why bring him out here in the wretched cold and dump him behind the DA's Office?"

"Lots of reasons," Gregor said. "Markey may have died in a place that could incriminate the murderer, although I doubt it. I can't see any of the people we've looked at in this case so far, not even any of the people on Ellen Harrigan's list, inviting a man like Sherman Markey onto their property for any reason. It would make more sense for them to pick a neutral place to meet. My guess is that somebody needs us to know that Sherman Markey is dead."

"Needs us to know that?" Rob Benedetti said. "Why?"

Gregor shrugged. "There's something somebody gets if Sherman Markey is dead. Rather than just missing, I mean. I don't suppose it's possible that Sherman Markey made a will."

"I'll ask the people over at the Justice Project about it," Rob Benedetti said, "but somehow, I doubt it."

"So do I. Is it possible Sherman Markey was left anything of value in Drew Harrigan's will?"

"If he was, I'll join the circus."

"My feeling exactly," Gregor said. "I don't know. There has to be a reason to go through all this elaborate nonsense to make sure we found the body, right away, and to make sure we got it identified right away. I don't believe in detective story murderers who go through a lot of elaborate rigmarole in order to commit the perfect crime. Murderers don't do that kind of thing in real life."

"Charles Stuart," Rob Benedetti said solemnly.

"Yes, well," Gregor said. "Any man stupid enough to shoot himself in the stomach is a wild card nobody should make any predictions about. Let's get inside."

"Let's get inside," Rob Benedetti agreed.

He walked over to the teams surrounding the crime scene, and had a few words.

2

Gregor Demarkian liked crime scenes. He liked the concreteness of them, the mundane specificity of forensics before the analysis got underway and the medical examiner started to think of himself as a cross between Conan the Barbarian and Sherlock Holmes. He liked them a lot better than having to investigate in their absence, which happened sometimes, as it had with Drew Harrigan. The problem was that, in a way, it had happened now, too. Sherman Markey, assuming it was Sherman Markey, had not been killed in that back alley. There was too much of that going around in this case. None of the bodies was ever found where they died, and none of them was found where he'd been murdered. It made Gregor wonder how it had been done and why it had been done that way. To kill someone as Drew Harrigan had been killed, you either had to not care how long it took before the death occurred, or you had to be sure that the victim would ingest the poison close to immediately. If there was no urgency to the murder, why commit it? And was it ever possible to be absolutely sure that your victim would swallow a pill just when you wanted him to? Drew Harrigan could have taken those pills on the bus coming up to the monastery, or right away, as soon as he got them. He could have stepped out the murderer's door and chugged them down dry and dropped dead half a block away.

Actually, there were a lot of questions to be asked about Drew Harrigan that nobody was asking yet, and others that were being asked, but without results. Back up in Rob Benedetti's office, Gregor looked around again at the prints on the walls and the furniture, utilitarian and drab, so much like what anybody would expect the furniture to look like in a District Attorney's Office that Gregor wondered if the person who had decorated it had taken her cues from old episodes of *Perry Mason*. He didn't like the unusual in murder cases. He didn't even believe the unusual in murder cases. When the unusual did exist, it was the sign of a serial killer, and that was not what was happening here.

Rob Benedetti was on the phone. He got off and came over to where Gregor was looking at a print of Connecticut's Charter Oak. Gregor had no idea why the print was there.

"Marbury and Giametti will be up in a minute. I just talked to the ME. He's standing by waiting for the body to be brought up to him. I want identification and confirmation of identification within the hour. This is making me crazy. I used to be a police officer, did you know that?"

"No," Gregor said, "but I guessed."

"Marbury and Giametti are good officers. It's not that. It's that the whole thing is taking too much time. I know. I shouldn't lose my grip. But from the beginning, the whole thing—when I get my hands on Bruce Williamson, I'm going to kill him."

"People threaten that all the time," Gregor said.

"I know," Rob Benedetti said, "but I mean it. I mean, you know, you absolutely know, that Drew Harrigan could never have been in rehab. If he had been and had gone missing, they would have notified the court. They would have had to. That's a condition of these things. Always. Which means Bruce Williamson knew that wherever Drew Harrigan was going, it wasn't rehab."

"Not necessarily," Gregor said. "He might just have agreed to rehab without the controls. He isn't required by law to impose the controls. He's the judge."

"He'd have known something was wrong if they didn't want the controls," Benedetti said. "I hate these guys, did you know that? Guys like Bruce Williamson. And he isn't the only one. Guys who are so damned impressed with money and fame that they think they're doing the right thing running an entirely separate justice system for the big guys. Williamson is not known as an easy judge, did you know that? If you're a black fifteen-year-old caught with a handful of coke in your pocket, you're going to jail. If you're a black sixteen-year-old, you're going to an adult prison, and to hell with what we all know is going to happen to you there. But if you're Drew Harrigan, or Alexandra Brand—"

"Alexandra Brand lives in Philadelphia?"

"She was here filming a movie," Benedetti said. "Got drunk as a skunk one night at some private club downtown, got in her car, ran a red light, hit a homeless woman pushing around one of those carts, and just up and left the scene."

"Wait," Gregor said. "I remember that. I do. It was in the papers nonstop for about three days and then it disappeared."

"She pled and Williamson gave her probation. No community service, nothing. Just probation. And the old woman was dead. This is the problem, Mr. Demarkian. This is supposed to be a country of laws and not men, and we're neck deep in a celebrity culture that makes the way the Brits treat royalty look egalitarian. It's insane."

"Why didn't Drew Harrigan plead guilty and get probation?" Gregor asked. "If Williamson will sit still for a movie star who commits a hit-and-run homicide, why wouldn't he sit still for Harrigan?"

"We weren't buying," Benedetti said. "We went in there—I went in there—and told them flat out that I wasn't going to accept a plea bargain. I was going to insist on going to trial, and if Williamson and Harrigan's people tried to get around me, I was going to go to the press. That put what's his name, Savage, that put him up the wall, and there was a guy there from Harrigan's sponsoring network, Liberty-Heart, those people. That guy wasn't happy, either. Maybe they were worried about the audience."

"I take it you weren't around when Alexandra Brand had her problems?"

"No," Benedetti said, "and she'd have had more problems if I had been. But it's not just judges like Williamson. It's some of the cops, too. You know what all that means with Harrigan screaming and yelling. Somebody was paid off. Maybe more than one somebody. The guys don't even see it as bribery. They're starstruck. Everybody is. And I guess they don't see the point in bothering people who matter with what they do to people who don't, which is what they think of the people who live on the street. Does it bother you that we've all seen pictures of this guy Sherman Markey, and I've even seen him in person on at least two occasions, and none of us can recognize him when we see him?"

"I've never seen pictures of him," Gregor said.

"Yeah, I know, but it's like I said. I saw him in person. And if he passed me on the street today, I wouldn't know who he was. I wouldn't even begin to know. It's things like that that get me nuts. This doesn't even feel like a case, do you know what I mean? If it wasn't for the Harrigan connection and we found this guy in the alley out back, the entire system would conspire in making us drop it. It isn't important. These people die all the time. Move on to something that needs to get done."

The door opened and Marbury and Giametti came in, looking more than a little exasperated.

"It's not our precinct, and the only reason we're here is to report back to where we belong," Giametti was saying. "They've got detectives to handle cases like this, and we've got a job to do we aren't doing."

"I thought our job was to bring the bad guys in to justice,"

Marbury said. "Whoever killed this guy is a bad guy, and he's connected to our bad guy, he probably is our bad guy. You don't have enough imagination. The city isn't divided up into little grids that are completely sealed off from each other. Bad guys go from one precinct to the other all the time. If we get stuck in the bureaucratic maze, we won't get anything done."

Gregor gave a moment's thought to the fact that the lines of jurisdiction were becoming hopelessly blurred. The one constant in this case, the one person who arguably had the right to be in it who was actually following it, was John Jackman, and he was keeping very carefully in the background. Gregor didn't think that the precinct where Drew Harrigan had actually died had detectives on the job yet. He didn't know if they knew they were supposed to.

Benedetti waved Marbury and Giametti into seats. "I've been complaining about celebrity justice," he said.

Marbury shrugged. "Everybody does it. If we'd gone along the night we picked up Drew Harrigan, we wouldn't all be sitting here now. And at least two people probably wouldn't be dead."

"You don't know that," Giametti said. "You don't know what this guy died of. You know what it's like with these guys. They die all the time. We don't know he was murdered."

"If he wasn't murdered, why push the cart into the alley and then call us up to find it?" Gregor said.

Giametti shrugged. "Maybe he died where somebody didn't want him found, but that doesn't mean he was murdered. He could have just been somewhere, with somebody, who'd rather we didn't know . . . something."

Gregor thought about it. "What about the phone call?" he said. "Who took the phone call?"

"Carol in the outer office did," Benedetti said. "The phone rang, she picked it up, she did her usual thing with 'District Attorney's Office,' or however she says it. Some guy said he had a message for 'her boss,' by which she presumed he meant me, and then he said that we ought to look out back because there was a dead body on our doorstep.

She's a bright woman. She asked him to hold. He didn't buy it. He hung up."

"Did she get the number?" Gregor asked.

"We always get the number," Rob Benedetti said. "We've got the kind of caller ID system an ordinary citizen couldn't buy if his life depended on it. We've got the number. It's going to turn out to be a public pay phone, probably in the neighborhood. If I was this guy, I'd go use the one right down there on the street."

"I wouldn't," Gregor said. "Remember, I saw him. He was dressed to look like a homeless man. Is that usual, homeless men using public pay phones?"

"The thing is," Benedetti said, "he might not really have been dressed to look like anything. You see a guy with a cart—"

Gregor thought about it. "Okay, possible. I did pay more attention to the cart."

"I'd really like to see a study done on what it is about people that makes us tag them as homeless on the street," Rob Benedetti said. "I know they did a study where somebody went out to Grand Central in New York dressed really nicely and asked for money, and people gave it to him by the fistful, where they wouldn't give it to the people who looked like they obviously needed it. I think the cart would have been enough."

"Maybe," Gregor said. "I'll admit I can't remember a thing about the man except that he was tall, and I don't really know he was a man. It was just a general impression. I wish I knew where Drew Harrigan has been these last four weeks or whatever it was."

"Me, too," Benedetti said.

"I wish I knew more about Ellen Harrigan and her list," Gregor said. "Did that strike you, that that wasn't the kind of list you'd expect a woman like that to make up herself? Jig Tyler, okay, he's a celebrity himself. He goes on television. But that other one, that Alison Standish. She might be important at the university, I don't know. But she's not—well, quite frankly, she's not the kind of woman I'd have expected a woman like Ellen Harrigan ever to have heard of. And then there are some of the others. Ray Dean Ballard does what, runs an organization that works with the homeless? Would she have known who he was? Why?"

"Good question," Benedetti said. "Ballard isn't even one of the people Harrigan went after on his show. Most of the others are, except for Marla Hildebrande, who does the scheduling for LibertyHeart. What've we got?" He looked around the top of his desk and pulled a sheet of paper from the mess. "Jig Tyler. Alison Standish. Ray Dean Ballard. Marla Hildebrande. Kate Daniel. That's Kate Daniel of the Justice Project, by the way. I assume Ellen Harrigan knew who she was, if only because she was the one spearheading the effort to sue Drew Harrigan on behalf of Sherman Markey. Sherman Markey isn't on the list, though. That's interesting. It seemed to me that Ellen Harrigan was blaming Sherman for everything."

"It seemed like that to me, too," Gregor said. "But mostly it seemed as if this wasn't her idea. Would Neil Savage pull this kind of stunt?"

"You mean, ask her to come to us with a list? Maybe. I don't know what lawyers would do. I never know what Savage is going to do."

The phone on Benedetti's desk rang, and he reached for it. Gregor went back to looking at prints on the walls. There were a couple of judges and lawyers, meant to look old. The judges were in wigs. There was one of Clarence Darrow from some newspaper's editorial cartoon so ancient that the man was hooking his thumbs into his suspenders in front of the jury.

Rob Benedetti put down the phone and said, "Shit."

"Excuse me?" Gregor said. Here was a difference between the Federal Bureau of Investigation under J. Edgar Hoover and the real world: in the Bureau in those days they had been trained not to swear with more diligence than they had been trained how to shoot, and if they were caught swearing in public they were suspended from duty for two weeks.

Rob Benedetti was staring at his phone and running his hands through his hair. "That was the ME's office," he said. "They got the body first thing. They've got it up on a slab. In the meantime, there's something he thinks we need to know."

"What's that?" Gregor asked.

"They did a fingerprint check," Benedetti said. "Whoever that is, it isn't Sherman Markey."

TWO

I

When Marla Hildebrande first saw the ID drawing up there on the television screen, her thought was: *Oh, God, Frank has robbed a liquor store.* Her next thought after that was, simply, that ID drawings were never any good. They never looked like the person the police were looking for. Then she began to feel uneasy. The sound was not on on the set. It never was, on the office set, unless somebody got interested in something and decided to turn it up. Marla was never entirely sure why Frank had the set in the office to begin with. He said he wanted to be ready if there was an assassination. Assassinations were one of those things he thought likely, on general principle. Marla had always secretly believed that he was interested in expanding the operation into cable. It was the kind of thing he would do, and he was young and ambitious, in spite of the lounge-around-the-office-couches-act he liked to put on for employees. That was Princeton. Never let them see you work.

She went across the field of desks to the little control panel for the screen and turned the sound up only slightly. It was past closing time and most of the women who worked in the bullpen were gone. It always bothered Frank that the secretaries and typists went home as soon as the closing bell rang, and Marla had never been able to explain to him about the differences between careers and jobs, or professions and simply earning a living. That was Princeton, too. Marla came from a long line of people who had had jobs and not careers and had been more interested in earning a living than establishing a profession. You didn't drive yourself into the ground physically and emotionally when you weren't much interested in the job and really only wanted to make enough to pay for the house, and the vacation, and a night out every month at the nearest chain restaurant. Marla had to give Frank this: he never *despised* those things. They weren't what he wanted for himself, but he didn't look down on the people who did want them.

Frank couldn't have held up a liquor store, she thought, and leaned in to hear what was going on. But the story had changed. The story on the screen now seemed to concern puppies.

Marla had a sudden urge to let it go, as if what she was about to do next was going to determine what that ID drawing meant. She knew you couldn't change the past. She knew that. She just felt as if she could. She reached out for the controls and flipped to CBS, but the story there was about the presidential campaign, which hadn't even started yet. She looked long and hard at the face of the Democratic candidate, who wasn't the Democratic candidate yet, since the convention hadn't happened, and then switched compulsively to NBC. It felt disloyal, somehow. Frank was devoted to ABC and Peter Jennings. He said he liked his Americans to be Canadians.

NBC had the ID drawing up. Marla turned the sound high, much too high, and then turned it back down again. On the other side of the room, one of the two lone secretaries still at her desk made an annoyed noise and shuffled papers noisily.

". . . police are asking the public's help in identifying this man, found dead this afternoon in an alley near the office of the Philadelphia District Attorney. Originally believed to be a homeless . . ."

Marla didn't hear the rest of it. She felt emptied of air.

Once, when she was very small, she'd fallen from the top of a slide in Roger's Park, right next to her house. It wasn't a high slide, but it was wavy, so you bumped and sank as you went down, and she'd wanted very much to know what it felt like to go down. Then she'd gotten to the top of the ladder, and all of a sudden it had felt completely hypnotic. She was up here, the ground was down there, it was calling to her. The next thing she knew she was on the ground, and she couldn't breathe. This was like that. She couldn't breathe. She couldn't think. She couldn't move.

She had heard the news at noon. She had listened to it on one of their own radio stations. At noon they were saying that the body of Sherman Markey had been found in the alley, and she remembered thinking that was good. Now that they'd found Sherman Markey, it wouldn't matter anymore about Ellen Harrigan's suspect list.

"Listen," she'd told Frank just yesterday. "You think it's funny, but you're not on it. I'm on it. Why that idiot woman thinks I'm more likely to kill Drew Harrigan than you, I don't know."

"Don't worry," Frank said. "It's just a red herring. If you don't want the police looking at you, you point them at somebody else."

She really couldn't breathe, but she had to be breathing. She really couldn't move, but she had to be moving, because she was sitting down, backing into one of those horrible ergonomic chairs with the wheels that always threatened to shoot the thing out from under her. She was also crying. The tears were coming down her face in sheets. She hadn't realized it until they dripped down onto her skirt and then through, making her thigh wet.

She looked up and the two secretaries who had been working at their desks only a moment ago were standing beside her. She couldn't remember either of their names, and that was ridiculous. She knew the names of everybody who worked in the office. Hell, she knew the names of everybody who worked for LibertyHeart Communications and had anything to do with scheduling, anywhere in the country.

They weren't that big a company yet that she could afford not to know people's names.

One of the secretaries was tall and young and African-American and looked as if she could have walked into any stray modeling agency on any stray day and picked up enough work so that she'd never have to use a word processor again. The other was a middle-aged white woman in a red dress that was much too young for her. What did it mean that clothes were much too young for somebody? Marla didn't know.

It was the African-American woman who spoke up. "Was that—I know this is ridiculous, but we thought that looked like, you know, like Mr. Sheehy."

"It did look like Mr. Sheehy," the white woman said.

"I thought it looked like Mr. Sheehy, too." Marla rubbed her palms against the sides of her face. She could breathe now, and knew she was breathing, but that didn't seem to be much help.

"Are they saying Mr. Sheehy is dead?" the African-American woman asked.

She had to make a decision, Marla thought. That was what she was paid for, making decisions. What would it mean, if Frank was really dead? What would happen to LibertyHeart? Who would own it? Frank had a large and extended family, scattered everywhere. He was the only one of them who worked very hard or did much of anything, but they all had money. When she had first come to work for this company, she had been endlessly fascinated by the parade of Ivy League colleges that seemed to be somehow attached to people Frank was related to. Later, she learned to be more impressed with the private high schools. It was odd, what people cared about, and what you learned to care about along with them. She wasn't afraid for her job. She was the best scheduler in the business. Other companies tried to head-hunt her three or four times a year. She was afraid for herself. If she had had a motive to kill Drew Harrigan—and she still didn't think she'd really had one; she couldn't imagine what it would be—she must have had an even better motive to kill Frank Sheehy. Didn't the employees always want to kill the boss?

"We have to call the police," she said.

The room around her was very quiet. The two other women were very still. The whole thing sounded absurd, sounding like an echo against the walls of this enormous room. You called the police if a disgruntled employee showed up with a shotgun. You called the police if you arrived in the morning and found that the place had been broken into. You called the police if the assistant with the abusive husband was getting beaten to a pulp on the front doorstep. You didn't call the police to tell them you thought that the homeless man who had been found dead in a shopping cart behind the District Attorney's Office was your boss and the owner of the company you worked for, and had at least ten million dollars in a trust fund that kept him happily on the mailing list of every good tailor in town.

"I have to call the police," Marla said again. That was when she realized that just being able to breathe, or just being able to move, didn't necessarily mean you were going to get anything done.

"You can use my phone," the African-American woman said, tugging at Marla's elbow. "Come on. I'd make the call myself, but under the circumstances—"

"You knew him better," the white woman said. There was an edge to her voice, as if she were just about to get hysterical. Marla remembered her now. Her name was Karin Kowalski. She did get hysterical sometimes, especially when the computers broke down.

Marla followed the African-American woman to her desk and sat down in her chair. She hated those chairs. She hated the wheels. She hated the small seats and smaller seat backs. She hated OSHA for insisting they have them. She couldn't remember the number she was supposed to call if she had any information about this man.

"Did either of you see the number?" Marla said. "They flashed a number on the screen, didn't they? Did either of you see it?"

"You can call the local precinct," the African-American woman said. "They'll have the number. They may even be able to transfer you."

"Yes," Marla said. She didn't know the number of the precinct, either. She was sweating. She was still crying. Everything about her was wet.

The African-American woman reached across Marla's lap to the computer, tapped on the keys, and brought up a list. "Second from the top. That's the precinct."

"Why second?" Marla asked. "Shouldn't the police be first?"

"The fire department is first. Do you want me to dial for you?"

"No," Marla said. "No, no. That's all right." She picked up the phone. The African-American woman's name was Charisse Johnson. That was it. Somebody ought to promote her. What would happen to the secretaries if LibertyHeart shut down, or was sold to another company, a bigger company? She punched numbers into the phone pad and listened to the ring. It wasn't true that if she didn't make this call, none of this would be real.

The phone was picked up by a woman with a voice like Arnold Schwarzenegger and a delivery like Speedy Gonzales. Marla didn't catch her name, and she didn't catch the number of the precinct, either.

"Excuse me," she said. "I know this isn't the right number to be calling but—"

"This number is for police business, ma'am. If you don't have police business, you shouldn't be tying up this line."

"But it is police business," Marla said. "It's just that I know this isn't the right number, and I hope you have the right number—"

"This is not directory assistance, ma'am."

Marla would have been on the verge of tears if she hadn't already been crying, and now she didn't know what to do next. The policewoman on the phone sounded angry at her. She was scared to death of people being angry at her. Maybe that was just something she used to be. She was having trouble breathing again.

"Ma'am?" the policewoman said.

"Give me that," Charisse Johnson said. She took the phone away from Marla, and Marla was glad to let it go. *I'm reverting,* Marla thought. *I'm reverting to kindergarten or something. I'm not making any sense at all.*

"This is Charisse Johnson," Charisse said into the phone. "I'm at LibertyHeart Communications. We're at—well, good, I'm glad you know where we are. That may save time. And there's no need to snap. We do have police business. There was a story on the news about two seconds ago, saying the police are looking for anyone who can identify a man found in a shopping cart behind . . . yes, that one . . . yes, we do think we can identify him . . . yes . . . thank you . . . yes . . . if I could have that number . . . yes."

Charisse Johnson hung up. "Cow," she said. "I hate women like that."

"She's only doing her job," Karin Kowalski said.

"Her job is to deal with the public," Charisse said, "and she's doing it badly. Do you want me to make the call to the hotline, Ms. Hildebrande? You still look very upset."

"Why are you a secretary?" Marla said. "Why aren't you a manager somewhere? What were we thinking when we hired you?"

"You were thinking I didn't have a college degree, which I never got because I had my daughter when I was sixteen. Don't worry about it. Do you want me to call the hotline?"

"Yes," Marla said. She would worry about it, though. If she landed another job in Philadelphia, she would steal Charisse Johnson away from whoever bought LibertyHeart and give her the kind of job she deserved. There was something wrong with a system that wouldn't let you hire a competent person who didn't have a college degree but would let you hire an incompetent one who did. She wasn't thinking straight again.

Charisse had sat down on the edge of her desk and punched in the numbers for the hotline. Marla closed her eyes and listened very carefully for the moment when she would say Frank's name into the receiver, and it would all be as real as it would ever get.

2

Growing up, Kate Daniel had always wanted, anxiously, to be perfect—to be perfectly obedient, really, so that nobody would ever be angry with her, and she would never do anything wrong. She remembered that time of her life with a kind of wonder. She could still feel the grinding anxiety of it just under the surface of her skin, like a ghost that had lost the capacity to haunt her. Other girls violated dress codes or rolled their skirts up in the girls' room after classes were over. Kate checked the dress code twice before she allowed herself to leave her room in the morning, and her skirts always fell precisely at the middle of her knees. Other girls smoked in the boiler room and told the housemother they needed to pick up feminine hygiene products at the drugstore so that they could meet boys in town. Kate never smoked anything, anywhere, and the only boys she knew were the ones who came to the subscription dances her parents brought her to over the long vacations. She could see some point in the way she had been when she'd still been a teenager and in boarding school, but the habit had followed her to college, and then into law school, and then into her marriage. Feminist magazines imagined the "pioneers," the women who broke the sex barrier in the law schools and medical schools, as bold and angry. Kate had been timid and afraid, and most afraid of all that she would be discovered doing something wrong. Maybe it was just that she felt guilty all the time, although at this moment she could not think of what she would have thought she was guilty of. She did know that she had always felt as if she were about to be caught at something.

Of course, it was possible that it was that very timidity, that long history of anxiety, that had made her what she was now. She had never smoked cigarettes in boarding school or college or law school, but she had smoked marijuana in that little one-room hole she had rented when she'd first left Neil and come to New York. She had never known any boys her parents would have disapproved of, but after she'd ended her marriage she'd lived three years with an activist lawyer from a working-class family who gave fiery speeches about how it was necessary to end private property and bring the rich to justice. If you start at one extreme, you go to the other. It bothered her that she was still going to extremes. Surely she should have grown out of all that by now. She ought to be more than ready to play by the rules. That was what the law was all about.

Chickie George was standing at the door to her office, looking—unhappy. Actually, he looked furious. That was the word Kate had been trying so hard not to think. That seemed to be left over, too. She still didn't want some people to be mad at her.

She had a pile of papers on the desk. She moved them around. She had a pen in a penholder. She took it out, put it down on the green felt blotter, picked it up, and put it back again. She wondered why they still had blotters for desks. People didn't use quill pens anymore. They didn't even use fountain pens most of the time. They didn't even use pens. Here was a way the computer had changed everything. The office wasn't paperless, but everybody's handwriting shat.

"Do you mind if I come in for a moment?" Chickie George said.

"I was just thinking about this man I lived with when I first came to New York," Kate said. "He was, I don't know, the kind of man women like me lived with in that time and place. His father worked in a factory. His mother was a school librarian. He'd gone to somewhere, the State University of New York at Buffalo, I think. He wanted the revolution to come tomorrow, with bells on."

Chickie came into the room and sat down in the guest's chair without asking if he could. "We need to talk about something," he said.

"Are there people like that anymore?" Kate asked him.

"People who want the revolution to come tomorrow? Does anybody take them seriously? It got to the point where I couldn't stand to be around them. The revolution isn't going to come tomorrow, and it shouldn't. Socialism is dead, and if any of us had had any sense to begin with, we'd have known that before the Berlin Wall fell. Stalin and Pol Pot are the revolution personified. It was never going to be any better than that."

"We need to talk about something," Chickie said again. "I don't think the revolution comes into it, at the moment."

"Don't you? I think the revolution comes into everything. People can't imagine incremental change. They want perfection. I don't want perfection anymore. I want a country where everybody who works for a living can live decently, eat decently, and send their kids to good schools right through their PhDs. And I want a country where the people who are really unable to take care of themselves are taken care of. And I want it now. But I don't want a revolution anymore. I don't expect the world to be perfect."

"Good," Chickie said, "but right now I've got a problem that's half-personal and half-not. I offered to go to Gregor Demarkian for you. You sent me there, and you know that I had history with that man, even if it wasn't much of one."

"It was hardly any at all," Kate said. "You were one of the suspects in a case he consulted on. Did he even remember who you were?"

"As a matter of fact, he did," Chickie said, "and I wasn't putting on the act I used to when he knew me last time. But that doesn't matter. What does matter is that my relationship to him is important to me, slight as it is. And there's more than that to be taken into consideration. I live and work here. I want to practice law in Philadelphia once I graduate and pass the bar. Gregor Demarkian is a very important person in this city, especially if you're a lawyer. He's tight with the commissioner of police and half the detectives and beat cops in the department. He can make or break a defense. I don't want him angry with me, and I don't want him deciding that I'm a dishonest jerk who's willing to use our acquaintance to make him look like an idiot."

"You're not making him look like an idiot."

"I know I'm not. I had no idea whatsoever what you'd done until about twenty minutes ago. But it's going to look like I made him look like an idiot, and that's all it's going to take. If you don't get on the phone to Gregor Demarkian and tell him what you've done, I'll do it."

"And would you tell him what I've done, that it was me?"

"Yes."

"You shouldn't be so harsh about it," Kate said. "I wasn't, I'm not, being deliberately meretricious. I'm not lying for the sake of lying. You can't defend these people without breaking some of the rules. The rules weren't made for them. They were made for people like you and me."

"That sounds like the revolution you say you don't want to have," Chickie said.

"No, it's not," Kate said. "It's just realism, that's all. This is a society—all societies are societies—where the rich count for more than the poor, the educated count for more than the uneducated, the able count for more than the disabled. I don't expect to make that disappear anymore, but I do have to do whatever I can to level the playing field when I get into a fight. I can't just go out there and behave as if my client were, well, you."

"Gregor Demarkian is a very decent human being," Chickie said. "He's not radical, and he's not particularly 'progressive,' but he's a decent human being and he's a fair one. You're making unwarranted assumptions about how he will behave—"

"It's not just him," Kate pointed out. "It's the police and the district attorney, too. They're part of this. You act as if nothing and nobody existed but ourselves and Gregor Demarkian."

"Two people are dead, Kate. Including that poor idiot from LibertyHeart Communications, who seemed to me like a pretty decent human being, too. This is not a game anymore. This is not a chance to stick it in the eye of Drew Harrigan."

"He was the first one who was dead," Kate said.

"Call Demarkian, and tell him what you did."

Kate swiveled the chair around so that her back was to Chickie and stared at the posters on the wall. They were somebody else's posters, or else some secretary's idea of what would be suitable for guest lawyers who wouldn't be around very long. "It's still about Drew Harrigan, you know," she said. "It's still about who he is, and what he can get away with, and what men like Sherman Markey can't. It's still not impossible that we'll lose this fight and Markey will end up on the run or in jail."

"He's already on the run."

"I know. I'm just saying that you have to be more careful than you're being. You can't just charge into the breach and blunder around and expect it all to work out like an episode of *Law and Order.*"

"Call Demarkian or I will."

"All right," Kate said, making up her mind. She swiveled the chair around again so that she was facing forward. She was struck, as she was sometimes, by just how young Chickie George really was. She wondered how much of his attitude had to do with the fact that he had a very good friend who was becoming a nun. She put her elbows down on the desk and her face in her hands. "All right," she said again. "First thing in the morning, I'll call him. You get me his number, and I'll call him. But you have to understand. I don't really think this is the right thing to do."

"Why not call him now?"

"Because it's late," Kate said. "It's very late. If he's home, he's going to want to rest, or he's going to be already resting. If he's not home, he's not in a place where I can talk to him in peace. I'll call him first thing in the morning. Get me the number. You were the one who said he wakes up early every day to have breakfast at some restaurant."

"At the Ararat on Cavanaugh Street at seven," Chickie George said. He hesitated. "All right. I suppose. I'm not happy about the delay, but I suppose. But no later than that. If he still doesn't know by tomorrow afternoon, I'm going to tell him."

"How will you know if he knows?"

"I'll ask him." Chickie leaned forward and took the note-pad that sat beside the telephone—another guest-lawyer note, Kate thought, another message from the land of the secretaries. Chickie took the pen out of the inside pocket of his jacket and wrote the number on the pad. "There it is," he said. "You don't even need an area code."

Kate picked up the notepad and put it squarely in the mid-dle of the felt blotter. "First thing tomorrow morning," she said. "I get in here at seven anyway."

Chickie stood up. "It's the one thing I don't like about public interest law," he said. "Too many of the people who do it seem to assume that the world is full of enemies, and offense is the only defense they can play."

"The world is full of enemies," Kate said. "The fact that human nature won't allow the revolution to succeed won't change that."

"I've got to go downstairs and do some work on the single-room occupancy thing," Chickie said. "The people who are on the other side of that aren't enemies. They're just trying to do what they're trying to do."

"Trying to throw the poor into the street and let them starve?"

"You don't believe that any more than I do," Chickie said. "Never mind. I'm going to go work. First thing tomorrow morning, or I do it myself."

Kate waited patiently as Chickie left the office and went down the hall. He was very young and very angry, and it wasn't certain that he'd learn to understand all the things she had learned to understand in the long years since she'd left Philadelphia and stopped being a society wife.

She waited until she was sure he must have gone down the stairs, that he couldn't possibly be about to pop back in again to give her one more part of this lecture. Then she pulled the piece of paper with Gregor Demarkian's phone number on it off the notepad and tore it into very tiny pieces.

She didn't know what she would say to Chickie tomorrow

afternoon, but she would think of something. She had no intention of giving up what little advantage she had in this case just because Chickie George thought Gregor Demarkian was "a good guy."

THREE

I

It had been a long day, and not a good one, and Gregor Demarkian wanted to walk. It was what he usually did to clear his mind. He hated being in truly rural areas for very long, because there were no sidewalks, and walking any length in any direction was difficult. He hated bad weather, for that very reason, although he'd gone long distances in heavy rain and moderate snow. He left Rob Benedetti's office after it was already dark and realized, in less than a block and a half, that this was never going to work. He didn't mind wind, but he minded it when it pushed hard cold at him like needles. All his joints had begun to ache. His neck felt stiff enough to snap off his body like a plastic pearl on one of those little add-a-pearl necklaces the girls used to have when he was a child. He knew he was in trouble when he started thinking about himself when he was a child. Other people were sentimental about their childhoods. He was not. Growing up poor was either a lifelong ticket to neurosis or a prelude to something else, and he had the something else.

He stepped into a tiny hole-in-the-wall magazine store just to get out of the cold and think. There was a television on the wall showing the news, and the story that was up was the one about Frank Sheehy. Gregor could still hear the noise in Rob Benedetti's office when the confirmation had come through, but he didn't want to think about that, either. There was something all wrong about this case. He just couldn't put a finger on what it was. Everything was sideways. Nothing fit what it should. He wished he knew something more about Drew Harrigan, but when he asked people he got nothing more than clichés and nothing less than venom. To know him—or to know of him—was to hate him. That was clear. What wasn't clear was the personality behind the bombast. It was as if the man had been invented, from scratch, out of old bits and pieces of political speeches.

They were saying something on the news about Frank Sheehy and his life: his years at Princeton, his struggle to found LibertyHeart Communications. Gregor reached into the pocket of his coat and came up with a crumpled copy of Ellen Harrigan's list. There was something else that bothered him, and that should have bothered Rob Benedetti and the police much more. They seemed to take it as a ruse on the part of Ellen Harrigan to draw suspicion away from herself, and Gregor thought that was certainly possible. He didn't think it began to explain either why she'd made the list to begin with or why these particular people were on it.

It was a silly idea, but it at least involved moving around, so he decided to go ahead with it. He went back out onto the street and looked up and down for the cab. Rush hour appeared to be over. He had no idea what time it was. At any rate, the traffic wasn't back-to-back here. He saw a cab in the distance and raised his hand for it. It sped up until it got to him and then pulled over to the curb.

It was one of those things. It was as if God were trying to tell him something. He got in and gave the driver the address he'd noted beside one of the names. Then he explained he was talking about one of the buildings at Penn. He'd been an undergraduate at Penn, years ago, but he'd never become really familiar with its campus, because he'd commuted from home instead of living in a dorm. It was a different time and a different place. The Ivy League was really Ivy. Poor boys on scholarships didn't get around very much with the rich boys who ran everything from the Chess Club to the campus newspaper.

They were closer than Gregor had realized. He probably could have walked—but then, you could walk almost anywhere in Philadelphia, if you were willing to take long enough to do it. He paid the driver and got out. The campus looked deserted, or close to it. The security lights were on everywhere. Did they lock the doors at night in these places? They would have if he'd been running things.

The door to this one, the closest thing he could find to a "front" door, was not locked. He walked in and looked around. The address gave an office number on the second floor, and now that he thought of it, that was interesting. Why give Alison Standish's office address instead of her home address? He got the list out again and looked down it to find Jig Tyler. It gave his office address, too. Either Ellen Harrigan hadn't known the home addresses of the two professors at Penn, or she hadn't wanted to look them up.

He went up to the second floor, feeling more idiotic by the minute. The building was nearly empty. He did see one or two people at their desks, pecking away at computers, but it was obvious that most of the people who worked here had gone home long ago. He had no reason to think that Alison Standish hadn't gone home, too. He would have, if he was her. He walked down past the offices. Most of their doors were closed. Some of those doors had posters hanging on them: the New York City Ballet; the imminent release of Milan Kundera's *The Unbearable Lightness of Being;* Che. He stopped for a moment in front of the Che. It astonished him that anybody still took Che seriously.

Alison Standish's office was far at the end of the hall, and he saw before he reached it that it was open. Light was flowing out of it into the dark corridor. He went up to the door and looked in. A blond woman in her forties was standing on a ladder with her back to him, trying to get a book off a high shelf.

Gregor hesitated. He didn't want to startle her, and he

didn't want her to fall. He cleared his throat and knocked lightly on the door. She turned around.

"You're very tall," she said.

"Ah," Gregor said. "Yes. Yes, I am."

"Could you come up here and get this book for me? I should have known not to let them put books up on that shelf. I'm going to kill myself here."

She got down off the ladder. Gregor came into the office and got on. The top shelf was all the way up to the ceiling, and even for somebody as tall as he was, it wasn't comfortable to try to get a book from it.

"What you need is a taller ladder," he said.

"It's the thick navy blue one right about where your head is. It's called *Ecclesiastica Romana*."

Gregor got it. It weighed a ton. He came down the ladder and handed it over. "What is that, anyway?"

"It's a book on the evils of the Roman Church, written by a monk in twelfth-century Provence. I have to bless Latin, really, because if he'd written it in Provençal, I wouldn't be able to understand a word. Not that we really understand the Latin, even ecclesiastical Latin, after all this time. The context is gone, and we can never get it back again. It makes you wonder what people are thinking when they say that they understand the Bible."

"My guess is that they're thinking that the Bible, being divinely inspired, is also divinely delivered, so that God prevents us from making mistakes we would make with ordinary texts."

"You sound like you're quoting somebody."

"I am," Gregor said. "I'm quoting Father Tibor Kasparian, who is the pastor of Holy Trinity Armenian Christian Church and a good friend of mine."

"The Tibor Kasparian who wrote 'The Aesthetic Roots of the Nestorian Controversy'?"

"I don't know. The Nestorian controversy sounds right. He talks about Nestorians quite a lot. I just don't understand him. My name is Gregor Demarkian, by the way."

"I know," Alison Standish said. "The Armenian-

American Hercule Poirot. I recognized you from your photographs. And that would be the same Tibor Kasparian, by the way. I met him at a conference on The Problem of Art in a Time of Heresy. He's an interesting man."

"Yes," Gregor said. "He is."

"I take it you've come about that list, and about that man who died. I didn't know him. I didn't know Drew Harrigan, either. I've got no idea why all this is happening to me."

Gregor got down off the ladder and looked around. It was like being in Tibor's apartment, in among the Serious Books. He saw English, French, German, Latin, Greek, and a few he didn't recognize.

"Rob Benedetti's people looked it up," he said. Then he paused. "Rob is the district attorney. After the list came out, they looked it up. They said that Drew Harrigan had talked about you 'repeatedly' on his show, and called for you to be investigated for bias, and that the university had responded by opening an investigation."

"I know."

"That's a fair indication of why all this is happening to you."

"Except that Harrigan's original accusation is part of what's happening to me," Alison said, "and I don't understand why. I teach medieval literature and intellectual history. I'm not in the Women's Studies program. The people in the Women's Studies program don't even like me. I'm too blindly wedded to the repressive hermeneutic of dominant heterosexism. Or something. I never get the jargon straight. My last book was about the influence of Scholastic theology on English common law."

"From what I understood, Harrigan claimed that he was in contact with a student of yours who claimed that you deliberately gave lower grades to students with conservative political convictions."

"I know. The problem is, I wouldn't know which of my students had conservative political convictions to save my life. Modern politics doesn't tend to come up in a course concentrating on marital imagery in medieval devotional poetry."

"What about the student in question. Do you remember him?"

"I don't even know if it was a him," Alison said. "I've never had his name, and the university investigating committee wouldn't give it to me short of a court order. Which, by the way, I was threatening to get. I've wracked my brains for weeks, but I can't think of a single student in any class I've taught for the last five years who said anything at all about his politics one way or the other. I keep thinking that has to be wrong, somebody must have made an offhand comment during the last elections, and somebody probably did, but it didn't stick with me. And if you're about to ask me why somebody would go to all the trouble of contacting Drew Harrigan if that was the case, don't bother. I don't know."

"What did you mean, the university wouldn't give you the name of the complaining student?" Gregor asked.

"They wouldn't," Alison said. "That's the way university inquiries are run. We're better than the criminal justice system, you see. We're really interested in getting to justice, and not just in a competition. It's not an adversary system here."

"So you aren't allowed to face your accusers?"

"If they had to face me, they might be too intimidated to make the accusation."

"That's the idea," Gregor said. "It helps guard against false accusations."

"I know," Alison said. "Which is why I was threatening a court order. They backed down after that, though. I knew they would. The public doesn't understand the spirit of disinterested inquiry which is the function of the university, so they're liable to get all worked up over what they mistakenly see as a university committee running roughshod over a professor's due process rights."

"You sound very, very sarcastic."

"I am feeling very, very sarcastic," Alison said. "But that's all I can be. I really don't know why this started, or why anybody would pick me to start it about. First I was all over the airwaves. There was even a piece up about me on Matt Drudge's Web site. Then I was the object of the inquiry. Then the inquiry was called off but I was suddenly on Ellen Harrigan's list. And, trust me, that one is all over campus by now. I'm going to have to change my name to Red Emma if this keeps up."

Gregor thought about it. "You never met Drew Harrigan, not even once?"

"Not even once."

"What about Dr. Tyler, do you know? Had he met him?"

"You'd have to ask him," Alison said, "but I think he had. But that makes sense, doesn't it? Dr. Tyler writes political books, lots of them, so far off the left end of the spectrum they're practically on Mars. The evil corporations are brainwashing us all to believe we really want to eat hamburgers instead of raw vegetables and tofu on whole grain bread. The United States planned and carried out the 9/11 attacks itself, to give the government the excuse to restrict civil liberties. Drew Harrigan had something about Jig Tyler on nearly every broadcast. But I've just been sitting here, worried about Thomas Aquinas and the concept of property in twelfth-century Britain."

"Had you ever met Ellen Harrigan?"

"No," Alison said. "And from what I could see, I wouldn't want to."

"Is she right? Did you have a motive for wanting her husband dead?"

"Well, I was being investigated by the university, and that investigation did disappear as soon as Drew Harrigan's body was found; but it would have disappeared anyway, because I had every intention of filing a suit, and the university wouldn't risk that kind of publicity unless it had a lot stronger evidence against me than anything it could have had. I would think that, to kill somebody, you'd have to be desperate, and I wasn't desperate."

"What about Dr. Tyler? Would he have had a reason to want Drew Harrigan dead?"

"If you believe his books, he wants half the world dead. I don't know, really. You'd have to ask him. I've met him exactly once, and that was yesterday, when the news came out that it was Drew Harrigan who'd died, and not that homeless man. He walked over here to tell me about it."

"Why?"

"To offer commiseration from a fellow sufferer, I suppose," Alison said. "Maybe he just wanted to see what I looked like after all the reports. Anyway, that's the only time I ever set eyes on him in the flesh. I really couldn't tell you much about him, not even what he was like. He seemed nice enough here yesterday. He seems anything but nice on television."

"One more thing," Gregor said. "This accusation by a student, did it actually have to exist? Did there actually have to be a student making a complaint? If you weren't allowed to question your accusers, what would stop the administration from claiming that such a complaint had been made in order to, I don't know, harass you, force you out of your job?"

"The answer is nothing, I suppose, but why would they want to? I'm not a thorn in anybody's side that I know of. I don't have an endowed chair that somebody else might want. I don't get involved in politics, campus or otherwise, or at least I didn't before all this started. Why would anybody want to go to the trouble?"

"I don't know," Gregor said.

And it was true. He didn't. He had no idea where this line of questioning was going. It was just that here was one more thing that had no reason to be here, one more complication for the sake of complication. He didn't like it.

What he did like was Alison Standish, and under other circumstances he would have offered to buy her dinner.

2

Most of Cavanaugh Street was dark by the time Gregor Demarkian got back, a three-block stretch of quiet in a city that had recently become so revitalized he sometimes thought it was threatening to turn into New York. There was light spilling out of the Ararat, but he never went there after eight in the evening anymore. There were too many tourists looking around for "exotic" food, and for him. That was what happened when your life became the subject of newspaper articles over and above the ones that reported the cases you were involved in or the testimony you gave at trials. Bennis would understand this. Bennis had spent a good deal of her life being an object of public curiosity. That was something you wanted to happen to you when you wrote books and wanted to sell as many of them as possible, which Bennis did. She took great pride in how many bestseller lists she'd been on and how long she'd been on them. But Bennis wasn't home, and he was damned—he really was—if he was going to go rushing up to the apartment to see if she'd left a message on his answering machine. She hadn't left a message on his answering machine now for over ten days, and he'd checked for one far too often.

He passed his own apartment and looked up at the windows at Lida Arkmanian's on the other side of the street. The big bank of glass on the second floor was dark. If Lida was home, she wasn't in her living room. He crossed the street so as not to be directly in the line of fire when he passed the Ararat. He had to pass the church first, and that was all right. The spookiness he'd gotten from it before it had been rebuilt was gone now that its entire facade was lit up all night long, framing the tall new stained glass windows and the broad stone steps as if they were works of art. If he went up the steps and tried the door, it would be open. Tibor insisted on it. There was always the possibility that somebody, passing, might need to pray. They took care of the security problems by having a tandem team of parishioners sit vigil all night. You could come in to pray, but if you tried to leave a package under the pew, it would be discovered before it could blow the church to pieces again. He had sat vigil a few times himself, to fill a gap in the schedule, or because he knew he wasn't going to be able to sleep anyway. Most of the time it was the Very Old Women who stayed up all night, and who didn't mind spending the time in a church.

The Ararat was packed. He was glad for the Melajians at the same time he was sad for the days when he could always stop in and eat, because there was always a place at the tables and never much of anybody around he didn't know. He passed Ohanian's and considered stopping in to buy *loukoumia,* or something else he could shove down his throat without thinking about it. He was starving. He should have eaten hours ago. He went another half block, crossed another street, and went another half block again. By now, the street was very, very quiet. It was all residential here. Most of the buildings were private houses that didn't rent their ground floors out to businesses. He went up the steps of the one that was wrapped up to look like a box of chocolate candy—Donna must be getting ready for Valentine's Day early—and rang the buzzer.

It was Tommy who came to the door, a book in one hand and a pair of glasses in the other. The glasses were new this year, and he had been very careful to get wire rims, like the kind Harrison Ford wore when he was teaching college classes in the Indiana Jones movies.

"Hi, Mr. Demarkian. Have you talked sense into Grace yet?"

"Grace is in New York playing the harpsichord," Gregor said. "What does she need to have sense talked into her about?"

"About the name of that dog," Tommy said. "I mean, it's undignified. It's undignified for the dog."

Down at the end of the long hall that ran past the stair, a door opened. Donna Moradanyan Donahue stuck her head out and said, "Oh, Gregor. Hello. We weren't expecting you. Aren't you on a case?"

"Relax," Gregor said. "I haven't come to pump you about Bennis."

Donna relaxed so visibly it was practically the punch line to a comedy routine. Gregor ignored it, and kept coming down the hall toward the kitchen. "I'm looking for Russ, to tell you the truth. I've got a few things I want to ask him."

"Is it private?" Donna asked. "If it's private, you can go into the study."

"It's not particularly private. I don't care where we are. Would it be wrong of me to ask if you had a ham sandwich somewhere around? It's been a long day and I forgot to eat dinner."

"Did you remember to eat lunch?"

"Lunch, yes," Gregor said. "For that, I had Tibor come to keep me company."

"I've got a lot of dinner left over. I'll throw some into the microwave. Russ is watching something or the other on cable."

Gregor turned to his left and went into the door that led to the "study," which the Donahues sometimes called the "television room." Whatever it was, it was the place where the television was left to rest, because Donna had strong views on having a television in a place where people were supposed to socialize. Gregor always thought it was one of those things she must have picked up at college before she dropped out.

In the study, Russ was camped out in an enormous overstuffed chair, watching *Forensic Files*. Gregor had seen some of those programs on Court TV, and although they'd seemed accurate enough, he couldn't understand why anybody watched them. It seemed to him there was far too much information out there about crime and forensics as it was.

Russ looked up and said, "Hey, Gregor. What's up?"

"I'm looking for a lawyer," Gregor said.

"Has John managed to get you arrested? I saw you on television, by the way. Jackman's out of his mind. He's going to cause a nuclear explosion by the time he's finished with this."

"It's Rob Benedetti running the show, as far as I can tell."

"It ought to be a homicide detective running the show," Russ said, "and Rob Benedetti is going to do what John

Jackman wants him to do, because he thinks John Jackman is going to be the next mayor of Philadelphia."

"Is he?"

"In a walk."

"I don't understand why you'd want to watch something like this," Gregor said. "Don't you get enough of this at work all day?"

"I don't get any of this at work all day," Russ said. "I don't practice criminal law. I probably should. What do you need a lawyer for that you'd come over here in the night?"

The door to the room swung open a little farther than it was, and Donna came in carrying a long tray with enough food on it to keep Gregor for three days, plus a tall glass of mineral water, a linen napkin, a full set of silverware, and a little white ceramic cup full of whipped butter. There was a TV table open and discarded against the wall near the bookcase. She put the tray down on that and straightened up.

"There," she said. "That should keep you. I'll leave you two alone to talk."

"You don't need to leave us alone to talk," Gregor said. "It's nothing confidential."

Donna was out the door and gone.

"It's because of Bennis," Russ said. "She doesn't want you—"

"Oh, I know," Gregor said, moving the TV table, tray and all, in front of the other overstuffed armchair. "She should know better, though. I haven't pumped her about Bennis yet. Do you know what's going on with Bennis?"

"No," Russ said. "It's like the seal of the confessional or something. I'll admit to its being incredibly annoying."

Gregor sat down in front of the food and thought that no matter what else was going on, Donna was a true Armenian woman. If somebody said they were hungry, she assumed they had been starving in the desert for forty days and fed them accordingly.

"So, what is it?" Russ said. "You need help solving a case, for once? What will the papers think if they find out the

Armenian-American Hercule Poirot comes to a lowly local lawyer when he's stumped by a fiendish archvillain?"

"You watch too much television," Gregor said. "And I'm not stumped, if by stumped you mean not able to figure out who committed the crime. I know who committed the crime. I knew it halfway through the morning of the second day. There were really only two or three possibilities. One of them is now dead, and another one isn't capable."

"I'd be careful about that if I were you," Russ said. "I think it was even you who told me that everybody is capable, and it's bad policy to rule out a suspect because you think he has too fine a soul to commit a murder."

"I'm not talking about fineness of soul," Gregor said, "I'm talking about capacity. You can't murder somebody with a knife unless you can raise a knife and bring it down. That kind of thing."

"There is somebody in this case of yours who isn't physically capable of, what, putting arsenic into prescription painkiller capsules?"

"No. Well, not exactly."

"How did the other one die, this, what's his name, Sheehy?"

"Frank Sheehy. We don't know yet, but we're going to assume poison. They almost always go on the way they've started. It's easier. The ME's report will be in tomorrow. The thing is, I know who, and I know why, in general at least, two people are dead. But there are other things going on here that I don't understand, and it bothers me."

"Are you sure they're connected with the killings, assuming that should be a plural?"

"No," Gregor said. "I'm not sure. And that's part of the problem. Let me ask you something, even if you don't practice criminal law."

"Shoot."

"Does it come under attorney-client privilege if an attorney knows that his client is in the process of committing a crime, and does nothing to stop it?"

"Gregor, attorneys know their clients are guilty of crimes all the time."

"No, I didn't say guilty, past tense. I said in the process of. Committing a crime now. Right this second. Is the attorney still protected by attorney-client privilege?"

"I don't know," Russ said. "It's not that easy. Attorneys are friends of the court. That means they have a responsibility to see that trials and court proceedings are carried out ethically. And to an extent I think it would depend on what kind of a crime it was. An attorney can certainly be an accessory, before, during, and after the fact. Some things, though, would be nearly impossible to prove, so impossible that nobody would ever bother, and the attorney involved could certainly stonewall a long time on the principle of privilege."

"What about if the person was committing a crime with the full knowledge of the judge whose order he was violating?"

"Wait now. Are you talking about a crime, or a court order?"

"Both."

"They're different things," Russ said. "The court order brings in that friend-of-the-court thing. And the judge couldn't be in on it."

"Why not?"

"Because if he was, there would be no violation. Judges have broad discretion in their own courtrooms. Absent something like a mandatory minimums law, they can pretty much do what they want. I've seen murderers walk away with nothing but probation in my time, which is how we got mandatory minimums to begin with."

"What if the judge said one thing in the courtroom on record and something else in chambers in private?"

"Doesn't matter much, as long as you can prove what was said in chambers. Like I said, he's got broad discretion to do what he wants. He's supposed to. You write laws for the general rule, but you try particular cases, and they've all got quirks. I don't like mandatory minimums, myself. They're—"

"Do you like Bruce Williamson?"

"Oh God," Russ said.

"Oh God?"

"Some of us would like to see Judge Williamson go to Hollywood, get an agent, and enter the acting profession legitimately. The man is a disaster, Gregor. He's never met a celebrity he doesn't have an excuse for, and he doesn't care what it is the excuse is needed to cover. Every defense lawyer with a prominent client in the city of Philadelphia does cartwheels trying to get Bruce Williamson on the case, and the worst of it is that when the person involved *isn't* a celebrity, Williamson is the next best thing to a hanging judge. Is all this about Bruce Williamson? Because if it is, good luck."

"No," Gregor said, "it isn't really about Bruce Williamson. It just starts there. Well, no, it starts with Drew Harrigan's drug problem, I'd guess. Williamson isn't the only one who has a celebrity fixation, is he?"

"You mean some of the uniformed police officers do? Yeah, they do. But that's minor, compared to the havoc a judge can wreak."

"It starts with Drew Harrigan's drug problem," Gregor said, "but I think it only gets to the point where a murder is imminent once Harrigan was arrested and brought in front of Williamson. And even then it would have been all right if Williamson had been another kind of judge."

"You do realize you're making no sense," Russ said.

"I'm making sense to myself," Gregor said. "The problem with situations like this is that they look like puzzles, and they really aren't. Not in the sense we usually use the term."

"A mystery wrapped in an enigma," Russ intoned.

Gregor picked up his fork and started in on dinner. "I met a very interesting person today," he said. "Her name is Dr. Alison Standish, and she knows Tibor."

FOUR

I

Ray Dean Ballard had heard the rumor in dozens of places over the years, and read it in the *Philadelphia Inquirer,* so when he started out that morning he had the feeling of doing something so rational, and so sure of success, it gave him no more worry than brushing his teeth. He didn't bother to buy a map and work out the bus routes. He would have, ordinarily, but over the past week or so the whole charade he had been putting on for work had seemed more shallow and less necessary than ever. It shouldn't be a requirement for employment, anywhere, or friendship, ever, to pretend to be something you are not. Exactly how he would go about being what he was, or even how he'd know that if he saw it, he wasn't sure. It had been years since he had thought all this through. Even then, working it out on page after page of a narrow-ruled legal pad on the desk in his dorm room at Vanderbilt, he hadn't come to any hard-and-fast conclusions. He was not the kind of person who found solace in revolutionary posturing. He wasn't about to turn vocal Communist wannabe just because his father was the icon of global capitalism. He didn't want to show up on the evening news with a Kalashnikov and a beret and declare the overthrow of oppression to be right around the corner. God only knew he didn't want to plunge himself into that half-world of un-

happy resentments populated by rich-girl socialist independent filmmakers and rich-boy volunteers for the Cuban Har-
vest. Hadn't there been a time, somewhere back there, when
it was possible to want to do good in the world just because
you were unhappy that so many of your fellow citizens were
doing badly? Hadn't there been a time when everything,
even the food you ate, wasn't politics?

He got a cab outside his apartment, and thought that it
was time to change that. He wasn't going to buy a town
house in Rittenhouse Square, but he could do better than
this, and there was really no reason to go on putting up with
bad plumbing when he didn't have to. On the other hand, he
didn't want to turn out like Tony Benn, living like the lord
he'd been born to be and spouting off about the miserable
conditions suffered by the world's downtrodden poor. He
didn't know what he wanted to be. It seemed impossible,
considering how much thought he'd given to it back in Tennessee, but he didn't actually seem to have figured out his
life yet.

The cab deposited him outside the big plate glass windows of a small restaurant, and as soon as he got out onto the
sidewalk he could see that it wasn't much more than one of
those hole-in-the-wall diners that dotted the city from one
end to the other. Etched gold lettering across the top of the
largest window said: ARARAT. Ray Dean looked up and
down the street. It was a nice street. The houses were expensive as city houses went, but not as expensive as the kind of
thing his father would have bought. Of course, very few people could afford the kind of thing his father would have
bought, but it was amazing how many people tried. He saw a
small grocery up the street a little. It was a "Middle Eastern"
grocery, and he wondered if that meant they would have
loukoumia and halva. He could buy packages of both and
bring them home when it was time for him to leave. He
looked through the big plate glass window at the people at
the tables and then realized that the man he was looking for
was right there, sitting in the window booth, facing off
against a plate of eggs, sausages, and hash browns that

would have given a cholesterol-induced heart attack to a fifteen-year-old Olympic athlete.

Ray Dean went into the restaurant and looked around again. There didn't seem to be a hostess waiting to seat him. He went over to the window booth and looked down at the man he knew to be Gregor Demarkian and the other man with him, a little man, very thin and gnarled, who was making do with buttered toast. For the first time, Ray Dean began to think he should have called in advance. He hadn't because . . . because he'd thought of this as going into the police station to make a report. It was ridiculous, but there it was.

The two men were looking up at him now, the smaller one with a look of calm inquiry, Gregor Demarkian with a look that was not so calm. Ray Dean cleared his throat.

"Excuse me," he said. "Mr. Gregor Demarkian? I'm sorry to bother you, but I thought—I'm sorry. My name is Aldous Ballard, and I run an organization called Philadelphia Sleeps."

Gregor Demarkian was staring at him. Ray Dean didn't think he was blinking. Finally, Gregor Demarkian coughed a little and said, "Aldous Ballard. Well, you're too young to be the original, so that would make you . . . what? The grandson?"

"The son. But my father doesn't use Aldous. He uses William."

"In the papers, he's always William Aldous Ballard."

"True enough," Ray Dean said. "At the coalition, they call me Ray Dean."

"Why?"

Ray Dean sighed. "Because when I went to work there, it seemed the better part of valor. Can I sit down? I have this thing." He stuck his hands in the pockets of his coat and came up with a typewritten list. "I have something I thought you ought to see. I didn't do it to bring it in here. I don't know why I did it. Because I was pissed off at being jerked around, I think."

"Sit," Gregor Demarkian said. "This is Father Tibor Kasparian."

"How do you do, Father?" Ray Dean sat.

A young woman was at the side of the table instantly, with a cup and a saucer and the coffeepot. Ray Dean allowed her to pour for him, and thanked her, and told her that he didn't need any breakfast just yet, but it was good of her to ask. He sounded to himself like a decade before, at Parents' Day at St. Paul's. That was a blast from the past.

He put the typewritten paper on the table before him and said, "I went to the bank. My father's bank. The branch of it here, you know. And I got this."

"What's this?"

"A list of the people connected to the disappearance of Sherman Markey who have accounts with the Markwell Ballard Bank."

Gregor Demarkian's eyebrows rose. "Isn't that kind of information supposed to be confidential?"

"Absolutely," Ray Dean said.

Gregor Demarkian cocked his head. "You're a very interesting man, Mr. Ballard. I assume you've got hold of the names on that list through connections."

"I've got something better than connections," Ray Dean said. "I own a fifteen percent interest in the bank. In trust, mind you, and I can't sell it, but there it is. It's all right, you know. You could get this information with a court order. We don't allow absolute bank secrecy in the United States, for which I am truly grateful. If it makes you feel any better, my father is probably grateful, too."

"Why did you want a list of people connected to the disappearance of Sherman Markey who had accounts with your father's bank?"

"Because the nuns got an offer for the property Drew Harrigan parked with them," Ray Dean said, "and the offer came through the Markwell Ballard Bank. Which, by the way, is why you could get the information with a court order, and why I could get it. The person who gave it to me knew that my father was going to have one of his patented fits as soon as he found out about it. And trust me, my father's patented fits are something to see."

"I've heard about them. He won't have a patented fit about your obtaining the information and giving it to me?"

"I was hoping you wouldn't say anything about my giving it to you," Ray Dean said, "and he won't mind that I went and got it. He'll probably think it means I'm finally taking an interest in the family business, which I'm not. It's not that I look down on the family business, or anything like that. It's just that I'm not cut out for it."

"Why would you look down on the world's most important investment banking firm?"

"You'd be amazed at how many of the people I went to prep school with would do just that. Take a look at that list, Mr. Demarkian. It's interesting."

Gregor Demarkian picked up the list off the table and began to read it, and Ray Dean, finally relaxed, looked around the restaurant with more interest and concentration. At a table near the center of the room there were three extremely old women, all thin to the point of emaciation and all wearing black. Something at the back of Ray Dean's head labeled them the three witches from *Macbeth* and started waiting for them to leap up and chant. He looked around some more and found mostly small groups of people having breakfast quietly, but somehow all together, as if they all knew each other.

Gregor Demarkian had put the list back on the table. Fr. Tibor Kasparian was trying to read it without looking as if that was what he was doing. Ray Dean turned his attention back to them.

"It's a very interesting list, Mr. Ballard."

"Call me Ray Dean. Or call me Aldy. Most of my life, I've been known as Aldy. I know it's an interesting list."

"Drew Harrigan isn't on it," Gregor Demarkian said. "Is that because he's dead?"

Ray Dean shook his head. "Drew Harrigan couldn't get an account at Markwell Ballard if he offered to die for it. The bank has criteria for accepting accounts, and the criteria are so outrageous that nobody can meet them. I mean nobody. My father can't meet them. Bill Gates can't meet them. Somebody like Drew Harrigan couldn't come close."

"But Mr. Harrigan is likely to have had a lot more money than, say, Dr. Richard Alden Tyler."

"Sure," Ray Dean said. "But it's not about money. In the world my father lives in, everybody has money. My father has, uh, principles, about who he will enable to get richer and who he won't. He wouldn't touch the Drew Harrigan/Rush Limbaugh/Ann Coulter axis with a ten-foot pole. Not that he's much in favor of Democrats, either, you understand. Do you know why I starred Jig Tyler's name?"

"No," Gregor Demarkian said.

"Because I'm pretty sure he's the one who made the offer on the land to Our Lady of Mount Carmel Monastery."

Now, Ray Dean saw, he had Gregor Demarkian interested. "That's not legal, is it, to ask about a particular transaction like that? Or to tell me. You really do need a court order for that sort of thing."

"I didn't ask for it directly," Ray Dean said. "They wouldn't have given it to me if I had. But I grew up around people who know how to ask the questions that will get them the answer without crossing the line, and I got this one. Look at that list. There's Neil Savage."

"Yes, I noticed that," Demarkian said.

"Savage almost certainly didn't make the offer," Ray Dean said, "because he's Harrigan's attorney, and doing that under the circumstances would have been illegal and it would probably have gotten him disbarred."

"If it ever came out," Demarkian said.

"He couldn't know it wouldn't," Ray Dean said, "and he wouldn't take that kind of risk. Not for a low-rent putz like Drew Harrigan. I've known a million Neil Savages. Trust me. Then there's me, of course, and that's perfectly possible, but I promise you the right to look through all my records at the bank, no matter how confidential, so you can check."

"Fair enough."

"Then there's Kate Daniel, but the times don't work. She didn't have anything to do with this case until well after the offer was made. Of course, she was married to Savage once—"

"Was she?"

"Years ago, when they were both just out of law school. She had a feminist epiphany and ran away from home. Of course, they could still be close. I have no idea if they are or not, but I've met them both, and I'd doubt it. And it goes back to that risk thing. It's too close a connection to trust that it wouldn't get caught."

"How does a woman like Kate Daniel get enough money to open an account in an investment bank?"

"She inherits it," Ray Dean said. "Then we've got Frank Sheehy. That's a real possibility. A lot of the success of his business depended on Drew Harrigan. He was losing money because of the rehab thing. It was worth his while to do anything he had to do to get Drew Harrigan straightened out and back on the air. I can't really rule out Frank Sheehy. Even the murder fits, if you think about it. Whoever was getting Drew Harrigan the drugs killed Sheehy because Sheehy knew all about it, or maybe Sheehy was getting Harrigan the drugs. I'm not very good at this, am I? I've thought about writing a murder mystery, but I keep getting worried I'd end up at the end of the book babbling like this."

"I want to know why you think it was Dr. Tyler who tried to buy that piece of land."

"Because Jig Tyler was feeding material to Drew Harrigan," Ray Dean said. "He'd been doing it for months, at least. He might have been doing it for longer."

"And you know that—"

Ray Dean looked at the ceiling. "Because he fed something to Drew about me. Last November. Three days before Thanksgiving, we were at a party together. He contributes to causes. The causes have parties. He goes. I've always found that one of the oddest things about him. Anyway, I had just come from the office, where I'd realized that I was going to have to turn down a donation we'd gotten that very afternoon, a big donation, in six figures, because I'd finally figured out who the donor was."

"Who was it?"

"Charles Scherver. He doesn't call himself that anymore. He changed his name when he got out of prison, but it was Charles Scherver nonetheless, the most famous American traitor in the history of the Cold War. If we'd taken the donation, it would have come out. We're required to make our list of donors public. Anyway, by the time I tracked it down it was late, and there was nobody in the office, and I went to this party. And I got to talking to Dr. Tyler, and then, just as we were waiting for our cars on our way out, I told him about it. We were talking about donations versus public financing of charitable works, and Tyler was doing one of his shticks about the evils of capitalism, and I let loose with all the checks and balances there are on donations, and I told him about it. And then his car picked him up, and he was gone. The next morning—the very next morning—eleven o'clock sharp, Drew Harrigan led with the story on his broadcast."

"Maybe somebody overheard you."

"There was nobody there to overhear."

"Maybe he told a friend, who told Harrigan."

"Maybe," Ray Dean said, "but I don't believe it, and neither do you. It was too fast. He must have gone home and gotten on the phone right away, if he didn't use a cell in the car. It's the kind of stupid little thing that causes us no end of trouble because it gets all the 'patriot' groups mad at us—note that I've got mental scare quotes around the word 'patriot'—and they make a lot of noise, and they bring our donations down."

"Even if he did give that information to Drew Harrigan," Gregor Demarkian said carefully, "that doesn't mean he also tried to buy the property from the nuns, does it?"

"No," Ray Dean said. "But." He shrugged. "It was the connection. That started me looking. That's what made me ask questions. Jig Tyler is the person who tried to buy that land from the monastery, Mr. Demarkian. I know it for sure."

"How?"

"Telling you that would be illegal," Ray Dean said. "You're going to have to get a warrant and ask those questions yourself. But it's true. I don't know what kind of a connection Jig Tyler had with Drew Harrigan. I've met Tyler on a number of occasions, and I can't imagine it. Tyler hates idiots. Harrigan was practically the definition of one. But there you are. Get the warrant. Ask the questions. Find out where Sherman Markey is and bring him back to me."

"You think Jig Tyler has Sherman Markey, too?"

"I don't know," Ray Dean said. "I just know that he's out there somewhere, dead or alive. He's being used by people who should know better than to . . . I don't know than to what. It's freezing out there. He's been gone for weeks. I want him back. I want him now."

"I'll do my best," Gregor Demarkian said.

Ray Dean felt suddenly awkward—more shades of St. Paul's, more memories from the kind of childhood he would never have wished on himself. He stood up a little stiffly and said good-bye in that oddly formal way he couldn't help. He hadn't noticed it before, but Fr. Tibor Kasparian hadn't said a word. Ray Dean said it was nice meeting him, anyway, and then he heard his mother in his head, telling him that manners had to be glued on tight, especially in the most awkward situations.

A moment later, he was out on the street, looking up and down again. He would go to that Middle Eastern food store, he thought. He would buy *loukoumia* and halva. He wasn't the kind of person who usually used sugar to make himself feel better, but he didn't usually use liquor, either, and he didn't usually use pills, and he thought that, the way things were going, he might as well try something.

2

It was one of those things, an accident at the end of a long string of accidents, an impossibility dressed up as a moment of revelation. Jig Tyler had been trained well enough to know that coincidences happen. He didn't believe in the supernatural, or the paranormal, or fate. Still, he wasn't usually out of bed and out in town this early in the morning. He liked to read late at night, because it was quiet, and nobody thought to call him. He'd been up until at least three, plowing his way through the latest piece of idiocy by Mona Charen. He didn't know why he went on reading books like that. They were aimed at an audience with an IQ of under a hundred and average cultural literacy of even less than that, and it was just as bad in the books by the "liberals" on the playing field. He wished he could take all these people and sweep them off the board, the way angry women swept chess pieces off boards in melodramatic movies. He wished he had a melodramatic movie to go to. He wished he were still asleep, but the alarm clock had gone off for some reason probably having to do with the fact that it was very old and beginning to malfunction, and he hadn't been able to get to sleep again once he'd finally managed to stop its buzzing.

He had gone out because he'd started feeling claustrophobic staying in, and he had gone into the drugstore because it had been handy and open when the wind started. He never wandered around in drugstores. He always headed straight for whatever it was he was looking for. He didn't know what to make of the plastic toys and decks of cards and boxes of candy that drugstores had everywhere. He couldn't imagine anybody paying the extra freight to pick up a three-ring binder here to get out of walking the few blocks to a regular stationery store. The people in drugstores made him nervous, because they always seemed to be confused about what it was they were supposed to do next. Now that he was out and awake and cold he was also fuzzy, the way he got when his sleep had been interrupted at the very worst time.

He went back to look at the magazines because they were there to look at, and because they at least constituted something to read, sort of. He looked over the covers of *Time, Newsweek,* and *U.S. News & World Report.* He marveled at the sheer number of cooking magazines, all with glossy four-color photo spreads of things that probably tasted terrible once you had them in front of you, but that looked so perfect on the page you wanted to have every one of them now. He looked at the car and motorcycle magazines. He looked at the women's magazines, which all seemed to assume that women were spending their time at home all day the way they had in 1950. He was about to go back out into the cold when he saw the nuns.

Here was another accident—what were the odds that it would be the same nuns, all the way out here, miles from Hardscrabble Road and their convent? Monastery, Jig reminded himself, and then the younger of the two turned, looked around absently, saw him, and stopped. Jig was holding a copy of *Women's Wrestling Today*, which he found to be one of the most remarkable examples of popular culture he'd ever encountered. The women must have been taking steroids. There was no possibility that they could have developed that kind of musculature without them. He put the magazine down very quickly. The women were all wearing very skimpy clothing, thongs and postage stamp bra tops, not the kind of thing that would suit a nun. The nun didn't seem to notice. She was staring at his face. Then she tugged sharply at her companion's sleeve and started to come over.

This was not an accident, but a mistake. He should have turned away and left the store, immediately. He should not have stood still where he was, with his left hand resting on the big magazine rack, as if he was seriously considering finding something to buy.

"Excuse me," the nun said. "I'm sorry to bother you. It's Dr. Richard Tyler, isn't it?"

"That's right," Jig said. Then he thought that that, too, was another mistake. He would never make a spy. People recognized him from television, or from magazines. He was used to admitting who he was.

"I'm sorry," the nun said again. "I really don't mean to bother you. It's just—I have such a strong feeling I've seen you somewhere before."

"You've seen me on television, probably," Jig said. "I'm not really on all that often, but people remember."

"We don't watch television," the nun said. "And it's not

that, it's that I could swear I've seen you somewhere in person, face-to-face. Very closely face-to-face. Do you come out to the monastery?"

"The monastery?"

"Our Lady of Mount Carmel on Hardscrabble Road."

"Is that in Philadelphia?"

The nun bit her lip. She was, Jig thought, a remarkably beautiful young woman, more like an actress playing a nun than most of the nuns he'd met. She was also very intelligent. It showed in her face. For once, it did not make him very comfortable.

"I'm sorry," she said finally. "I'm being ridiculous, and I'm intruding. It's just—never mind. I don't know. I'm not making any sense. Please excuse me, Dr. Tyler. I shouldn't have intruded on your privacy."

"Not at all," Jig said.

The nun gave him one last searching, worried look. Then she turned away and went back to the other nun, who had bought something she was now carrying in a white plastic bag. Jig realized that he couldn't remember nuns like this, with full habits to the floor, carrying anything in their hands. He couldn't remember them wearing coats, either, and now he knew why. They had heavy wool capes to wear instead.

The two nuns went out together, to the front of the store, to the street. Jig watched them go until he couldn't see them any longer. His mouth was as dry as paper. He looked at the clock on the wall and saw that it was barely quarter past eight.

There were things he was good at, and things he was not good at. When he was good at something, he was so good at it that he could not be compared to other people who did it. In mathematics, in physics, in research medicine, he was so far out ahead of the pack that he might as well have been in the field alone. When he was not good at something, he was incapacitated. There were not a lot of things he was not good at, but they were there, and one of them was lying to other people face-to-face.

No, he thought, that wasn't true. Sometimes he did that

very well. It was more complicated than that. It was just that he had been so very bad at lying to that nun, just a moment ago, and it was one of the few times in his life when he had wanted his lies to be effective.

3

Beata was on the bus and reaching for her breviary before it struck her, and then she found herself torn by the sort of procedural guilt she had always thought was the least attractive thing about religious life. It was quarter after eight. They were absent from prayers because they had errands to do, and they were later than they should have been because Immaculata had had three coughing fits in half an hour and wanted to pick up lozenges so that she didn't cough and hack her way home. They were supposed to take the first opportunity to "make up" prayers, and that first opportunity was now, a half-hour ride on this bus with nothing to worry about in the way of missing their stop, since it was the last one before the bus turned around. The Office sat in her hand, thick and red. They had separate volumes now for Advent and Christmas, Lent and Easter, and Ordinary Time. In *The Nun's Story,* Audrey Hepburn had carried a prayer book so small it almost fit into the palm of her hand, but that was the Little Office, and nobody said the Little Office anymore. Beata couldn't even fault the rule, really. The idea was to have the whole Church praying the same words at the same times every day, to lift up praise and supplication in one voice, *ad maiorem Dei gloriam.*

Next to her on the seat, Immaculata was already hard at prayer, her finger moving carefully from line to line, her lips moving. The Office was in Latin, and the rule had made much more sense when all the Offices were in Latin. These days, though, there were religious orders and churches saying the Office in every possible vernacular. Somebody had told her once that the Office had been translated into Klingon and posted on the Internet.

Beata opened the Office to the relevant day, to the beginning of Morning Prayer, and stopped. The words came. The visions did, too. She had seen Dr. Richard Tyler before, she just hadn't realized it was him. She'd not only seen him, she'd stared straight at his face and exchanged at least half a dozen sentences with him. Even at the time, something about him had been nagging at her, some feeling that he was somebody she knew or somebody she ought to recognize. But, of course, she'd pushed all that away. She'd just assumed that she'd seen him before at the barn. She saw so many of them, and so many of them came over and over and over again.

Out the windows of the bus the day was dark and cold and windy. The few sickly trees that lined the sidewalks were bent under the force of winds that whipped back and forth with no indication of what they would do next. It wasn't just that she knew where she'd seen him, it was that she knew when she'd seen him, and that was, well, crazy. It got crazier the longer she thought of it. She should pray her Office. She should offer this up. God was supposed to provide you with answers to dilemmas like this.

At the moment, though, God was not providing, and Beata knew she was going to have to take it up with Reverend Mother.

FIVE

I

It was Rob Benedetti's idea that they should all meet at Neil Savage's office, and then his further idea that he himself shouldn't be there, since he wasn't really investigating "the case." Gregor Demarkian had come to the conclusion that nobody was investigating "the case." In several important respects, there was no "case" to investigate. There was only a series of not-quite-connected happenings, a lot of conjecture, and a confusion of jurisdiction. Surely a homicide detective working out of the Hardscrabble Road precinct should be investigating the death of Drew Harrigan, and a homicide detective out of whatever precinct it was where the DA's Office was should be investigating the death of Frank Sheehy. Even assuming cooperation between those two detectives—or, more likely, detective teams—that would be confusion enough, without taking into consideration the fact that Frank Sheehy had almost certainly not died in the place he was found, and the further fact that a man dressed as a homeless person pushing a shopping cart could have walked for miles without being intercepted by anybody. Even the police gave the homeless people a wide berth. It would be easy for all this confusion to sink whatever case there might be altogether, and Gregor thought John Jackman should know that, but he didn't want to tell him, yet. The lack of any clear jurisdiction was having the oddly salutary effect of leaving him free to work out the problems presented on his own, which was something he'd almost never had the luxury of doing, even at the FBI. There was always somebody around to second-guess you, or to insist that you do this first rather than that. Right now, they were all doing whatever he told them to do, in whatever order he told them to do it. Nobody else was competing for their time.

It was Marbury and Giametti who would be coming to Neil Savage's office. Rob Benedetti had told him about it when he called last night to run the details of the ME's report.

"Arsenic, again," he'd said. "I know we suspected it, but it's kind of disappointing. If it's another case of filling a bunch of pill capsules with the stuff, it's going to be impossible to trace to anybody in particular."

"Did Frank Sheehy take pills?"

"I don't know," Rob said. "I had one of the uniforms up here go over and talk to that woman again, that Marla Hildebrande, and she didn't seem to think so, but she was an employee. She could have not known."

"The impression I got was that she was very close to Sheehy," Gregor said, "but that doesn't matter, because it almost surely won't be another case of putting the arsenic in pill capsules. When you do that, you have to be prepared to wait. Unless you doctor every single pill, you've got to assume it could be a week or more before your victim is actually dead, and I'm pretty sure nobody could wait that long to get rid of Frank Sheehy."

"So how would he deliver the arsenic?"

"In a cup of coffee," Gregor said. "In a drink. Anything sweet would be all right. After that, all we need is somebody who would not be seen as out of place handing Frank Sheehy a drink—no, beyond that. Somebody who wouldn't seem out of place talking to Frank Sheehy in the first place. Somebody Frank Sheehy talked to often enough so that nobody would take much notice of the fact when he was around."

"That sounds like it has to be Marla Hildebrande herself," Rob Benedetti said.

Gregor got out of the cab in front of a magnificent town house with a double wide front facade and steps that curved out to the left and right as if they belonged in a ballroom instead of on a city street. Gregor kept forgetting that in Philadelphia, unlike Washington, Really Important Law Firms didn't take up several floors of a high-rise building, the more modern the better. He went up the steps and rang the front door bell. The front door was not open to the public. Nothing else took up space in this building but the firm. A woman came to the door and let him in, and he found himself in the wide front lobby of what could have been a private club. Marbury and Giametti were already there, in uniform, looking something worse than out of place. The redheaded woman who had admitted Gregor was paying no attention to them. She did pay attention to Gregor Demarkian, but just.

"Mr. Savage will be out in a moment," she said. Then she nodded toward the little cluster of chairs and couches near the front windows, where Marbury and Giametti already were.

"I keep expecting Katharine Hepburn to come down the stairs and talk about calla lilies," Marbury said.

Gregor took in the rugs—Persian, and real—and the porcelain. The paintings were all portraits of men who looked at once too prosperous and too smug to also look intelligent.

Another woman came out, this one small and neat and middle-aged. "Mr. Demarkian?" she said. "Come with me, please. Mr. Savage can see you now."

Marbury and Giametti rose when Gregor did, and followed the middle-aged woman when Gregor did, but neither the middle-aged woman nor the redhead at the front desk paid any attention. *Maybe,* Gregor thought, *this is how they meant it to be.* They would deal with the fact that the police were in the building by pretending that the police weren't in the building, and the police would help along the delusion by never talking directly to anybody in the firm. The hallway was a masterpiece of masculine interior decorating.

The paneling went halfway up the walls and was topped with a flat plaster wall papered in dark green. The runner carpet was dark green, too, but narrow enough to show the hardwood underneath, the same hardwood that had been used on the walls. There were more pictures, one after the other, in a long line. There had to be a hundred years of partners, or more.

The small, middle-aged woman opened a door and waved Gregor inside. "He'll be right in," she said, and then disappeared.

Gregor, Marbury, and Giametti found themselves in a long conference room, with another Persian rug, another four half-walls of paneling, and another cluster of partners' portraits.

"I think everybody who ever worked for this firm had a burr up his ass," Giametti said.

The door opened, and a man Gregor presumed to be Neil Elliot Savage came in. He was tall and thin and "patrician," in the way newspapers meant that word. In other words, he seemed arrogant. He had nothing with him, not so much as a folder. His suit was expensive but not new.

"Mr. Demarkian," he said, holding out his hand. Unlike the receptionist and the middle-aged woman, he didn't behave as if Marbury and Giametti didn't exist, only as if they almost didn't. "Gentlemen," he said to them, turning his head to one side. When Gregor sat down, Neil Savage sat down as well. He didn't wait for the uniformed officers.

"Well," he said, laying out his long fingers on the table in front of him, "I'm not really sure what information we can give you. Even though Mr. Harrigan is dead, considerations of confidentiality restrict what I can tell you about his affairs, unless I'm ordered to do so by a court, and the courts are restricted in what they can order me to do."

"Did you know the man who just died, Frank Sheehy?" Gregor asked.

"Of course I did. Mr. Sheehy owned the company that syndicated Mr. Harrigan's radio show. Of course, Mr. Harrigan had an agent to negotiate contracts and that kind of thing, but we in this office looked over everything Mr. Harrigan signed, one more time, so to speak, and just in case. It's a good policy."

"I'm sure it is. Will there still be contracts to look over, now that Mr. Harrigan and Mr. Sheehy are both dead?"

"Of course there will be," Neil Savage said. "There's the matter of the corporation, for instance, which owns all of Mr. Harrigan's copyrights and which handles material under his name. He's got a publisher for his books, but he was very popular on the lecture circuit, and every lecture he gave was tape-recorded and reproduced for sale on his Web site. Those tapes will go on selling, and so will the books. And the corporation itself will not necessarily disband. It will depend on how the fans respond to the fact that he's dead."

"Do you think they'll respond well?" Gregor asked.

Neil Savage gave an elaborate shrug. "I've got no idea what they'll do. Mr. Harrigan was not a typical client for this firm. Most of our clients are either individuals whose families have been with us for generations, or the businesses those families engage in. Of course, there are some exceptions. No firm could survive in this day and age without making some concessions to modernity, and we do. But Mr. Harrigan was our only media celebrity."

"How did he happen to come to this firm for representation?"

"He was recommended by a longtime client."

"I'm sorry, Mr. Savage, but you must admit—I've seen something of what Drew Harrigan did, and what he was like. And I've talked with his wife at length. Somehow, they don't seem the sort of people to have friends of the kind that would be longtime clients in this place."

Neil Savage hesitated. "One of our longtime clients," he said, "is the Philadelphia Republican Party. They've got a state firm in Harrisburg, of course, but Philadelphia is a large political operation on its own, and it has legal issues of its own."

"Do you also handle the Democratic Party?"

"No."

"As a matter of conviction?"

"As a matter of tradition," Neil Savage said. "My grand-father was lieutenant governor here, a long time ago. My great-great-grandfather was mayor of Philadelphia in the days when people like us could be elected mayor of Philadelphia."

"Did you know that Drew Harrigan was addicted to pre-scription painkillers?"

"Everybody knew it," Neil Savage said. "Not the fans, of course, but everybody who came in contact with him on a daily basis. It was hard to miss. I think even Ellen knew, al-though she's something of a . . . she looks on the bright side of things."

"You believe Mr. Sheehy knew?"

"Of course. In fact, I know he did. We talked about it on several occasions. It was obvious a year ago that something was going to happen eventually if we couldn't get Mr. Harri-gan to enter treatment voluntarily, and, of course, eventually something did."

"What about the names on Ellen Harrigan's list of sus-pects? Did you know them?"

"I knew the names, yes. I didn't necessarily know the people."

"Why did you know the names?"

"Because," Neil Savage said, "they were mostly the names of people we had reason to believe might file a law-suit against Drew Harrigan or *The Drew Harrigan Show*. Miss Hildebrande's name seemed to have been thrown in to make the list longer, but the rest were people Drew Harrigan had commented on on the air. He was not a temperate man."

"No, he wasn't," Gregor agreed. "Did any of them in fact have a lawsuit pending?"

"No," Neil Savage said. "But there have been lawsuits in the past. That's chiefly the work we did for Mr. Harrigan, dealing with the lawsuits. There were a lot of them."

"Did that bother Mr. Sheehy? Did he get sued when Drew Harrigan did?"

"Most of the time, no," Neil Savage said. "People who

sue, well, they tend not to get very good representation. Of course, Mr. Harrigan made comments about public figures, and if they'd decided to sue they would have had very good representation indeed, but they wouldn't. It's nearly impossible for a public figure to sue a media company for libel or slander and win. The courts err far too much on the freedom of the press side of the issue. But other people, professors at the University of Pennsylvania, for instance, who were among Drew's favorite targets, those people do sometimes decide to sue. And they can neither afford, nor do they know how to find, representation that would be of any use to them."

"Do you know who was getting the extra prescription drugs for Drew Harrigan?"

"According to Mr. Harrigan, it was a homeless man who did occasional work for him, named Sherman Markey."

"According to everybody I've talked to," Gregor said, "it wouldn't have been possible for Sherman Markey to have done any such thing. For one thing, he looked the part of a homeless person far too well for druggists to hand pills to him on a regular basis."

Neil Savage shrugged. "According to Drew, that was who it was. I've got no reason to disbelieve him."

"Have you met Sherman Markey?"

"I've seen him," Neil Savage said. "He was in court on a couple of occasions because of the lawsuit he filed for defamation. That the Justice Project filed for him. He was in court."

"Do you know where Sherman Markey is now?"

Neil Savage looked honestly surprised. "Of course I don't. I wish I did. The disappearing act has caused no end of trouble. Not that I'm surprised, mind you. Taking off instead of taking responsibility is the kind of thing a man like that specializes in."

"A man like what?"

"A homeless person," Neil Savage said. "An alcoholic. A drug addict, presumably. You don't end up on the streets like that unless you lack organization, determination, and pride. Don't you think?"

2

The worst thing about not having a settled status—aside from the very good possibility that he was never going to get paid—was the fact that he had no settled place to work out of. The sensible thing would have been to use his own apartment on Cavanaugh Street. If he was going to behave like the Armenian-American Hercule Poirot, he might as well have the comforts of a Hercule Poirot, and at the moment luxury railway carriages were not available in the Commonwealth of Pennsylvania. Unfortunately, Cavanaugh Street was convenient to nothing in this case, and there was no Hastings to sit beside him and fumble about badly among his ideas. He found himself sitting in the back of a police car again, wondering why it was strictly necessary for them to have this cagey-thing between the front and back seats, and making notes in a little bound book with stiff covers that Tommy Donahue had given him for Christmas. State police cars didn't have it, or at least the one he'd last ridden in hadn't. If it had, he'd have noticed. The little bound book looked precious, but it had the advantage of those stiff covers, half an inch thick, make of cardboard but very sturdy.

He had just started to make a list of questions when his cell phone went off, and the radio in the front seat went off as well.

"Mr. Demarkian?" a female voice said. "Mr. Benedetti needs to see you and Officers Marbury and Giametti as soon as possible. Do you think you could tell them so?"

Marbury turned around in the front seat and said, "That was for us. They want us to go to Benedetti's office as soon as possible. You have any reason you can't?"

Gregor thanked the woman on the phone and shut off. Then he went back to his list. It was a simple list, but he thought it pretty much covered everything he wanted to know to wrap this all up. What he wanted to know was a lot more than he, or Benedetti, needed to know. In real-life police cases, a lot of questions went unanswered. There were always side issues and subplots it made no point to pursue.

Fortunately, he was not a professional law enforcement person any longer. Right now, he didn't even know if he was a professional consultant to law enforcement persons.

He shied away from examining his use of the word "persons" and wrote: *Where is Sherman Markey?*

He was fairly sure he knew who had gotten him out of the way. There was only one person, or group of people, who actually needed him out of the way. Gregor would bet on the single person and not the group, though. Groups leaked like sieves. He picked up his pen again and wrote: *Why was Alison Standish falsely accused of political bias?*

Gregor was not naive about the politics of Ivy League universities, and especially not of the Ivy League university he had himself graduated from. It was within the realm of possibility that there really was a disgruntled former student and that Dr. Standish had been politically biased when she dealt with him, but Gregor doubted it. It didn't feel that way. She didn't present herself as somebody who would discriminate against a student because of political views that arguably had nothing at all to do with the subject matter of the course at hand, or as somebody who cared much about politics in any sense.

He turned the pen over in his hands and then wrote: *Why is there so much overlap between Ellen Harrigan's list and Ray Dean Ballard's list?*

Some of the overlap made sense. Some of the people involved in the case were the kind of people who might reasonably be expected to have accounts at Markwell Ballard. Some of the overlap was just eerie. What was Ray Dean Ballard doing on Ellen Harrigan's list at all? Yes, Drew Harrigan had attacked Philadelphia Sleeps, and called it practically a Communist organization, but that wasn't personal, and it wasn't likely to get Ray Dean fired or even inconvenienced in any other way. There was another question, too: *Who had drawn that list up for Ellen Harrigan in the first place?*

If there was one thing Gregor was sure of, it was that Ellen Harrigan hadn't written it herself. She wasn't that well wrapped. He doubted if she'd heard of all the people on it. He doubted even more that she had any idea why any of those people would "hate" her husband enough to want to kill him. Ellen Harrigan was a woman who ran on a very narrow array of emotions, and the most important of the ones she had was fear.

He dropped down what would have been another line if the paper had been lined and wrote: *Where was he getting the prescription medication?*

Gregor didn't mean Drew Harrigan. He knew where Harrigan was getting the prescription medication. He meant Drew Harrigan's source. It all came down to this: it made no sense to kill Harrigan if you couldn't be sure that nobody would discover that you were the one feeding him the pills in the first place. That meant that you had to be getting those pills in a way that you believed could not be discovered in almost any circumstance.

They were at Rob Benedetti's door. Gregor put the little bound book into the inside pocket of his coat and waited until Marbury came around to let him out. This was a car for transporting criminals. The back doors didn't open from the inside.

Getting out, Gregor looked around, carefully checking for homeless people, but found none. The last few days had made him hypersensitive to an issue he'd never thought about much before, and that made him more than a little uncomfortable to think about now. They went through into the lobby and waited for the elevator. They walked into the elevator and pushed the button for Rob Benedetti's floor. The building felt deserted, although Gregor knew it couldn't be. It had to be the time of day.

"Places always spook me when they get like this," Giametti said.

"Everything spooks you," Marbury said. "You thought aliens were going to land when the planets aligned."

The elevator stopped on Rob Benedetti's floor and they all got out. They walked down to the woman who served as Benedetti's gatekeeper. She didn't need to be told who they were. Gregor thought he himself would probably stick in her memory forever, because he was the one she'd had to find after being told there was a body in the back in a shopping cart.

She got Benedetti himself on the intercom, told him they were there, and then turned back to Gregor. "It's the nuns," she said. "I can handle anything but nuns. And nuns in habits like that." She waved her hands in the air. "I thought they stopped wearing habits like that. They're not anywhere near as scary in ordinary street clothes."

Benedetti came out and began waving them all into his office. He looked harried and triumphant at once. Gregor did not think this was a good sign. Investigations were not usually aided by investigators who imagined themselves marching through the last act in a Verdi opera.

"Wait until you hear this," he said, in what was supposed to be a muted tone under his breath, but wasn't. "Just wait until you hear this."

The two nuns Gregor remembered from the police station were sitting in Benedetti's office, their feet flat on the floor, their hands folded in their laps and out of sight under their voluminous sleeves. At least, Gregor thought it was the same two. He was sure about the young one, who was unusual in both her looks and her manner. He admitted to himself that he hadn't paid attention to the other nun yesterday, and wasn't paying much attention to this other nun now.

Benedetti waved them all to chairs and sat down on the edge of his desk. "This is Sister Maria Beata and Sister Mary Immaculata. I think we've all met."

"Yes, of course, Mr. Benedetti," Immaculata said. She looked disapproving, but she probably always did.

"Tell Mr. Demarkian what you told me," Benedetti said to Sister Beata. Then he turned to Gregor. "They came marching in here about forty-five minutes ago and told me the most amazing thing."

"We didn't know where else to go," Beata said. "Our first thought after talking to Reverend Mother was to go to the precinct at Hardscrabble Road, of course, but that didn't seem to make sense, since it didn't seem as if anybody there knew anything about this. Then we tried to call you, Mr. Demarkian, but we got your answering machine. We know you have a cell phone number, but we didn't know what it was."

"We weren't sure if there was directory assistance for cell phone numbers," Immaculata said.

Beata brushed this off. "The thing is, I never would have remembered. I mean, I did remember, in a way, but I couldn't put my finger on it. Even at the time, you see, the man in the red hat looked familiar, but I just thought that was because he came to the barn often. And the odd thing is, he did come to the barn often. Or rather, often enough. At least a couple of times a month this winter."

"People come in and out," Immaculata said. "You can never tell with the barn, who will show up and who will not. We have regulars, but there are other people who come and go."

"And later," Beata said, "when it was Drew Harrigan in the red hat, I thought that was it. I must have recognized him as Harrigan and not realized it. But I knew that couldn't be true. Mr. Harrigan was Reverend Mother's brother. I hadn't seen him often, but I'd seen him often enough to know when somebody wasn't him, and the man in the red hat that night couldn't have been him. He was too thin, for one thing."

"Listen to this." Benedetti was practically dancing.

Beata ignored him. "Then this morning," she said, "we were in town, and Immaculata wanted a throat lozenge, because she was coughing. So we stopped at a drugstore to buy her some Halls mentholeucalyptus, and he was there, standing by the magazine rack. And then I knew, you know, because he was wearing a hat. Just not a red one."

"Jig Tyler," Rob Benedetti said, nearly crowing. "It was Jig Tyler who showed up at the barn that night, dressed up like a homeless person."

"Are you sure?" Gregor asked Beata.

Beata nodded her head. "Absolutely sure. It's like when you're trying to remember the name of an actor you're watching in a movie, or where you've seen him before, and then the next day or so it comes to you, and you can't imagine you ever didn't know. I'm sure. I looked straight into his face as we were getting out of the car."

"Did you look straight into the face of Drew Harrigan when he was found dead?" Gregor asked.

Beata shook her head. "I really couldn't have told very much from the body, Mr. Demarkian. It was slumped, and fouled with vomit. I'm not a doctor and I'm not a pathologist. It was . . . unnerving . . . to be with a dead body at all, never mind one who'd been sick. I took a pulse. I checked for breathing. I wasn't looking into his face. I'm sorry."

"No, that's quite all right. I don't blame you. You say that Dr. Tyler had been to the barn before on more than one occasion?"

"Oh, yes," Beata said. "He'd been coming all winter. I don't know why I never realized who he was, because that wasn't the first time I'd thought I recognized him. But you see, we don't really spend that much time in the barn. We hire a man for security, and then we leave the place open. It's not really a shelter. Any other winter, the city would have shut us down if we tried to do this the way we're doing it. Now, of course, with the temperatures so awful, they look the other way. But it's not as if we're out there managing things all the time."

"Did you ever see anybody else you thought you recognized?" Gregor asked.

"No, Mr. Demarkian. I'm sorry. You're wondering if I might have seen Mr. Harrigan. I'm almost certain I didn't. But that doesn't mean he wasn't there. You might ask one of the other extern sisters, Immaculata here or Marie Bernadette."

"I didn't recognize this one," Immaculata said. "I still can't believe you did."

"You wouldn't happen to know the specific dates on which you saw Dr. Tyler?" Gregor said.

Beata shook her head. "I really don't. It wasn't that big an issue for me, you see. It wasn't that I thought anything was wrong or going on. I suppose I should have."

"I don't see why," Gregor said. "I don't see why anybody

would think that perfectly ordinary people with decent homes to go to would be lined up to get a spot in a homeless shelter so far out on the city limits it's almost in the next township. Although I suppose that was the point. The remoteness, I mean."

"This is the point," Benedetti said. "Jig Tyler poisoned Drew Harrigan. He was supplying Harrigan with pills, and Harrigan was out of control, and he was afraid Harrigan was going to implode and take him down, too, so he filled a bunch of pills with poison and killed him."

"And he killed Frank Sheehy, why?" Gregor said.

"We'll find out," Benedetti said.

Gregor sighed. "Never mind. You've actually almost got it right. Almost, not quite. You know what part you got wrong?"

"What?" Benedetti said.

"The part where Jig Tyler kills Drew Harrigan. Jig Tyler didn't kill anybody, and certainly not Harrigan. Although I suppose we're going to have to shut down his antics anyway."

SIX

I

Ellen Harrigan truly hated Neil Savage's offices, and Neil Savage, and Neil Savage's law firm, and everything about Neil Savage and all his works. She hated him, and them, more than she hated the women who had worked for Drew, who seemed to her to exist for no other reason but to make the point that women who hadn't attended the Ivy League or the Seven Sisters weren't fit to live. She hated him more than she hated liberals, and with more concentration, because she knew who and what he was. She had come to the realization, over the last few days, that she didn't actually know what a "liberal" was, except for somebody who voted for the Democratic Party, which didn't make sense. Her father voted for the Democratic Party. All the men she had known growing up did, the ones who worked the line at the factories that ringed the small city near their town, the ones who worked as garage mechanics, even the ones who managed the local IGA and wore a short-sleeved white collar shirt and thin stringy tie to do it in. She was beginning to think that she had understood even less than she had thought she had. Being married to Drew, it had been much too easy to let him take care of everything, including the thinking, and the fact was that she didn't care that much about politics anyway. Liberal, conservative, Republican, Democrat, it was all pretty much the same to her, except that she was sure that whoever Drew had liked was a Good Person, and whoever he didn't was not. That was fine when he was alive, but he wasn't alive anymore. He was lying in a morgue somewhere. People suspected her of killing him. She thought that people suspected her now more than they had when she'd first gone to Gregor Demarkian with that list. She thought they hated her now that she had done that press conference. It hadn't been a good idea. She had let herself be panicked, and she knew what she was like when she was panicked.

Standing in the front waiting room with its pictures of overdressed old farts on the walls and leather furniture that looked like nobody was allowed to sit on it, Ellen checked herself for signs that she was losing her resolve, but there were none. She used to be intimidated when she came into this room. She wasn't anymore. She still thought the over-dressed old farts would have looked down their noses at her, but she didn't care. She still thought the furniture cost more, altogether, than what she'd paid for her first car, but she didn't care about that, either. She had been panicked because she had been thinking the way they wanted her to think, and in the . . . She groped for the word. There was a word. She'd heard it at a dinner in Washington once when she had been seated at the same table as Michael Novak and his wife. Michael Novak was an intellectual. He intimidated her, al-though right now she wasn't sure he'd meant to. Still, she'd listened to him, and she'd come up with a word.

"Categories." That was the word. She thought in the cat-egories they wanted her to think in, and because she did that, she believed the things they wanted her to believe. And the issue wasn't liberal or conservative, Republican or Democratic, left or right, or any of the other things that they said were so damned important to them. The issue was smart and stupid, and when it came right down to the wire, that was all they cared a flying damn about one way or the other.

The door that led to the offices at the back opened, and Neil himself poked his head out. Ellen was surprised, but only a little. Neil Savage would have sent out a secretary to greet his own mother, but he probably thought she was out of control, and dangerous. That was one of the things Michael Novak had been saying about "categories" at that dinner. When people started thinking in categories and forgot they were doing it, they ended up buying into the very myths and stereotypes they'd invented themselves. It had been some conversation about religious people and politics. She didn't remember what it was about. She only remembered that she'd thought at the time that it made sense he was an intellectual.

Neil decided she wasn't about to scream and cause a scene. He came out and held out his hand. "Mrs. Harrigan," he said. "Ellen. Come on back and let me know what I can do for you."

Ellen looked around again at all the overdressed old farts on the walls—she'd almost thought of them as "over-stuffed," which made her smile—and then walked past Neil through the door and into the long corridor beyond. There were more old farts here, and more expensive carpets, and that muted amber lighting very expensive hotels used to give the impression of intimidating elegance. In the end, though, it was just a law firm. It was no different from the offices her father went to on the clotted Main Street of their town when he wanted to buy a house or make his will. It was all an illusion, everything these people had. They used it to make you afraid of them.

She walked right by the doors to the conference room and into Neil's office, because she knew he would try his best to get her to sit at that big table while they talked. That was more of trying to make her afraid, and she wasn't having any. She sat down in the big visitor's chair, feeling the softness of the leather under the palms of her hands. What wasn't illusion was money. She wondered why it was people were always so intimidated by money.

Neil came in and went around to the other side of his desk. Ellen had noticed that he liked looking "official." He would have made a good judge. He was tall and intimidating. His face looked like it was hewn out of stone. He walked as if he were already wearing robes.

"Well," he said, sitting down.

"Do you know who you look like?" she asked him. "You look like what's his name, the senator. You look like John Kerry."

Neil Savage blinked. "Yes. Well. As a matter of fact, I think we have a common ancestor in the Massachusetts Bay Colony. My mother would have known."

Ellen looked around at the walls. There were no old farts here, only hunting prints and dark paneling. Everything in this building was dark paneling.

"I want to do something about the will," she said.

Neil Savage blinked again. "Yes," he said. "Well. We will have a reading, of course, as soon as possible, but it's only been—"

"We can have it the day after tomorrow," Ellen said. "That should be enough time for you to get the word out to the other people who will need to be here. You can send messengers if you have to."

"Well, yes, but that will depend on who is named in the will, won't it? We may have to bring somebody down from New York, or up from Washington."

"You won't. I know what's in the will, Neil. I have a copy of it."

"Do you?"

"I've got copies of everything. The will. The deeds. Everything he owned, and everything we owned together, and everything I owned by myself. Not that I would have known what to do with the money if I'd been left to myself, but Drew bought stock for me, and real estate. I know you have all the originals, but I have copies. Drew said it was safer."

"It is. It's a lot safer."

"I want to do whatever we have to do about the will. I control a lot of things now. The franchise, isn't that what it's called? The merchandising. I don't suppose that will last all that long now that he's dead, but it's got to be taken care of."

"I can take care of those things for you," Neil said. "And Drew had a business manager. She can—"

"Yes, I know Drew's business manager."

Neil hesitated. "If it's, well, if it's a personal thing, I can assure you that nothing Drew ever did gave me the least impression that—"

Ellen was genuinely startled. "Do you honestly think I'd suspect Drew of having an affair with that woman? Or with any of the women in his office? Drew was a lot of things, but one of them was not the kind of man who gets attracted to that kind of woman. Do you know what he used to say about Danielle? That she probably took her briefcase to bed with her. And he didn't mean when she was sleeping alone."

"Ah," Neil said, "yes."

"It bothered you when he talked like that, didn't it? It bothered all of you. The women in the office, too. I mean, after all, what was he? Some small-town hick with a tenth-rate education. That's not mine, by the way, I heard a woman at a party say it once, when she thought she was alone with a friend in the ladies' room. But you think that about all of them. Rush Limbaugh. Alan Keyes. Oliver North. They're your version of slumming."

"I really don't think I know what you mean," Neil said.

He was stiff now. She could feel it. She got up and began to walk around the office, doing the unthinkable, the one thing she had been told by everyone, even Drew, that she was never to do. She started picking up the bric-a-brac. It was ancient and venerable bric-a-brac: a painted wooden duck decoy that had never been in the water; a picture of a woman in a shirtwaist dress in a thick silver frame; a little canoe made out of birch bark and tailored into a perfect miniature. She could feel him flinching every time she picked up something else. There were no Steuben glass crystal hand warmers here, and there never would be.

"You know," she said, "I know you think I'm stupid, and it's probably true. I'm not very quick at a lot of things, and there's a lot I don't understand. But I understand this. All those people you can't stand have rights, too. They have the right to be heard. They have the right to be taken seriously."

"Nobody has the right to be taken seriously. You earn that by the content of your ideas."

"That's not what I meant, and you know it. But maybe you don't, so I'll let it pass. The thing is, I've thought it all out, and I've decided that I'll be a lot better without you than with you. And that goes for Drew's staff. There have to be people out there who can run an office without thinking their shit doesn't stink because they got their degree from Mount Holyoke. There have got to be people with skills that I can actually work with."

"You've never had any problem working with me," Neil said.

"That's because I've never had to work with you. You could ignore me while Drew was alive. You can't ignore me now. I don't want to spend my time meeting in offices surrounded by all your dead partners who probably thought the Irish were the next worst thing after refrigerator mold, if they even knew what refrigerator mold was. I don't care if people hate me for being Catholic, but I care when they laugh at me for it."

"I've never laughed at anybody for being Catholic."

"Not in public, no. But you do. At least, you laugh at my kind of Catholic, at rosaries and scapulars and pictures of us making First Holy Communion in a white dress and a veil like a make-believe bride. I didn't make that one up, either. That was one of the women at the office. I want the will read, and settled, and then you're fired. You never wanted Drew's business anyway. Now you're rid of it."

"I think you're making a mistake," Neil said.

"You think I'm too stupid to think for myself," Ellen said, "and that could be true. We'll just have to see. As soon as we get the will read and it becomes official that I'm taking over the franchise, I'm going to fire the office staff. All of them."

"But they know where everything is. They know things you can't possibly know, that even Drew couldn't possibly know."

"I've got a friend from home who's been a secretary all her life. I'm going to bring her in to run things. I'll bring her in a couple of weeks early so they can show her what she needs to know. And no, Neil, I'm not so stupid that I don't know that they'll probably sabotage her—or is it that I think they'll probably sabotage her that's the stupid part? That's something I heard once, too. That people like Drew think the things they think because they're just stupid enough to know they don't get it, so they suspect everybody all the time of trying to pull one over on them. But Drew wasn't stupid, you know. No matter what you thought."

"I didn't think he was stupid."

"Maybe not. Maybe you only thought he was vulgar. I don't see where it matters. After I get Janice installed at the office, I'm going to take off for two weeks and take my nieces to Disney World. No fancy restaurants where I don't know how to pronounce the food. No being stuck with mineral water and a salad because that's what everybody else is eating and I'm afraid to look like an idiot having a hamburger. I'm going to drink Coke, eat pizza and Tex Mex, and go on rides. And you'll never hear from me again."

"I don't think you can just take off for Florida like that," Neil said. "You're a suspect in a murder investigation. You may have to get permission from the court."

"Don't be ridiculous," Ellen said. "The only reason I'd need that is if I'd been arrested and I was out on bail, but I'm not going to be arrested, and you know it. Nobody suspects me of killing Drew. Not even Gregor Demarkian suspects me of killing Drew."

"You can't possibly know that."

"But I do know it," Ellen said. "And do you know how I know it? Because the person he suspects is you."

2

It had been bothering her since Gregor Demarkian had come to see her the night before, and now it was impossible to keep out of her mind on any level. Alison wasn't even able to keep it out of her mind while she was teaching, and usually teaching was better than a memory drug. She found it all too easy to retreat into the Middle Ages and to experience that as more real, and more immediate, than anything in the present. Maybe that was because the Middle Ages *were* more real and immediate than anything in the present. The passage of time did a lot of good things for whatever cultural periods it didn't completely destroy. It washed away the trivial and the dross. It eliminated the extraneous. Chaucer's *Canterbury Tales* and Hildegarde von Bingen's music stood out like shining beacons of culture, taste, erudition, and sanity next to the violent confusion of a world full of Madonna and Beethoven, Steven Spielberg and Shakespeare, *The Weekly World News* and *The Portrait of a Lady*. But Chaucer's world had been a violent confusion, too, and on every level. It was a world where people died young of diseases we didn't have the names for anymore, where maiming and mutilation were par for the course in war, where the cultural landscape included hundreds of truly execrable morality plays and drama from traveling troupes with no more thought to the artistic integrity of what they were doing than for the feelings of the playwrights whose works they were plagiarizing. Then there was the really gruesome: the art of religious relics, manufactured wholesale from bits and pieces of dead animals and, yes, dead human beings. There was the art of the Chapel of Bones, with its facade made of human bones stacked one on top of the other and, in the sanctuary, the bodies of a dead man and a dead child hung by hooks over the congregation, to remind them of the fleetingness of life. There was the Plague, and there were the flagellants, monks who walked through the streets of towns and cities in formation, scourging themselves with metal-tipped leather whips until their upper torsos spurted blood. *Hell,* Alison thought, *give me World Wrestling Entertainment anytime.*

She looked up now at the building she thought was the one she wanted, and tried consulting the visitor's map one

more time. It was astounding that she had managed to be at
Penn for all these years and still not know where the Math
Department was, but she wasn't in the Math Department,
and she didn't usually need them for anything, so that was
the way that went. The visitor's map was more than a little
surreal. It showed the university buildings as if they were
made of Lego blocks, but it didn't show anything of the city
that not only surrounded the campus but interweaved with
it. It was disorienting. People who came to visit here must
feel as if they'd entered a virtual reality game, or exited
from one.

This looked like the right building. She went inside and
looked at the information board just inside the door. Not all
buildings had them. She was glad this one did. Maybe it had
something to do with this being a science building, and committed to modernity and reason. Or maybe not. The information board didn't give much in the way of information. It
didn't list professors' offices. It did say that the Math Department was in "Room 217," by which Alison supposed it
meant that the office with the Math Department's secretaries
was there. She wondered sometimes why academic departments always wanted to make having to deal with them
something that was very hard to do.

She found the stairs and ran up them. This building might
have an elevator. It was hard to tell which ones did and
didn't. On the second floor, she went down the corridors
counting doors, looking for Room 217, and then she got
lucky. She heard his voice, sailing out into the corridor as
clearly as if he had been speaking into a microphone.

"No more hegemonic discourse, Delmore," he said. "I'm
very, very serious."

Alison was startled for a moment. She didn't think math
people talked about hegemonic discourse. She got tired just
hearing literature people talk about hegemonic discourse.
She slowed down a little and tried to listen, but whoever Delmore was, his diction was deplorable. All she could catch
was mumbles.

"The revolution won't be destroyed because you learn to speak in plain English," Jig Tyler said then. "It might be destroyed if you don't."

Alison went up to the door and looked inside. Jig was sitting behind his desk, with his legs up, wearing a ratty old crew-necked sweater over even rattier khaki pants. "Delmore" was wearing jeans, but he shouldn't have been. He was too fat, too round, too soft, and far too earnest-looking.

Alison was just wondering if she should clear her throat, and knock, when Jig saw her there. He put his feet down and sat up straight. "Dr. Standish," he said. "Get yourself together, Delmore. This is Dr. Standish. She teaches in the English Department and writes articles about the development of vernacular poetry and heresy."

"Heresy is good," Delmore said earnestly. "Heresy is inherently transgressive, and because of that it almost always has subversive and underminic effects on the hegemonic—"

Jig cleared his throat. Delmore shut up. He had thin hair pulled awkwardly across the top of his head, over what was becoming a bald spot.

"Well," Delmore said. "I've got Dr. Markham's seminar in about twenty minutes. I should go."

"Good idea," Jig said.

Alison watched Delmore leave the office and go down the hall. He looked dejected. She thought the oppression he most needed to alleviate was his own.

"Do you always behave that way to him?" she asked. "Is it—I don't know—some sort of tradition in the Math Department, like it used to be at Chicago, when people said you were presumed guilty of stupidity until proven innocent?"

"I'd never presume anybody guilty of anything until proven innocent," Jig said. "Delmore proved his stupidity long ago. He's an entirely mechanical actor. He's flawlessly conscientious. He comes to every class. He does every assignment. He studies for every test. He's always prepared. It's taken him this far, and that isn't a small thing. Getting admitted to the graduate program in this department these days makes getting elected God look like a piece of cake.

But the mechanics are all Delmore can do. He has no imagination, and he has less knowledge of the real world and how it operates. You don't want to begin discussing his problems understanding people."

"Is that necessary in a mathematician? That he understand people?"

"Probably not. Lord only knows there have been enough mathematicians who don't. And in some highly technical fields, a lack of understanding and empathy could even help. You wouldn't want a surgeon standing over you with a knife and feeling your pain. But it's necessary to a human being that he—or she, excuse me—understand people, and I'm afraid Delmore isn't ever going to be much of a human being."

"But he does what you tell him to do, doesn't he?"

"Oh, yes," Jig said. "Delmore tries to compensate for his lack of interrelatedness with people by committing himself to what he thinks are left politics and hero-worshiping me. In the beginning, I thought the hero worship was what bothered me. Lately, it's been the left politics."

"I thought you had left politics."

"I do," Jig said. "I have real left politics. Delmore is sunk up to his neck in the intellectualized crap that's become the security blanket of the embattled academic class. A transgressive hermeneutics of grammar. Ad infinitum."

This room, Alison thought, was exactly what you would expect the office of a two-time Nobel Prize winner to be like. There were books everywhere, and not only books related to his field. There was Aristotle and Kant and Heidegger. There was Jane Austen and James Joyce. There was a copy of Einstein's essays on society and politics. If they gave you something besides a check to mark your Nobel Prize—a plaque, or certificate, or a statue—that wasn't here. She folded her arms across her chest and looked back at Jig. He was exactly what you would expect him to be, too. The intellectual giant as Brahmin WASP. The genius as preppie.

"I came," she said, "to find out why you told Drew Harrigan I was discriminating against my students with conservative views."

Jig didn't even blink. "Why do you think I did that?"

"I don't know, but I'm sure you did. I don't think you went to the administration, or the department. Once the accusation is made, it takes on a life of its own. But I think you told Drew Harrigan that. I think you fed him the original story. That's why you came to my office the other day."

"I came to warn you about Ellen Harrigan's list."

"I don't think so," Alison said. "I wasn't in danger from Ellen Harrigan's list. If I'd thought about it for two seconds, I would have realized that. Gregor Demarkian came to see me. The police are no more interested in me than they are in the Easter Bunny. And why should they be? I never met the man. Either man, I suppose it is now."

"I was trying to be helpful to a fellow sufferer from Drew Harrigan's allegations."

"I don't think you ever suffered from Drew Harrigan's allegations," Alison said. "You're untouchable, really. You'd have to rape a child to get into any real trouble on this campus. You've got the two Nobel prizes. You've got tenure. You've got the political books, and they sell, which means they probably also make money. I went on the Internet and paid twenty-nine ninety-five to join Drew Harrigan's Web site. Then I listened to a bunch of the archived programs. It wasn't just me. There was a woman in the Spanish Department who got accused of teaching the Inquisition from a Marxist perspective, a man in the Philosophy Department who got nailed for supposedly having said that the United States was the greatest danger to human life the world has ever known, a man in the Sociology Department who was called out for supposedly saying that the family was obsolete and ought to be abolished. Do you know what they all had in common?"

"What?"

"They were all pretty obscure, and the complaints came from their upper-level and graduate courses. In other words, the courses with the fewest number of students in them."

"So?"

"So the probabilities are low that it would have happened

that way that many times," Alison said. "The more you look at just who Drew Harrigan went after at Penn over the last year and a half, the more it looks like an inside job. We had Angela Davis come and speak at this campus not six months ago, and Drew Harrigan never mentioned it. Do you want to tell me what it is you were trying to do?"

"Why do you think it was me who was trying to do something? Even if your analysis is correct, and in my opinion it's logically weak to the point of feebleness—"

"Oh, stop," Alison said. "Nobody else came to me. Nobody else 'warned' me. Nobody wanted to find out how I was feeling. Of course it was you. The question is, why was it you?"

"I was a victim, too, you know," Jig said.

"Nonsense," Alison said. "You throw your ideas out there for all to see and somebody attacks them; that's not being a victim, that's being a part of the debate. I was damned near a real victim. I had an inquiry launched into my teaching, into my integrity—"

"A secret inquiry," Jig said quickly.

"I know."

"But don't you see, that's the point," Jig said. He got up so suddenly, Alison flinched. "Secret inquiries. Speech codes. Star Chamber proceedings where the accused is presumed guilty until proven innocent and isn't even allowed to know who is testifying against him. Do you know how that looks in the outside world, how it looks to our students?"

"Yes, it looks terrible," Alison said. "The speech codes should be abolished. More professors should do what I did when faced with secret inquiries and threaten to sue. Why does that justify giving Drew Harrigan lies to spout on his radio program about people who've done nothing wrong in the first place?"

"How do you know that they've done nothing wrong?" Jig said. "Cavellero, the man in the Philosophy Department, was one of the principal architects of that speech code you think should be abolished. And during the water buffalo thing, he was one of the biggest advocates of expelling the kid outright for daring to cause trouble. The woman in the Spanish Department helped design the 'Orientation' program all new faculty hires are required to take. That's after your time. Do you know what that's like?"

"I've heard rumors," Alison said.

"Re-education camp," Jig said. "Emotional bullying in the name of antidiscrimination. It's insane. Do you know what we're doing, on campuses like this across the country? We're raising a generation of Republicans, because we're raising a generation of kids who think it's the Republicans who stand for freedom of speech and of the press. And do you know why that is?"

"Why?"

"Because on college campuses, it *is* the Republicans who stand for freedom of speech and of the press. It's the Republicans who fight against the shouting down of speakers, and against censoring campus newspapers, and against criminalizing speech. The Campus Republicans are the single strongest force for civil liberties at Penn. What are we doing to ourselves? What are we doing to the world when we send kids out of here determined to vote for right-wing nutcases because they mistake the campus reality for reality in the real world?"

"And that justifies giving a nationally syndicated radio talk-show host false information about my teaching and grading practices so that he can call me a Communist and get me investigated by my department?"

"The investigation didn't happen because of what Drew Harrigan said. It happened because a student complained."

"Maybe," Alison said. "But I'm going to look into that, too. Because I've got my suspicions."

Jig sat down again. Everything he did was abrupt, Alison thought. Watching him sometimes was like watching jerky animation.

"We have to do something to stop it," he said. "Just talking about it won't help. I do talk about it. I talk about it all the time. Nobody listens."

"Nobody is listening to this," Alison said.

"You would have sued," Jig said. "They would have listened to that. Just watch them change if not changing means they lose money."

"They're not going to change," Alison said. "They're just going to retire. I've got to get back to my office. I have to teach in a little while. I never have supported the speech codes, you know. Why pick me?"

Jig shrugged. "It was a paper you wrote. I forgot what it was called, now. About women and heresy."

" 'Women and Theology in the Albigensian Crusade.' "

"That's the one."

"I really do have to go now," Alison said.

She watched him sitting there behind his desk, perfectly at ease with himself and the world, perfectly at ease with his conscience. There were people who said that the great danger of a scientific education was that it lacked insight into the human condition. For that, you had to study the humanities. Here he was, though, with his Heidegger and his Jane Austen, and he was just as arrogant and brutal as any witch-hunting thug.

SEVEN

I

For a few moments, Gregor Demarkian thought he was going to have to stage an escape from Marbury and Giametti's car. It was suddenly obvious why there was no settled chain of command in this case. Without one, Rob Benedetti could play crusading district attorney, like a character in a John Grisham novel, and run the whole show himself. He didn't even have to leave the office to do it, since Gregor had the cell phone, and Benedetti had no compunctions about dialing its number. It had gone beyond the point where Gregor was worried about whether or not he was ever going to be named a formal consultant on this case, or whether or not he was going to get paid. He'd gone without getting paid before. All he wanted was to be able to do two things in a row without having to check in and explain himself. He especially wanted not to have to listen to Benedetti's ideas on how a criminal should be hunted down and cornered. It was a shame young men were no longer required to spend a couple of years in the army. The army would have taught Rob Benedetti that the last thing you wanted to do with something panicked and dangerous was corner it.

"I know who the killer is," Benedetti insisted, his voice coming over the air like a squawk.

"No, you don't," Gregor told him. Then he shut the phone all the way off and stuck it in his pocket. Benedetti could still get to him on Marbury and Giametti's radio, but he'd have to work at that, and that would take time. "I want to go over to LibertyHeart Communications," Gregor said. "I want to talk to Marla Hildebrande for a while."

"Do you think she'll be there?" Marbury asked. "The day after her boss was killed?"

"I'd think she'd have to be. There's the network to run. There's the direct stations. Somebody has to be doing all that."

Neither Marbury nor Giametti could think of a good objection to that—Gregor himself could think of two—and neither of them seemed very interested in waiting around to be told what to do by headquarters, so they all piled into the patrol car again and started back out into city traffic. By now the day had started for serious, and there were a lot of cars on the road. Gregor wondered whether that hadn't been part of the reason to choose Hardscrabble Road as the place to meet. It had to be an advantage not to have to dodge gridlock and backups when time was going to be important to you.

But no, that didn't matter. He was making things unnecessarily complicated. They were pulling up alongside a line of parked cars somewhere in the very center of downtown. There wasn't anywhere to park.

"We can double-park because it's us," Marbury said, "but the department doesn't like it. You want to go in on your own and let us get this straightened out?"

Since Gregor didn't need them at all, except as a substitute for real credentials—*don't ask what I'm doing here, I've got these nifty uniformed policemen coming with me*—he climbed out of the car and went to the pavement. Liberty-Heart was not CBS or ABC or Fox. It didn't have an entire building with an enormous logo sign out front. In fact, it didn't have a sign out front at all. Gregor finally found it by going into the lobby of the nearest high-rise building and checking the information board. He was spending far too much time these days checking information boards.

LibertyHeart was on the ground floor. He tried to figure out whether that made sense or not, and then decided it did. If they were broadcasting from here at all, all it would take would be some equipment on the roof, and it was a very high roof. He went down the hall until he found a door that finally had a logo on it—the Statue of Liberty inside a heart; this did not bode well for the general level of originality in this organization—and went in. The receptionist at the front desk was distinctly Not Ready for Prime Time. Her hair was pulled back in an elastic band. Her skirt was made of denim.

"Yes?" she said.

"I'd like to see Marla Hildebrande," Gregor said. "Could you tell her that Gregor Demarkian is out here waiting."

The receptionist was chewing gum. Gregor half expected her to make some crack about the Armenian-American Hercule Poirot. She just got on the phone and called for Marla Hildebrande instead.

It took no time at all for Marla to come to the reception area and collect him. The receptionist might not be ready for prime time, but Marla definitely was. In spite of the fact that she had obviously been crying, and that she hadn't had much sleep, she was turned out like an ad for Brooks Brothers women's suits and made up with the skill of a professional. She could have walked into an interview with Bill Gates or the president of the United States and looked entirely at home.

She held out her hand to him. "Oh, Mr. Demarkian. It's good to see you again. I'm sorry about last night. I know I wasn't being coherent—"

"You were fine," Gregor said. "You were distraught."

"Oh, dear. I can't think of that word anymore without remembering the Harry Potter movie. You know, Moaning Myrtle."

"Mm," Gregor said. He did not know.

"I didn't know what else to do but what I did, you see," Marla said. "I mean, we saw the picture on the screen. And you know how it is with those pictures, you see the pictures when they're looking for somebody, and then you see the somebody when they pick him up, and the person they pick up never looks anything like the pictures. But the picture looked just like Frank. It was uncanny."

"It wouldn't have happened the way it did last night under normal circumstances," Gregor said. "If you ever make another identification, they'll just take your information and your contact numbers and that will be it. The district attorney felt, because the case has been so—"

"Overpublicized?" Marla Hildebrande smiled slightly. "Yes, I know. We used to say around here that everything Drew Harrigan did was overpublicized."

"Could we go someplace and talk? I've got two officers with me, Marbury and Giametti, and they ought to be in soon, but I'd still like someplace we could close the door."

"Come back to my office. Ginny, please. When the officers get here, send them back."

" 's'okay," the receptionist said.

Marla Hildebrande rolled her eyes and waved Gregor through the door to the offices proper. They consisted of an enormous bullpen full of secretaries' cubicles, all of them separated by glass, and a few offices at the back. One of those offices also had a glass wall that left it open to the bullpen. That was the one Marla Hildebrande took him into.

"I'm sorry," she said. "Frank had the only office you could really close off. I really need to be able to see what's going on. It's usually bad news. Will it matter, that they can see us?"

"No. It probably wouldn't matter if they could hear us, although that makes me a little nervous."

"I'll close the door. They won't be able to hear anything. We're operating on a full schedule today. We have to be. But it isn't like we're a huge corporation. Yet. Frank would always say yet. He wanted to be a huge corporation. But we're not, not yet, and so everybody has to work."

She closed the door and waved him onto the couch, which was worn but looked comfortable. He sat down. Marla Hildebrande sat on the edge of the desk.

"So," she said. "I'm sort of surprised to see you here.

Surprised and pleased. I know this is being taken as part of the Drew Harrigan case. I know that. And I know what happens when that happens, when you're the secondary victim in a celebrity case. Goodness only knows, we report on enough of them. Celebrity cases, I mean. Although it's usually the celebrity who's the perpetrator. Listen to me. I'm not making any sense at all, am I?"

"You're doing fine," Gregor said. "I just want to ask you a few questions. They're really the questions I should have asked Frank Sheehy when he was alive."

"All right."

"Did he know that Drew Harrigan was addicted to prescription drugs? Did you?"

"Oh, of course we did," Marla said. "It was an open secret throughout the industry. These things usually are. And of course we had to cover for it, at least potentially. Although I'll admit, even when he came stoned to work, Drew really could work."

"Did you know where he was getting his information?"

"Drew, you mean? Well, he wasn't an investigative reporter, if that's what you're thinking. He wasn't anything like one. The impression I always got was that he got his stuff from informants. It's a snowball kind of thing. In the beginning it's hard, but after a while people come to you. People who want to feel important. People with grudges. You have to be careful, of course, because people with grudges can feed you false information and get you sued, but it isn't the end of the world to get sued in a business like Drew's."

"Did you like Drew Harrigan?"

"God, no."

"Did Frank Sheehy like Drew Harrigan?"

"Frank liked the money Drew made for everybody, and beyond that I don't think he cared much one way or the other. He was a very practical man when it came to business. We had Drew, but we also have three shock jocks. They're popular, too. We're an equal opportunity offender."

Gregor let that one go, and put it up to the fact that she

was . . . distraught. "Try this," he said. "Did you know that Frank Sheehy had an account with Markwell Ballard?"

"The investment bank? Really? I'm impressed."

"But not surprised."

"No," Marla said. "Not really. Frank came from a wealthy family, a really large wealthy family, with everybody at prep school and Princeton and that kind of thing. And the business has been successful. I could see him with an account at Markwell Ballard."

"Did he try to buy the property Drew Harrigan gave to the nuns at Our Lady of Mount Carmel?"

"No, that I know he didn't do," Marla said, "because he was pissed about it. He said Drew was going to end up shanghaiing himself into jail by pulling this kind of thing."

"He thought the sale of the property was something Drew was pulling?"

"That it was a setup, yes, to bulletproof himself from a court judgment in case Sherman Markey won in court. I thought that, too. Didn't you?"

"I think everybody did. Was Frank Sheehy getting the prescription drugs for Drew Harrigan? Did he know who was?"

For the first time, Marla hesitated. She seemed to be making up her mind about something. "Well," she said finally. "He's dead, isn't he? No, he wasn't the person getting the drugs for Drew, but he knew who was. He told me once that drug addictions were miraculous things, because they could make two people who were otherwise complete enemies into allies. I think on one level he thought it was funny. Oh, he didn't think the drug addiction itself was funny. That was making him crazy, because with a guy like Drew, with a show riding on him, people's jobs riding on him, dysfunction is never funny."

"Do you know who Frank Sheehy thought *was* buying the drugs for Drew Harrigan?"

"Not really," Marla said. "I mean, I've got a suspicion, but it really doesn't attach itself to anything. I mean, it's not based on evidence, or anything solid—"

"A suspicion about whom?"

Marla flushed. "You're going to think I'm nuts. A suspicion about Jig Tyler. You know, the genius, the guy with—"

"I know who Dr. Tyler is, yes. Why do you think it was Jig Tyler?"

Marla threw up her hands. "It was just something he said once, about how it was amazing how the oddest people would bend over backwards to accommodate Drew. But he said that about a lot of people. About Neil Savage, for instance. And Ray Dean Ballard. And even the people at the Justice Project. And everybody did bend over backwards for Drew. Half of them because of the celebrity thing, and half of them because they were afraid of him."

"So why do you think Mr. Sheehy was referring to the drugs when he said what he said about Dr. Tyler?"

"Because of when it was," Marla said. "It was the day they found out that the body at Hardscrabble Road belonged to Drew."

"Did Frank Sheehy know that Drew Harrigan had never gone into rehab?"

"Yes," Marla said. "To tell the truth, so did I. The judge—"

"Yes, we all know about the judge. What about the night Drew Harrigan would have died. That would have been the twenty-seventh of January. Was Mr. Sheehy in the office that night?"

"All night," Marla said. "And so was I. In fact, he was in this office most of the time. We were discussing what we were going to do if Drew had to go to jail. Or worse. What we were going to do if we had to replace Drew permanently."

"Did you reach a solution?"

"Absolutely. Frank authorized me to audition a prospect and get the ball rolling, and we made an offer to a new guy this week."

"What about the last few days, since the body was discovered," Gregor said. "Did Mr. Sheehy do anything out of the ordinary? Did he seem nervous?"

Marla shook her head. "It's really been business as usual. And, like I said, we'd already made the arrangements for the new guy. We were already looking ahead. You have to, in a business like this. The one kind of dead you don't want around here is dead air."

Gregor looked out into the bullpen. The secretaries were all at work doing something at computers. He'd never understood what happened in offices to require so much typing, not even what happened in offices where he himself worked. He wondered where Marbury and Giametti were. Maybe they'd taken their squad car and disappeared.

"Thank you," he said to Marla Hildebrande. "Just tell me one more thing. Whose idea was it to go looking for a replacement for Drew Harrigan? Yours or Mr. Sheehy's?"

"I brought it up, but he had to authorize it. I can't authorize it on my own."

"But you brought it up, on the twenty-seventh?"

"Absolutely."

"Did Mr. Sheehy resist the idea?"

"No, not at all," Marla said. "If you want to know the truth, he seemed to be relieved. We both knew we were going to have to do something about Drew someday."

2

Gregor Demarkian had graduated from the University of Pennsylvania so long ago, he could remember when it was a matter of campuswide discussion that the number of African Americans admitted to undergraduate study had reached a total of five. Of course, there was no discussion at all of what happened to students like him, bright, hardworking, local, and "foreign" in spite of the fact that they'd been born and raised in Philadelphia. The feeling at the time had been that the Gregor Demarkians of the world weren't "really" American, although they weren't really "international," either. There was respect for international students, because they almost always came from wealthy or influential families in their home countries, and shared that vision of the world Penn tried so hard to instill in its graduates in those days. People like Gregor Demarkian were almost always poor and almost always "striving." They not only worked hard, they looked like they worked hard, and that was the big no-no. Never let them see you sweat. But it went beyond that. Never let them see you care. Never let them see you want to better yourself. If you have to better yourself, there's something wrong with you already.

The truth was, Gregor Demarkian got neurotic whenever he had to set foot in that part of the city that housed the University of Pennsylvania, and there was nothing he had been able to do in all these years to change that. He distinctly remembered a July during his third year in the Bureau when he'd done everything but shot himself in the foot not to be assigned to a kidnapping case that had involved a business professor at the Wharton School of Finance. He didn't follow Penn football, or any other sport, and the only reason he contributed to the alumni fund was because he felt he had an obligation. Whatever else Penn had given him, it had given him a first-rate education. He had gone on to the Harvard Business School as ready to compete as any third-generation inheritor of a major merchant bank. He just couldn't help hating the sight of the place. He always ended up thinking of the endless bus rides he'd had to take, from school to Cavanaugh Street and back again. He wondered if it would have been different if Cavanaugh Street had been then what it was now. He considered the possibility that if Cavanaugh Street had been then as it was now, his parents would have had enough money to let him live away in a dormitory, and he wouldn't have gone to Penn at all.

Harvard probably wouldn't have been much better, he thought, climbing out of the police car and going up the steps to the building he knew the Math Department was in. Still. He'd checked the map, and the Math Department was *still* in this building. He'd thought it was only the humanities that were stalled physically and institutionally. He wondered if Penn's Math Department was a good one, or a filler to stuff the vacant spaces between Physics and Chemistry. There was Jig Tyler, but you could never tell.

Marbury and Giametti didn't want to come in. Penn, it

seemed, was deliberately intimidating to local law enforcement.

"It's not that they don't cooperate when they need to," Marbury said. "If they did that, we could nail them. It's that you don't want to make a mistake with one of their people."

"You especially don't want to make a mistake with one of their people like Jig Tyler," Giametti said.

Gregor could actually see the point. He left them his cell phone—Rob Benedetti had called him at least six times since he'd been to see Marla Hildebrande, and he hadn't done anything but ride across town in a patrol car—and went in, through the front doors, and up the stairs. It was not like last night, with Alison Standish. The building was full of people. The students looked the way they had always looked, except that there were more "different" faces among them than there had been in his day. There were not, however, as many "different" faces as the brochures and Web site made it appear. These days, all recruiting materials from the Ivy League looked as if they were advertisements for the Model UN.

He knew where Jig Tyler's office was because he had looked it up on Penn's Web site before coming in to see Rob Benedetti this morning. Tibor should get credit for another bit of work on the case, because without him Gregor couldn't find anything on the Internet. Tibor had gotten him Jig Tyler's teaching and office hour schedule, too. He just wished he'd been able to think of a way to get Dr. Tyler out of this building and down to a precinct station, where he wouldn't feel as if he were about to be stopped and questioned at any moment. Gregor had spent his entire time at Penn waiting for somebody—a security guard, maybe—to tell him he didn't belong there and had to go home.

Jig Tyler was sitting behind his desk behind piles of books, reading down through a page of text with his finger following the lines. Gregor wondered if he always did that when he read, or if he was only doing it now because he knew Gregor was standing in the doorway. You had to wonder what that was like, to have that kind of mind, to be able to do the things Jig Tyler was able to do. Maybe it was like nothing. Maybe he experienced it as normal.

Gregor cleared his throat. He felt silly doing it. They were not only playacting with each other, they were playacting badly. "You can put the book down," he said. "You know I'm here. You had to know I was coming."

Jig sat back. He had the kind of tall ranginess basketball players had, but Gregor didn't remember hearing that he'd ever played basketball. He took his wire-rim glasses off and put them down on the book. "I take it the nun called you," he said.

"She came to talk to us, yes," Gregor said. "You had to know she was going to do that."

"Oh, yes. Do I get any points for not taking the day off and going to New York?"

"Not really. You're smart enough to know that wouldn't work."

"You'd be astonished to know what kinds of stupidity smart people can get themselves into," Jig said. "Or maybe you wouldn't. You graduated from Penn. I looked you up."

"And?"

"Very impressive. I'd say very impressive especially considering your background, but I know better than that, too. Those were the days before affirmative action and diversity goals, and you probably wouldn't have qualified for either anyway. So, very impressive. I liked the dual major in history and philosophy. I liked the fact that you didn't major in literature."

"You don't like literature?"

"I like it fine. I don't like literature professors."

"You have to know by now that you delivered the poison to Drew Harrigan," Gregor said.

Jig rubbed the sides of his face with the palms of his hands and then picked up his glasses and put them on again. "Yes, of course I know. I knew as soon as they found the body. I suspected before that. I just wasn't sure he was dead. Do you know that I didn't deliver the poison intentionally?"

"Do you mean that you didn't think you were delivering poison?" Gregor said. "Oh, yes. You had absolutely no reason to kill Drew Harrigan. In fact, you had a few decent reasons to want him to stay alive. What was it you thought you were doing?"

"Saving the left from itself," Jig Tyler said. "The older I get, the more I think the distinctions are wrong. Left and right. Conservative and liberal. It's not that. It's libertarian and authoritarian. It's people who want freedom and people who want control. Never mind. I'm not making any sense. It was his idea, by the way, all the cloak-and-dagger stuff. Pretending to be homeless men and meeting at that monastery. His sister is the Mother Superior."

"I know. Didn't it occur to you to tell anybody about all of this? Come to me, if to nobody else, if you didn't want any exposure?"

"But there's going to be exposure, isn't there?" Jig said. "There's going to be no way around it. I'm going to be the only person who is able to put our man in the right place and the right time."

"You could have gotten yourself killed," Gregor said. "He's killed two people already. If you've got a cold capsule anywhere in this office or at your house, anywhere he could get to it, I wouldn't bet on your surviving a week."

"I've been very careful to take individually wrapped caplets. I hate that word. Caplets. Why is it that multinational corporations have to invent new words every time they produce a not-all-that-new product?"

"Are you the one who tried to buy that property?"

"No," Jig said. "He did. Drew blackmailed him into it, essentially. Drew pointed out, entirely legitimately, that he wouldn't be the only one who went to jail on prescription drug charges, if Drew wanted to start talking. And Drew was getting, ah, a little nuts. By the time I saw him that last time, at the monastery, he was damn close to raving. He could have passed for one of the regular schizophrenics."

"What was he raving about?"

"The usual paranoid bullshit," Jig said. "He was being persecuted. It was all politics. The Clintons were out to get him—"

"The Clintons?"

"Yes, well," Jig said. "Drew was still very obsessed with the Clintons. They're supposed to be leading a worldwide conspiracy of Communists and socialists to do, I don't know what. He got lucky with the judge, or Neil Savage got smart. Bruce Williamson would set bail for a man who gunned down a hundred babies and old ladies in front of Independence Hall at high noon if the man was a celebrity. Still, he was out and he was in hiding. He couldn't go any of his usual places. He was going to end up in court no matter what else happened, and that drove him nuts. And then there was Sherman Markey, a stooge, in Drew's words, who only existed as a scheme to deprive him of his property. Deprive Drew of his property. If you see what I mean."

"So he blackmailed our friend into buying the property and holding it until his legal troubles were over and he could get it back," Gregor said, "and he did it through Markwell Ballard because there was no way that Markwell Ballard would release any information about the deal to anybody, even the authorities. Not bad."

"Not bad that Markwell Ballard was available," Jig said. "Not everybody can get an account there, and they don't do retail checking. Drew couldn't get an account there."

"Whose idea was it for you to bring the pills?"

"Drew's, I think," Jig said. "I didn't know that our friend was the one who was getting him the pills until I got a call asking me to take the little package with me when I went out to Hardscrabble Road. I don't approve of prescriptions, did you know that? I think we should just leave everything out over the counter and let people go to hell in their own handbaskets. So I took the little envelope out there."

"Did you see him die?"

"No. I didn't even see him take the pills. I gave the package, we talked for a while—"

"About what?"

"About Penn," Jig said. "I think the meeting might have been a ruse to get me to deliver the drugs, but I couldn't know that. I went because I always went when he asked me to. I thought he'd be back, back on the air, back at the same old stand. And I needed him."

"You gave him the hat you were wearing."

"Right. I'd got it from our friend, believe it or not. I take it he got it from Sherman Markey."

"I think so," Gregor said.

"If he knows where Sherman Markey is, Sherman Markey is dead," Jig said.

"He doesn't know where Sherman Markey is," Gregor said. "I know who does, but I'm not all that interested in screaming at somebody just yet. What about Frank Sheehy? He knew about the drugs?"

"I don't know. But I'll tell you what he did know about. He knew about Ellen Harrigan's suspects list."

"Did he?"

"Yes," Jig said. "I talked to him, to Sheehy, maybe ten hours before I saw his picture on the news. I ran into him downtown and started railing at him, because I thought he'd written it. I knew she hadn't. It was the wrong list. She'd have thought of other names. And he stopped me in the middle of ranting and told me that it hadn't been his idea, but it was a good one nevertheless, because it diverted suspicion from the people who were on it. Nobody took Ellen seriously. The cops wouldn't take Ellen seriously, either."

"The idea was to divert suspicion to possible suspects whose names *weren't* on the list?"

"I think so."

"That almost worked," Gregor said. "But only almost. He should never have given me the second list, the one with the names of the people who had accounts at Markwell Ballard. It drew attention to himself, and to the fact that he was the one person on Ellen Harrigan's list *nobody* would have thought to put there. He wasn't one of the people Drew Harrigan went after. Harrigan went after Philadelphia Sleeps, but not Ray Dean Ballard personally. Are we going to have to subpoena you or are you going to come down and make a statement voluntarily?"

"Oh, I'll make a statement voluntarily," Jig said. "There's no reason not to, is there? No matter what anybody thinks, I'm pretty safe here. I could get away with things nobody else on any other campus could. Two Nobels will do that for you."

"That isn't a small thing, two Nobels."

"I didn't say it was," Jig Tyler said. "And I worked very hard to get them. Do you know what makes me the most angry about all of this? Good old Ray Dean Ballard never worked very hard at anything, except maybe pretending he wasn't who he was."

"Good old Ray Dean Ballard is likely to have a date with a lethal injection," Gregor said. "Except I think they'll probably call him Aldous on the execution order."

3

They were on their way to Rob Benedetti's office with Jig Tyler in the car—and pleased beyond belief to be riding in the back of a patrol car—when Gregor's always sketchy sense of direction kicked in and he realized they were only a few blocks from the offices of the Justice Project. He told Marbury and Giametti that he wanted to stop, and they turned in and out of a few narrow streets until they got to a place where they could double-park right in front of the Justice Project's doors. They did not have any intention of parking for real and getting out. It wasn't the kind of neighborhood where you would feel safe parking a police car.

Gregor waited until they let him out and then went up to the front door and rang. The building was old beyond telling, and badly kept up. There was garbage on the sidewalk, untouched and unnoticed by the people who passed. A good number of the people who passed were homeless men and women. They were moving with purpose. Gregor didn't know if they had somewhere to go, or had become good at this particular illusion.

A young woman let Gregor in, took his name, and called back for Kate Daniel. Gregor found himself wondering when they'd gotten to the point where buildings with institutions and businesses in them felt the need to keep their front doors locked and on a buzzer as a protection from . . . what? The pictures on the walls here were nowhere near as well-done or as oppressively expensive as the ones in the lobby at Neil Savage's offices, but they were equally didactic. Everybody wanted to teach everybody else something.

The woman who had let him in put down the phone and said, "Ms. Daniel isn't available at the moment. Would you like to make an appointment?"

"No." Gregor sighed. He could always bring in Marbury and Giametti and have them arrest her, but it would be showing off. "Tell her for me," he said, "that if she doesn't produce Sherman Markey from wherever she's got him stashed in the next three hours, I'm going to send those two police officers in the car out there to arrest her for obstruction of justice. Oh, and tell her I said I like her work."

EPILOGUE

Mon, February 16
High 21F, Low 7F

The God that holds you over the pit of Hell,
much as one holds a spider over the flame, ab-
hors you, and is dreadfully provoked.
—JONATHAN EDWARDS

Gravity is a habit that is hard to shake off.
—TERRY PRATCHETT

On the morning that the office of the Philadelphia District Attorney announced the arrest of Aldous Raymond Ballard for the murders of Andrew Mark Harrigan and Francis Xavier Sheehy, the Justice Project threw a press conference for Sherman Markey. Gregor Demarkian wouldn't have been invited to the press conference under the best of circumstances, and these weren't the best of circumstances. For one thing, the mayor was refusing to admit that Gregor Demarkian had been a part of the case at all. There were no contracts, no notes, no official references of any kind. If the press insisted on putting Gregor at this interview with that suspect or in that back alley where a body was discovered, that was the press's problem, not the mayor's, and as far as the mayor was concerned, it was all hype and dazzle. It was the Philadelphia Police who had solved the mystery of the murder of Drew Harrigan, under the able direction of Commissioner of Police John Jackman—and, in the process, arrested the son of one of the most influential men on the planet, and one of the largest contributors to Philadelphia political parties. The mayor of Philadelphia might be, as John Jackman suggested, an incompetent idiot at being mayor, but he was not an incompetent idiot at being a politician.

For another thing, even Gregor wasn't sure what he could

claim to have done in this case. It wasn't that he didn't know what it was he *had* done. It was that he usually had an agreement with the police department who hired him as a consultant. That way everybody knew up front who was going to get credit for what, and Gregor didn't mind letting the police have it all. Police detectives were like any other professionals. They talked among themselves, and word got around. Gregor always had more requests for his time than he had time to give.

For a third thing, he wasn't a reporter, didn't want to be a reporter, and couldn't understand how anybody ever managed to stay in journalism more than a week without getting either bored to tears or thoroughly disgusted with himself. He had no idea what it was the reporters thought they were going to get out of Sherman Markey, but he wished them well. He just hoped Rob Benedetti wasn't planning on calling Markey in as a witness. Gregor still hadn't met the man, but he thought that Markey was likely to be as good a witness as he was a plaintiff in a lawsuit. Benedetti would get better testimony out of a hamster.

The cab pulled up to the front of Our Lady of Mount Carmel Monastery, and Gregor reached into his pocket for his wallet. When he'd come out here in police cars, he hadn't really paid attention to the neighborhood. Now that he did, he saw that it was run-down and shabby, but not as remote as he had assumed at first, merely because it was all the way out at the edge of the city. He got out and paid the cabdriver. He looked up and down the street and saw small grocery stores, small shoe stores, small "dollar stores" that promised that everything inside cost ninety-nine cents. There was also a McDonald's, two blocks down, lit up and crowded. Gregor did not see any homeless people. He took the time to look, hard, to make sure he wasn't missing them. Hardscrabble Road was clear.

He went up to the monastery's front door, rang the bell, and waited. The door opened in less than a second, and Sister Beata let him in.

"I've got the television out here," she said as she closed

up behind him. "It's the only television in the place, and we never see it except when something awful happens, but I've got it today. I convinced Reverend Mother that somebody from the house had to hear Sherman Markey's press conference, and she gave right in. I was a little surprised, really. Maybe she just wants to know what he's going to say."

"Has he said anything?" Gregor asked.

"Not really. He's such a confused old man. I keep asking myself if I'd have recognized him if he'd ever come to this house and I'd seen him, but I don't really know. I keep trying to console myself by saying that I recognized Jig Tyler, but that isn't the same thing, is it? Jig Tyler is the sort of person you notice. He radiates—something."

"Well," Gregor said, "an IQ over two hundred, a driving ambition to beat Napoleon's, and a Messianic complex that should only be brought out of the closet at Easter would tend to make a man radiate—something."

Beata smiled. The little receiving room had a couch in it for visitors. She waved Demarkian to it and turned the television set so that he could see. "He's a very nice man, Dr. Tyler," she said. "He's come out to see me a couple of times since all this happened. He brought us a cake. I told him I never understood why people always seemed to be trying to make nuns fat. The next time he came, he brought us a vegetable tart. It was very good. He sits in here some nights and we talk about political economy and Carmelite spirituality."

"I'm warning you, Sister. It's very hard to get a man to believe in God when he already thinks he is God."

"I don't think Dr. Tyler thinks he's God," Sister Beata said. "I think he thinks he sees more clearly than the rest of us. I've been trying to convince him he's wrong."

There was a sudden loud sound on the television, and they both turned to look at it. There was nothing to see. A grizzled, confused-looking old man was standing at the podium next to Kate Daniel, who had a hand on his shoulder. Chickie George was standing in the background, looking grim. A reporter asked a question, and Sherman Markey mumbled through an answer that had nothing to do with what he'd been asked.

"Why are they putting him through this?" Beata asked. "It's so obvious he's in no shape at all to answer questions. I wonder if he even knows where he is. He looks like he's in pain."

"He's in need of a drink," Gregor said. "And they're doing it to protect him, in case the police decide to name him as an accomplice. It's going to be pretty hard to do that and have it go over with the public after this performance."

"But that would have been true all along, wouldn't it?" Beata asked. "Why didn't the Justice Project produce him weeks ago? Anybody who looked at him had to see he wasn't capable of doing what he'd been accused of doing. Even with clean clothes and a bath and a haircut and shave and everything else they gave him so that he could appear up there, he doesn't look capable of getting prescription drugs for anybody, never mind himself. I mean, if I were a doctor, and he showed up at my door asking for OxyContin, I'd think he was an addict and boot him out into the street."

"I agree," Gregor said. "But they did suspect him. Police investigations are strange that way. And my guess is that the Justice Project didn't produce him because Kate Daniel didn't want it to. Like I said, she was protecting him. When the time came for the suit to go forward in court, or if the case had gone forward and he was needed in criminal court, she would have produced him. She just wanted him out of the limelight and away from anywhere he could be asked questions, because she could never be sure what he was going to say. Look at him. Get him addled enough and he might confess to the murder of Jimmy Hoffa."

"It made him look guilty of murder, though," Beata said. "I'm not sure that was much better."

"If he'd ever been thought guilty of murder by the police, he was dropped from the suspect list after I saw Ray Dean Ballard pushing Frank Sheehy's body into that alley. And yes, I know I didn't know it was Ballard and I didn't know it was a body at the time. But I did know that that man was tall and thin, and Sherman Markey is neither."

"If you'd really paid attention to him, would you have known it was Ray Dean Ballard?"

"No," Gregor said. "I was hypersensitive to looking at the time, but he was too far away from me. The fact that I got the height and weight ratio even within the ballpark was a miracle of concentration as it was, and I was only concentrating because you and other people had pointed out to me how seldom we actually look at the homeless."

"And you were feeling guilty?"

"Yes," Gregor said. "You'd made me feel guilty, Sister, you and, oddly enough, Ray Dean Ballard had."

"He must care about the homeless," Beata said. "He worked at Philadelphia Sleeps. He didn't have to. He could have done anything."

"I know," Gregor said. "I suppose he must have cared about the homeless. I don't know how to determine something like that. I do know that he truly, truly hated Drew Harrigan and all the Drew Harrigans in the world, what he thought of as the Clone Army. Rush Limbaugh. Ann Coulter. So, when he realized that Harrigan was addicted to prescription drugs—"

"Yes, but how did he realize that?" Beata said. "How could he know that?"

"You forget that they'd met socially," Gregor said. "At fund-raisers, as he put it to me, one of the times he talked to me. There were charity events to raise money for Philadelphia Sleeps, and Drew was invited. But it was more than that. There were charity events to raise money for all kinds of things, soup kitchens, children's nutrition, and Ray Dean Ballard was invited because he ran Philadelphia Sleeps and Drew Harrigan was invited because he was a prominent Philadelphian with a lot of money."

"Somehow, I can't see Drew Harrigan giving a lot of money to the homeless."

"I don't know that he did," Gregor said, "but he was like a lot of men in his position, up from the bottom or near bottom. Whether he liked giving money to the homeless or not, he liked meeting important people. And with some kinds of important people, the only way a man like Drew Harrigan would get a chance to meet them would be at a charity event. Most of old-line Philadelphia, even most of old-line Republican Philadelphia, thought he was a buffoon."

"He was, wasn't he? Just a little. I read his book. So did Reverend Mother. She said it wasn't the sort of thing you wanted to read aloud in the refectory."

"I think it's a little lightweight for Our Lady of Mount Carmel," Gregor said. "Anyway, they met at charity functions, and Ray Dean figured out that Drew Harrigan was hooked pretty easily. It wasn't exactly a secret in the first place. My guess is that Sheehy may have been getting Harrigan the pills at least on and off for a while before Ray Dean stepped in. I say I guess because Ray Dean's got better lawyers than the Vatican, and I'm not expecting him to be admitting to anything anytime soon. But anyway, Ray Dean took over the task of getting Drew his pills."

"But why? Why would he want to?"

"Power," Gregor said. "Ray Dean may like working in the nonprofit sector, he may like helping people, but he also likes power. Most people do. Here was this man he despised, who spent more time than was necessary excoriating Philadelphia Sleeps as a 'Communist' organization or a 'socialist' organization or whatever it was that week, and it turns out that he's got a deep dark secret that you could hold over his head. I think Ray Dean thought he was going to be able to control the situation, and control Drew Harrigan."

"And he couldn't."

"Hell," Gregor said, and then blushed, for the first time in twenty-five years. "I'm sorry, Sister."

"It's really all right, Mr. Demarkian. I heard worse in district court."

"Yes. At any rate. Ray Dean couldn't control Drew Harrigan because Drew Harrigan couldn't control Drew Harrigan. You know, a political writer named Al Franken wrote a book called *Rush Limbaugh Is a Big Fat Idiot,* and Limbaugh went out and lost weight. Limbaugh was picked up for illegally buying prescription drugs, and he really went into rehab and got clean. But Drew Harrigan was a mess. When people called him fat, he ate more. When he saw himself getting addicted to OxyContin, he took more. He was out of control in his life. He was out of control on the air. He was out of control in every possible way, and one day the wrong cops stopped him."

"There were right cops?"

"Oh, yes," Gregor said, "and if John Jackman gets elected mayor, we're going to find out which ones. They've already started looking into it. Harrigan was stopped dozens of times for 'driving erratically,' given a Breathalyzer test, and sent home. Rob Benedetti's office has demanded copies of the records, and he'll get them. But it's more than that. Marla Hildebrande knew about it."

"Marla Hildebrande is—?"

"Frank Sheehy's program manager. Sheehy had made oblique references to the fact that they were having to keep the cops sweet, given Harrigan's behavior."

"But that's Frank Sheehy. That's not Ray Dean Ballard."

"No, but it doesn't have to be," Gregor said. "It only matters that the cops were in on the game, except these two cops, Marbury and Giametti, were not. So, when they found Drew Harrigan in a car full of pills, they arrested him and impounded the pills. And once that had happened, once it was out in the open, there was no way to just fix it and make it go away. Neil Savage tried, and he's very good. He's probably one of the two or three best attorneys in Philadelphia. But if celebrity means you're not likely to get much of a sentence for what you do, it also means you're not likely to get let go once you get caught. There's too much publicity. No police department, no district attorney, wants to get tagged with the charge that he let you off just because you were famous."

"So Drew Harrigan got arrested, and he got arraigned," Beata said. "And then that judge let him go into rehab instead of sending him to jail."

"Bruce Williamson," Gregor said. "Yes, well. Bruce is famous. Famous for loving famous people, I mean. Yes, he let

Drew go into rehab without the usual controls on that, and of course Drew had no intention of going into rehab. He had no intention of doing anything about his drug habit instead of keeping it stoked. So he just kept out of sight. He had sixty days for his lawyers to work something out so that he didn't have to go to jail."

"Where was he?"

Gregor shrugged. "Not in homeless shelters, I can assure you. Neil Savage has a vacation house up in the Catskills. He was supposed to be there. Then he found out he couldn't get the pills he wanted, and he called Ray Dean Ballard to come out to see him. Which Ray Dean wasn't about to do, and I don't blame him. That's when Harrigan started threatening him. Because the power hold goes both ways. Ray Dean had power over Harrigan because Harrigan needed the drugs, but Harrigan had power over Ray Dean because he could finger Ray Dean as his supplier. So, Harrigan made a few threats, and Ray Dean agreed to get him the pills if he could get himself into the city."

"And here," Beata said.

"No," Gregor said. "Not the first time. Remember, Harrigan had been out of the way for weeks by the time January twenty-seventh rolled around, and a lot happened in that time. For one thing, Harrigan needed to protect his property. Drug cases are notorious for costing people everything they own. So there was this monastery, with his own sister at the helm, but that wouldn't work by itself, because he didn't really want to give up the property. So there was Ray Dean Ballard, with lots of money and lots to lose, and a perfect intermediary in the shape of the Markwell Ballard Bank."

"But that didn't work," Beata said, "because the Justice Project sued Harrigan for defamation on behalf of Sherman Markey."

"Right," Gregor said. "The judge they got for that one wasn't Bruce Williamson, and he liened everything Harrigan owned. I think that at that point, Harrigan probably went completely over the edge. He wasn't a man who handled stress well. You can see that in his book and if you listen to enough of his radio programs. So he wanted more pills to calm him down, and Ray Dean decided to give them to him."

"And that's when he came here," Beata said.

"Actually, he'd been coming here for weeks," Gregor said. "From the start of the winter, long before he got arrested. Jig Tyler was feeding him information about the University of Pennsylvania to use on the air, and Tyler didn't want to get caught talking to Harrigan. So Harrigan cooked up what he thought was the perfect cloak-and-dagger role-playing game. They'd been coming here since the monastery opened the barn to the homeless at the beginning of the winter. They'd get dressed up in old clothes, stand in line, go into the barn, talk for a while, and then both leave separately. Nobody was likely to notice them. This isn't a secure facility, the way some of the regular homeless shelters are downtown. This is an emergency accommodation because the temperatures have been so low. There was no staff to speak of. The men weren't checked in and out."

"Reverend Mother has had a fit at the Cardinal, if you want to know," Beata said. "It's not that we mind opening the barn to the homeless, but she always did think it was done in haste and without proper preparation."

"If I were Reverend Mother, I'd insist on hiring at least one professional security guard," Gregor said. "Anyway, Harrigan wanted more pills, and Ray Dean didn't want to risk another obvious run into the city with the chance that they'd be caught together. So Harrigan suggested giving the pills to Jig Tyler and getting Jig Tyler out here for a meeting, and to Dr. Tyler the whole thing sounded perfectly plausible. He didn't know he was carrying pills full of arsenic. He didn't know he was carrying pills at all when Ray Dean Ballard gave them to him. If Harrigan hadn't insisted on swallowing them the first chance he got, Jig Tyler would never have known he was carrying pills at all."

"So Dr. Tyler will be able to testify that he got the pills from Ray Dean Ballard," Beata said. "That's something."

"That's a lot. If I was Ballard, I'd have gone for Tyler before I'd gone for Sheehy, but I think Ballard thought that he was safe from Tyler because Tyler didn't want to risk what he has risked. Meaning that Ballard's lawyers would try to make out that Tyler physically gave Harrigan the poisoned pills, and that meant that Tyler was the one who wanted to and deliberately did kill Harrigan. Sheehy probably looked like a much more pressing danger, since Sheehy knew about the pills and he knew about the cops and he knew about the murder."

"What did you say?"

"I said he knew about the murder," Gregor said. "I'm not going to be able to prove that to anybody, but he knew about the murder. On the night of January twenty-seventh, Frank Sheehy had a conversation with Marla Hildebrande about finding a talk show to replace Drew Harrigan's permanently. Marla Hildebrande thinks it was just a matter of being realistic about the prospects for the show if Harrigan went to jail, which he very well could have. I think it was that Sheehy knew he was going to have to replace the show because Harrigan wasn't going to be alive to go on with it. And that, you know, is the best motive for murder in the world."

Beata looked at the television screen. The press conference had gone on far longer than Gregor would have suspected it could have. Sherman Markey was slumped over the microphone in front of him, a vague-looking old man that normal people would pass on the street without noticing, a man with too many bad habits, too much bad history, and no damned luck at all. Kate Daniel looked brisk and confident. Chickie George looked as angry as he had sounded when he'd called Gregor in the middle of the night to apologize for Kate Daniel's behavior.

"I'd never have gotten you into this if I'd realized she knew where he was all along," Chickie had said, and then he'd gone on to rail endlessly about people who thought the end justified the means. "You'd think that's the first thing they'd learn the problems with in Philosophy 101, or wherever."

Beata leaned forward and turned off the television. "I still wouldn't recognize him if I saw him on the street," she said. "It's a terrible thing, isn't it? We don't want to look, and they learn to be so self-effacing that nobody takes notice of them. And they manage it. We're supposed to be self-effacing, you know. The nuns at Carmel. We don't ever quite seem to manage it."

"I think walking around in brown and black robes designed in the Middle Ages is likely to make you stick out on the bus, Sister."

Beata laughed. "Most of us never do get on the bus. The nuns in enclosure stay in the house all the time. But when they do go out, to vote, for instance, they wear exclaustration veils. Black net veils that cover their entire faces, more concealing even than a burkha. That's pretty self-effacing, too."

Gregor got up. "With any luck, we'll be able to find out where Ray Dean Ballard and Frank Sheehy met on the day Sheehy died. I've got a terrible feeling it's going to be in a public restaurant, like a diner, so that Ballard could slip him the arsenic when he wasn't looking and we'd never be able to find a trace on it; but there's always the possibility that he was worried about Sheehy collapsing in public and picked a more private place. We'll see. One way or the other, there's no way Ballard stays out of prison. He may end up in the death chamber."

"I don't approve of the death chamber," Beata said. "It always seems to me that there's enough killing without having the government create more."

"I don't approve of the death chamber either," Gregor said, "but only because I'm far too aware of the fact that innocent people end up there, and I don't think we should go on with it as long as even one innocent person could even possibly be unjustly executed. But morally—morally, I think that there's not a single thing wrong with putting a man to death if he's committed deliberate and premeditated murder, and I won't lose a millisecond's sleep if Ray Dean Ballard dies."

"Well, then," Beata said. "I'd say I'll pray for you, but I'm doing that already. I pray for Ray Dean Ballard and Frank Sheehy and Drew Harrigan, too. That's what we do in this place. We pray for the world."

"If you try praying for them individually and by name, Sister, there won't be enough time in the history of the universe."

2

Back on Cavanaugh Street, Father Tibor Kasparian was walking Grace Feinman's dog. Or rather, he was trying to walk it. He had the dog on a leash, and the dog was jumping around and getting tangled, terribly excited to be out in the world with people and hydrants and trees to sniff. Gregor watched them both as he paid for yet another cab—he felt as if he'd spent the day paying for cabs—and then crossed the street to where they were, halted temporarily as Godiva made a huge fuss over Lida Arkmanian.

"Tcha, Krekor," Tibor said. "She's a very friendly dog. I was taking her to your building to see if Grace is home yet. She is due this afternoon sometime."

"She *is* a very friendly dog," Lida Arkmanian said, leaning down to rub her under her chin. Godiva sincerely loved this. She showed it by leaping a foot in the air and barking in ecstasy. Lida stood up. "I don't know how Grace thinks she's going to keep a dog like this in an apartment. They get big, Labradors do."

"She will take the dog to a park and let it run around," Father Tibor said. "She will take it to obedience school, too, I hope. It is a wonderful dog, really, but it is very active."

"Come on," Gregor said. "I'll let you into my place and you can stay there if Grace isn't home yet."

They went into the building and past old George Tekemanian's door. Old George was out on the Main Line with his nephew for the duration of the very bad cold, although why Martin and Angela thought the apartment on Cavanaugh Street wouldn't be properly heated was beyond Gregor's understanding. They went upstairs past Bennis's apartment, where Tibor had stayed for the months the church and his own apartment were being rebuilt after the bombing. They went up to Gregor's floor and let themselves in. Tibor leaned his head back and tried calling out "Grace" in his loudest voice, but his loudest voice wasn't worth much. When the new church was built, they had convinced him to get a microphone set up so that people could hear him when he sang the liturgy, and it had been a great relief for everybody concerned.

"Don't worry about it," Gregor said. "She's not home yet. There's no music coming out of there at all. She can't sleep without music."

"On the CD player," Tibor said.

Tibor went down the short front foyer hall into the living room, and Gregor followed him. The apartment looked the way it always looked, except that it had been empty the second before they'd walked in, and empty for hours before that. Really, it felt as if it had been empty for months before that, although he knew it hadn't been that long that Bennis had been on her book tour. Emptiness was more than the absence of people. Or something like that. He shrugged off his coat and threw it over the back of the couch. He wasn't at his best when he was trying to be profound.

"I'm going to change," he told Tibor. "Go into the kitchen and make yourself a cup of coffee. I bought those coffee bags Bennis suggested a few months ago. They at least mean that we don't have to drink what we percolate, and that's something."

"I'll make for both of us, Krekor, no? And there's food?"

"There's a refrigerator full of food," Gregor said. "Lida and Hannah and the rest of them think I'm starving to death now that Bennis is away, which is funny as hell, if you think about it. You couldn't get Bennis to cook if you threatened her with death. Be right back."

"Take your time, Krekor."

Gregor went down the long hall to his bedroom, closed the door, and sat on his bed. He could see the answering machine from where he was sitting, and there was no question at all that the green light on it was blinking. He took off his jacket and tie and tossed them toward the chair. He missed. He got up, picked them up, and put them over the chair's back. He sat down again. His hands felt cold. His face felt cold. His brain felt frozen in place. He was not a man who found relationships with women easy. He could not keep his distance or look at sex as a game for players who knew when to hit and run. He had been in love exactly twice in his life, and in both those cases it seemed to him that the woman he loved had disappeared from existence exactly when he needed and wanted her the most. But the green light on the answering machine was blinking, and that meant somebody had left him a message.

"It's going to turn out to be John Jackman," he said, to the air. Then he reached out to the night table and pushed the play button.

"Mr. Demarkian?" a woman's voice said, the wrong woman's voice. "This is Alison Standish. I'm at 555-4295. That's home. I'm sorry. I'm a little addled here. I just wanted to say thank you for everything, and especially for the heads-up about Dr. Tyler. It's made all the difference in the world. Thank you again."

The machine went dead. Gregor stared at it. A woman's voice, but the wrong woman's voice, or just the wrong voice. He wondered where Bennis was now, and what reason she had for not calling. He had her schedule someplace. Women didn't make any sense to him, and they never had.

He could hear Tibor on the other side of the apartment, banging around coffee mugs and the big teakettle. He needed to get a sweater on and get up and out of here and have something to eat. He needed to think, but this was the kind of thing he wasn't good at thinking about.

Bennis's schedule wasn't "someplace." It was on the night table next to the answering machine. He picked it up and looked at it. There was the date, and the hotel in Salt Lake City, and the time the signing started at a bookstore whose name he'd never heard before. All he had to do was call.

He picked up the phone, put it in his lap, and put the schedule down next to him on the bed. Then he picked up the receiver and dialed 555-4295.

Keep reading for an excerpt from
Jane Haddam's new mystery

GLASS HOUSES

NOW AVAILABLE FROM
ST. MARTIN'S / MINOTAUR PAPERBACKS

Sometimes Henry Tyder thought that the real problem would always be the blood. Bodies could be stashed under tables or cut up and put into trunks. You could take pieces off them or settle for pieces of clothing instead, in case you were worried about how you were going to smell on the bus. Evidence was nothing at all. Evidence was what you made it be. If you wanted it, you went and got it. If you wanted to get rid of it, you had only to point out that you were who and what you were: living on the street half the time; drunk to the gills half the time; out of your mind half the time. No, it was the blood that was the problem because blood went everywhere.

It was five o'clock on the evening of March 23rd, and not as cold as it should have been. A fine drizzling rain had been coming down most of the day. The streets were slick and wet and shiny under streetlamps that were just going on. Down at the end of the block, half a dozen people were huddled near the curb, hoping for taxis. This was not Henry's ordinary neighborhood. It was not a place where he felt safe.

He checked out the people one more time and then retreated to the narrow alley between two brick buildings. They were the kind of buildings he remembered from his childhood, with stoops at the front and tall windows that looked out onto the city. It was as if the people who lived inside cared not at all about who could see them. On the alley side, though, there were no windows, except one very high up on the fifth or sixth floor. That would have been a maid's room in the old days. Now it was probably a place where a law firm stowed the kind of files it expected nobody to ever want to see again.

The body was halfway between the two ends of the alley. It was the body of a young woman in a red cloth coat, with fingernails painted to look like American flags. Henry crouched down next to it. His mind was clear. It really was. He'd been living "at home" for weeks now—or at least he'd been living with Elizabeth and Margaret, which was as close as he came to home. He was cold and his bones ached, but he thought he understood what he was doing. The young woman must have been one of those people who liked to call attention to herself. The coat would have stood out in a crowd. The fingernails would have started conversations. Maybe that was what she had wanted. Maybe she had hoped that somebody would make a comment about her nails, some man, and they would talk, and the talk would lead to other things.

Henry got down closer, and looked into her face. Her eyes were open, staring blankly, the way they did when the person who owned them was dead. The side of her face was all cut up. The glass that had been used to do it—thin, wide jagged plates from a glass window, broken God only knew where—was lying around her as if it had fallen from the sky like snow. The glass was covered with blood, and so was the face, and so was the collar of the coat. Blood was in the puddles at the body's sides, diluted and spread by the falling rain. Henry put his hand out and rubbed his palm across the body's face. When he took his hand away, it was red and sticky and smelled like something that made his stomach churn.

From here to the end, it was an easy thing: it was just a question of finding a policeman and bringing him here. It would have been easier in the days before most policemen rode around in cars. He picked up one of the small plates of glass and turned it over in his hands. He put it down and picked up another. He picked up the woman's purse and opened it. She had twenty-six dollars and change in her wallet. He took that and put it in his pockets. She wouldn't need it anymore, and he did. If he could find some money someplace, he wouldn't have to face his sisters until he was ready to.

He stood up and looked around. He knew how the woman had died. She'd been strangled from behind with a thin nylon cord people used to tie some kinds of packages for mailing. You found the stuff all the time in Dumpsters. He bent down again and felt around her neck. The cord was buried deeply into the high collar of her jersey turtleneck. It was folded back on itself, but not tied. The cords were never tied. He remembered that from the newspapers. He pulled at it until it came loose in his hands. Then he put it into his pocket with the change.

The drizzle was turning into something heavier. It was so very warm for March, but still cold enough for wet to be something he did not want to be. He leaned over one more time and put his hands in the blood again. He liked the feel of it under the tips of his fingers. He stood up and turned his hands over and let the rain fall on them. The blood washed to the edges, but it did not wash clean.

Henry put his hands in his pockets and started for the street. It was better to go to the street than to the back courtyards after dark. The courtyards were unused and uncared for and often without working lights. Kids hung out in them when they wanted to do drugs and make trouble. He felt the money one more time to make sure it was still there. He came out onto the sidewalk where the people were and looked around.

It was another woman in a red coat who saw him first, an older woman this time, somebody paying attention. Most people didn't look at Henry Tyder at all.

"Oh, my God," the woman said, backing away from him toward the stoops. She caught the back of her leg on a step and stumbled. "Oh, my God," she said again. "Oh, my God."

A man in a dark raincoat stopped to see if he could help her. "Is there something wrong?" he said. "Is there something I can get for you?"

Nothing succeeds like success, Henry thought. If you looked pretty much all right, everybody in the neighborhood wanted to help you.

That was when the woman started screaming.

Margaret Beaufort had a whole list of things she considered too outrageous to be tolerated, and on the top of that list were police departments that couldn't do their jobs. The job of a police department was both simple and undeniable. It was to keep the peace, and keep the people who were likely to cause trouble off the streets and away from decent people. If Margaret had had her way, the people who needed to be kept off the streets would include garbage collectors (unless they were collecting garbage) and day laborers (at any time at all), and the only people allowed to walk around neighborhoods like this one would be the people who lived in them and the people they hired as staff. Margaret was sure that life had been like this once when she was a child. She couldn't remember ever seeing rough men walking the sidewalks when she was on her way to school. She was sure her mother had never been knocked into by some teenager carrying an enormous music player and paying no attention to where he was going. In fact, her childhood was a golden haze that sometimes seemed more real to her than the life she was living now: going to school every morning in the navy blue uniforms that marked her out as a Sacred Heart girl; stopping on the way home at a little store that sold nonpareils and red hot dollars; driving up into the mountains at the beginning of August to escape the heat. She'd especially liked the driving, even though it had meant riding in the backseat of the Pontiac with her sister, Elizabeth, and later—much later, when things were already beginning to go wrong—with her half-brother Henry. It had been a long time since she had had a vacation.

It had also been a long time since she had been this nervous. Margaret was not, usually, a nervous woman. She had seen herself through three pregnancies and three miscarriages. She had weathered her late husband's serial affairs in a manner that would have made her mother cheer. She had even managed to tough her way through that most awful time of all, during the protests in the sixties, when it seemed like all the people who should be kept off the streets were actually in the middle of them, carrying signs. She was tall and fair and florid and just slightly running to fat; and if she wanted someone to know she was unhappy with him, she didn't have to raise her voice.

Now she tried raising the volume on the television set they kept in the spare room, as if by doing that she could change the content of the story being repeated on it. She'd already listened to this story once, half an hour ago, when it had appeared on the first of the local nightly newscasts she made it her business to watch every evening. The newscasts were the excuse she made for not putting her foot down and making Elizabeth get rid of the television entirely. In their childhood, people of good family didn't own televisions. They had them in the maids' rooms for the maids, who couldn't help watching them because they were uneducated. She didn't like to think of what it said about both of them that Elizabeth was now addicted to at least three soap operas and would give up an afternoon at the Philadelphia Museum of Art to watch the latest installment of *Days of Our Lives*.

Elizabeth was in the kitchen, sitting calmly at the little round table in the breakfast nook drinking tea. Her response to this crisis had not been satisfactory. As far as Margaret was concerned, nothing Elizabeth ever did had ever been satisfactory. Even in their childhood, she had been both an embarrassment and a thorn.

The kitchen was just across the hall from the spare room. Margaret gave one last look at the television set—they'd gone on to something else anyway; there was corruption in the mayor's office, again—and went to find her sister. She could hear the light *chink* of china on china as Elizabeth put her cup into her saucer and picked it up again. If she was running true to form, she'd be doing the crossword puzzle when Margaret came in.

Elizabeth was doing the crossword puzzle. She was also wearing sweatpants and a sweatshirt, both black and over-sized, ballooning around her small, spare frame.

"Really," Margaret said. "You look like one of those women in the park, the old ladies who jog and think it's going to make them younger."

"I don't jog."

"I know you don't. You don't do anything anymore. Why wouldn't you come and listen to the story?"

"I did come and listen to the story."

"I mean this time, on CBS."

"It was the same story, Margaret. You can't honestly tell me they gave you any new information."

"They might have," Margaret said defensively. "It's a breaking story. It just happened. There could be new information at any moment."

"But there wasn't."

"No, there wasn't. But still."

"It will all come out in the paper tomorrow, Margaret, or on the news. It's not so important that I have to hear about it right away. Sit down and relax a little."

Margaret didn't sit down. She went to the window over the sink instead. In their childhood, the family never came into the kitchen except to check on what the cook was doing. Now they ate in here all the time.

"Doesn't it matter to you at all? She was our maid. We knew her. A little, at any rate, because she didn't speak English. But we knew her. And then there were the police, and all that trouble over Henry. He could have been arrested."

"Maybe he has been," Elizabeth said.

"Do be serious."

Elizabeth put down her crossword puzzle. "I am being serious. They said a man had been taken in for questioning, but they didn't say who the man was, did they? Why couldn't it have been Henry?"

"Henry could never commit a murder," Margaret said, "never mind eleven of them. This was the eleventh, did you know that? Anyway, we discussed all this when Conchita

died. You agreed with me that Henry is not, well, not mis-
formed in just that particular way. He isn't a *violent* man."

"No, he's not," Elizabeth said. "But I wasn't saying that
he *might* have committed the murder; I was saying he might
have been *arrested* for it. It's not that farfetched, Margaret.
The story said the body had been found on Society Hill."

"There are a lot of people who live on Society Hill.
Henry isn't one of them. He lives here with us."

"He stays here with us when he's sober," Elizabeth said,
"but he's not sober a lot of the time, is he? And he does like
to hang out on Society Hill. He's got less of a chance of getting rolled there. He may be a drunk, but he's not an idiot."

"So you think he's the man in the story, the one they
didn't name? You think that's Henry. But when the police
were here they said he couldn't be the Picture Window
Killer, or whatever it is—"

"Plate Glass Killer."

"—because he had an alibi for one of the deaths. Or
something like that. There was a reason he couldn't be. So
they wouldn't arrest him, would they, since they already
knew that."

"I don't know," Elizabeth said.

Margaret came back to the table and sat down. Now she
was more than nervous. She had reached a level of panic the
like of which she hadn't had since menopause, when everything in her life was in panic. It was odd how it went. It was
when you were young that you were supposed to be excited
and frightened. When you got older you were supposed to
mellow into a mature wisdom that made you both calm and
happy. She reached into the fruit bowl in the middle of the
table and took out an apple. She didn't really like apples.
She didn't want to eat one.

"We knew she was going to be trouble, didn't we?" Margaret asked, noticing with a certain amount of annoyance
that Elizabeth was doing the crossword again. "When she
first came here. When she first married Daddy. We knew she
was going to be trouble."

"She's been dead and buried for thirty years."

"She was an alcoholic," Margaret said stubbornly. "That's why Henry is an alcoholic. We should have seen that coming a long time ago. We should have had him committed."

"You can't just have people committed against their wills," Elizabeth said. "Not unless they're convicted of something, and Henry has never been convicted of anything. He doesn't even drive."

"Still. We should have done something. Daddy would have done something. He did something about her in the end."

"She was hospitalized for alcohol poisoning. Daddy had nothing to do with it."

"I keep expecting him to show up on one of those programs. *American Justice*. Or *Investigative Reports*. They'll do a program on the black sheep of prominent families, and there he'll be, sleeping on the sidewalk with newspapers all over him and his shoes in shreds. I don't understand why he doesn't just come home. I don't understand why he has to live his life out in public like that."

"He isn't living his life in public, Margaret. He's just living it away from us."

Margaret put the apple back and went to the stove. She'd make herself some coffee. If it was earlier in the day, she could have had the new maid get it for her, but the new maid wasn't living in. Nobody wanted to live in at their house at the moment because of what had happened to Conchita and the fact that it had happened right in their own back courtyard. Conchita. In her childhood, maids were either Irish or black. They had names like Kathleen and Lydia. They spoke English with accents, but they spoke it well.

Margaret pulled the coffeemaker out of the little roll-front wooden appliance port they had had built into the kitchen counter. "I think you'd care more," she said. "You found her. Wasn't it horrible? Doesn't it matter to you that our own maid was strangled with a nylon cord and her face was all cut up by pieces of glass?"

"Of course it matters to me."

"You don't act like it. You act as if it had nothing to do with us, but it does. Because it was our maid. Because of Henry. Because of a lot of things. I was thinking before about what it was like, growing up in this house."

"It was a nightmare."

"Not for me, it wasn't. It was a wonderful thing. It was calm. And organized. I remember something Mother said once when we were very small—not to me, to one of her friends. I was playing in the room and they didn't notice me. She said that somebody they knew 'lived a very disordered life.' And I knew what she meant. Immediately. That's the problem with all this. It's as if we live very disordered lives."

"Henry does."

"I know he does. But I don't want to. I don't want that to be me."

"If Henry's in trouble, there's not much either one of us can do about it. Drink decaf instead of the regular stuff. It's only going to make your nerves even worse."

Margaret did not think her nerves could be any worse than they were, and she did not drink decaffeinated coffee for the same reason she did not eat potato chips. There was a difference between real food and fake, and decent people—people with ordered lives—didn't eat the fake kind. She got a thick ceramic mug out of one of the cabinets and put it to the side. She'd take the coffee into the spare room and see if there would be any mention of the story on the national news, although she doubted it. Philadelphia didn't have the same influence on the rest of the country that it used to have.

She was just carefully filling the coffeemaker with coffee when Elizabeth cleared her throat.

"You know," Elizabeth said, "there's one good reason not to worry about any of this yet. One sensible reason, I mean."

"And what's that?"

"Henry hasn't called. They get one phone call when they're arrested, and Henry knows the number here by heart. If he'd been arrested, he would have called."

Margaret brightened. "That's right," she said. "That's right. I'd forgotten about that. I wish you'd said that in the beginning. It must have been hours since all this happened. They don't get these things on the news right away. If he'd been the one they picked up, he would have called by now."

She poured water over the coffee, fitted the lid back on the coffeemaker and stepped back to wait for actual coffee to come out the other side. She felt relieved, very relieved, so relieved she almost thought she must have lost weight.

It wasn't as good as time traveling back forty years or so, but it would have to do.